VI KEELAND
PENELOPE WARD

WELL PLAYED

Cover designer: Sommer Stein, Perfect Pear Creative
Editing: Jessica Royer Ocken
Formatting and proofreading: Elaine York,
Allusion Publishing www.allusionpublishing.com
Proofreading: Julia Griffis
Cover Photographer: Celso Colaco
Cover Model: Gonçalo Teixeira

ONE

Presley

"SO, HAVE YOU at least run into one of those southern gentlemen the movies always show? Like Ryan Gosling in *The Notebook* or Matthew McConaughey in...well, anything?"

I sighed and set my cell on the bed so I could get undressed while I finished my call with my best friend, Harper, on speakerphone. "No. But I did speak to a man at the post office yesterday named *Huck*. He spoke with such a heavy accent that I initially thought he was speaking a foreign language. I apologized and told him I only spoke English. He wasn't too amused. I don't sound like that, do I?"

"Only after a few drinks. Some people start to drool after too much liquor. You start to drawl and say things like *howdy*."

"I *do not* say howdy. But I definitely met a man this week who does. Atticus Musslewhite."

"Is that seriously a person's name?"

"Sure is. He's a mechanic at the gas station in town. We went to high school together, but I'm pretty sure he

1

didn't recognize me. When I got here on Sunday, I pulled up to the pump, and he was standing there like the welcome wagon. He looked me up and down with a piece of actual straw hanging out of the side of his mouth, lifted his hat, and said, "Howdy, pretty lady. Welcome to Beaufort. If you need anything at all, you just give Atticus a call. I'll *buttah* your biscuit."

"Oh my God. I demand you pack up and move back here immediately."

I laughed and sat down on the bed to untie my sneakers in front of the air conditioner. "Yeah, no Ryan Gosling yet. Though I am happy to be home. When I made the decision to move back down here, I worried maybe I wasn't cut out for small-town life anymore. But I feel like my shoulders are relaxed for the first time in years."

"Hmmm... Then maybe I should move to Beaufort. My massage therapist just raised his rate to a hundred and fifty an hour."

"Pretty sure your head would explode after more than a few days. It's definitely a slower pace than you can handle."

Harper sighed. "I hate that you're so far away. But I'm glad you're finding peace. How's The Palm Inn?"

I looked around the bedroom I was staying in, which was in better shape than most of the other rooms in the B&B. Paint was peeling from the walls, the carpet was worn so thin you couldn't make out the pattern anymore, and a termite-damaged wood-framed window held the world's shittiest air conditioner. "Ummm... It needs some TLC."

"How long do you think it'll take to get it fixed up?"

"I'm not sure. I'm working on a budget to figure out what we can afford to have done. I'll figure out a timeline after that. But it's going to have to be before I start my new teaching position."

I'd lined up a part-time job teaching art and photography at the local high school. It wasn't the glamorous life I'd had back in New York where I managed a gallery and had shown some of my own photography and artwork. But I wasn't a glam girl at heart anyway, and I was looking forward to teaching something I loved.

"You'll get it done," she assured me. "My girl can do anything."

"I hope you're right."

"And how's the best boy in the world?"

I'd had to pull my seven-year-old out of the last few weeks of classes in New York when my lease was up and we made the move to get things started down here. School in Beaufort was already out for the year, but he still had a few things to finish up, so I was trying my hand at homeschooling—just to finish up second grade.

I smiled. "Alex is happy. He made some friends right away. I was worried it might be difficult for him until he starts school here in the fall. But my mom took him to lunch with her friend and her friend's grandson, and they really hit it off. They've been hanging out the last few days playing football. They're both planning to join the junior peewee team, and they'll be at the same camp this summer. Once the kid heard who Alex's father and uncle were, he became sort of an instant celebrity."

"What team does his uncle play for again?"

"The Broncos."

"Is that the same team Alex's dad played for?"

"No. He was with the Jets. That's how I wound up in New York, remember?"

"Jets, Mets, Nets—I have no idea where any of the teams are from."

I laughed. That was another thing different about living in a big city versus how things were down here in the

South. In New York, football was a sport that played in the background at bars. Here it was more like a religion. The whole town came out for Friday nights under the lights—not just the family and friends of the kids playing. Before his injury, my ex, Tanner, had been a second-round pick in the NFL draft eight years ago. His brother had been a first-round pick two years before that, and their dad had played in the NFL for fifteen years, too. When I left to go to New York with Tanner almost a decade ago, our little town had already sent fifty-two kids to the NFL. I was sure it was more by now.

"How am I supposed to do this?" Harper said. "I miss you already, and you've only been gone six days. You know I don't like people enough to make a new friend."

I smiled. "You have plenty of friends."

"Not real ones like you."

I sighed. Harper wasn't wrong. She'd been the one thing that had kept me up north the last year or two. Lord knows, in the six years we've been separated, Alex's dad didn't give us a reason to stay. He barely ever saw his son even though we'd lived in the same city.

"I miss you, too. But you're going to come down and visit soon, right?"

"Of course. I can't wait."

"Alright, well... That's how we'll get through this—looking forward to vacations and visits. But listen, I gotta run. Alex is down the block at his new friend's house. I just finished cleaning out the attic in the B&B, and I really need to jump in the shower. It was so hot and dirty. I think I might smell. The heat down here is enough to *roast a lizard.*"

"They roast lizards down there?"

I chuckled. "Not that I've ever seen. But my mom said that the other day, and Alex looked at her like she had two heads. The lingo is going to take some getting used to for him."

She laughed. "I'll talk to you in a few days, my little *buttah biscuit.*"

"Bye, Harp."

After I hung up, I peeled my yoga pants down my clammy legs, unstuck the thong glued to my ass, and stood in front of the unimpressive air conditioner in my bedroom. The thing was producing the equivalent of me filling my cheeks with hot air and blowing out. I needed to add *find an AC repairman* to my mile-long to-do list if there was any hope I was going to make it through the summer heat.

A Bose SoundLink speaker sat on the nearby nightstand. I'd turned down the music when my cell phone rang, and the low sound of Justin Timberlake's "SexyBack" wafted below the loud clanking of the dysfunctional AC. I walked over and cranked it up, pulled the tie from my ponytail, and returned to let the air blow my blond hair back, Beyoncé-video style. Shutting my eyes, I began to move to the rhythm of the song.

It felt like forever since I'd danced. I used to love it. In high school, I'd been the head of the dance squad, and Harper and I liked to go out dancing on occasion. But really dancing? Dancing like no one was watching? It had been years. So I went with the urge. Why not? I was the only person in the B&B, and the blinds were shut.

I started slow, swaying back and forth, until my hips decided to join in on the fun. By the time the chorus came around the second time, I was full-on shaking my goods all over. Tanner had been an ass man. Years ago, after the Miley Cyrus VMA twerk had gone viral, I'd caught him watching it on his laptop. So I'd surprised him and learned to twerk. Now, at the ripe old age of twenty-nine, I wasn't sure I could move like that anymore. But when Justin asked to see what I was *twerking w*ith, I obliged. And I'll be damned if I didn't still have it. So I went to town— twerking my jiggly, naked ass like nobody's business while the air conditioning continued to blow my hair back.

When the song ended, an odd, euphoric feeling came over me, and I couldn't stop smiling. Maybe being back in Beaufort, South Carolina, would be good for me after all.

And maybe naked dancing was just what I needed.

Or maybe not.

I turned around to head to the shower, and my heart leapt into my throat as I found a man leaning casually against the bedroom doorframe.

I jumped and let out a blood-curdling scream. My self-defense mechanism kicked in, and I picked up the nearest thing I could get my hands on and hurled it across the room. Fortunately, I'd grabbed the Bose SoundLink, and that thing packed a wallop. The hard plastic connected with the intruder's head, and he went down for the count.

Shaking, I looked around for another weapon, but the room was pretty sparse. So I grabbed my cell phone from the bed and called 9-1-1, hoping they'd arrive before he came to.

The operator asked my name and address and then said the police had been dispatched. "Is the intruder breathing, Presley?"

My eyes widened. Could I have killed him? *Oh my God.* I thought I might throw up. "I don't know. But he's not moving."

"Okay. Just stay on the phone with me. The police are en route. Can you make your way outside safely?"

I shook my head, though the woman obviously couldn't see me. "He's lying in the doorway, and there's no other way out. There's an air conditioner in the window."

"Okay. Try to stay calm. Let's just keep talking until the police arrive."

I nodded, but couldn't focus on anything else the woman said. *What if I killed him?* My heart ricocheted against my ribcage as if it were trying to escape. I peered over at the man. He was dressed in jeans and a button-down shirt, but his face was turned away from me, and I couldn't get a good look from where I stood huddled in the corner.

Though something struck me as odd. An intruder didn't usually dress that well, did he? Shouldn't he have a stocking over his face and filthy clothes from his years of doing drugs and living on the streets?

I pushed up on my tippy toes to get a better look. His crisp, white shirt had a little horse embroidered on it. My intruder wore a hundred-dollar, Ralph Lauren dress shirt?

A bad feeling settled into the pit of my stomach. I needed to see this man's face. "Are you still there?" I asked into the phone.

"I'm here. Is everything okay?"

"Yeah. I'm going to take a few steps toward him. He's still out, and I want to see his face."

"Okay. Stay on the line, and see if it's safe to maneuver around him and get outside."

I nodded. Realizing I was still naked, I tugged the sheet from the bed and wrapped it around me. Then I took one hesitant step and waited to see if the man moved. He didn't. So I took another step, and then another until I was close enough to lean to one side and get a look at the intruder's turned-away face.

I gasped.

"Presley? Are you still there?" the 9-1-1 operator asked. "Is everything okay?"

"Oh my God!"

"What's going on, Presley?"

"I think it's Levi!"

"You know the intruder?"

"Yes. He's Tanner's brother."

"And who's Tanner, Presley?"

"He's my ex-fiancé."

"What's Tanner's last name?"

"Miller."

"Miller?"

"Yes."

"Okay. So the man on the floor is Levi Miller, then?"

"Yes."

"The same name as the football player?"

I shook my head. "No, not the same name as the football player—the *actual* player. I think I just killed the Super Bowl MVP quarterback."

XOXO

"I'm fine," Levi growled at the paramedic from the other room.

The police had separated us, asking me to take a seat in the kitchen and keeping him in the adjoining living room. I peered around the police officer sitting across from me to see what was going on.

"Sir, you lost consciousness. There's a good chance you have a concussion. Plus, you need a few stitches."

"I'll walk over to Doc Matthews' house down the block. He'll stitch me up and check me out."

The paramedic frowned. "That's not a good idea. We need to take you to Memorial." She fussed, trying to wipe his head with gauze.

The police officer sitting across from me finished writing notes in his pad and shut it. "So you didn't know it was your ex-fiancé's brother when you attacked him? You didn't recognize a famous football player you've known all your life?"

"I didn't attack him. I told you. I was dancing, and he walked in on me. He has a full beard now, and I'd never seen him with one before. I got scared and picked up the first thing I could grab and threw it at him. It was an accident. I thought he was a robber or something."

"And you were dancing...naked?"

"Yes."

He flipped open his notepad and started to write again.

"Can you...leave that part out of your report? It's so embarrassing."

The officer glanced up at me and then continued to write. "They're just the facts of the case, ma'am."

Levi again raised his voice from the other room, causing even the officer sitting across from me to turn in his chair. He towered over the short female paramedic. "Give me whatever you want me to sign. I'm not getting into an ambulance for a little cut on the head."

One of the two paramedics who had been attending to Levi walked into the kitchen and spoke to the officer. "The victim's vitals are stable, and he's refusing treatment, so we're going to have him sign our Refusal of Necessary Medical Care form and be on our way."

The officer shut his notebook and looked at me. "Excuse me for a minute."

While the paramedics packed up their transporter bed and all of their equipment, the officer spoke to Levi. He lowered his voice, but I could still strain to hear.

"Are you sure you don't want to press charges, Mr. Miller?"

Levi looked over at me. His glare was icy, but he shook his head no.

"Alright, then. We'll have to do a full report. But we'll put it down as a domestic accident."

Fifteen minutes later, the last of the responders walked out the front door. The paramedics and police had arrived just as Levi came to, and they'd immediately sprung into action to treat him and then separated us. I hadn't had a chance to apologize.

"Levi, I'm so sorry I did that to you. But why were you watching me anyway? It's creepy."

"It's kind of hard to not watch when I find a naked woman in my house, twerking. I had no idea it was you."

I folded my arms across my chest. "It's *our* house. And I had no idea it was you either. You look so different. Your hair is long, and I've never seen you with a full beard like that." I looked up at the cut on his head and grimaced. "You should have let them treat you. You're still bleeding."

"Cuts to the head bleed a lot. It's fine."

"Please go over to Doc Matthews' at least."

"What are you doing here?"

"I moved back."

"Why?"

Right about now, I was asking myself that very question. "Because it's a good place for my son to grow up."

He looked me up and down. "Why are you so dirty?"

"Oh. I cleaned out the attic. I finished right before you came in."

"Why would you do that?"

My brows furrowed. He had a lot of questions, and some of them seemed pretty obvious. "Ummm...because it was a disaster."

"The builder doesn't care if the attic is clean. He doesn't care if the entire place is a mess. He's going to tear it down."

"Tear what down?"

"This place."

"*What?* What are you talking about?"

This time it was Levi who looked confused. His forehead wrinkled. "Didn't you get the offer?"

"What offer?"

"For the B&B. Franklin Construction made an offer of more than twice the value of the property. My lawyer said he sent it over to you. I assumed it was a done deal."

I shook my head. "But I don't want to sell."

Levi put his hands on his hips. "Well, then, we have a problem. Because I do."

TWO

Presley

HOURS LATER, LEVI stood on the porch of the B&B as I opened the door to let him in.

"You don't have to knock. This is your home."

He pointed to his bandaged head. "Eight stitches says otherwise."

I covered my mouth. "Oh my God. *Eight* stitches? I'm so sorry. I can't believe I did that to you."

"It's fine. Doc Matthews said I'm good as new."

I squinted. "Doc called five minutes ago. You left your wallet at his office. He also mentioned that you really should've been admitted to the hospital and need to be watched closely for forty-eight hours for signs of slurred speech and vomiting."

Levi shook his head. "I forgot no one gives a shit about things like HIPAA and privacy laws in Beaufort." He looked around the living room. "Do you know where my suitcase went? I left it in the hallway earlier when I went to see where the music was coming from."

"Oh. Yeah. I put it in the Woodward Suite."

His brows drew down. "Aren't you in there?"

"I moved to a regular room. I don't need that much space."

"Don't be ridiculous. I'll stay in any room that's open."

The Woodward Suite was a full efficiency apartment on the ground floor of the B&B. It was never rented to the public and always available to whatever family member or friend might be in town visiting. "It's your family's room, Levi. I'm fine."

He glowered at me and walked over to a locked box on the wall where all the room keys were kept. Fishing a set of keys from his pocket, he unlocked the box and grabbed a key.

"Room thirteen." He scoffed. "Fitting for me. You take the suite."

XOXO

The next morning, I was cleaning up breakfast in the kitchen when Levi came downstairs.

"Do you think we can talk for a minute?" I asked.

"About what?"

I eyed the open envelope sitting on the kitchen counter. Last night, after Levi went to bed, I'd sifted through a large pile of mail I'd brought down with me last week. I hadn't had a chance to sort through it all, much less open any of it. But I'd found the letter from the lawyer Levi had referred to yesterday.

He nodded. "We're not going to get a better offer than that for this place. It's falling down. Only one of the outlets in the room I stayed in works, and the AC is blowing hot air."

"I know. It's a lot of money—an awful lot of money."

"Good. I'll tell my lawyer to get the ball rolling."

"Actually..." I bit my nail. "I know it's a really good offer and all, but I don't want to sell The Palm Inn."

Levi's eyes narrowed. "Why the hell not?"

"Because it's been in your family for three generations. It's a landmark and a special place, Levi."

"It *was* fifty years ago. But there's a very nice chain hotel five minutes out of town now, one where all the amenities actually work. People don't need to stay here."

"The Palm Inn isn't about needing a place to sleep. It's about experiencing Beaufort."

He scoffed. "What do you know about *experiencing* Beaufort? You didn't look back when you got your meal ticket out of here."

I blinked, taken aback. Tanner had never been my meal ticket. We'd been a couple all through high school and then for four years of college. "Excuse me?"

He shook his head. "Whatever. I don't understand why my grandfather left half to you anyway."

"He didn't leave half to me. He left it to my son."

"With you as trustee. Why not leave my brother in charge, so someone reasonable would be making the decisions?"

My face grew hot with anger. "He *did* leave someone reasonable in charge. *Me*. And as for why your grandfather didn't put Tanner in charge, the answer is because he was a very smart man."

"When was the last time you even spoke to my grandfather?"

"The week before he died. I spoke to Thatcher just about every Sunday, and so did Alex. Why don't you ask your brother the last time he spoke to him?"

"Why?"

"Why what?"

"Why did you speak to my grandfather every Sunday?"

"Because he meant a lot to me, and I wanted my son to know him, too. He was an amazing man."

Levi looked skeptical.

"You think I'm lying or something?"

"I don't know what you're up to. And at this point, I'm not sure I care. Just tell me what it's going to take for you to agree to sell. Will an extra five percent do it? Ten? I know you have a number. If you didn't care about money, my nephew wouldn't be deprived of his father."

I blinked a few times rapidly. "What the hell does that mean?"

"Save the insulted act and just let me know what you want, Presley."

I was seething. "You know what I want?"

"What?"

"I want you to go screw yourself, Levi."

xoxo

I spent the majority of the afternoon stewing over my ex's brother and his attitude. Maybe it had been naïve of me to think he'd want to preserve his grandfather's legacy rather than sell this place to the highest bidder. But I damn well wasn't going to give up without a fight.

As I went in search of my son, I thought about how big The Palm Inn was. We'd been here for several days already, and I'd barely run into the little old woman who inhabited one of the rooms. Fern was an old friend of Tanner's grandfather. I suspected she might have been a little bit *more* than a *friend* to Thatcher from time to time. He'd let her pay a reasonable rent to live here. Aside from a quick greeting on my first day, the only sign of her thus far had been the size G bras she'd left hanging to dry in one of the bathrooms. Despite the fact that she'd been close to his grandfather, I assumed Levi would have no trouble kicking Fern out on her ass, if it meant selling the place for top dollar.

After much searching, I finally found Alex in the backyard—throwing a ball back and forth with his uncle. Levi might have been a dick, but it warmed my heart for a moment to see him playing ball with my son. This was always what was missing in Alex's life—male camaraderie.

Tanner and Levi had grown up with a father who was constantly paying attention—almost too much attention— vested in their every move as he groomed them for careers in football. Up until Jim Miller's death a few years back, he'd been heavily involved in both sons' lives. That's why it made little sense that Tanner was an absentee father. Considering the examples he'd had growing up—between Thatcher and Jim—you'd think he'd want to be closer to his son. But Tanner lost a little of his mind when his football hopes were shattered after an injury only a couple of games into his NFL career.

As much as my cheating ex had treated us poorly, I did feel for what he'd been through. Though that was no excuse for his behavior. While he'd remained close to his dad until his death, Tanner's relationship with Levi had changed. They'd grown more distant, probably because Tanner was reduced to living football vicariously through his older brother; and that was hard.

I took a spot under a tree behind where Levi and Alex were playing and listened in on their conversation.

"You play a good game, but you're not perfect," my son told him.

Levi's brow lifted. "You watch me play, eh?"

"Yeah. All the time. I like telling people you're my uncle. It's more fun when you're winning, though."

Levi bent his head back in laughter. "For me, too, buddy, believe me." He passed the ball back to Alex. "So tell me. How can I do better?"

"A lot of people say you're too focused on staring down your target. You're not paying attention to the other players who can intercept you. That's what happened during the last game in Philly."

Levi nodded, catching his nephew's return throw. "Yeah. You're right about that. But you know, making mistakes is good sometimes, because they help you realize what you need to work on to get better." He tossed the ball back to Alex. "Anything else I can fix?"

Alex threw it. "You're not that great of an uncle."

Levi caught the ball, but then froze. My heart clenched.

He blinked, looking like he was trying to figure out a response.

"How come you never came to visit me in New York?" Alex asked.

Levi was silent for a bit. "I don't have a good answer for that. Adults sometimes get too wrapped up in their own lives and forget what's important. I'm sorry if you've been waiting for me to come visit. Hopefully we can make up for some lost time while I'm here, though." Levi walked over, knelt down, and ruffled Alex's hair. "Seriously. I'm sorry I've been a crappy uncle."

"You're a cruncle."

"What's that?" Levi squinted.

"Crappy uncle—cruncle." Alex laughed. "Actually, you're a better cruncle than you are a quarterback."

Levi flashed a rare, genuine smile, seeming amused at the little ball-buster his brother's son had become. "Thanks a lot."

"You're welcome, Uncle Levi."

×○×○

Late that night, when I caught myself ruminating about whether I was right to fight Levi on selling The Palm Inn, I decided I needed a reminder of why I'd come back to Beaufort in the first place. So I took out the letter I'd written to myself years ago. I'd penned it right around the time I'd moved away to attend college at Syracuse with Tanner. At the time, I'd had no clue just how messed up things would get between us, or with my life, in general. I'd always kept the letter tucked inside an old book in the hopes that I'd find it at just the right time. It had come in handy a lot since finding out Thatcher had left Alex half of The Palm Inn. When I was considering whether to move home, I'd referred to the letter several times.

The thick, stiff paper crinkled as I unfolded it. Sitting back on the bed, I let the gentle night breeze coming in through the window comfort me.

Dear future self,

I sure hope you haven't screwed up your life. Because as of right now, as a high school senior, it's really great. You have no reason to have gone and messed it up. Maybe you haven't—maybe you're extremely successful. If that's the case, this might be an even better opportunity to remind you of some things you might have forgotten over the years.

No amount of success in the world is worth forgetting what's really important. So, either you're doing really well and need to hear this, or you're in a bad place and need to hear it. Either way, you NEED to hear this.

Where is this all coming from? Well, from Mamaw, if you recall. You just had a long conversation with her out on the porch. And something told you that you needed to write it all down so you'd never forget any of the things she talked about tonight, because she might not be around by the time you read this. God, I can't even fathom that. Anyway, I've documented everything for you here in this letter. So, here are all of the things Mamaw wants you to remember about life:

Be the type of woman who gives up your seat on the bus for someone who needs it. Even though this should be obvious, don't get so wrapped up in your own head that you don't notice when someone needs a seat. That's just one example. Bottom line, don't be self-absorbed.

Next thing is that there's no such thing as not having time for the people you care about. You can always make time. Any excuse is bullcrap. Someday when you're old and gray, it's not gonna matter how much you worked or how much money you have. All you'll have left are the memories you made time for.

Remember, if you're not where you think you should be in life, it's never too late to change. But you don't need to be successful to be happy, because happiness IS success.

Find your purpose. It doesn't have to be anything grand. Even the man who shines shoes on the corner has a purpose. People walk away from him with an extra pep in their step, with an air of confidence they didn't have before. Maybe that person went on to ask out the future love of their life that day or took a job that would start their career. All because of that shoe shine.

That said, shine shoes or clean floors for a living if you have to—just don't become dependent on a man. Always work hard so you can support yourself and never have to rely on anyone.

Don't go to bed angry. Because you might not wake up. And that would just suck.

Pick up your trash. Because who are you to pollute the Earth?

In summary, be nice to others, work hard, but also recognize that money and success aren't anything if ya ain't happy.

And most of all, according to Mamaw: never, ever forget where you came from.

A place where people say hello when they walk by you.

A place where connections with the people around you are more important than the type of car you drive or the brand of watch on your wrist.

Never forget the comfort of just sitting under an oak tree and watching that amazing southern sunset.

Never forget the taste of sweet tea made right.

And down-home cooking—if you don't find someone who can make it like Mamaw, make it your damn self! (Or learn if you still don't know how.)

And if for some reason you're reading this and missing home, maybe it's damn well time you went back.

Love,
You

Wiping a tear from my eye—as I always did when I thought about my grandmother—I carefully folded the paper and placed it back in my hardcover copy of *I Know*

Why The Caged Bird Sings by Maya Angelou. Mamaw had passed away a couple of years after Alex was born. I liked to think she would have been proud of my plans to revive Thatcher's place.

After I put the book back on my shelf, I looked out the window and noticed something moving out front. It was Levi. He was using a tree branch to do pull-ups. Apparently, I wasn't the only one who was restless and unable to sleep tonight.

THREE

Presley

THE FOLLOWING MORNING, Levi walked right into me as he exited the bathroom off the kitchen.

Flustered, I stammered, "Oh...uh, I'm sorry. Didn't expect you."

He simply nodded and brushed past me, heading toward the kitchen table.

His cologne lingered in the air when I entered the bathroom. I looked down to find goosebumps covering my arms. This forced me to deal with the uncomfortable realization that my body had reacted to his hard chest against mine. I cringed. This was proof that you absolutely can't choose who you're attracted to, even if it's the most inappropriate person on Earth. After years of not being touched by a man, it seemed any contact could cause a visceral reaction. I just wished it wasn't my ex's brother, who I was pretty sure hated me.

After I used the bathroom and washed my hands, I found him sitting at the table eating some cereal. His knees bounced up and down, like he couldn't wait to eat and run. His jeans were ripped, and his knee poked out of the right leg. It was a sexy look, particularly with his strong, muscular legs. Again, I cursed myself for noticing such things.

But Levi's appeal was undeniable. Half of America likely agreed. He was ruggedly handsome, his features a bit stronger than Tanner's. Levi's jawline was more angular, and right now he had quite a bit more facial hair than his brother. When you looked at Levi, you knew he was someone who wasn't afraid to get his hands dirty. Tanner was more of a pretty boy. But they were both handsome in their own ways, and both had dark hair and blue eyes. Whatever their mama fed them growing up had helped turn those boys into very beautiful men.

Just when I'd decided to sit across from him and try to make conversation like a reasonable adult, Levi got up and put his bowl in the dishwasher before booking it out of the kitchen.

Well, so much for that.

A few minutes later, Fern came up behind me.

"What's this mess you're making? Is Grumpypants getting under your skin?"

The paper napkin I'd been holding now resembled white confetti strewn all over the countertop. I hadn't even noticed I'd done that.

Fern might have been tiny, but she was a spitfire. She wore hot pink lipstick and currently had a smear of it on her teeth. Her hair was the type of gray that looked blue. Unlike most older women around here who wore the standard puffball hairdo, Fern kept her hair in a long braid. It whipped around sometimes when she spoke.

I nodded. "Yeah, Levi *is* getting under my skin. He just left faster than a bat out of hell so he wouldn't have to talk to me. I think my being here upsets him."

"Not that hard to do, sweetheart. He seems like a loose cannon. I heard you and him arguing the other day. He seems to have a stick up his ass. The air blowin' upsets him. And he certainly has no respect for this place."

My son suddenly entered the room. "Uncle Levi has a stick up his butt? For real?"

Fern answered before I had a chance to. "It's just an expression. It means uptight."

"What's uptight?"

"You know that grumpy character, Luey, in that show you like?" I asked. "The one who always disagrees with everyone and never wants to do anything with his friends?"

"Yeah?"

"That's sort of what being uptight is."

"But what does that have to do with Uncle Levi having a stick in his butt? I bet that hurts."

I shook my head. "He doesn't really, Alex. That's just something people say to describe people who are uptight. It's a figure of speech."

"Oh."

"Yeah, don't worry."

The sound of Levi's voice froze me in my tracks.

"It doesn't hurt, buddy."

I cleared my throat. "I didn't realize you were still here."

"Yeah. The Big Bad Wolf with the stick up his butt forgot his wallet." He took it off the counter and tucked it in his back pocket. "Incidentally, wanting to do what's right for everyone involved in this situation doesn't make me the bad guy." He turned to Fern. "Or *Grumpypants*."

He turned to my son. "Alex, go grab your ball and meet me in the yard, okay? We'll play a quick game before I leave."

Alex ran out to retrieve the ball, and once he'd disappeared, Levi turned to me with daggers in his eyes. When he took a few steps toward me, I got chills.

"You seem to think I have no regard for my grandfather's legacy. Wanting to do the sensible thing is *not* disrespect."

I swallowed. "*Sensible* doesn't make it the right decision or what he'd truly want."

"My grandfather certainly never said he wanted *you* to run this place. You show me where he wrote that down. He left half of it to Alex so the money from the sale would go to him. Period. You're taking his intentions and twisting them into some convoluted fantasy to suit your own needs."

I put my hands on my hips. "Fantasy? Well, if that means wanting to do the right thing, then bring it on."

"The *right thing* is to sell." He blew out an exhausted breath. "You're in way over your head."

"I'm just attempting to do what I think your grandfather would want."

"By trying to turn his fucking house into a goddamn Hallmark movie for your own damn entertainment?"

Seriously? "Fuck you, Levi." I felt steam coming out of my ears. I hadn't meant to be so abrupt, but he'd brought it out in me.

Fern interrupted our fiery exchange. "With all due respect, I spent more time with Thatcher than *either* of y'all in recent years. And I can tell you one thing he absolutely *wouldn't* want, and that's to see you fighting!"

Levi and I looked at each other.

Fern got in his face and pointed her index finger. "Now listen to me, ya big lug. I don't care what you *think* is right here. Your grandfather would've never wanted your nephew—or me, for that matter—out on the street. And as long as we *want* to live here, you have no right to sell this place."

"So glad we could have a mature conversation about this," he said, glaring at me before turning to her again. "Not really sure what say *you* have in all of this, Fern. But I *am* trying to do right by my nephew by selling this place. I don't owe you any explanation for that. I'm sure you'd love to stay here with the minimal rent you've been paying, but I have to think about the big picture—not anyone's selfish needs."

She stomped her foot. "The big picture is me cutting off your balls if you sell this place with me or your family in it. End of story!"

He raised his voice. "I can't sell it without *her* approval anyway. Our hands are both tied if we can't agree on the fate of this place. So my goal is to knock some sense into Presley here and get her to see the light."

I straightened, pushing my shoulders back. "Well, *my* goal is to get *you* to see that preserving this place as a local landmark is doable. We can make more money over time renting it out, while also upholding an important part of Beaufort's history."

"Sure. Go ahead. Keep practicing that ridiculous pitch." He rolled his eyes.

I had a very long battle ahead of me. But I was willing to fight. I had to wonder if I needed my head examined for wanting to take all of this on, yet something deep inside me told me it would be worth it. I just needed to get through to this stubborn man first.

After he stormed off and went outside to play with Alex, Fern turned to me.

"That man is just as pig-headed as his grandfather. But sexy as all hell like Thatcher, too."

I'm not going to touch that comment.

xoxo

That afternoon my phone rang, and when I managed to pull it out, I was kind of sorry I'd bothered. *And here I thought my shitty day couldn't get any worse.*

I blew out a deep sigh and closed my eyes for a few seconds before taking a calming breath. When I opened them, I felt only marginally better, but nonetheless, I swiped to answer and used my best cheery voice. "Hi, Tanner."

"Have you come to your senses and left Beaufort yet?"

I rolled my eyes and shifted the bag of groceries to my other hand so I could dig in my purse for the car keys.

"Alex and I are actually very happy here."

That statement was only partially true. While Alex seemed settled, the last couple of days—full of run-ins with Levi—had me considering packing up my entire life and moving back to New York. I clicked the key fob and unlocked the trunk of my car.

"How can my son be happy when his mother moved him a thousand miles away? A boy needs to be near his father."

I dumped the groceries into the trunk and slammed the hatch closed. "Actually, Tanner, a boy doesn't need to be *near* his father. He needs to spend time with him."

"And how am I supposed to do that with you living all the way down in Beaufort?"

I sighed. Back in New York, Tanner had only lived a few miles away, yet he'd seen his son maybe six times over the last year. Distance had nothing to do with why Alex and his father weren't very close.

"I'm busy running errands, Tanner. Did you call to have this argument again, or was there another reason you needed to speak to me?"

My ex cleared his throat. "I need you to hold off on depositing that check I gave you."

My forehead wrinkled. "A new check? The last one I received was the one you gave me before I left, almost two weeks ago?"

"Yeah, that one."

"I deposited that a few days ago."

"Well...it's not going to clear."

I closed my eyes. I'd written a check for Alex's football camp with that money, not to mention the phone bill and a few other things. "Why this time?"

"I ran a little short this month."

The last few years had taught me how to translate the language I called Tanner Speak. I swear, if I popped *I ran a little short this month* into Google Translate, it would return *I lost a big bet.* Unfortunately, after his injury, when Tanner couldn't play for a living anymore, he'd started getting his action fix by betting on games. At first it had been just football, but over the years it had spread to most sports.

I sighed. "That check was only half of what you owe me, Tanner. You were supposed to send me the other half by this week, and now you're telling me you can't even make good on the first half?"

"What's the big deal? You have plenty of dough these days since you scored *my half* of The Palm Inn."

Though he hadn't come out and said it, I was pretty sure Thatcher left half of the property to Alex and not Tanner because he knew about Tanner's gambling addiction.

"First of all, the inn isn't even covering its costs right now. And second, even if it was showing a profit, that money would be Alex's, not mine."

"Why don't you just sell the damn thing?"

I balled my hands into fists. "*Ugh.* Now you sound just like your brother."

"Well, there's a first. You mean my big brother and I actually agree on something?"

I shook my head in frustration. "I have to go. Is there anything else you needed to discuss?"

"No, I'll call Alex in the next few days."

Sure you will. "Whatever." I didn't bother to say goodbye before swiping my phone off. Honestly, he was lucky I didn't hang up on him the minute he told me about the bounced check.

I drove home with a giant knot in my neck, grumbling a string of curses about the Miller men. If there were ever a day I was entitled to an afternoon glass of wine, it was today. And since Alex wasn't being dropped off until later, that's exactly what I was going to do—sit on the couch, prop my feet up on the coffee table, and let the wine take the edge off. Yep, that was my plan.

At least it was until I walked in the door and promptly slipped and landed on my ass...from the flood.

xoxo

"What the fuck?"

"Don't just stand there!" I yelled. "Find me another bucket!"

Levi disappeared back out the front door. He jogged in ten seconds later holding a garbage can and shook his head. "Really? You couldn't find anything else?"

I'd been using Alex's football helmet to catch the water pouring from the ceiling. This was the third leak that had sprung in the half hour since I'd gotten home. I was starting to worry that the entire ceiling was going to crash down on my head. Since the helmet was almost full, I pulled it away, and Levi slipped the can into its place.

He looked around at the disaster I'd been dealing with. "What the hell happened?"

"I have no idea. I walked in the door and fell on my ass. The ceiling was leaking in two places. It finally started to slow down, and I'd just finished mopping the floor when this third leak started pouring water."

"And the best thing you could find to catch it in was a football helmet?"

"*It was the closest thing I could grab!*"

Levi thumbed out front. "Got six empty cans right outside."

This day had really gotten to me. It had chipped and chipped at my sanity, and I finally lost it. I stood and glared at Levi. The look on my face must've forewarned him that I'd snapped, because he smartly took a step back.

Though I followed and jabbed a finger into his chest.

"I'm." *Jab.*

"Doing." *Jab.*

"The." *Jab.*

"Best." *Jab.*

"I." *Jab.*

"Can." *Jab.*

Levi held his hands up. "*Okay. Okay.* Calm down."

"Calm down! You're telling me to *calm down*?!"

The six-foot-three man of muscle actually looked a little scared. "Just...take a few deep breaths. Everything is going to be fine."

I growled at him. *Literally growled.*

Levi's eyes widened.

Feeling like I might explode, I did what I always did—though usually, my self-calming breathing technique was reserved for *the other* Miller brother. I shut my eyes and took a few deep breaths, inhaling through my nose and exhaling through my mouth. When that didn't help, I decided a much stronger remedy was in order.

I stomped to the refrigerator and whipped open the door. Inside was an almost-full magnum of white wine. Using my teeth, I uncorked it and spit the top on the floor. Then I swigged straight from the bottle.

Levi didn't budge as I continued to glare at him while I drank.

When I finally stopped chugging to take a breath, he raised a brow. "Bad day?"

I cocked my head. "You think?"

He motioned toward the ceiling. "I'm going to go take a look at what's going on upstairs with the pipes and turn off the water in the house. You got everything under control here?"

I waved the wine bottle around like a crazy person. "Doesn't it look like it?"

I saw a hint of a smile threaten at the corner of Levi's lips, though he did his best to hide it. He disappeared to God knows where, while I continued to slurp wine from the bottle and watch water drip into buckets and cans.

Ten minutes later, my cell phone rang. The last thing I felt like doing was answering, but since it was a local number, and Alex wasn't home at the moment, I had no choice.

"Hello?"

"Hi. Miss Sullivan?"

"Yes."

"This is Jeremy Brickson. I run the football camp you signed your son, Alex, up for last week. We met at registration."

Great. Just great. I knew what this was going to be about. When it rains, it pours—through the ceiling apparently. "Yes, sure. Hi, Jeremy."

"I'm really sorry to bother you. It's just that the check you gave us for Alex's camp tuition... Well, it bounced."

I shut my eyes. "Yeah, I just found out about that a little while ago. I'm very sorry. I'd planned on calling you to apologize and find out if I could replace the check or if it would be possible to redeposit the one I gave you a second time, but I got sidetracked."

"We can deposit it a second time. That's no problem. But I thought I'd let you know about a program we have for kids who can't afford football camp, just in case that's something that might help you out. I know you just moved here and all."

The anger I'd felt a few minutes ago morphed into something else. Why did he have to be so nice about it? Why couldn't he be a dick like Tanner and Levi? That I could deal with. But him being kind brought me to a new breaking point. The taste of salt filled my mouth, and a large lump lodged in my throat.

I struggled to swallow it down. "No, that's okay, Jeremy. Thank you for the offer, but I don't need any help. I just...I was supposed to move money from one account back to the other, and I didn't. That's all."

"Okay. Well, I'll hang on to this check for a few days before we redeposit it to give you a chance to do what you have to do. I'm sorry for bothering you."

I'd bounced a check, and *he* was apologizing. I definitely wasn't in New York anymore. "Thank you, and I'll cover whatever bounced-check fees you incur."

"No need. It's fine. You take care, Miss Sullivan. We're looking forward to seeing Alex in action. Rumor around town is he's got the Miller arm."

I smiled sadly. "Yeah, I think he might."

"Bye now."

After I hung up, I felt defeated. I didn't even have the energy to wipe the tears that started to flow. I just let them fall from my cheeks to the wet floor.

"Everything okay?"

Shit. How long had Levi been standing there?

I wiped my face. "Everything is fine."

"Didn't sound too fine. Sounded like you're in some financial trouble."

"I'm not. It was just a little mix up."

"Uh-huh."

You know what? Fuck it! He wants to poke his nose into my business? Let him. But he's going to hear the truth.

I straightened my spine and pulled my shoulders back. "If you must know, your brother bounced a check that's caused a ripple effect now. He owes me about four months of the measly child support he pays, and even though he only paid me *half*, he still bounced it. *Again.* I didn't know the check wasn't good when I wrote a check for Alex's football camp."

Levi looked at me like he wasn't sure if I was telling the truth. So I swigged another mouthful of wine from the bottle and decided to keep going.

"And since you seem to need to know *everything,* why don't we back up and start from the beginning, shall we? First off, *I* didn't leave Tanner like you apparently believe

I did. He left me—after the *second* time I caught him cheating. Oh, and your wonderful brother? He also has a serious gambling problem and only saw his son a handful of times over the last few years. And about Thatcher... You're so suspect of the reason I kept in touch with your grandfather? Well, the truth is, we bonded over Tanner. The two of us tried to intervene and get him help for his addiction on multiple occasions."

I took another swig from the wine bottle and started to feel a bit lightheaded. "And if you don't believe what I'm saying, you can probably verify everything with Fern." I pointed the wine bottle toward the back of the house where she lived. "Because I'm pretty certain she was fucking Thatcher and wasn't just his *friend*."

Levi blinked a few times. He opened his mouth and then shut it. Then opened it. And promptly shut it again. He looked down for a few minutes and then slowly walked over to me and held his hand out. I wasn't sure what he was asking for until he motioned down to the wine with his eyes.

I hesitated, but let him have the bottle.

His swig finished nearly a quarter of the contents. When he was done, he let out a loud *ahhh* and offered the bottle back to me. "So Gramps and Fern, huh?"

I smiled sadly. "I'm pretty sure."

He nodded. "Good for Gramps."

We stayed quiet for a long time, each sipping from the bottle and passing it back and forth. Eventually, Levi broke our silence.

"Tanner made it seem like you left him because he wasn't going to be a football star anymore."

"I figured that. I think he spewed a lot of misinformation around to your family. And I never said anything because the only one who gets hurt when I fight with Tanner is

Alex. Your brother really changed after his injury. It was like he didn't know who he was without football. You boys and your dad have the sport running through your veins. So I tried to understand as best as I could, even when he was treating me badly. That's why I gave him a pass the first time I caught him with another woman. I knew he was hurting. But the second time, I couldn't get past it, and we were fighting all the time. Eventually, he moved out." I caught Levi's eye. "You've known me as long as Tanner has, Levi. Do you really think I'm the type of person who would've left someone I cared about because life threw us a curveball?"

Levi's eyes moved back and forth between mine. He shook his head and looked down. "No."

After he gulped some more of the wine, he extended the nearly finished bottle to me. But when I went to take it, he pulled it back. Switching it to his other hand, he replaced the wine offering with his hand. "Peace?"

I nodded and put my hand in his.

A heavy silence fell between us as we shook. I figured Levi was busy trying to grasp everything I'd just said, or maybe wondering how the hell he was ever going to get the crazy person standing across from him to sell this mess of a place. But I was tongue-tied by the electricity I felt running up my arm from where our hands were joined. It was so incredibly strong—my eyes jumped to Levi's face to see if he felt it, too.

But his eyes were cast down, and he seemed unaffected. Unfortunately, that only gave me the opportunity to soak in his face. He'd shaved the beard he'd had a few days ago and now sported a close crop of day-old stubble along his masculine jawline. Levi really was incredibly attractive.

Oh God. It's the wine. It has to be. I need my head examined for thinking these thoughts.

Our hands were still joined, so I abruptly pulled mine back, which caused Levi to look up.

"Yeah, sure. Peace would be good," I said.

Levi nodded and looked down once again as he shoved his hands into his jeans pockets. "Okay, good. Ummm... why don't you, uh, go change?"

"Change?"

His eyes came back up, stopping on my breasts.

I followed his line of sight. *Oh! Shit.* I had on a white tank top with a sheer, nude bra underneath. The water from the flood had soaked them both, and my pink nipples were practically piercing through the wet fabric. I quickly folded my arms to cover up.

Our eyes met again briefly, and for the first time, I saw something other than disdain blazing in my direction. Unless I was crazy, that *something other* was the exact same thing I'd been failing to control around him lately: *desire.*

Oh God.

"Sorry...yeah... I'll, uh, be right back."

FOUR

Levi

I MANAGED TO avoid Presley for four days after that. And right now, if there had been any question in my mind as to why I'd steered clear of her, *this* was a giant, glaring reminder. Presley was in one of the guest rooms, up on the bed on all fours.

Jesus Christ. What the hell was she doing? But also, damn...*what an ass.*

It didn't help that I could still picture her naked from the day she'd greeted me with a radio to the head. Or that I remembered she shook that ass better than a five-night-a-week stripper.

When she reached one arm between the headboard and the mattress, I cleared my throat. "Lose something?"

She whirled, startled, and I put my hands up. I guess I should've been grateful there was nothing sharp or heavy nearby.

"I didn't hear you come in. And yes, I dropped some photos behind the bed, and I can't reach them."

I walked into the room. "Let me see. My arms are longer."

Presley parked her ass on her heels on the bed. "That would be great. I never realized these headboards were nailed to the wall."

I stuck my arm down behind the bed and reached around until I felt something. Pulling up some old photos, I held them out to Presley. "How many were there?"

"I think just those three. Thanks."

I pointed to the headboard. "There's a story behind why those are screwed into the wall."

"Oh yeah?"

"When we were little, Grams and Pops used to have us stay over once a month to give my parents a night off. I was probably about six this one time we came for our visit, and I was staying in a room two doors down from here. A young couple was staying in the room next to me. All night long, the headboard banged away. There was also some grunting. When I asked Pops if he'd heard the noise the next morning, he told me the couple must've been jumping on the bed, and he was going to have a talk with them about it, because the beds weren't for jumping."

Presley smiled. "I take it they weren't jumping on the bed?"

I shook my head. "Definitely not. But the next afternoon, the sound was back again. Pops had run out to the hardware store, and Grams was busy in the kitchen. So, being the man of the house, I decided to knock on the door and tell the guests the beds weren't for jumping. They didn't answer at first, but then I heard the woman yell, '*Yes!*' so I opened the door."

Presley's big, green eyes widened. She covered her mouth. "You walked in on them?"

"Yup. I'll never forget it. The woman was blond, and the only thing she had on was a black cowboy hat. She was sitting on top of the guy. It took me a few years to figure out she was riding him. At the time I just thought she was jumping up and down on the bed naked."

Presley cracked up. "Oh my God."

"I told them to stop jumping because they were going to break the bed. A few minutes later, the man stormed out half-dressed and spoke to Grams. When Pops came home from the hardware store, she turned him around and made him go back to get screws. All the headboards were bolted to the wall from that day on. No more banging to attract curious kids."

"That's hysterical. And I can totally see your grandmother pushing your grandfather right back out the door."

I smiled and nodded, feeling warmth in my chest. This old place had a million memories.

"By the way, where have you been?" Presley asked. "I haven't seen you the last few days. At first I thought maybe our peace treaty had been short-lived. But then I went down to pick up Alex's equipment for football camp and spoke to Jeremy Brickson. I came to your room earlier to talk to you. You didn't have to pay for Alex's camp. My bounced check would've cleared this time. I have some savings. I just hadn't transferred any money over to my checking when Tanner bounced that check."

"I wanted to pay for it. It's the least I could do for being such a cruncle."

Presley smiled. "Well, thank you. That was really generous."

"It was nothing."

"Are you in a rush right now?"

"Not really. Why? You need something?"

"No, but I've been cleaning out this room all morning, and I found some old albums. They have some incredible photos. I didn't realize how much Alex looks like you when you were a kid."

"Me?"

"Yeah, come look."

She showed me a photo from Little League. I almost did a double take. Everything from the expression on my face to the shape of my eyes matched my nephew's.

"You're right. I thought that was him for a split second."

"I know. Genetics is pretty crazy." Presley laughed. "I thought the same thing."

Even though Alex wasn't mine, the fact that Presley had given birth to this human who looked like me made me feel oddly connected to her. Who knows if I'd ever have a kid of my own someday.

She flipped the pages of the album and stopped at a photo of a lemonade stand Tanner and I had set up in front of our house when we were around Alex's age.

"That little side hustle made us some good moola back then. Too bad it never helped my brother learn the value of a dollar. He likes to piss money away now."

Presley's smile faded. "Well, yeah. Unfortunately, it's his way of dealing with…everything."

Her empathy surprised me a little—especially now that I knew he'd cheated. It takes a big person to sympathize with someone who shit all over them.

"On some level, I understand it—how he could get caught up in an addiction like that," I said. "But on another, I feel like smacking him upside the head. At some point you have to get your shit together before your life passes you by."

She sighed. "Yeah."

I turned to the next page of the album to find a photo of Tanner and me on a boat with Gramps. "Man, look at this one. I remember this day like it was yesterday. Gramps took us fishing, and Tanner caught a spotted bass. It was the first time either of us had ever caught anything. I remember being so damn jealous. I barely spoke to him the rest of the day."

That was kind of ironic now. I knew my brother had to endure a lot watching me continue a successful career in the NFL when his own dreams had been cut short. The jealousy I experienced over the bass that day was nothing compared to that.

"See?" Presley said. "Stuff like this is why I want Alex to have the experience of growing up here. Beaufort is nothing like New York, where the kids are inside all day messing around on their devices. This is the kind of life I want for him, playing out in the sun with his friends and family."

Family.

"Tanner couldn't have taken you moving so far away very well."

"He gives me shit for leaving, yeah. But he never took advantage of having us there, Levi. That's the difference. I would've never left if he'd been there for Alex, day in and day out. But he barely ever was."

It disappointed me to realize how absent Tanner had been all this time. "Yeah, I get that, Presley."

It was one thing to suck as an uncle—which I absolutely had, as my nephew was quick to remind me. But it was another thing entirely to suck as a father.

"Anyway," she said. "You can't beat the experience of growing up in a small town like Beaufort. I wrote a letter years ago to remind myself of how important this place is to me."

"You wrote a letter...to yourself?"

She blushed a little. "Yeah. It's about all the lessons I learned from my mamaw growing up." She smiled. "Want to see it?"

"Sure."

She left to go get it. As much as I knocked her for having delusions of grandeur when it came to the future of this place, I did admire her respect for where she came from.

Presley returned holding a book.

"What's with the book?" I asked.

"Just a hiding place for safekeeping."

I looked down at the title—*I Know Why The Caged Bird Sings*. "Why that one?"

"I remember reading it in high school. It left an impression on me. I always found it inspiring. Maya Angelou was amazing. I love what she has to say about learning to love yourself and showing kindness to others. So her book seemed like a fitting place to keep my letter."

Presley handed the paper to me, looking a bit shy, which I found kind of adorable. *Yeah, she might be growing on me a little.*

I spent the next couple of minutes reading Presley's letter as she watched, seeming to try to gauge my reaction. Reading these words made me feel even worse about the misconceptions I'd had about her until our chat the other night. I'd had no clue my brother had cheated on her— twice. That was certainly not the story he'd told us. We all assumed she'd left him selfishly, when in fact, she'd had damn good reason for it.

When I got to the end, I handed it back. "Your mamaw was a smart woman. I think it's cool that you wrote this. We could all use a reminder of what's truly important from time to time."

She took a deep breath in. "So..."

I suspected what she was leading up to. "What?"

"If you truly *get it*—if you appreciate the importance of Beaufort and growing up in this idyllic place—why can't you understand wanting to preserve The Palm Inn?"

Here we go.

And we were getting along so well.

"You can still have the kind of life you want here in Beaufort without running the inn, Presley."

"But what about preserving your family's history?"

"The Palm is a building. It doesn't have a heart that beats. Moreover, I don't think it's important to preserve something that's not relevant anymore. It would be much smarter to take that money and invest it—make a new history for yourself and Alex so you can have a fresh start."

Her expression turned almost sad. What the hell was she thinking? Why did she want this so badly? There had to be more to it.

"I feel like you're searching for something in this place that's just not here," I told her. "Maybe you're searching for the innocence of a time that doesn't exist anymore. Beaufort is still a nice place to live, but things have changed. The memories of this place will always be here, but my grandfather never specified that he wanted us to run it forever. I think even *he* knew it wouldn't work out. Otherwise he would have told us that's what he wanted."

She blinked. Even though she didn't say anything, I got the sense that she was really hearing me for the first time. I took advantage of the rare opportunity to try to get through to her.

"Hear me out, Presley. Even if you were able to fix it up, there's just not enough draw. People stay in Airbnbs now, not bed and breakfasts. And even if the demand were there, it's a fuck ton of work. You'd regret it."

Her frown deepened, the look on her face growing sadder by the second. And now I regretted pissing on her parade. It made me feel like shit. I knew her intentions were good, but I couldn't stand by and let her make a huge mistake.

But I'd done enough damage for one day. So I sighed and lay back on the bed, staring at the ceiling. "Okay. I'm done with the lecture."

"I guess we're just going to have to agree to disagree until one of us backs down," she finally said. "Hopefully that person will be you."

God. Presley was stubborn. A part of me admired her resilience, as much as it fucking annoyed me.

No way was I getting into it any more today, though, because we'd been getting along. Actually, maybe playing nice would be more successful than being combative in getting her to see the light.

I changed the subject as I bounced on the bed. "This mattress is hella comfortable. The one in room thirteen is hard as a rock. Mind if I switch it out with this one?"

"Go to town," she said as she proceeded to pack some stuff away in the corner of the room.

"Don't you mean go to hell?" I cracked.

"I'm trying to be nice to you, Levi."

"Is that your new strategy?"

"Maybe."

I laughed to myself. I'd thought I was so clever a minute ago, planning to kill her with kindness. Apparently, we both had the same idea.

XOXO

Later that night, Presley and I were cleaning up after dinner, and I insisted she let me do the dishes. She'd made a damn good chicken pot pie and thought she'd have leftovers for lunch tomorrow. But I'd demolished three huge pieces and squelched all hope of the pie surviving past supper. After my gluttony, the least I could do was help her clean up.

"Mom and I eat like birds," my nephew said. "But, Uncle Levi, you eat like a tyrannosaurus. I've never seen anyone eat like you."

I knew damn well that my brother could throw down some food. The fact that Alex couldn't remember the last meal he'd had with his dad wasn't lost on me.

"Wait until those Miller genes catch up with you, buddy. It's only a matter of time before you're eating everything in sight, too. I bet you'll end up taller than me."

Presley chuckled. "Actually, I'd forgotten what it was like cooking for an athlete. I have to remember to make double next time if I want leftovers." She winked.

"Well, it was really good. Thank you again."

"You're welcome." She smiled.

Here we were seeming to get along again. I had to wonder if this was all part of her "kill him with kindness" plan.

After Alex went upstairs to his room, Presley became suddenly anxious. I turned to find her looking like she wanted to tell me something.

I slapped the hand towel over my shoulder. "What's up?"

"I've been doing a lot of thinking about our conversation earlier."

I took a seat across from her at the kitchen table. "Okay..."

"What you said definitely made some sense, but my gut is still telling me selling The Palm Inn *isn't* the right decision."

Damn. The first part of her statement had gotten me excited for a moment; I'd thought she was coming around.

"It's one thing if you think it's a lot of work for me. That's my problem, and shouldn't be a concern for you. But I do understand your worries about lack of demand. Still, I feel like you could be wrong." She licked her lips nervously. "So, I have a proposition."

My brow lifted. "What is it?"

Presley rubbed her hands together. "Once we get this place presentable, if I can sell out the first month, I think that will be a good indicator of how things will go. So, what I'd like to propose is that if I *can* sell out August...you agree not to sell."

I twiddled my thumbs as I thought about it.

She prodded. "We can always sell later if we need to, Levi. At any point."

It didn't make sense to invest too much in making this place nice if the developer was just going to tear it down anyway. But he wasn't pressuring me to close the deal fast, so I had some time to let Presley have her way—for now. In any case, this was going to be the easiest win ever because there was no freaking way she could sell out the first month. I felt completely confident in agreeing.

"You got a deal."

Her eyes widened. "Really?"

"Really."

Presley got up from her seat and wrapped her arms around me. "You're the best."

Something happened to me in that moment, as I felt the warmth of her arms around me, smelled her sweet scent. I hadn't been hugged by a woman in God knows how long. I'd kissed plenty. Screwed plenty. But this? Just having someone's arms around me? It felt foreign. And nice. *It felt nice.*

And I had to wonder whether it was the hug or the woman giving it.

Either way, I needed to check myself before I wrecked myself. *What the hell are you doing even thinking about your brother's ex this way, Levi?*

I pulled away. "I, uh... I'm actually late. Supposed to be meeting some of my old high school buddies at Dale's Pub."

Disappointment crossed her face. "Ah. Okay." She took a few steps back and smiled. "Have fun."

"Yeah. Thanks."

Now, I'd have to call my friends and actually get the hell out of here. I'd completely made that shit up to avoid the tension in this room.

FIVE

Presley

LEVI AGREEING TO my proposition left me on cloud nine for the rest of the night, so much so that I had the worst time sleeping. Well, it wasn't only Levi's decision that gave me insomnia. Alex had also come to my room and fallen asleep in my bed. He'd had a nightmare and asked if he could lie with me. While I was always happy to let him do that, my son was a restless sleeper and kicked a lot. So anytime he slept in my bed, I had to accept that I'd be awake most of the night.

I did need to get at least a few hours of sleep since I had a full day of house chores and errands tomorrow. I decided to leave Alex here and move to the empty bedroom I'd cleaned out earlier today.

As I lay my head down, I realized Levi was right—this mattress was definitely pretty comfortable compared to others in the house. It didn't take long for me to fall right asleep.

Sometime in the middle of the night, though, a train in the distance woke me up again. Except this time, when

I rolled over, I felt something next to me. It took a few seconds to realize it was a warm body.

Someone's in the bed!

My first instinct was to scream. After my loud yelp, the body jerked and fell to the ground in a loud thud.

"Ow, what the fuck?" I heard him growl.

I grabbed my phone and activated the flashlight. I pointed it to find Levi rubbing his head with one hand and his knee with the other.

Levi? What was he doing in bed with me?

Not only that, he was virtually naked aside from his tight boxer briefs.

My pulse raced. "What are you doing in here?"

"Me?" He stared up at me, his eyes groggy. "What the hell are *you* doing in here? This isn't your room, either."

"I know. I couldn't sleep because Alex is in my bed. So I came in here."

He stayed on the ground and kept rubbing his knee. "I must have had too much to drink because I didn't even notice you in the damn bed. I came back from the bar and decided to sleep in this room since I hadn't had a chance to swap mattresses yet. The damn lights in here don't work, so I couldn't see you."

"Are you hurt?" I asked.

"Just the knee I injured the last time you nearly killed me. No biggie."

"Shit, I'm sorry," I said, bending down and placing my hand on his knee.

He moved back suddenly and stood up.

Jesus. I wasn't trying to be inappropriate; but maybe it came off that way? *Shit.* Earlier he'd pulled back from our hug, too. Did he think I was crossing the line?

"Don't worry about it," he said. "That's what I get for scaring you."

"I'm sorry I caused you an injury...again."

"It'll be a miracle if I make it out of this house unscathed."

Crap.

When I didn't say anything, he added, "I'm kidding, Presley. I'll be fine."

Somehow I hadn't noticed that the flashlight on my phone was pointing straight at his crotch. It wasn't my intention; I was just so flustered. His body looked so damn good right now, and I was shining a spotlight on his cock! I needed to get out of here.

"I'm going back to my bed," I announced.

He held out his hand. "No. I'll go."

"I *insist*, Levi. I won't be able to sleep knowing you're injured and uncomfortable on top of that. Not taking no for an answer."

I ran out of the room before he could argue with me.

Back in bed, my pulse pounded a mile a minute, and the insomnia was worse than ever. I couldn't get the encounter with Levi out of my mind. *Why am I still thinking of him, and why am I feeling so guilty?*

I didn't owe my cheating ex the courtesy of feeling guilty about being attracted to another man, although his *brother* might have been the only exception to that. I cringed when I thought about how Levi had moved away when I touched his knee. Being attracted to Levi Miller was an extremely unfortunate circumstance, but one I couldn't stop. You can't help how your body reacts to someone. And Levi was insanely hot, even if I didn't think it was *appropriate* to see him that way.

I finally came to the conclusion that staring at the ceiling with Alex's leg wrapped over me was getting me no closer to sleep. So I carefully slipped out from under him and ventured into the kitchen.

I stopped short at the sight of Levi sitting at the table drinking a beer. He was still wearing nothing but his damn underwear.

"Isn't it a little late to be drinking?"

He looked up before lifting the bottle. "Or is it early? Practically morning, right? Anyway, you judging me or something?"

His gaze landed on my chest, and it hit me that I was dressed no more appropriately than he was. The silk camisole I wore left little to the imagination.

"I was actually going to make myself some warm milk. That sometimes helps me get to sleep."

"Warm milk?" His voice was low. "I've got something better to knock you out."

My nipples hardened as I freaked out for a millisecond.

Levi walked over to the cabinet and took out two shot glasses. I felt like an idiot for wondering if that comment had been suggestive.

I held up my hand. "I can't drink that at this hour."

"Sure, you can. It's easy. I pour it in the little glass here, and you chug it down. I guarantee it'll help you sleep better than anything else." He pointed to the seat across from his. "Sit."

His demanding tone gave me chills, and for a moment I wanted nothing more than to hear him give me command after command. *I have issues.*

"I guess it can't hurt to try," I said, sliding a chair out.

As he threw his shot back, I took a moment to admire his body, the ripples of muscle lining his abs.

He slammed his glass down and said, "Your turn."

I took the glass in my hand and gulped the contents. I wasn't a hard-liquor drinker and couldn't even identify what I'd just consumed. But nevertheless, it was down the chute.

The alcohol burned my throat, and I let out a single cough. Then I nearly choked when Levi blurted out a question.

"Have you been with anyone since Tanner?"

I swallowed carefully. "That's...sort of a random question. What made you ask that?"

"Sorry if I'm being intrusive." He crossed his arms. "You're a really involved mom, obviously. And you certainly love biting off way more than you can chew. Doesn't seem like that leaves much room for...anything else."

"I've gone out on a few dates here and there over the years, but nothing serious."

"No sex?"

Whoa. "Don't hold back with your questions. Do I ask you about your sex life, Levi Miller?"

He smiled. "You don't have to tell me shit. I was just curious since you and Tanner haven't been together in so long."

I'd been trying to skirt giving him a direct answer, but screw it. Why not be honest? No better time to talk about sex with your ex's brother than when he's sitting across from you half-naked in the middle of the night after you've just had a shot of something, right? *Ugh.*

"I've slept with one man since Tanner. He was a nice guy. Luke. Sort of a friend with benefits—not someone I saw myself with long term." I shrugged. "It's not easy to find someone you're compatible with, want to have sex with, *and* who'd make a good role model for Alex. It's nearly impossible to find all three, actually. I certainly haven't brought anyone I've dated around my son, though. I wouldn't do that unless it was serious."

"Yeah. That's smart."

I lifted my chin. "What about you? I'm sure you have no problem finding women to pass the time with. You probably have the opposite problem I do. I mean, how do you choose when you can have anyone you want?"

My face felt hot as it hit me that I was bracing for his answer. This jealousy was eye-opening—and uncomfortable.

"It's not that simple," he answered.

"Yeah, I would imagine it's hard to pick." I chuckled through gritted teeth.

"That's not what I meant, Presley." He blew out a frustrated breath. "Do you have any idea how sucky it is to never know if someone wants to be with you because of who you are as a person, or just the fact that you're a famous athlete? Some women just want to say they fucked the Broncos' quarterback. I mean, sure, I'm not gonna complain *too* much. I don't have any problem finding someone attractive to have sex with whenever I need it, but that gets old real fast. When it's *too* easy, it's just not... invigorating, you know?"

His eyes met mine, and his stare burned the damn skin off my arms.

"I suppose I can understand that," I whispered.

Levi rubbed his index finger along the rim of his empty shot glass. "When I was younger and first starting out in the NFL...yeah, the sex aspect was exciting because it was new. I didn't care as much about what was up here back then." He pointed to his head. "You know? But as I get older, I need more mental stimulation to get me off. Sometimes you just want to have a fucking conversation with someone, or hang out without having sex and just watch a movie. Everyone has this impression of what being with me is like, and I always feel pressured not to disappoint them. Sometimes all I want to do is to just fucking *be*—just talk, or sit in comfortable silence with someone I trust." He sighed. "That's not easy to find at all."

What he'd just said hit me in the feels, but I tried not to show it. Instead I joked, "You poor baby. It must be so hard being you."

He bent his head back in laughter. "I know. Woe is me, right?"

"I'm kidding," I said. "Honestly, I never gave much thought to how difficult it would be for someone in your shoes to trust. I always assumed you had the pick of the litter. But I guess that's just on the surface, huh?"

"You know how when you were a kid and got birthday money to go to the toy store, you couldn't figure out what to get? You had enough to get almost anything in the place, but for some reason because you *had* the money that day, there was nothing you wanted? That's sort of what it's like. It's too easy sometimes. I like a challenge. At the same time, if I found her now—that special person—how would I know she'd want to be with me if I wasn't Levi Miller?"

As much as I'd teased him a minute earlier, I did feel bad that he saw things this way. It must suck to never know who to trust or who might be using you.

"Do you sometimes regret your career?"

He bounced his head back and forth silently. "That's tough to say. I don't regret getting to play for a living. In that sense, I'm living the dream. But I could do without some of the other bullshit that goes with it. The problem is, you can't have it both ways, and it's futile to think about now anyway."

"Yeah."

"But I do know the right person for me would have to be someone who doesn't give a shit about Levi Miller the quarterback. Because a career in the NFL has a shelf life. As my brother knows all too well, it can end in an instant."

The mention of Tanner sent a wave of guilt through me. I was enjoying this intimate conversation with his brother a little too much right now.

Levi once again looked me straight in the eyes. "Part of my negative feelings toward you in the beginning were because I thought you'd left Tanner when things got bad—even though that never lined up with the way I remembered you, the type of person I believed you were. I'm sorry for making assumptions."

"I would never have left your brother, Levi. I loved him. But he betrayed me twice. And those are just the times I know of. His lying was the reason it didn't work out. I can assure you it had nothing to do with his injury."

His stare was penetrating. "I know that now." Then he shook his head, seeming to snap out of it. "Anyway, this conversation is way too deep for nearly four in the morning. You'd better get some sleep before Alex wakes up."

As much as I didn't want to leave, I pretended to agree. "Yeah. I'd better."

"Take the guest room," he insisted.

"I injured you, remember? You need the comfortable bed."

"Not up for negotiation, Presley. Take the bed."

"Thank you." I smiled.

"You're welcome."

As I turned around and headed to the room, I felt my entire body buzzing with desire. Hearing Levi say he wanted more than just sex with a woman made me want to have sex with him, if that made any sense. I was losing my mind. Then when I lay down in the guest bed, I immersed myself in his scent. His cologne had infiltrated the bedding where he'd been sleeping earlier.

Damn.

I tossed and turned in the sheets, moving my legs around and thinking about our time together in the kitchen—the way he'd demanded that I sit, the way he was looking at me, the way he so very directly asked me about sex. There was something so unapologetic about it all, and somehow I knew he would be the exact same way in bed. I suddenly imagined him bending me over his knee and smacking my ass so hard it burned.

What in the ever-loving fuck, Presley?

Somehow the thought of that led to me closing my eyes and imagining his naked body over me. He was physical perfection. I slipped my hand down my panties and began circling my clit as I imagined what his cock would feel like sinking into me. When I'd shined my flashlight on his crotch earlier, I'd gotten a clear view of his bulge. I could tell he was massive.

It took me all of one minute to give myself one of the most intense orgasms I'd had in ages. I continued to throb between my legs and wondered if I needed another round to calm down enough to sleep.

Panting, I wiped the sweat off my forehead.

You just got off thinking about Tanner's brother. Real nice.

And damn it, I wanted to do it again.

Sitting across from him at breakfast tomorrow would be interesting.

SIX

Presley

"THE COACHES CERTAINLY didn't look like that when we were in high school."

I looked up to find my old friend Katrina walking up the bleachers toward me. We'd reconnected a few days ago when football camp started, and we realized our boys were the same age. It was nice to have someone to sit with.

"Hey, Kat."

She sat down next to me, and we shielded our eyes with our hands as we looked down at the sideline of the field. Jeremy Brickson was using the hem of his T-shirt to wipe sweat from his forehead, revealing a glistening, tanned six-pack.

Kat sighed. "Last week I saw him at the gym. I couldn't walk for two days after. You know the machine where you put the cushioned things on your shoulders and lift up and down while standing on the edge of the grate?"

"The calf machine?"

"Yeah, that's the one. I was using it. I normally do two reps of six, but Jeremy was using the arm machine right across from me. Every time he lifted, he made this grunting sound. Between the bulge of his biceps and that grunt, it was better than porn. So I lost track of how many lifts I did and stayed on the machine for *way* too long. My calf muscles were in knots for days. I legit couldn't walk."

I laughed. "Oh no."

"Totally worth it, though."

"He seems like a really nice guy. Alex can't stop talking about him when we get home. He calls him Brick. It's really cute."

"Yeah, I heard the other coach call him that, too. Of course, it totally escaped me that his last name was Brickson, and my mind automatically went to wondering if he had a brick in his pants." She leaned forward and squinted. "I wish he'd wear tighter shorts so I could get a look at the outline."

I shook my head and laughed. "You haven't changed a bit since high school."

"What? Like you weren't wondering the same thing. A man that nice, who donates his time to coach football, and has a body like that... There's got to be a catch. No one is the full package."

My mind instantly flashed to Levi in his boxers last week, the night he fell out of the bed. Now that man had a *very full package*—one I'd thought about too often lately.

"What's his deal, anyway?" I asked. "He mentioned the other day that he's lived in Beaufort for five years. It's not a place people usually move to without a reason."

Kat nodded. "He owns a construction company. Came to town to build the new high school and never left. I think he lived up in Charleston before. He's divorced. He and his wife lost a child—born with some sort of heart defect and only lived to age four. He played college football at

Clemson, and his son was a huge football fan. So now he donates his free time to teaching kids football. Honestly, I'm not sure I could do that—be around a bunch of kids who are probably about the same age his son would be now, playing his son's favorite sport."

"Wow. I had no idea. That's really sad that he lost a child."

"He's pretty private. Keeps to himself mostly. But my friend Annemarie was his receptionist for a while, so she gave me the skinny." Kat opened her purse and dug out a ChapStick. She rubbed it on her lips as she spoke. "So what's going on with you? Are you seeing anyone?"

I shook my head. "I'm still getting settled in."

"Well, if you want to go out sometime, I'm game. There's a new bar a few miles out of town that has a good crowd. Travis stays at his dad's Thursday through Saturday morning since we share custody, so I'm always up for a Friday night out."

"That sounds good. I'm sure I'll be more settled in a few weeks."

After practice, Kat and I walked down to the field together to help our boys carry their equipment. They might be playing football, but God forbid they carry a duffle, helmet, and pads. Jeremy walked over while Alex was shoving his jersey into his bag.

"Alex is doing great. The rumors about him having a killer arm were all true."

I smiled. "Thanks. He's been practicing a lot with his uncle lately."

Alex finished packing his bag and zipped it shut. When he stood, Jeremy rested his hands on my son's shoulders. "He told me. How am I supposed to take credit for all of his accomplishments someday when he's drafted into the NFL if Levi Miller is also helping him train?"

I chuckled. "Ummm, if he stands on the podium and thanks anyone other than his mother, both you and his uncle will be hearing from me."

"Mom?" Alex interrupted. He pointed to the parking lot. "The ice cream man is here. Can I get something, *please*?"

"Sure." I dug into my purse and pulled out a five. Alex snatched it and took off running. "Hey! What about your equipment!" I yelled after him.

"Thanks, Mom!" he yelled without looking back.

I shook my head and bent to lift the duffle. But Jeremy took it out of my hand. "Let me. I'm heading to the parking lot, too."

"Thanks."

We started to walk side by side. "So Alex said you guys live over at The Palm Inn?"

"We do. Alex's grandfather passed away six months ago. He left part of it to Alex as an inheritance. So we're living there while I work on trying to make a go of it."

"It's a beautiful building. I stopped in once when I'd first moved to town and Mr. Miller gave me a tour. I do construction, but I'm a closet wannabe architect."

"Yeah, it's a pretty incredible place."

"It's got something like ten bedrooms, right?"

"Fourteen. But *ugh,* don't remind me. That just means more work. It's pretty run down. I got an estimate for new air conditioning this morning, and it's more than I expected to spend on the entire refurbishment."

"Do you have a GC?"

"A general contractor?" I shook my head. "Well, I guess I do. You're looking at her. I'm trying to save money by coordinating everything myself."

"Well, if you need any help or any recommendations for reliable workers, just let me know. I'm sure I don't need to tell you to get a few estimates for any big jobs. It still surprises me how much one company's price can vary from another."

"Thanks. That's very nice of you to offer."

"It would be my pleasure. Is the B&B open for business while you're working on it, or do you have it shut down?"

"It's closed right now to guests. Well, except Fern. But she's not really a guest. She's more like a permanent resident. She was a good friend of Thatcher's. Levi is also staying there while he's in town, too. He owns the other half with Alex."

"I hope you don't mind me asking, but are you divorced?"

I shook my head. "No, but only because I was never married. Alex's dad and I were engaged, but we didn't actually make it down the aisle. He lives in New York. We haven't been together in a long time."

"Well, why don't I give you my number in case I can offer any help with finding good contractors?"

"That would be great." I dug my phone out of my pocket and handed it to Jeremy. As he typed, I said, "I might bug you for the name of a plumber, if you don't mind. We had a few pipes burst the other day."

Jeremy looked up and smiled. "No problem at all. I'm happy to help. I'll send you some later."

He had a really warm smile and was also pretty cute. I'm not sure I'd even noticed that when I'd spoken to him at registration.

As he went to hand back my cell, Kat caught up to us. She noticed the phone passing, and her eyebrows rose with a smirk. "Hi, Coach. You look really good out there. I mean, the kids—*the kids* look really good out there."

"Thanks. They're picking things up fast."

"Hey, Brick!" one of the other coaches called. "You got a minute?"

"Sure." Jeremy looked back at us and nodded. "Have a good night, ladies."

Kat wiggled her fingers. "We sure will."

"Bye."

When he was barely out of earshot, Kat was all over me. "You lucky bitch."

"What are you talking about?"

"Don't play coy with me. I saw him give you his number."

"To give me a recommendation for a plumber for The Palm Inn. We need some new pipes."

"Uh-huh."

I laughed. "No, really. That's all it was."

"Are you that oblivious? Coach wants to give you some pipe, alright."

Alex walked over with two ice creams. "I could get two with the money you gave me!"

I ruffled my son's hair. "Just because you *can* get two, doesn't mean you needed to."

Alex shrugged. "You can have one, if you want."

"Hmmm. A SpongeBob popsicle with gumball eyes. Tempting, but I think I'll pass."

"I gotta go." Kat leaned in for a hug and whispered in my ear. "Hope his pipe is really long."

I laughed. "You're nuts."

XOXO

That night, Alex and I were getting ready to eat dinner when Levi walked in.

He sniffed. "Did you fry chicken or something? It smells great in here."

I lifted the basket of golden brown chicken from the kitchen counter and tipped it so Levi could see inside before I set it in the middle of the table. "I did. It's your grandmother's recipe. I found a book of them when I was cleaning out room eight today. They're all in her handwriting, too. Would you like to join us?"

He licked his lips, staring at the chicken. "You sure you have enough?"

"I learned from last time and made enough for a small army. Sit and eat."

He pulled out a chair before I'd finished my sentence. It made me happy that he seemed to enjoy a home-cooked meal. I'd always loved to cook, but the only man I'd ever done it for was Tanner. While he liked southern cooking, he was always concerned about eating healthy and gaining too much weight. Levi, on the other hand, seemed less worried about that. I set out mashed potatoes and green beans, and he filled his plate to the brim.

"Do you always eat like that? Or is it just because it's the off-season?"

Levi's brows drew together. "Eat like what?"

"I don't know. You seem to eat whatever you want."

He bit into a drumstick and shrugged. "Food is fuel. I'll burn it."

I realized I'd forgotten to put out the butter for the mashed potatoes, so I grabbed it from the fridge. Walking back, I held up the stick. "You make it sound so easy. I might as well glue this thing to my hips, because that's exactly where it will wind up."

Levi's eyes dropped to my hips and flickered back up to meet my eyes. He didn't say a word, but bit into his drumstick a bit more aggressively. *Oh my.*

I cleared my throat as I sat and changed the topic. "I have someone coming tomorrow to give us an estimate on fixing the pipes upstairs."

Levi had capped them after the flood, but they needed a permanent repair before we could turn the water in that part of the house back on. Luckily, we didn't need use of the second-floor bathrooms.

"Oh yeah? Is it Morrow Plumbing? Pete Morrow's father's company?"

"No, actually. It's called Universal."

"Never heard of them. Are they local?"

"I'm not sure. They were recommended to me, and I just called and made the appointment."

"I thought Coach was going to fix it," my son chimed in. "Didn't Travis's mom say Coach Brick has a pipe he wants to give you?"

My eyes flared wide. I'd been chewing a piece of chicken and started to cough.

Levi's eyes narrowed. He looked between Alex and me. "The coach wants to give you his...pipe?"

I pointed to my throat as my face reddened. "Swallowed wrong."

Levi seemed to lose interest in his food as he waited for me to explain. I washed my chicken down with a glass of water, glad I at least had a reason for my red face.

"I don't think that's quite what Travis's mom said, Alex."

My son was oblivious to the innuendo. He shrugged and kept on eating.

"Coach Brick is a general contractor," I explained. "He offered to give me some referrals for the contractors we need."

Levi studied my face. "Uh-huh."

"He also gave me an air conditioning company to try. Did you see the estimate that the first company gave us?"

"Yup. It'll drain almost the entire operating account, and we won't see a dime more if we wind up selling the place since the buyer plans to tear it down."

"We're selling The Palm Inn?" Alex asked. "It's going to get torn down?"

I hadn't explained that as a possibility. "We're still trying to figure that out, honey."

Alex shoveled mashed potatoes into his mouth. "I like it here."

"Don't talk with your mouth full of food. But I like it here, too."

Alex looked over at his uncle. "Do you not like it here, Uncle Levi?"

"Of course I do. It's just that...sometimes as adults we have to make decisions that aren't always based on what we like."

"What are they made on then?"

"Well, lots of things. Money and time, for example. A place like this takes a lot of both to keep running."

"So you don't make a lot of money playing football?"

I sat back and enjoyed my son's impromptu inquisition.

"I do, buddy. But—"

Alex frowned. "Oh, I get it. You're too busy. You're going to go back to being a cruncle, aren't you?"

Levi looked to me for help. When all he got was a grin, he rolled his eyes.

"How did we get from the pipes to me being a crappy uncle so fast?"

I chuckled. "I'm not sure, but I'm glad we did."

Levi shook his head. "Why don't we talk about neither? What plays do they have you running at football camp?"

For the rest of dinner, the boys talked football. I was impressed at how much my son had learned already. He'd memorized most of the plays and was able to describe them to Levi using the right terminology. Just as we were finishing, one of Alex's friends knocked at the door and asked him to ride bikes.

"Can I, Mom?"

I looked at the time on my phone. "For an hour. And no going off the block."

Just like earlier today, he bolted before I'd finished my sentence.

Levi and I cleared the table. I set our plates in the sink and turned on the water to rinse them. "These are the little things I love about living here," I said. "Never in a million years would I tell my son he could go outside and ride his bicycle unsupervised in New York City."

"Yeah, I get that."

As I loaded the dishwasher, Levi leaned against the counter next to it. He folded his arms across his chest and lifted an inquisitive brow. "So...the coach wants to give you *his pipe*?"

I waved him off. "That's just my friend Kat being cheeky. Jeremy was being polite and offered to help with referrals for The Palm. He's a general contractor, so he has a lot of contacts. Kat is making it more than it is."

"You sure about that? Men don't generally offer a woman help without wanting something in return."

"So you're saying there's no such thing as nice people anymore? Everyone just wants to get in each other's pants?"

"Not necessarily. It's not always about getting into someone's pants. But there's usually something people want in return when they're nice."

"Yes, they want *kindness* in return, Levi. When did you become such a cynic?"

"I'm not a cynic. I'm a realist. Half the time, we don't even recognize we're doing it. It's just human nature. If your rent is late, you're a little nicer to your landlord because you're going to need an extension. You have two weeks to return something and it's been two and a half since you bought it? You walk into the store and smile at the lady behind the counter. You want in a woman's pants, you offer to help her find the contractors she needs."

I folded my arms across my chest. "Oh really? Well, you just helped me clean up after dinner. What exactly would you like from me?"

Levi's eyes flickered to my lips a moment. It was so fast that I almost thought I'd imagined it. But the heat between my legs told me I hadn't. He looked away. "We'll agree to disagree. But don't say I didn't warn you if *the good coach* wants more than to be helpful."

xoxo

The following afternoon, I again sat with Kat on the bleachers, waiting for camp to end for the day. That woman had some sort of radar, because she didn't seem to miss any hot-guy sightings.

"Holy crap." She lifted her chin toward the bottom of the bleachers. "I'm glad *that guy* wasn't standing in front of me at the gym this morning. I was doing thigh presses, and I might not have been able to open my legs to pee later."

A man stood at the railing watching the field. His back was to us, but the view was pretty damn great anyway. He had broad shoulders, tan skin, and the tapered V-shape of a swimmer. Not to mention, he wore a backwards baseball cap, which I'd always found sexy, for some reason. I was just about to comment that I might join a gym if that guy was a member, when the man turned around and faced the bleachers.

Shit. I shut my eyes. Seriously? I did not need to see any more of Levi's skin. As it was, I'd spent too much time daydreaming about piercing it with my fingernails. I was really glad I hadn't commented to Kat now.

But what was Levi doing here, anyway? And more than that, why didn't he have a damn shirt on?

Levi scanned the bleachers. Spotting me, he smiled and jogged up the stairs.

Kat nudged me. "Oh my God, is that Tanner's brother, Levi?"

"It is."

"Christ on a cracker. Wow. He's even more gorgeous in person than he looks on TV. You have to introduce me."

I inwardly rolled my eyes, but put on a southern smile as Levi approached.

"Hey," I said. "What are you doing here?"

"I was passing by on my way back from the store, so I thought I'd stop and watch Alex play for a bit."

"Did you...lose your shirt at the store?"

"No, wiseass." He thumbed toward the other end of the bleachers. "There's a kid down there in a wheelchair. He recognized me when I walked in and said he was a big fan. I had on a Broncos T-shirt, and he said he liked it. So I gave it to him."

"Oh...that must've been Cody Arquette's older brother," Kat said. "He's got spina bifida, and he does love football. Comes to every game at the high school." She held out her hand. "I'm Kat, by the way."

"Levi Miller. Nice to meet you."

"Does that always work, Levi?"

"Does what work?"

"You give away clothing when someone compliments you on it? Because if so..." Kat paused for a dramatic lash-batting. "I really like your shorts."

Levi laughed. "You ladies mind if I join you to watch for a while?"

I'd been sitting at the end of the row, but Kat practically jumped out of her seat to make room. She scooted down and patted the empty bleacher between the two of us. "We'd be delighted."

That time, my eye roll wasn't inward. As Levi took the seat, he leaned in and whispered in my ear. "Your friend is very nice. Wonder if she wants something..."

I'm sure she does.

Over the next several minutes, Levi watched the game closely, criticizing every other move Jeremy made with the kids.

"I'd love to tell him how it's really done. But I don't want to embarrass Alex. So I'll shut up."

"Well, the technique doesn't have to be perfect," I said. "This is camp, not *training* camp."

Levi huffed and behaved for the most part after that.

When camp ended for the day, Levi had stopped to sign autographs as Alex and I waited beside him. After, the three of us were headed toward the parking lot when Jeremy came up behind me for a moment.

"Do you have a second, Presley?"

"Sure." I turned to Levi. "One second, okay?"

Jeremy led me several feet away. "I didn't want to do this in front of Alex, but I was wondering if you might like to go out for a drink sometime?"

Oh. Taken aback, I wasn't entirely sure what to say. *Damn, Kat and Levi were right.* But ultimately, I couldn't find a reason to say no.

"Sure. Why not?" I smiled.

"Great. Are you free tomorrow?"

I bit my lip and thought for a second. "I just have to make sure I have someone to watch Alex. Is it okay if I text you in the morning?"

"Sure. And no worries if you can't find anyone. I'm flexible most nights this week."

"Okay, good to know."

His eyes lingered on mine. "Alright. I'll let you get back to Alex. Have a great night."

"You too."

After all, I needed to get out, and taking my mind off the tension with Levi would be a good thing.

Speaking of Tanner's brother, he was now glaring at me as we continued to walk to our cars in silence. Was it my imagination, or had my escaping with Jeremy for a couple of minutes ticked him off?

SEVEN

Levi

I'D JUST GONE to the kitchen to grab some coffee the next morning when I heard Presley on the phone with her mother.

"I was wondering if you could watch Alex tonight, early evening."

Great. I bet my suspicions were correct—the coach had asked her out yesterday. She was probably planning for her little date with the dude who wanted to *give* her his pipe rather than help her fix them.

"Oh, shoot. I forgot you had that," she said after a moment. "No biggie. I'll figure something out or change my plans."

She wrapped things up with her mother and hung up before she noticed me. "Oh...hey."

"Hey," I said, stirring some sugar into my coffee. "I can watch Alex if you need me to."

Presley looked surprised as she picked out a mug for herself. "Oh. I wouldn't have thought to bother you."

I arched my brow. "Why?"

"I guess I just assumed you might have plans."

"I'm free tonight, if you need me."

She paused. "Actually, that would be great."

I used this as an opportunity. "Where are you headed?"

She looked over her shoulder and whispered, "I'm having drinks with Coach Jeremy, actually."

Shocker. "I should've known after he pulled you aside yesterday. I was wondering if he was going in for the kill."

"You make it sound so...*aggressive*," she said as she poured her coffee.

"Isn't it, though? Making a move on one of your camp kids' mothers?"

"I didn't realize there was a rule against that. Did you make it up?" Her tone was sarcastic.

"I hope you see now that his offer to *help* you was officially bullshit."

"He can be both helpful and want to take me out. That doesn't make him a bad person."

"Alright. I didn't take you for gullible." I took a long sip of coffee that nearly burned my throat.

"Gullible? Because I choose not to see the worst in everyone?" She set her mug down hard on the table. "Anyway, let's suppose he was simply making a play for me when he offered help—who really cares? It's not a crime."

"I'm sure Alex will care."

"Why is that?"

"You're dating his coach. The other kids will give him shit for that when they find out."

"First of all, I'm not dating him. Second, Alex won't know where I'm going tonight. I'm telling him I'm meeting a friend."

"Well, don't worry. Your dirty little secret is safe with me."

"Dirty?"

"There's nothing clean about his intentions. I hope you know that."

"I still don't understand how you're so sure of that."

"I'm a guy. I know how we look at women we want to bang. That's exactly how he was looking at you yesterday."

"Well, luckily, this is none of your concern. So you can stay out of it."

"My nephew *is*, though."

Fuck. I'd been completely inappropriate playing the Alex card. I'd gone too far, but it was too late to take it back. She looked at me with daggers in her eyes and decided to hit me where it hurt.

"Since when do you take responsibility for your nephew? You never came to visit him once in New York, even when you played there, and suddenly he's your concern?"

"I'm trying to change."

"Look, I'll have you know… Jeremy Brickson could have all of these bad intentions you're warning me about. But I bet I'd still be safer with him than I ever was with your brother."

She's probably right. I sighed. "I'm not saying my brother was the right man for you, either. You probably dodged a bullet there." My tone softened. "Listen, I'm sorry. Alright? I'm just…stressed about a few things today. I shouldn't be giving you shit. Go have a good time."

Presley sighed. "Well, I appreciate you offering to watch Alex. I think he'll be excited about that."

I sucked it up. "What time are you leaving?"

"Jeremy told me to let him know. But I'm flexible. You tell me what works for you."

"Anytime is fine."

"Okay, I'm gonna tell him five. That way it's early enough that if I'm not feeling it, we don't have to do dinner. I can make up a story that I have to prepare something for Alex."

"And if it's working, you're gonna stay out late?"

"I don't know. I guess it depends."

I swallowed. "Okay, well...I have all night anyway."

"Thank you. Again, I really appreciate it."

Presley put her cup in the dishwasher and walked out of the room. My eyes might have lingered a little too long on her tight, round backend.

What is wrong with me?

"Sucks, doesn't it?"

For a second, I thought my damn conscience was talking to me.

But it wasn't. It was Fern.

I blinked. "What?"

"Watching her pretty ass go out with someone," she clarified. "It sucks."

Apparently, she'd been listening to our conversation.

"What are you getting at?" I snapped.

"Presley and you. Don't think I don't see that y'all secretly want to...explore each other. Why else would you be buttin' heads all the time? Two attractive people don't get that heated with each other on the regular unless they be wantin' something more."

My face heated as I dismissed her. "You're nuts, old woman."

"Am I, now?" She cackled. "Why are you so invested in her going out with a decent man? Not like her son's coach is some guy she picked up in a bar. You're manipulatin' her by pushin' guilt cuz you know you want a piece yourself."

This woman is going to drive me crazy.

74

"Fern, who the hell made you the expert on what's going on inside my head?"

"Your gramps, actually. You're just like him. Wouldn't know a good woman if she smacked her titties in your face. How do you think he and I got together?"

"Well, I hope it had nothing to do with you smacking your titties in his face. But please spare me the details."

"You remember his friend Roland?" she asked.

"Yeah, of course."

"You know Roland and I used to be together. We were a thing."

"I didn't know that, actually."

"Yeah. Roland kicked me to the curb to go back with his ex-wife, and it took your gramps two years before he grew the balls to ask me out. He was too afraid of what Roland would think, even though Roland and I weren't with each other anymore. I know that's what's going on here. You like Miss Presley, but she's your brother's ex girl. So you're not making a move. You're just taking your frustration out on her."

"You know what I think? That you're making shit up right now." I shook my head. "You are right about one thing, Fern. I wouldn't be pursuing any ex of my brother's—but especially not Presley."

"Why?"

"I don't have to list the reasons. Plus, I don't trust your big mouth—with all due respect."

She flashed a mischievous smile. "How much are you gonna give me if I'm wrong, rich boy?"

I squinted. "Wrong about what, exactly?"

"About you two hooking up someday?"

"That's a losing bet for you."

"Ten grand," she demanded.

This woman is out of her damn mind. "I don't place bets."

"Liar. You got one goin' right now with Presley about whether she can book up this place."

"That's my one exception." I scratched my head. "Anyway, what the hell would *I* get out of this?"

"Maybe I'll consider leaving this place quietly so you don't have to kick me out."

"Now you're tempting me." I laughed. "Anyway, ten grand? You're not asking for much, are you?"

"I know you're good for it. Many times over."

"I'm not gonna end up giving you shit, except maybe a few months' rent after I have to kick your ass out when we sell this place," I teased.

"If you're so sure of yourself, why are you scared to bet me?"

She was starting to piss me off. Mainly because her challenge made me feel so on edge.

"You know what? You got it, Fern. Ten freaking grand. That's how confident I am that you're smoking crack right now."

XOXO

That afternoon, I brought over a realtor who'd been recommended to me to look at The Palm Inn. Even though Presley seemed determined to make a go of the bed and breakfast, I still needed to prepare for when she inevitably couldn't since the Franklin Construction offer wouldn't last forever.

I texted Presley to let her know Harry Germaine would be coming by around two that afternoon.

After I greeted him at the door, I let him in and began showing him around The Palm.

I suddenly heard loud music coming from the kitchen. *What the fuck?*

I made my way over there, and Harry followed.

Fern and Presley were dancing—fucking dancing. And Fern was drumming a spoon against a pot. There was an ancient-looking tape recorder on the counter playing the music. After a few minutes, I realized what it was. The voice was all too familiar.

"Is that Gramps singing?" I asked.

Fern smiled wide as she banged on the pot. "Sure is."

My grandfather used to play the banjo out front and sing along to old country songs. The neighbors would sit on the lawn and listen with their beers in hand. Those were some of the best memories. I never realized we had any of his performances recorded. I closed my eyes and took a few moments to transport myself back to that time.

"He kept a stash of himself singing on tape. Loved to listen to himself, that man," Fern said.

"Just another wonderful memory here at The Palm Inn." Presley smiled at me exaggeratedly.

"I know what you're doing." I groaned. "Don't think I'm stupid."

"Oh, I'm not even trying to pretend. My intentions are no secret, Miller."

She winked at me, and I got the strangest urge to bend her over the counter and slap her beautiful ass. I definitely would be keeping that to myself.

Harry and I left the kitchen, and the music faded as we made our way around the house. I noticed Fern had left bras hanging to dry in several of the rooms. More than usual.

Harry cleared his throat. "I'm sensing a common theme here."

"Not sure why she needs to do that. We have a damn clothesline out back."

Actually, I knew why she'd spread them all around today. She was trying to mess with me.

"Well, hopefully once we start showing the place, you can clear them out," he said.

I eagerly changed the subject. "So, what do you think in terms of a listing price?"

"I think we can go even higher than previously estimated, actually. Not to mention, now is a really good time to sell, given the market. I would highly suggest getting the ball rolling."

That was excellent news, but somehow I felt a pang of guilt. Those two *had* gotten to me.

After we finished the tour, I walked Harry to the door. We stepped out front together.

I shook his hand. "I appreciate you coming out."

"I'm just a phone call away whenever you're ready to pull the trigger."

Back inside, I found Presley and Fern in the kitchen.

"So did we scare him away?" Fern laughed.

"Hardly. He thinks we can get even more for The Palm Inn than Franklin wanted to pay. We really need to have another serious discussion, Presley."

"Yeah, well, that won't be happening tonight," she said. "I have to get ready to go."

After Presley exited the room, I looked over at Fern, who smirked at me.

"Already planning how I'm gonna spend that 10K."

Determined not to dignify her comment with a response, I simply rolled my eyes before going in search of Alex.

I found him in his room. "Do you know what you want to do tonight?" I asked. "I get you all to myself."

"I know. Mom's going out. I love it when she goes out because I get to have takeout."

"What's wrong with your mom's cooking? I like that better than takeout."

"You'll eat anything, Uncle Levi."

"I guess that's true."

"I think my mom is going out on a date," he suddenly announced.

I played dumb. "What makes you say that? I thought she was just meeting a friend."

"I saw her putting on makeup and a pretty dress. It's what girls do in the movies when they're going out on a date."

"Well, I think your mom deserves a night out whether it's a date or not, right? She works hard to make sure you're happy every day. She deserves some happiness, too."

I stopped to take in my own words, which were a reminder that I really needed to stay out of Presley's business. I regretted my conversation with her this morning. I should've never tried to make her feel guilty about going out with this dude just because he was Alex's coach. That was a sad excuse to interfere. Why was I even doing it? It was messed up that I had a vested interest in whether or not she dated this guy.

I snapped myself out of my thoughts. "So what do you want to order tonight?"

"Is Iggy's still around?" he asked.

"Yeah. How do you know about Iggy's?"

"My dad told me about it the last time I saw him. He said he used to go there when he was my age. I haven't asked Mom to take me there because I didn't want to make her sad if I told her why I wanted to go."

"Your mom can handle that. Just because your parents aren't together anymore doesn't mean they make each other sad."

"I know. But I thought maybe it would make her *mad*. So I didn't say anything."

"Your dad and I both used to love Iggy's, you know. They have the best fried chicken and biscuits—even better than the chicken your mom made the other night, which was really good, by the way."

"Yeah. That's what Dad said, that they have the best chicken. I wanna try it."

"Iggy's it is, then. I haven't been there in ages."

"Can we eat there?"

This town wasn't very big. Without knowing where exactly Presley might end up tonight, I didn't want to commit to taking Alex out where he could potentially spot her with the coach, so I made up a story.

"I was kind of looking forward to a night in. Is it okay if we just pick it up and bring it back here?"

He shrugged. "Yeah, okay."

Presley interrupted us as she entered the room. "I just wanted to hug you before I leave, baby. I shouldn't be gone too long."

I felt my eyes widen. She wore a tiny black dress and high heels. She'd even put a flower barrette in her hair. It was a damn sexy look, and it made me all kinds of messed up inside to think of the message she'd be sending that guy.

"It's no rush," I managed to tell her. "We're gonna have an early dinner and maybe watch a movie or something. Stay out all night if you want."

"It shouldn't be *that* late," she said.

"Like I said, doesn't matter if it is."

She wrapped her hands around Alex's. "Be a good boy for your uncle, okay?"

"Okay, Mom. Have a good time."

"I will, baby. Thank you."

Soon after she left, Alex and I drove to Iggy's. He came inside with me as we fetched the paper bags filled with fried chicken, French fries, and biscuits. I told him about the time his father won a chicken-eating contest right out front and reminisced about the times we'd gone to Iggy's with the whole family on a Friday night after our dad got off work. Friday nights were the only time we ever ate out. My mother always said she deserved a night off once a week, so we'd visit a different local place for dinner. In those days, I'd had no idea that my parents' marriage was on the rocks. They divorced when we were much older. I got to at least enjoy my parents together for a while— unlike my nephew, who can't remember his ever getting along, thanks to Tanner.

Back home, Alex and I set up a table out in the yard. It made me happy to see him scarfing down the Iggy's food. There was something cool about watching another generation discover the things you'd enjoyed. I couldn't figure out how it was fair that I was the one here enjoying this moment and not his father. But it was Tanner's loss.

Taking a bite of my chicken, I decided to probe him a little. "Are you happy to be in Beaufort?"

He nodded. "I love it here. I just wish we weren't so far from my dad."

His answer was a little heartbreaking.

"Yeah. I know. I can imagine how hard that is."

"We didn't see him much in New York, but if he wants to come see me now, it's even harder."

"I'm sorry, Alex. You deserve better. But you know, I grew up with your dad, so you might say I know him better than a lot of people do. I know who he truly is. And I do think one day he's going to wake up and realize he's not been the dad he should have been. And he'll make it up to you."

Did I just make a promise on my brother's behalf that I wouldn't necessarily be able to keep? I had no proof Tanner would ever make things right, but I wanted to give his son some damn hope.

"And one thing I can definitely promise is that I'm gonna be a better uncle to you. I want you to count on me. There aren't all that many Miller men left anymore. It's just the three of us. We need to stick together. You got it?"

"Got it," he said as he ripped a big piece of chicken off the bone with his teeth.

"You know what we used to do after we'd come home from Iggy's on Friday nights when I was a kid?"

"What?" he asked with his mouth full of chicken.

"We'd have ice cream for dessert. I picked up a couple of different kinds earlier. Want some?"

He jumped in his seat. "Yeah!"

It was getting a little chilly out anyway, so after we finished eating, we moved our party into the kitchen.

Fern, who seemed to be everywhere I was lately, was also in the kitchen.

As I prepared two bowls of Rocky Road for Alex and me, I turned to her. "Care to join us for some ice cream, Fern?"

She smiled. "Sure. Don't mind if I do." She looked at the container. "Rocky Road. Sounds like the path a certain someone is going to be on if he keeps pushing to sell this place."

"Very funny."

The three of us sat at the table, and we were able to have a relatively jab-free few minutes enjoying our ice cream—until my phone chimed.

Fern reached her hand toward my phone on the table. "Presley's textin'!"

I went to grab it so fast that I hit my damn injured knee on the leg of the table.

"Fuck." I quickly turned to Alex. "You didn't hear that."

He giggled.

"Are you okay?" Fern asked. "Seems like something got you a little excited there."

I glared at her and looked down to read the text.

Presley: We're gonna do dinner after all. Hope that's okay.

My stomach churned. Why did it upset me that things were apparently going well? I knew I should've been happy for her, but I couldn't be.

I'd pretend, though.

Levi: Cool. Yup. We're all good here.

Presley: What did you end up doing?

Levi: Took him to Iggy's but we ate it here. Told him some old stories. Having ice cream now. Nice night.

After about a minute, she texted back.

Presley: Aw, nice. Okay. Thanks again.

Levi: Anytime.

I turned to Alex. "That was your mom. She's having a good time, so she's heading out to dinner now. I told her we were all good here."

Fern stirred the pot. "Dinner and hopefully some *dessert*."

She was enjoying this way too much. But since she seemed to see my weird, territorial feelings toward Presley, I had to ignore her and not engage. The last thing I needed was for her to say something Alex picked up on. He was sharper than she realized.

After I cleaned up our bowls, Alex and I turned on a movie in the living room. He fell asleep before the ending, so after the credits rolled, I carried him to his room and tucked him in.

I took a few moments to look down at his sleeping face, once again marveling at how much he looked like me. The fact that he'd wanted to go to Iggy's really had touched me. And our conversations tonight only added to that. It had been an emotional evening. I just wished one of the emotions wasn't anxiousness over the fact that Presley still wasn't home.

Finally, the door opened around 10PM.

I was watching TV in the living room when she walked in. I started to chastise her about how late she'd stayed out, but then stopped myself. "How was it?" I asked instead.

She threw her purse down on a chair. "It was...nice."

I gritted my teeth. "Just nice?"

"Yeah. You know, about what I expected."

As she sat across from me, I felt a sharp jolt of pain in my bad knee. I started to massage it.

She looked at it. "Is your knee still hurting you?"

"I reinjured it tonight."

Her mouth dropped. "How?"

"I banged it against the damn leg of the table."

"Seriously? That's crazy. At least I can't take credit for it this time."

"Actually, it *was* kind of your fault."

Presley's nose wrinkled. "What?"

"When you texted me, nosy-ass Fern was looking at my phone and tried to grab it. I jumped to take it from her, and that's when I hit my knee."

"That's *my* fault?"

"No. I'm teasing. It was my fault. I was on edge about you being out, so I overreacted." *Why did I just admit that?* "But tell me about tonight."

She looked a bit confused before she answered. "Jeremy is really nice. Like *really, really* nice. And smart and funny..."

Swallowing the lump in my throat, I said, "Okay..."

"But honestly, after I texted and you told me what you guys had done tonight—going to Iggy's and reminiscing—I sort of lost focus. All I wanted was to be home. Which is weird, you know? That shouldn't have happened so easily."

My heart began to beat faster. "I wished you were with us too," I admitted.

She rubbed her palms together. "So, you said you were on edge tonight...because of me?"

I nodded, but it took several seconds before I could respond. "I can't properly explain it. But yeah." I shook my head, not wanting to elaborate. "Anyway, I apologize for trying to make you feel guilty about things this morning."

Her mouth spread into a smile. "There are worse things in the world than having a handsome football star acting all protective over you. I appreciate you looking out for me."

"It wasn't exactly as noble as that. But I will look out for you from now on, Presley. You and I, we didn't know each other all that well before. But I feel like after I leave in a couple of months, things will be different. I don't plan to lose touch with you guys."

"I'm kind of getting used to having you around, Levi. It's gonna suck when you leave."

I hadn't realized I was still rubbing my knee until Presley moved from her seat and positioned herself next to me. She placed her hand on it and began to gently massage. My body stirred.

"Does that feel okay?" she whispered.

"Yeah. It does. More than okay."

I bent my head back, swearing at myself for enjoying her damn touch more than I'd enjoyed...well, hell, the last time I'd had sex. What the fuck was wrong with me? Getting off on Alex's mother?

But I saw her as so much more than that now, didn't I? And it was starting to become a problem.

EIGHT

Presley

"SWEETHEART, WILL YOU do me a favor and go see if Uncle Levi wants any banana-nut pancakes?" The stack on the side of the stove had to be eighteen inches high.

Alex got up from his chair, but instead of heading to his uncle's room, he walked over and put his hand on my back. "Are you okay, Mom?"

My forehead wrinkled. "Sure, why wouldn't I be?"

My son shrugged. "I don't know. But you usually make a lot of food when you get upset. Last time Dad didn't show up for his visit, you made like a hundred cupcakes."

Though a hundred was a bit of an exaggeration, I *did* tend to cook when I was lost in my head. I'd had no idea Alex realized that. This morning, I'd gotten out of bed at six and roasted a whole chicken before chopping it up and making chicken salad. My growing feelings toward Levi had me very unsettled.

But I didn't want Alex to worry, so I smiled. "I'm fine, sweetie. I made extra to freeze in case you're hungry after practice, that's all. You can just pop them in the toaster oven later when you get home."

Alex shrugged. "Okay, Mom." Then he walked back over to his chair and sat down.

I turned with the spatula in my hand. "Umm... Did you forget you were going to go ask Uncle Levi if he wanted pancakes?"

"No, I didn't forget. Uncle Levi's not home. He left already."

"He left?"

Alex nodded.

"When did he leave?"

"While you were in the shower. I was in my room getting dressed, and he came in with his suitcase to say goodbye."

"Suitcase?"

"Yeah. He said he was going away for a few days."

"Did he say where?"

"No."

Alex was completely unfazed as he shoveled a pancake into his mouth. I, on the other hand, felt oddly bothered. Levi had gone out of town for a few days and didn't even mention it to me? It wasn't like he had any obligation, yet it still made me feel sort of bad that he hadn't told me or said goodbye.

"Did he say when he'd be back?"

"No. He just told me not to drop my right shoulder when I cut to my right at practice. Coach Brick taught me to do it that way, but Uncle Levi said it should be the opposite—I need to drop left to fake out the defender."

"Hmm... Well, I'm sure your uncle knows what he's talking about. Though I'm not sure you should ignore the direction of your coach without discussing it with him first."

"What's a wet noodle, Mom?"

"A wet noodle?"

"Yeah. When I told Uncle Levi Coach Brick taught me to cut right, he said Coach Brick was a wet noodle and didn't know his butt from his elbow."

Oh boy. "Umm...a wet noodle is... What I think your uncle meant was that he didn't agree with the information Coach gave you. But I don't think you should repeat what he said when you talk to your coach, because it's sort of not nice. Maybe just say your uncle told you to check with him because he thinks you should drop the other shoulder."

Alex shrugged. "Okay."

I sighed. "We need to get going in a few minutes to get you to football camp on time. So finish up, and then go wash your hands and grab your equipment bag."

After I dropped Alex at camp, I decided I didn't have time to wallow in my silly hurt feelings or micro-analyze everything going on in my head. I had an enormous job to do in order to get the B&B up and running, and that needed to be my priority. So I stopped by the paint store and picked up a few gallons of primer, then dove into the monumental task of getting all of the bedrooms ready for paint. It took me almost five hours, but I cleared the furniture out of the first three rooms I planned to work on, removed everything from the walls, spackled all the small holes, and covered all the moldings and corners with painter's tape. By the time I was done and ready to pick up Alex at camp again, I felt invigorated, rather than deflated like I had this morning.

At the end of practice, Coach Jeremy walked over to my car while I was putting Alex's equipment in.

"Hi, Presley." He seemed a little apprehensive, and I hoped Alex hadn't mentioned what Levi had called him.

I smiled. "Hey."

He shoved his hands into his pockets and glanced around the parking lot. My son was talking to a few boys near the fence and not paying the least bit of attention. Jeremy rubbed the back of his neck. "So, I was wondering if maybe you'd like to go out again?"

While I was relieved that Alex hadn't mentioned Levi's comment, I also wasn't sure how I felt about going on a second date. He was a nice-enough guy, and handsome, too; I just didn't feel any spark. Though, I was pushing thirty now, so was a spark really necessary? In my experience, sparks that burned too hot generally led to a fire. Maybe I needed more of a slow-burn person.

I managed a smile. "Umm... Sure, why not?"

"Great." He smiled. "Do you like country music?"

"I do."

"I have tickets to a country festival in Charleston the weekend after next, if you're up for it. It's an all-day, all-night type of thing. But we can go and come back whenever you want."

"Could I...let you know about that? I'd need to figure out a sitter for Alex and stuff."

"Sure." He nodded. "Of course."

I closed my trunk. "I'll figure it out within a few days, okay?"

"That sounds perfect."

Alex ran over. "Mom, can I go over to Timmy's after dinner?"

I smiled and mussed the hair on the top of his head. "We're not even back from one thing yet, and you're already asking to do something else."

Jeremy smiled. "I miss having that energy. The only thing I want to do after a long day of practice in the sun is put my feet up and drink some sweet tea. You two have a good night. I'll see you tomorrow, Alex."

I smiled back. "Have a good night, Jeremy."

Later that evening, I'd just gotten Alex to bed and settled in the living room to watch TV when someone knocked at the door. I hadn't been expecting anyone, but people occasionally stopped in for a room even though we had the *Sold Out* sign hanging under the main sign for the inn. It looked to be exactly the case as I unlocked the door and saw a woman standing on the porch with her back facing me, a suitcase next to her.

"May I help you?"

The woman turned and lifted her arms in the air, each holding a bottle of wine. "*Surprise!*"

"Oh my God!" My mouth dropped open. "Harper! What are you doing here?"

My best friend swamped me in a hug. "I took on a new client in Charleston and flew down to visit him. I figured I'd drive over and see if there was any room at the inn."

"Of course there is!" I squealed. "I can't believe you're really here. Come in! Come in!"

Harper grabbed the handle to her Louis Vuitton-monogrammed luggage and wheeled it inside. She always dressed like a million bucks, and after a few weeks of living in Beaufort, I'd realized just how different the people down here looked compared to her. Harper was tall and model thin, and she had on a white linen pantsuit. The stylish bottoms had a high waist and wide legs, and a matching double-breasted jacket covered a sheer, white, lacy tank top. The only color in her ensemble came from a thin, blood red belt, matching pointy high-heeled red shoes, and a fully lined mouth with bright red lips. I couldn't help but think how out of place she'd look at the local supermarket.

I brought her in and smiled, shaking my head.

"What?" she said.

"Nothing. You just look so...*New York*. Like the one-woman PR powerhouse you are."

She looked down. "I specifically wore linen, so I'd look more casual."

"If *that's* casual, what the heck do I look like?"

I had on gray sweats with a rip at the knee and a ribbed white tank top. My hair was tied up in a messy bun on top of my head, and I'd just washed off what little makeup I wore these days.

Harper looked me up and down and grinned. "Do you really want me to answer that?"

I laughed. "Definitely not."

She gazed around the spacious house. "Wow...this place is great. I feel like I stepped back in time."

"It's a mess right now. But I'll give you the grand tour anyway."

I walked Harper through the inn, giving her some of the history of the place as we went room to room. When we came to Levi's room, I pointed to the door. "This is Levi's room. He's out of town."

"How are things going with him? Last time we spoke, you said he was giving you attitude."

I hadn't filled Harper in on the weirdness between Levi and me lately, so I chose my words carefully. "No, we sort of worked out our differences. It's a long story, but Tanner had been feeding his family a bunch of crap about me for years—basically led them all to believe I'd left him high and dry when he got injured."

"Ugh. Figures. Can't say I'm surprised with that man."

I sighed. "Yeah."

"So things are okay between you and the brother now?"

While I debated how to answer, a voice boomed from over my shoulder.

"All's good, except the two of them want to boink like rabbits!"

Fern. I turned and shook my head.

"What?" She shrugged. "Don't look at me like that, young lady. It's true, and you know it."

"Levi does not want to...boink me."

Fern *tsk*ed. "You and that boy have been blowin' up a storm since he rolled in. Only two things happen with that much whirling going on. Either you wind up fornicating or a house lands on a wicked witch."

Harper's entire face wrinkled. She shook her head. "Fornicating? Witch? I'm so confused."

Her look made me chuckle in spite of myself. "Harper, this is Fern. She lives here at the inn. Fern, this is my very best friend, Harper Langley. She lives in New York and came down for a surprise visit."

Harper extended her hand. "Nice to meet you, Fern. But who's fornicating with whom and where's the witch?"

Fern ignored Harper's hand and instead pulled her in for a hug. "Nice to meet you, too, darlin'. Any friend of Presley's is a friend of mine." When she pulled back, she held Harper's shoulders and gave her the once-over. "Is this a uniform you're wearing? Are you a flight attendant for American Airlines or something?"

Harper looked down, seeming utterly confused. "A uniform? No, I'm not a flight attendant. This is Christian Dior."

"Who?"

I chimed in, "It's a designer, Fern."

She shook her head. "Shame. Someone should be paying you to look that fancy."

Harper's brows were still pinched tight when Fern excused herself. "I'd love to stay and chat, but it's my

Mahjong night, so I need to get myself cleaned up. You two enjoy your evening now."

After Fern walked away, Harper shook her head. "You're going to have to explain what that woman just said."

I laughed. "Come on. I think we need that wine you brought for me to do that."

xoxo

"I cannot believe you didn't call and tell me you're hot for your ex's brother." Harper sipped her second glass of wine. "Do you think maybe deep down you want revenge on Tanner?"

I shook my head. "I have zero desire to get even with Tanner. Maybe I did six years ago when I caught him cheating on me again and he walked out, leaving me with a one-year-old, but I'm long past that. I actually feel bad for him. He can't seem to get over the life he lost enough to start making a new one. And that's a shame, because he's young and healthy with a great son, and he's missing out on some of the best years of his life—and Alex's."

"Okay... Being with your ex's brother still sounds kind of messy. I mean, how do you think Tanner would take the news if that happened and he were to find out?"

Just thinking about that scenario had me guzzling the rest of the wine in my glass. "Oh, I know exactly how he would take it—*horribly*. Tanner has always lived in Levi's shadow. Levi was a first-round draft pick into the NFL. Tanner was a second. Tanner is six-feet tall. Levi is six foot three. But things got much worse after Tanner's injury. He resents his brother's success. Last year, their entire family went to Arizona for the Super Bowl to watch Levi play, but

Tanner refused to go. Instead, he stayed home and bet *against* his brother's team. Levi wound up with a Super Bowl ring, and Tanner wound up five-thousand dollars more in debt."

I shook my head. "Tanner sees Levi's life as the one *he* should be living. So I'm certain seeing Levi and me together would not go over well. It would be a disaster, really."

Harper wrinkled her nose. "That doesn't sound pleasant. I guess we're just going to have to find you another man to—what did Fern call it?—*boink*. We're going to have to find you another man to boink. That shouldn't be too hard. I read an article on the flight down that said there're a hundred-and-sixty-million men in the United States. Finding one to make you forget all about Levi shouldn't be so hard."

I nodded and smiled, though all I could think was... *A hundred-and-sixty-million men in the United States, and of course, the only one I've wanted badly in years is the one I can't have. Great. Just great.*

NINE

Presley

"I STILL CANNOT believe how much we got done this week." After returning from the bathroom, I looked around the inn in amazement.

Apparently a visit from Harper was just what I needed. Over the last four days, not only had we painted six of the fourteen bedrooms, we'd also painted the living room, ordered new window treatments, and had all of the rotted pipes on the second floor replaced by a reasonably priced plumber whose name I'd gotten from Jeremy.

Harper had also offered to help with publicity for the grand reopening, and somehow talked both the local paper and local news station into agreeing to cover the *huge event* she told them I'd be throwing to celebrate next month. It had been a whirlwind few days, and I was exhausted, but also sad that she was flying back home tomorrow.

Earlier we'd gone to dinner at one of the local restaurants, and now we were sitting around drinking spiked lemonade. Mine was going right to my head. I'd dug out some old photo albums to show Harper what the inn had looked like back in the day, and she sat flipping through the pages.

"Wow, Tanner was super hot in college."

I peeked over her shoulder at the photo she was checking out. "Ummm...that's not Tanner. That's Levi. I think you're looking at one of the scrapbooks his grandfather made. He made books of both his grandsons. But Levi has a few more since his career didn't end as soon as his brother's."

She flipped a few more pages and stopped on a shirtless picture of Levi taken in front of the inn. He was all dirty and had on work gloves, leaning one elbow on a shovel. His bare chest glistened in the sun.

Harper lifted the book closer. "Damn, I might need to start watching football. He's something else all sweaty."

"That picture looks like it was taken in the last few years, probably during spring planting," I told her. "As far back as I can remember, the brothers would come over to The Palm Inn every year and plant all the flowers out front. They were probably only six and eight years old when that tradition started. I know from talking to Thatcher that Levi was still doing it even last year. He's a Super Bowl MVP and flew home for a weekend every April to plant his grandfather's flowers. Obviously, he could have afforded to send a gardener in his place, but he never did. I guess it's things like that that confuse me about how Levi can sell this place so easily. The Palm Inn meant so much to his grandfather and the entire family."

Harper flipped another page. "Did Tanner come home every year to help, too?"

I shook my head. "He stopped doing it in college."

On the next page was a newspaper advertisement. Levi had done an underwear modeling campaign for

Adidas. Harper pointed to the very noticeable bulge in his gray boxer briefs. "They stuff these sometimes, you know."

"I've seen the man up close and personal in his underwear. There's no stuffing going on there."

"Wow." Harper picked up her lemonade and gulped back the rest. "Is it getting warm in here?"

I sighed. "Tell me about it."

Harper flipped a few more pages before shutting the book. "I think we need a plan B."

"For the inn?"

"No, for the innkeeper. Screw forgetting about Levi. I think you should fuck him out of your system."

I laughed. "I think you've had too many spiked lemonades."

"Oh, I definitely have. But hear me out." She shifted in her seat, pulling one knee up on the couch to face me. "Why does Tanner or anyone have to know? You and Levi are both adults. Clearly you want to boink him, and from everything you've told me, it sounds like the feeling is mutual. He's only here for a little while longer, so it's not like things could get too serious. Why not screw him so you can move on?"

"We're going to need refills for this conversation. Hang on a minute." I got up and went to the kitchen to get the pitcher of lemonade from the refrigerator.

"Hey!" Harper yelled from the living room. "Grab your notebook with your to-do list while you're in there!"

"Okay."

I emptied the remainder of the pitcher into our glasses and set the notebook down on the table.

"I think I was too shortsighted earlier in the week," Harper said.

I chuckled. "I think your vision miraculously improved when you got a look at what's in Levi's pants."

She pointed at me. "Maybe, but humor me for a minute anyway. You're lusting over this man, right?"

Considering I'd dreamed about Levi hovering over me *again* last night, I didn't bother to deny the truth. "I'm definitely attracted to him, yes."

"And if you continue to keep your distance, is that going to change?"

I shook my head. "I don't know."

She leaned forward and opened a random page on the scrapbook she'd been thumbing through. Of course, she just happened to open to the underwear ad again. Tapping the page with her nail, she said, "The answer to that question is a big, fat *no*. That is not going to change. How could it? We're attracted to who we're attracted to. So if it's not going to change, why suffer through the next month or however long he's here? Fuck him out of your system. Have a no-strings-attached fling—one no one has to know about."

I chewed on my nail. "I don't know. That sounds easy, but the reality would be different."

"Why? Because it will be tough when he leaves and it's over?"

I shrugged. "That's one reason."

"You're already into this guy. Isn't it going to be tough when he leaves after you spend another month secretly going to bed with your hand down your panties thinking about him anyway?"

She'd nailed that. "I guess."

"So why not enjoy that time? It's going to suck when he leaves either way."

"What if we get caught?"

"By who? Fern? Pretty sure she'd high five you both and keep her mouth shut. The only other person in this big, old place is Alex. That's easily solved with a lock on the door and your face pressed into a pillow to muffle the screaming from multiple orgasms."

"I don't know..." God, I must've been drunker than I thought because Harper was starting to make sense. Or maybe it was the thought of multiple orgasms. It had been a while...

She picked up the notebook that contained my to-do list from the table and opened to a fresh page. Clicking the pen open, she scribbled across the top.

To do with Levi

I chuckled. "Are we making a dirty to-do list?"

Harper wiggled her eyebrows. "We certainly are." She put the pen to the paper. "Tell me one thing you fantasize about doing with him."

Yep, I was definitely drunk, because sober me wouldn't have participated in this. Though, even in this state, I felt my cheeks blush. "Well, every day he goes out back and does pull-ups in that big oak tree. Sometimes I imagine he's naked while doing them, and then I walk out naked, too. I wrap myself around him like a koala and he's a tree, and he keeps doing the pull-ups. Hoisting us both up and down."

Harper smirked. "Nice start." She then jotted down *koala pull-ups*. "What else you got?"

"Well, I also have this running fantasy that I'm watching him do the pull-ups from my bedroom window with binoculars, and then I lie down on the bed and...you know...go to town on myself. And when I'm just about to orgasm, I look up at the window and see Levi with the binoculars. He's watching me masturbate from outside."

"Oooh... I like that one." Harper wrote down *voyeur masturbation*.

For the next half hour, we polished off our spiked lemonades, laughed a lot, and added more than a dozen sexual to-do tasks to my list. It was the most fun I'd had in ages. But Harper had to fly home in the morning, and I didn't want her to have a raging hangover. So rather than make another pitcher of spiked lemonade, I grabbed her a water bottle and some Motrin and told her to drink up before going to bed.

But as I walked around and shut off the lights, another fantasy hit me. "That peach cobbler we had for dessert at the restaurant was orgasmic, wasn't it?"

"It sure was."

I pointed to the notepad. "Sit on Levi's face while eating that pie."

Harper had been drinking water and spit it out all over the place. "Oh my God. That is most definitely going on the list!" She picked up the pen and spoke while jotting something down. "Double orgasmic peach cobbler."

We started to crack up, but a knock interrupted our laughter. At least it interrupted mine. I looked up to find Levi standing in the doorway to the living room.

My eyes widened. "Levi... What are you doing here?"

His brows lifted. "I own half the place."

"No, I meant I didn't know you were back."

He looked between Harper and me and seemed to smirk. "Oh, I'm back."

My palms started to sweat. "I didn't hear you come in. How long have you been...standing there?"

Levi tilted his head, and his smirk elevated to a cocky smile. "Not too long."

Oh my God. I wanted to crawl into a hole and never come out. What if he heard? I suddenly felt pretty damn sober. "Umm...well, this is my friend Harper. She's leaving early tomorrow, so we were just going to bed."

He nodded. "Nice to meet you, Harper."

Harper stood and hiccupped. She covered her grinning mouth. "Nice to meet you, too. Your family's inn is beautiful."

"Thank you."

Her eyes shifted to me. "Although there's a lot to do around here. Presley and I made a list. You might want to take a look at it and get going on some of the new to-do tasks we added."

My eyes nearly bulged out of my head, and I lunged for the notebook on the table.

Levi squinted at me. "Everything okay, Presley? You seem stressed."

"I'm fine!"

He nodded slowly. "Right."

"Alright...." I grabbed Harper's arm and tugged. "We're going to bed. Welcome home."

Levi never moved from the living room doorway as he watched me drag my friend out of the room.

Harper waved over her shoulder. "'Night, Levi. Enjoy your to-do list!"

Somehow I managed to get Harper to her room without her yelling anything too obscene. But for the next half hour, I lay in my bed with my heart pounding. What if he'd heard us? What if he'd been standing there listening the entire time? *Oh my God.* I covered my face with my hands. *The things I said I wanted to do to him.* My head began to ache, and tomorrow's hangover hadn't even started yet.

After another twenty minutes of lying there freaking out in the dark, my mouth was so parched that I needed a bottle of water. But there was no way I wanted to run into Levi again. So I cracked open my bedroom door and listened for any sounds of someone moving out in the common area. Finding it quiet, I snuck down the hall and peered around the corner to see if any lights were still on. They weren't, so I breathed a sigh of relief and went to the kitchen for a drink.

I guzzled half a bottle of water before turning to slink back to my bedroom. But I froze at the sight of Levi standing in the kitchen doorway. My hand flew up to cover my racing heart. "Oh my God. You scared me."

"Sorry. I was just going to head out to grab a bite to eat."

"Oh...there are leftovers from lunch in the fridge, if you want. I made chicken pot pies this morning."

Levi held my eyes for a moment. "Thanks, but I think I'm going to go out." He walked over and leaned down to whisper in my ear. "I have a real hankering for peach cobbler."

Oh.

My.

God.

My jaw dropped to the ground. I had no idea what to do or say.

Levi winked as he walked to the door. "Get some sleep. I wouldn't want you to be too tired to work on that to-do list."

✗○✗○

Late the following afternoon, I took advantage of the fact that Alex was at a friend's house and decided to sit out on the porch to enjoy the cool breeze.

Harper had gone back to New York this morning, and I'd been anxious all day, wondering when I might run into Levi and have to address what he'd walked in on and clearly overheard yesterday.

I'd brought one of my books to read, but soon after I opened it, Levi came out of nowhere holding a beer. He looked so amazingly good in his ripped jeans and a plaid shirt rolled up to his elbows, showcasing the prominent veins of his strong forearms.

My heart sped up as he sat down next to me.

Levi settled into an Adirondack chair. "Your friend went back?"

"Yeah. I drove her to the airport this morning."

"Glad she had a chance to come visit."

We sat in awkward silence for a bit. He took a long sip of his beer, and I didn't know if it was my imagination, but his tongue lingered in the opening of the bottle before he slowly pulled it out. It almost looked like...*yeah. Is he messing with me?*

He turned to me and smiled. Suddenly burning up, I quickly looked away.

Then Levi reached out and handed me his beer. I took a long sip—a really long sip. Maybe he sensed that I was going to need alcohol for the conversation that might ensue over the next couple of minutes. But it unnerved me to have my mouth on the same spot where I was pretty sure he'd been simulating oral sex just a few seconds ago. At the same time, I could've been so on edge that I'd misinterpreted that.

The next thing he said freaked me out for a moment.

"It's *really* hot..."

"Hmm?"

"In the house today," he clarified.

I realized he was referring to the AC—which was indeed broken. I hadn't had a chance to tell him yet since

I'd only discovered it after I got back from taking Harper to the airport.

"Yeah. The AC is broken again." I handed him back the beer and rubbed my eyes. "I don't know. Maybe you're right. Maybe we should sell this place." My shoulders sank in defeat.

Levi gave me a surprisingly empathetic look. "Let's not have this discussion now, okay? I'll get someone in to fix the AC tomorrow. I know a guy." He sighed and took another sip of his beer.

If we weren't going to be arguing about The Palm Inn, there was only one thing left to talk about. I needed to get what I wanted to say over with.

I cleared my throat. "About what you overheard..."

"Yeah." He smirked. "That was completely crazy."

My heart skipped a beat.

"I mean, *peach cobbler*? Chocolate cake would be *way* more appropriate for that scenario, don't you think?"

The fact that he made light of it gave me momentary relief.

"It's fine, Presley. You don't have to say anything about it. I know you were drunk."

"Yeah, but that's no excuse to drag you into my crazy, drunken..." I stopped short of finishing the sentence.

Unfortunately, he finished it for me.

"Fantasies?"

"It was more like delusions."

"So there was no part of you that actually meant any of it?" His eyes seared into mine.

I dodged his question altogether. "People don't really know what they're saying when they're drunk."

"You didn't seem all that drunk when I ran into you after, though."

Right. Of course. Because I wasn't *that* drunk.

"Okay, well, it was inappropriate regardless of how drunk I was."

"You know, sometimes the truth comes out when we're intoxicated..."

He was really trying to get me to admit to something here. I needed to nip this in the bud.

"Look, Levi, you're a very attractive man—you know that. We've been around each other a lot lately. You were fresh in my head. So my drunken mind latched onto you during that little to-do list game. But it wasn't more than that." I paused. "It's been a very long time since I've been with a man, as you already know. And I got carried away. You were the target of it. I'm sorry."

Levi's eyes narrowed. "Are you seriously apologizing? You didn't do anything wrong. There's no crime against a drunken fantasy."

I no longer tried to dispute his use of the word *fantasy*. "Maybe there's no crime against it, but there should be when the target is your ex's brother."

For a moment, you could have heard a pin drop.

"Well, Tanner didn't overhear anything, did he? So no harm done. What he doesn't know won't hurt him."

Is he sending me a message?

"How long has it been exactly?" he asked after a moment.

Playing with some lint on my shorts, I said, "How long for what?"

"I know you said you slept with one guy after Tanner. How long ago was that?"

I swallowed. "About...eighteen months ago."

"Damn." Levi nodded. "Alright." He chuckled. "You look so uncomfortable right now, by the way."

"I am. I'm still embarrassed about last night."

"Embarrassed? Why? For having fun with your friend and fooling around?"

"Yeah, but it was at *your* expense."

"You think I was insulted?" He shook his head. "No, Presley." He handed me back the almost-empty beer. "You're not the only one who's sexually frustrated. And I haven't been innocent either. I just haven't said what I'm thinking out loud. Even worse, I acted like a dick to you the other day because I was freaking jealous over you going out with the coach. That's worse than your drunken stuff, because I wasn't even intoxicated. That was *all me* acting like a jealous bastard."

Chills ran down my spine as I finished off the beer. "So...you were jealous?"

"Yeah. So who's out of line now?" He expelled a long breath. "Speaking of *Jeremy*, what's the latest there?"

"He asked me out again. I'm supposed to be going to a concert with him next weekend."

He nodded slowly. "How do you feel about him?"

"I don't know. He's really nice, but I'm on the fence."

"You're on the fence with him. And on the *face* with me. I think I win."

I burst into laughter. "You're bad."

"But you're laughing."

"Yes, I am."

"I have a confession," he said, taking the empty beer bottle from me and placing it on the ground next to his feet.

I wiped my eyes. "What?"

"I didn't really have anywhere to go the past few days. I just felt like I needed to get out of town to think. I basically put myself in a time out after my behavior with you. That night, when you were rubbing my knee... Well, that didn't help."

Batting my lashes, I asked, "Were you able to clear your head?"

"Any head-clearing I might have done went out the fucking window when I came back to that conversation." He stood up. "Speaking of which, I'll be right back."

Uh-oh. What's going on?

He returned a minute later with an aluminum tray and two forks.

My mouth dropped. "That's not what I think it is..."

"My mother made it. I asked her to, and I went and picked it up this afternoon."

I covered my face. "Oh no. I can't believe you asked Shelby to do that."

"Relax. It's not like she knew the context."

"I know, but it just seems wrong. What the hell did you tell her? The reason for your sudden craving for peach cobbler?"

He took the plastic top off the tray. "I told her you'd been dying for it. *Dying.*"

"You suck."

"I do—and lick. And sometimes I do this thing where—"

"Stop!"

We both broke out into laughter again. And when it finally died down, we dug into the peach cobbler. It was delicious, but I couldn't get my mind out of the gutter. I'd probably never be able to eat this dessert again without thinking about Levi.

xoxo

The following morning, a loud knock woke me up.

I groggily answered the front door. "Can I help you?"

A portly man holding a clipboard stood across from me. "Yeah, Mr. Miller called me in to replace the AC system. I got my crew with me to do the installation."

"Don't you mean repair?"

He looked back at his truck. "No. I mean replace. We're putting in a whole new system. Normally I wouldn't be able to do it on such short notice, but Mr. Miller made it worth our while."

I specifically remembered Levi telling me we shouldn't replace the AC system if we were going to sell the place. He'd said we could get away with repairing it until the sale, after which it would be the new owner's problem.

This was a huge investment. My heart filled with hope.

I nodded, the man called in his crew, and they got to work.

While these guys were invading with all of their equipment, I went to the kitchen to make some coffee.

As it brewed, I texted Levi.

Presley: You're replacing the AC?

My phone dinged with a response. But it didn't address my question.

Levi: I'm out getting supplies for some other stuff we need to do around here. I left you something in your bedside table drawer while you were sleeping, btw.

After I prepared my coffee, I walked to my room to find a large manila envelope in the drawer. Inside were a couple of pieces of yellow notepaper and what looked like a DVD. A large sticky note on top of the paper read:

Presley,

> *I made a to-do list so we can keep track of what needs to be done around The Palm.*
> *I'm handling number one—replace the air conditioning system.*
> *I've got items number four, six, and ten today and have already gone to Home Depot to get materials.*
> *Maybe you should work on number six on the second page?*

When I flipped to the second page, I realized page two wasn't part of his list. It was the Levi to-do list Harper had jotted down the other night. How the hell had he gotten this? He must have snuck into my room and found it. *Damn it!*

Number six was: *Masturbate while looking at Levi.*

My heartbeat accelerated. *What the hell is this disc?*

My hands were shaky as I popped it into the DVD player.

Before my eyes appeared a montage of Levi, a highlight reel of him—throwing the football with no shirt at practice, pouring an entire bottle of water over his bare chest. Clip after clip, every muscle of his gorgeous, bronze upper body was on full display.

He was giving me *material* to facilitate my work.

I was ready to burst into flames.

Oh my God.

TEN

Levi

"HOW'S YOUR TO-do list coming along?" I asked Presley the following morning at breakfast.

She took a sip of her coffee. "What *ever* could you be referring to?" Her face turned beet red.

Smirking, I decided to drop it. I didn't want to scare her out of the kitchen. I was enjoying this coffee time with her. Alex had a sleepover at my mom's last night, and I'd done everything to stay the hell away from Presley, making myself scarce after what I'd pulled with that DVD.

Maybe I'd crossed the line, but damn, it was fun watching her face change colors right now as she clearly thought about it. The elephant had stayed in the room all day yesterday. Neither of us had mentioned it. I had no idea whether she'd actually *used* the DVD. But the thought of that had kept me hard for a while as I lay in bed last night.

After her face returned to its normal color, we made easy conversation over coffee and eggs. We actually managed to talk about neither our sexual tension nor The

Palm Inn. And the more we talked, the more the feelings brewing in my chest grew as invigorating as they were unsettling.

Presley then decided to make smoothies. As she got out the blender, she asked me if I would trust her to put something in my smoothie I'd likely never agree to if I knew what it was. She bet me I wouldn't be able to taste it. Always up for a challenge, I let her do it.

She made me look away while she blended it.

When she finally told me I could turn around, she handed me a tall, green drink.

I took it and sniffed. "This better not be disgusting."

"Just drink it." She laughed.

As I drank it down, I tasted nothing but peanut butter and banana. It was actually really good—nice and icy, too.

After a few sips, I said, "Okay, tell me what you put in this."

She flashed an impish grin. "Chicken liver."

I nearly gagged. "Really?"

Presley giggled. "Yup."

I didn't want to seem like a pussy, so I drank more of the drink down even though it now grossed me out.

"Turns out," she said, "you can hide the taste of almost anything with ripe banana, sweet vanilla milk, and peanut butter. Besides the liver, I also put in spinach and ice." She smiled. "This is how I get Alex to eat his veggies. I hide them in shakes."

"So why does he just get veggies, and I got liver?" I asked, sucking the last of the smoothie down.

"You were my test subject. They say organ meat from time to time is good for your immune system. I pan fried some last night and planned to blend it for myself, but figured I'd have you try it first to make sure the flavor wasn't overbearing." She winked. "I actually had no clue whether you'd be able to taste it."

"I was your test rat. Great."

"Exactly."

As we cleaned up breakfast, I made some wise-ass comment, and she got back at me by grabbing the sprayer attached to the sink and pointing it in my direction. That turned into an all-out brawl for control of it. We were both laughing so hard.

I managed to grab it and spray her, proclaiming, "This is what you get for tricking me into eating liver, woman."

I hadn't thought that move through, though, and now she had a full-on wet T-shirt. Feeling bad and a little turned on at the same time, I let her win, loosening my grip on the sprayer. She proceeded to drench my shirt.

We were both still cracking up when my mother and Alex walked in.

"What the hell is going on here?" Mom asked.

Presley quickly placed the sprayer in its rightful spot.

"We were playing with the water," I said. "Things got a little out of hand."

Alex's eyes lit up. "Cool! A water fight!"

Realizing her shirt was wet, Presley quickly covered her chest. "Your uncle and I were just having some fun. But it's over now."

"Next time I wanna do it, too!" Alex said, rushing past us and toward his room.

Presley continued holding her arms over her chest as my mother looked between us.

"I'd...better go change," she said, disappearing from the kitchen.

This sucked. Presley and I were damn adults. But right now, I felt like we were two kids who'd been caught doing something bad. And I didn't like the way my mother was looking at me.

With Presley gone, she dug in. "I'll ask it again. What the hell are you doing?"

"Lower your voice," I whispered.

"Let's go outside," my mother said as she started toward the door.

To make matters worse, Fern was in the hallway snickering as Mom and I made our way out to the yard.

I hoped Presley didn't look out her window and get the impression we were talking smack about her.

Once outside, I faced my mother on the lawn. "What?"

"You *know* what." She crossed her arms. "It's obvious what's going on here."

"*Nothing* is going on, Mother. We were just having a little fun. You should want us to be getting along—for Alex's sake."

"Well, I'll have you know your nephew isn't stupid. If there's something going on between you two, he's going to figure it out. All he talked about last night is how you and she seem to be getting along now when all you used to do is fight."

"So you'd rather we fight?"

"I'd rather you not sleep with the one woman you don't have a right to."

Anger built inside of me. I took a deep breath and composed myself. "With all due respect, that would be none of your business if it *were* happening, but it's simply *not*. *Nothing* has happened with Presley. We're just two stressed-out people, finally seeing eye to eye. We have a mutual respect for one another. And I'll say it again: we were just having fun."

She moved her head from side to side. "You know I suspected something weird when you asked me to make that peach cobbler."

"That was just a nice gesture. It didn't mean anything."

Her eyes widened. "You mean to tell me you're not attracted to her?"

I looked up at the window to make sure Presley wasn't looking out. "Why does that even matter if we're not involved?" I whispered.

"Your brother would flip."

I raised my voice. "Really? Because he doesn't give me the impression that he gives a shit about anything or anyone lately."

"Trust me. This would most definitely wake him up. She left him, and now he's gonna find out there's something going on between *you two*? You think that's not gonna hurt him?"

Mom didn't know the story behind why Presley and Tanner had ended things. She had no clue my brother had cheated. But I didn't feel it was my place to share Presley's business. However, given that my mother was still under the impression Presley had done Tanner wrong, her attitude wasn't surprising.

Then she said, "And what's this I heard from Harry the realtor—that you told him you're putting a hold on plans to sell The Palm?"

"How the hell did you find out about that?"

"Ran into him last night at the market with Alex. He mentioned it."

"He should've kept his big mouth shut. He's probably just upset that he's potentially gonna lose a commission." I groaned. "Anyway, my plans aren't canceled. They're just...on hold."

"I don't think giving up that fight is a smart idea. Do you?"

"It's not about the financial aspect. I've just been thinking about the impact selling would have on Presley and Alex. They like it here, and Presley really wants to revive the place. It's like her...passion. I should at least give her a chance."

Mom squinted. "And your feelings for her have nothing to do with that?"

I had two choices. I could lie, or not say anything at all. I chose the latter.

My mother proceeded to say one more thing to piss me off before she left.

"I have an appointment, but before I go, I just want you to think long and hard about the repercussions of getting too close to Presley. This isn't some fling you can mess up like all the others. She'll be in this family forever. If something were to happen, not only will you mess up things with your brother, but Alex too. All I'm asking is for you to think on that for a while."

"I hear you, Mother," I said, gritting my teeth.

After she left, I decided to take a walk to let off some steam. It was a little unnerving that two people—my mother and Fern—had now picked up on the fact that something was brewing between Presley and me. It would only be a matter of time before Alex became the third. And then Tanner. It was one thing to enjoy being around her in secret, to be attracted to her on the down-low. But now it was on people's radar.

I was supposed to have come to Beaufort to handle the sale of The Palm Inn. But if I'd all but given up on that fight, what was the point of staying? My being here now was because I *wanted* to be. If I kept going, it was going to end in someone getting hurt, either Presley or Tanner.

And I couldn't let that happen.

ELEVEN

Presley

LATER THAT WEEK, things were really coming along around The Palm Inn. Between the new air conditioning almost fully installed and the fact that someone had booked a room for a weekend late in July, I was feeling more confident than ever.

Levi hadn't joined us for dinner tonight. He'd been out of the house most of the day, so it was just Alex and me cleaning up after supper. As my son handed me a plate from the table, he hit me with a question I definitely wasn't prepared for.

"Why do people call boobs *tits*?"

I wrinkled my forehead. "Where did you hear that term?"

"Some boys at the playground the other day were talking about Uncle Levi—how they saw some picture of him online with a woman who had really big tits. I had to ask them what that meant. They told me tits are boobs."

Letting out a long breath, I continued washing the dishes as I spoke. "I don't actually have a clear answer to your question. It's a name people use to describe women's breasts, sometimes when they're doing it in a derogatory way."

"What's derogatory? Is that like purgatory?"

"No, it means—"

"Why do people *like* boobs?" he interrupted. "The boys told me they did."

I chuckled. "It's just something they like because they don't have them, maybe? Well, guys do have breasts, but typically not large ones...most of the time."

"They said Uncle Levi's friend had *fake* boobs! How do you get those? Can I get them? I don't want them for me. I just want to know if I could, like, buy them for Uncle Levi for Christmas."

Bending my head back in laughter, I couldn't contain myself long enough to address that before he posed another question.

"Where do babies come from?"

Shutting off the water, I wiped my forehead with the back of my arm. "What made you bring that up now?"

"Well, when those boys were talking about boobs, they started telling me where babies come from, and I want to see if they're right."

Shit. I swallowed. "What exactly did they tell you?"

"I want you to explain it first."

"Why?"

"Because it's weird, and I don't want to have to say it out loud if it's not true."

As I stood there with my mouth agape, unable to figure out what to say, Levi walked in.

He threw his keys on the counter and looked between the two of us. "What's up?"

Alex turned to him. "I just asked Mom where babies come from, and I'm waiting for her to tell me."

Levi's eyes widened. He and I stared at each other with an oh-shit look.

This was a talk I'd always hoped Alex would have with Tanner, and I was certainly less than prepared to be having it now.

Levi cleared his throat. "What brought this on?"

"It started because of that girl with big tits you were with."

"Whoa, whoa, whoa." Levi shook his head. "Back up. And who taught you that word?"

"The kids at the playground. They were talking about some girl you were on the Internet with."

Levi sighed as he ran a hand through his hair. "This is a conversation I wasn't planning to have today, but if you want, let's all sit down and talk about it." He turned to me. "If your mom is okay with that."

I nodded.

The three of us took a seat at the table. I had no clue how this was going to go down.

Levi twiddled his thumbs while I bounced my knees up and down. Alex just kept looking back and forth between us, waiting for someone to answer his damn question.

"Okay, Uncle Levi's going to explain everything," I finally said, turning to him. "Right?"

Levi's eyes went wide. "I am?"

"Yeah, I think it would be nice if it came from you. You know, man to man."

I watched as Levi's ears turned red. Then he proceeded to grab his phone and scroll.

"What are you doing?" I asked.

"Googling *birds and bees talk*."

After a few minutes, Levi flipped his phone around and faced it toward Alex.

I momentarily panicked. "What are you showing him?"

"Relax. It's an e-book for kids about where babies come from. We're gonna read it together."

I exhaled. That was actually an amazing idea. I pulled my chair around to their side of the table. Over the next several minutes, I watched as Alex's uncle read him every page of the book, which illustrated the anatomical differences between males and females and explained the process of how babies are made in as innocent a way as possible.

I watched and listened as Levi stopped to answer each question Alex threw at him. For someone who didn't have kids, he certainly handled this situation like the champ he was—unlike me, who had totally frozen.

"How old were you when you found out where babies came from?" he asked Levi.

"I think I was about eight when my dad told me. So, only a little older than you."

"Thank you for explaining it, Uncle Levi." He stood up from his chair. "Now I'm gonna go puke, cuz it's sort of gross to think Dad did that to Mom."

Levi patted Alex on the shoulder. "You do what you need to do, buddy."

After Alex ran out, I shook my head. "You totally saved the day there. Thank you. I don't know why I froze up like that. I've often thought about the moment he'd ask me, but I totally wasn't prepared."

Levi shrugged. "I winged it."

"You did amazing."

"Well...anything for him."

"That was a conversation he should've had with his dad. But if not with Tanner, I'm glad it was with you."

"It's the least I could do for him." He paused. "Speaking of Tanner, have you heard from him at all?"

"No. Not in the past couple of weeks. I do expect him to check in soon, though. He doesn't usually let it go past a few weeks."

Levi shook his head. "It's shocking to me that he hasn't tried harder to be a better father. It makes me feel like he's struggling more than I realize. Only someone terribly wrapped up in their own head acts like that." Levi rested his head in his hands. "I do worry about him."

I put my hand on his arm. "I know. Me too. It's why I've always tried to give him grace. I never shut him out of Alex's life, when he wants to be part of it."

"You're a saint for the way you handle it all. And if I haven't said this to you already, you're an amazing mother. You try so hard every day. You're always smiling and attentive to Alex, even when I know you're having a bad day."

"Yeah, a bad day like today when you walked in and I couldn't even form a response when my poor kid asked me about sex."

"Well, no one's perfect. And if I hadn't walked in, you would've figured it out." He smiled. "Alex is really lucky to have you as a mom."

I got goosebumps. "Thank you. That's nice of you to say."

"It's the truth."

An overwhelming feeling came over me. I didn't know what plans Levi had tonight, but all I wanted was to spend more time with him. So I went out on a limb.

"Hey, after Alex goes to sleep, would you...want to watch a movie with me?"

He blinked a few times. It felt like minutes went by, though it was only seconds.

Levi toyed with his phone. "Actually, I told Patrick McGibbons I'd meet him for a drink."

My stomach sank. *I shouldn't have asked.* Faking a smile, I said, "Oh, okay. Yeah. Have fun."

That night, as I watched a movie alone, I couldn't stop thinking about Levi and how great he'd been with Alex today.

I shouldn't have, therefore, also been thinking about that DVD of him tucked away in my drawer. But after I went to my room, I was tempted to take it out and watch it. For some reason, though, it didn't feel right. It sort of felt like exploitation, even if he was the one who'd given it to me. After everything that happened today, what he'd done for Alex and the kind words he'd said to me after, it felt wrong to touch myself while looking at shirtless images of him. So, I would abstain—tonight.

There's always tomorrow.

xoxo

The next few days kept me too busy to spend much time dwelling on my infatuation with Levi. The air conditioning crew finished installing the new system while I painted two more bedrooms and planted flowers in the beautiful flowerboxes that hung beneath each of the windows in the front of the house. Unfortunately, though, as had been the case since I arrived, taking one step forward was immediately followed by taking two steps back.

Yesterday evening, when I'd started clearing out the furniture in the next bedroom I planned to paint, I discovered mold on one of the walls. The old air-conditioning system had only cooled three quarters of the house, mainly the common areas and eight of the fourteen bedrooms. The remaining four bedrooms on the south side of the house had been added after the original construction of The Palm Inn. Those rooms had individual AC units in the windows, and apparently one of them had been leaking water for a long time, which then spawned mold, and the heat and humidity had encouraged it to grow up the wall.

So yesterday, two guys wearing hazmat suits had ripped that wall down to the studs, and today the same men had been banging away all afternoon installing sheetrock.

"Hey, Miss Sullivan." Ned, the carpenter, came into the kitchen. "Sorry to be here so late, but we finished hanging the new boards and slapped on the first coat of Spackle. That'll need to dry overnight, so I'll be back tomorrow morning to sand the walls and apply the second coat. We'll be out of your hair by lunch."

I nodded. "Oh, that's great, Ned. I really appreciate it. I have six boys sleeping over Friday night for my son's birthday, and I was hoping I wouldn't have to find them little Martian suits like you guys had on yesterday."

Ned chuckled. "Nope. All good. I'll see you in the morning."

After I showed the two men out, I turned off the light in the kitchen and paused to listen to the noise in the house—or rather the lack thereof. There had been a constant barrage of hammers banging and electric tools whirring over the last week. The newfound quiet was music to my ears. There weren't even any voices since Alex was staying at my friend Katrina's tonight for a sleepover with her son, and Levi had gone to his mother's for dinner. Even Fern was out. She'd left early this morning with some friends to drive up north for the night to go on some river gambling cruise.

I figured I might as well take advantage of the rare quiet time and enjoy a bath. My muscles ached from all the stretching that painting and planting required, and a good, hot soak would probably help loosen things up.

While I waited for the tub to fill, I scrolled through the music on my phone to make a quick bath-time playlist and then grabbed a change of clothes before slipping into the steaming water. It only took a minute or two before my knotted muscles started to relax. So I popped in my earbuds, turned the volume up on an old jazz song I loved but hadn't listened to in forever, closed my eyes, and sank deeper into the water. The equivalent of a sigh rolled through my body. *This is exactly what I needed.*

A half hour later, I was pretty much a prune when I finally got out. If the water hadn't started to cool, I probably would've stayed in there all night. I rolled my head from side to side as I dried off, surprised by how much I'd loosened up. Only a deep-tissue massage or a good orgasm could've relaxed me more. Though the Zen feeling I relished came to an abrupt halt when a high-pitched alarm began to wail.

Beep! Beep! Beep!

What the hell?

I tugged on my PJs and whipped open the bathroom door to see where the sound was coming from. But the second I took a breath in, an overwhelming smell hit me.

Burning! Something was burning!

There wasn't any smoke in this hallway, so I ran to the kitchen to check if maybe I'd left the oven on, but I hadn't. Everything was off. The piercing alarm kept blaring as I ran through the rest of the house, trying to figure out what was going on. The burning smell grew stronger as I reached the south wing and approached the room that had been sheetrocked today. Smoke billowed out from under the door the workers had closed when they left.

Shit! I ran back to the bathroom to grab my phone and quickly dialed 9-1-1.

"I need the fire department," I blurted as soon as they answered. "There's a fire in my house!"

"What's your address, ma'am?"

"Six thirty-eight Palm Court. It's The Palm Inn."

"Okay." I heard the clickety-clack of typing, and then the woman spoke again. "I've dispatched the fire department. Are you inside the house?"

"Yes, I am. There's smoke coming from one of the bedrooms. The door is closed, so I haven't actually seen what's going on. Do you want me to open it to see how bad it is?"

"Absolutely not. Get yourself outside and leave that for the fire department. Is anyone else in the house with you?"

"No, it's just me."

"Okay, good."

I jogged outside and stood on the lawn, staring at the house. The room on fire was located at the front, but I didn't see flames or anything through the window, so I thought that was probably a good sign. Two minutes later, I heard fire engine sirens in the distance.

I still had my cell up to my ear, but had forgotten I was on the phone for a second. "I hear them," I said to the operator.

"Yes, ma'am. They'll be to you any minute. Let's stay on the phone until they arrive."

"Okay. Thank you."

When two big, red rigs and a black SUV pulled up, I said goodbye to the 9-1-1 lady and went to speak to the firefighters.

One of the men stepped forward as I approached. "I'm Captain Morales. Dispatch said the house was empty. Are you sure about that?"

"Yes, I'm positive. I was the only one home tonight."

He nodded. "Good. Okay. Tell me what's going on inside."

"I don't know. I was in the bath, and when I got out, the smoke alarm went off." I pointed to the room at the far right of the house. "There was smoke coming out from under the door of that room. We had construction done in there today."

The fireman waved for his crew to proceed to the house. "Levi Miller owns this place, right? The quarterback?"

"Yes. We own it together."

"Okay. Why don't you wait over by the truck while we check out what's going on inside."

I watched as at least ten firefighters in full gear ran into The Palm Inn. A few were carrying hoses, while others held axes and other tools. Neighbors started to gather and ask what was going on, and the block quickly became a scene. At one point, one of the firemen yelled for water, and the hoses connected to the truck started to pump. I felt a little sick watching all of the action, but also immensely grateful that no one else had been home tonight, especially Alex.

It seemed to take forever for Captain Morales to come back out again. But when he did, he walked right over. "So, you have a small fire in the walls. I can't be sure what happened until we take a closer look, but usually with a thing like this, it has to do with old wiring. You said you had construction done on that room today?"

"Yes, but not any electrical work. Just sheetrock."

He nodded. "They could have moved a frayed wire while they were working, or disturbed wires with rotted casings. It's an old building. I can tell you more once we make sure all the hot spots are out."

I nodded. "Thank you. I appreciate it."

Behind us, a pickup truck skidded to a loud stop. Both the captain and I turned toward the sound. Levi's door was wide open, and he was already running toward me.

"What happened?" His eyes darted around at everything going on. "Are you okay?"

The fireman lifted his chin to me. "I'll let you fill in Mr. Miller while I go check on things inside." He looked to Levi. "When I come back, I'll answer any questions you might have."

Before I could even finish telling Levi the full story, two news vans pulled up. Cameramen and reporters got out and started looking around.

"Shit," Levi grumbled. He wrapped his arm around my shoulder and turned our backs to them. "The vultures already heard. Let's move over here."

We walked to the big tree on the front lawn and stood behind it as much as possible. But just when we thought we were safely shielded from attention, the fire department threw on a huge spotlight. They aimed it at the house, but we were standing right in the line of fire, now completely illuminated. Levi's eyes dropped to my chest. "Uhhh..." He swallowed. "Your shirt is see-through."

Looking down, my eyes bulged. The flimsy pajama top I had on did nothing to cover anything. I might as well have been standing outside fully naked.

"Oh my God." I folded my arms across my chest. But then it dawned on me that my flimsy top *also had a matching bottom*. And I wasn't wearing any underwear. I squeezed my eyes shut. "Levi, please tell me my shorts aren't as see-through as my top right now."

He said nothing for a few heartbeats, until... "Hands up."

Confused, I opened my eyes. I was about to remind him that I *couldn't* move my hands because I was busy covering my boobs, but then I saw why he was asking. Levi had already pulled off his shirt and had it above my head, ready to slip over me.

"Raise 'em up," he grumbled.

The material fell to my knees like a dress, covering all the important stuff. Although Levi was now shirtless.

"Thanks," I said. "But the reporters are going to have a field day with you half-naked. Pretty sure your bare chest attracts more ogling than mine."

The corner of Levi's mouth twitched. "Stay here. I'll be right back. I think I have a jacket in my car."

He jogged off, ignoring two reporters trying to ask him questions and multiple neighbors whipping out their cell phones to take videos. Couldn't say I blamed them. Levi Miller's muscles were a hell of a lot more interesting than a fire. When he returned, he had a Broncos blanket in his hands.

"No jacket, but this should work." He wrapped it around my shoulders.

"Let me give you back your shirt. Just hold up the blanket to shield me so I can slip it off."

"Keep it on. You're safer with two layers."

"I don't think the cameras are going to see through a blanket."

Levi caught my eye. "It's not the cameras I'm worried about."

My brows furrowed for a second, but the intense look in his eyes gave all the unspoken explanation I needed. I felt a flurry of excitement in my belly that Levi thought I needed to be safeguarded from *him—while the house is currently on fire*. I really, *really* needed my head examined.

Luckily, Captain Morales walked over again, which helped refocus my attention. He put his hands on his hips. "So it looks like wires were indeed the culprit. You're very lucky you were home to catch it when it first started. Sometimes old wiring can act almost like a fuse and facilitate travel behind the walls. Next thing you know, the entire house is up in flames. We had to tear down the wall you just put up, and the room is pretty wet, but at least the damage is contained to the one area."

I let out a deep breath. "Thank you so much."

"Is it safe to go back inside and take a look?" Levi asked.

"You can for a minute or two once we're done. But I'd find somewhere else to stay tonight. Soot's gonna rain down like light snow for a while. Small particles get into the air and settle over the next few hours. You'll find it in most rooms in the house by tomorrow morning. Sometimes it even gets inside closed cabinets."

Levi extended his hand. "Thanks, Captain. I really appreciate it."

Captain Morales smiled, and the men shook. "No problem. But do me a favor?"

"Anything."

The captain rested his hand on Levi's shoulder. "Go easy on my Panthers next year. You're killing the confidence of our defense."

Levi chuckled. "Anything *but that*."

It took another hour or so before the fire department departed and the crowd that had formed thinned out so Levi and I could take a peek inside at the damage. The electricity was off in that part of the house, so we grabbed a flashlight and went down to see how bad things were. My heart sank when the light illuminated the wall we'd just put up earlier today. Half of the nice, new sheetrock was torn down, and the parts that remained were charred black. Not to mention, the entire ceiling was dripping water, and the beautiful oak floors were covered in a sludgy mix of water and ash.

I sighed. "God. Is this a sign, Levi? It feels like the universe might be trying to tell us something."

He turned to face me. "It's just a slight setback. That's all."

I shook my head. "I don't know."

"You probably don't remember this because you're a few years younger than me, but when I was seven, I fell off my skateboard and broke my ankle. It was about a month into my second year of playing peewee football."

"I didn't know that."

He nodded. "They gave the starting quarterback position to Eddie Andrews. I was in a cast for eight weeks and couldn't play, and then I had to work my way back to putting weight on it. By the beginning of the next season, I was back to myself. But the coach kept Eddie as the starting quarterback. He told me Eddie had earned it, and I'd need to earn it back. I did by midseason, but after starting only two games, I fell off my bike and dislocated my elbow—on my throwing arm. Eddie went back to being number one. After I'd healed again, Coach kept Eddie as the first-string quarterback for the season, no matter how hard I worked. So when the next year rolled around, I started getting up early and making my mom drive me to school at 5AM so I could run sprints around the track. I also stopped riding bicycles and skateboards, and had my dad throw the ball around with me every night until it got too dark to see."

I sighed again. "I get what you're trying to say. But this isn't football, and I'm not you, Levi."

He shrugged. "Maybe not. But the same principles apply. If you want something bad enough, you don't let anything stand in your way."

I nodded. "Okay. It's been a really long day. Hopefully things will seem brighter in the morning."

"I think they will."

"Come on, let's get out of here."

I'd already called my mom and told her what happened, and she'd invited me to stay the night at her house. But Levi had said he was going to stay at a hotel.

"It's late. Why don't I drop you at your mom's?" he said. "I can pick you up in the morning, and we can stop at the insurance broker's office first thing. They'll probably need a statement from you and stuff."

"Oh...okay, yeah. I hadn't even thought about insurance. But that sounds like a good idea. To be honest, I don't feel like driving right now. A ride would be great."

When we pulled up at my mom's house, she was waiting at the window. She bolted out the door and ran to the car before Levi could even park. "I'm so glad you're okay." She hugged me.

Levi got out and walked around to greet my mom. "Hey, Mrs. Sullivan. How are you?"

She engulfed him in a big hug. "Better now that you two are safe and sound."

We talked for a few minutes before my mom swatted a mosquito. "Why are we standing out here? It's so buggy."

Levi smiled. "You two go ahead in. I'm going to get going anyway."

"Are you staying at Shelby's?" Mom asked.

"Nah." Levi shook his head. "I was over there for dinner earlier, and she had a headache. When I left, she was going to lie down. She still gets those migraines. I didn't want to wake her. I'll fill her in tomorrow on what happened."

"Where are you staying, then?"

He thumbed behind him. "I'm just going to grab a room at the Best Western."

My mother frowned. "Nonsense. You'll stay with us."

If Levi thought he could politely decline and walk away unscathed, he obviously didn't remember my mother very well. "It's okay. I already got the room. But I appreciate the offer."

Mom wagged her finger at him. "It wasn't an offer, young man. If you're not going to stay with us, then you have to at least let me feed you dessert. I insist."

"It's okay. Really, I—"

Mom grabbed Levi's hand. "Come on now. I need to feed these pies to someone. When I'm nervous, I bake. I whipped up three different pies after Presley called to tell me she was in the house when a fire broke out. You know it's an unwritten rule that a good Southern man does not let pie go to waste."

Levi chuckled. He looked to me for help, but I shrugged and shook my head.

Mom started to drag the poor man toward the door. "Now what's your favorite pie? I made pecan, apple, and a peach cobbler."

Levi's eyes flashed to me. "Did you say peach cobbler? I *love* peach cobbler—almost as much as your daughter does." He grinned. "You know Presley likes it so much, sometimes she even *dreams* about *eating peach cobbler*."

"When she was little she used to dream about riding horses."

Levi chuckled. "You don't say..." He opened the door to Mom's house and held out his hand for her to walk in first. As I passed, he leaned to whisper in my ear. "Riding and eating pie. Can you guess what I'll be picturing while you eat that cobbler?"

I squinted at him, though my face was flushed. "I'll be having the apple."

"Pity. But hey, you were looking for a sign earlier to tell you what to do." He winked. "Maybe this is it."

TWELVE

Levi

THE NEXT MORNING I was on my way to pick up Presley at her mother's when my cell phone rang. *Tanner* flashed on the screen. It had been a long time since my brother had called, so I was curious about what he wanted. Maybe I had some latent guilt for rubbing one out to thoughts of Presley eating that damn pie last night, but I got a little nervous that maybe my mother had said something about Presley and me growing too close.

I took a deep breath before swiping to answer on speakerphone. "Hey. What's up?"

"The superstar decides to answer his phone..."

Tanner and I didn't speak much, but this was exactly the shit he did every time we did. To my knowledge, I'd never blown off a single one of his calls. Yet he had this passive-aggressive way of making it seem like my ego kept me from talking to him. "Have you tried to reach me recently and I missed your call?"

"Nah. I just know how busy you are. So I try not to bother you."

I gritted my teeth. "Always have time for family, brother."

"Yeah, well, speaking of family. What the hell happened at The Palm Inn last night? I just heard about the fire on the news."

"We had some work done, and the fire department thinks it disturbed some frayed wires and started a small fire in one of the bedrooms."

"I told Presley that place was falling down. Maybe now she'll come to her senses and move back to New York."

I felt defensive. "It's actually not falling down. She's done a lot of work, and it's looking pretty good already."

"Yeah, whatever."

I realized he hadn't asked how Presley or Alex were, even though he'd said he heard about the fire on the news. "Have you spoken to Presley today?"

"Nah. I left a voicemail, but she hasn't called me back yet. That's why I'm calling you to find out what went down."

"Did you talk to Mom?"

"No, why?"

"So how do you know Presley and Alex are okay?"

"The news said no one was hurt."

I shook my head. Unbelievable. Even if it were okay to accept what they said on the news, he should've at least asked about their emotional states. Being in a fire could be traumatic, especially for a kid. This fucker probably didn't even know Alex hadn't been home.

"Nice legs, by the way," Tanner said. "Are you sure whatever the two of you were doing didn't start the fire?"

My face wrinkled. "What are you talking about?"

"The news had a picture of you and some woman getting cozy on the lawn. Was your shirt off before the fire, or did you take it off when the reporters showed up?" He snickered.

Shit. I had no idea what picture he was talking about, but I didn't have a good feeling about it. I pulled over to the side of the road and took my phone out of the hands-free cradle. "Listen. I need to run into the insurance broker's office, so I have to hang up."

"Alright, yeah. I'll talk to—"

I swiped off before he'd even finished his sentence and typed into the Google search bar: *Beaufort fire.*

Sure enough, the picture he'd been referring to popped up.

Jesus Christ. I raked my hand through my hair. That *did not* look good. Thankfully, my bonehead brother didn't even recognize his ex-fiancée's legs. The photo showed Presley from the back, but her entire body was wrapped in my Broncos blanket, including the back of her head. So the only thing you could see was the rear of her bare legs. It was easy to assume she was naked under the fleece, and I stood close, with one hand on her arm, looking down at her. And of course, I'd given her my shirt, so I was shirtless. The shot captured what looked like a pretty intimate moment. I scanned the headline underneath the photo: Levi Miller and mystery woman get cozy as family's historic B&B goes up in flames.

I shut my eyes. *Great. Just freaking great.*

xoxo

After I picked Presley up, I showed her the news article and gave her a heads up on what Tanner had said while we drove to the insurance broker to open a fire-damage claim. Then I drove her home. Her friend was going to drop off Alex soon, and she wanted to break the news about the fire before he heard about it from someone else. I'd told her I had a couple of errands to run, and I'd be back in a little while to help deal with the cleanup.

Early this morning, I'd called Ned to tell him what had happened. Obviously there was no need for him to come to apply a second coat of Spackle anymore. I'd asked if he could come take a look at the damage and see what he could do to get us back on track, but he'd said he had a few jobs lined up, and it would be a while before he could get back over to The Palm Inn for any extended period of time. I'd initially thought that was fine, until I watched Presley walk into the house. The look on her face was so defeated.

So I'd decided to stop by and speak to Ned again, this time in person. I knew he had to start a big job at the hardware store in town this afternoon, so that's where I headed.

"Hey, Mr. Connor," I called as I entered. "Is Ned here? I saw his truck parked outside."

"Hey, Levi. Heard about the inn. Sorry, son. I know how much your grandpa loved that place. Hope the damage isn't too bad."

"It's not. We got lucky."

"Good. Good." He pointed to the back of the store. "Ned's in the back storage room. He's building an extension. Help yourself in."

I nodded. "Thanks a lot."

I found Ned with his nose buried in a set of blueprints. "Hey, Ned."

He offered me his hand. "Levi. How's it going over at the inn?"

I shook my head. "That's what I came to talk to you about. Is there any way you could juggle your schedule around to rip out that bedroom again and re-sheetrock it? The entire room, including the ceiling, needs to be done this time, not just the one wall."

Ned rubbed the back of his neck. "I wish I could, but I'm booked solid for the next month."

"Could your guys do some overtime, maybe? I'll pay for it, and I'll make it worth your while."

"That'd be pretty expensive, Levi. My guys are paid pretty well, and overtime is double for them."

"I can afford it."

He smiled. "I know you can. But I don't want to take advantage."

"You wouldn't be. I'm asking to pay the extra. Maybe your guys can come in the evening, when they're all done here for the day."

Ned still looked on the fence. So I thought I should sweeten the pot.

"And I'll get you and your entire crew box seats on the fifty-yard line when the Broncos play the Panthers next year."

Ned's brows jumped. "Wow. Box seats. I'd have to run it by my guys, but my guess is they won't pass up double time and seats on the fifty. Hell, they might've done it just for seats on the fifty and a few autographed balls."

"*Now* you tell me." I laughed. "I'm joking. I'm happy to pay the overtime and get them seats. Do we have a deal?"

"I have to talk to my guys. They're over at another job right now. But I'm sure they'll say yes with that offer."

"Great. Will you let me know for sure?"

"Give me an hour. I'll call you."

"I appreciate that."

Ned smiled. "I'm glad to see you decided to keep the inn. I'd heard through the grapevine that you were thinking about putting it up for sale."

Had I decided to keep the place? Fuck if I knew. But I didn't want Presley to give up. I extended my hand to Ned and avoided confirming my intentions. "Thanks again, Ned."

On my way back to the inn, I made some phone calls and managed to book one of those fire-damage-restoration places that could start this afternoon. When I walked into The Palm, I found Presley sitting at the kitchen table. Her shoulders were slumped, and she looked lost in thought.

"Alex take the news about the fire okay?"

She nodded. "He wanted to see the room because he'd never seen a house that caught fire before. I debated showing him, because the charred walls look ominous, and I wasn't sure if it would scare him. But he thought it was cool and asked if he could bring some friends over to check it out."

I smiled. "That sounds about right for his age. You gotta show your buddies anything gross, scary, or wrecked. It's sort of an unwritten rule."

Presley smiled, but it didn't quite reach her eyes. So I pulled out the chair across from her, flipped it around, and straddled it. "Alex is okay, but it seems his mother isn't. Talk to me. What's going on in that head of yours?"

She sighed and shook her head. "I don't know. I guess I'm just second-guessing, well, everything."

"You mean about the inn?"

She nodded. "And the move, in general. I think I might've bitten off more than I can chew here, Levi."

It would've been so easy to get her to agree to sell the place today. Hell, the fire damage probably wouldn't even matter to the developer who had made an offer, since he was going to tear it down. But I couldn't let Presley feel like she'd failed. She needed this, for more reasons than just a better life for her son.

"You didn't bite off more than you could chew. It was just a little setback, that's all. I stopped off and spoke to

Ned, and his guys are going to come start gutting that room tonight. We'll be back on track in a few days."

"But he said he had job after job lined up?"

"He does. But his crew is going to work nights here. Which reminds me, it's probably best if everyone finds somewhere to stay for at least a few more days. They'll be banging away here. Oh, and I also hired a fire-restoration company to clean up all the soot and stuff. They should be here early this afternoon."

She searched my face. "Why are you helping me when you'd rather sell the inn?"

I shook my head. "I don't know. Maybe it's because I like a good fight. It's not really a true win unless both teams are firing on all cylinders. If you bow out now, I won't get the chance to beat you fair and square."

Presley smiled. "I don't believe you."

"What do you mean, you don't believe me?"

"I've watched you trample teams that have their third-string quarterbacks in because of injuries. You don't go easy just because you like a fair fight. You know what I think?"

"What?"

Presley got up and walked over to where I sat. Leaning down, she kissed my cheek. "I think you're helping me because you're a good guy." She stood and took a deep breath. "I'll be right back. I'm going to go get my to-do list."

I watched her walk away—her beautiful ass swinging from side to side. Once it was out of sight, I looked up at the ceiling. *Not so sure you'd think I'm a good guy if you knew what I was thinking right now.*

THIRTEEN

Presley

"MOM? CAN WE have a tent sleepover for my birthday tomorrow?"

I paused with my fork full of pancake halfway to my mouth. "You mean like sleep outdoors?"

"Yeah. In the backyard."

"Oh...I'm not sure about that, Alex. We don't have any tents, and I don't really know anything about camping. Besides, I don't know how your friends' moms would feel about the boys sleeping outside."

"Freddie had one for his birthday." My son shrugged. "None of the moms cared, and he said it was the best birthday party ever."

Levi walked into the kitchen. "Morning."

I smiled. "Good morning."

He walked straight to the coffee pot, and Alex went straight to drafting his uncle to his side of this argument.

"Uncle Levi, can you tell Mom that tents aren't hard to set up?"

Levi poured his coffee and turned to look at me. "What am I getting in the middle of here?"

"Alex wants to have his friends sleep outside in tents for his birthday party tomorrow night."

Levi shrugged. "Sounds like fun."

My nose wrinkled. "Sleeping with bugs sounds like fun?"

He brought his coffee mug to his lips with a smirk. "Afraid of a few daddy long legs?"

"Oh my God. I was thinking more about ants. Daddy long legs are part of camping, too?"

Levi chuckled. "You won't even notice them. They like still bodies, so they mostly crawl on you when you sleep."

While my face twisted at that thought, my son laughed. "Come on, Mom. Don't be such a scaredy cat."

"I'm not a scaredy cat. I would camp...but...we don't have any tents." I smiled. "Such a shame."

Levi grinned. "I have tents. I'm pretty sure my mom still has all our old camping gear. We used to have these grilled-cheese makers that you use over the campfire. They made the best sandwiches. I'll see if she still has those, too."

"But—"

"Thanks, Mom!" Alex stood. "Can I go down to Billy's house to tell him I'm having a camping party?"

I felt like I'd just been bamboozled. I shook my finger at Levi. "You're helping set them up."

He laughed. "No problem."

XOXO

The next night, I watched from the back door as Levi and Alex set up the tents out back. It turned out Levi's mom had recently tossed all of their old camping gear, but Levi had come home with his truck filled with equipment anyway.

All brand-new stuff that he gifted Alex for his birthday—three tents, sleeping bags, lanterns, tarps, supplies to make a fire, headlamps, outdoor cooking utensils. He'd even found the cast-iron grilled-cheese makers he'd loved so much as a kid. And he bought me bug spray. I wasn't sure who was more excited about tonight's camp out—Alex or his uncle.

Levi pointed to the ground where the next stake needed to be set and handed Alex a mallet. I loved that he didn't just set up the tent; he took the time to show my son how to do it.

The doorbell rang, interrupting my thoughts, and two very anxious boys practically knocked me over when I answered. They were definitely eager to get to the yard. Levi walked over to the deck where I stood to give the boys some privacy as they said their hellos.

"Thank you so much for setting all that up," I said.

"No problem. It was fun. It's been a while since I did any of that. These days roughing it is getting put up at a four-star hotel instead of a five while the team is traveling."

I smiled. "I'd gladly take that version of roughing it over this one."

Levi shoved his hands into his jeans pockets. "Do you mind if I hang around tonight?"

"Mind? I'd be relieved if you did. I was playing with the little collapsible camping cups you bought and couldn't even figure out how to keep them open."

He laughed. "You have to twist them a certain way."

The doorbell rang again, and a few more boys joined the party. Over the next few hours, Levi and I were both kept pretty busy. We made a fire, roasted hot dogs on sticks, grilled-cheese sandwiches in the contraption Levi had bought, and sat around telling ghost stories once it got dark.

Though I'd been reluctant to have this type of party, it turned out to be one of the most fun nights I'd had in a long time. At eleven o'clock, I told the boys to go into the house and brush their teeth and then got them settled for the night. Since there were six of them, Levi had set up a few tents for them to sleep, but they all squished into one. When I was done, I found Levi sitting by the fire, staring into the flames.

"Mind if I sit with you?" I asked.

He smiled. "Not at all."

"Would you want to sneak a beer?"

"Hell yeah."

I laughed. "I'll be right back."

I went to the fridge and grabbed two cold Coors Lights. Handing Levi one back at the campfire, I sat and let out a big sigh. "Well, I can't thank you enough. Tonight turned out pretty great."

Levi drank his beer. "Feels like I should be thanking you. I had a really good time."

"I'm glad."

"I was just thinking...you're a really cool mom, Presley."

"I am? Well, that might be the best compliment anyone has ever given me. Though I think I'm usually a dork, I'm going to allow myself to feel like a cool mom—tonight anyway."

He chuckled. "You do that."

Levi was such a natural with the boys. "Do you want to have kids someday?"

"I do." He nodded. "If you'd asked me that a few days ago, I probably would have said six. But after tonight, I think that might be too ambitious."

I chuckled. "I agree. Six might be too many."

He lifted his chin and sipped his beer again. "What about you? You want more kids?"

"I'd love to have another one, or maybe even two. To be honest, I would've liked to have had them close together, but that obviously wasn't in the cards."

Levi frowned and nodded. He was quiet for a moment. "My brother is an idiot."

It was my turn to frown. "Alex asked me three times today if his dad had called for his birthday. I even sent Tanner a text to remind him about it a few hours ago, but nothing."

Levi shook his head. "He doesn't deserve you guys."

We were both quiet for a while after that. Bringing up Tanner felt like a mood killer, but I refused to let him put a damper on what had been an amazing evening. So I grabbed the bag of marshmallows. "One more before we call it a night?"

He nodded. "Definitely. Maybe you could manage not to set yours on fire this time?"

I stuck out my tongue.

He smiled, but his gaze lingered on my lips. He lifted his beer to drink again, never taking his eyes off me until he lowered it. When his eyes finally rose to meet mine, they were filled with enough heat to make my belly do a little somersault.

He sat up and cleared his throat. "I'll go find us some sticks."

For the next hour, we roasted marshmallows and talked. I was completely stuffed and about to slip into a sugar coma, yet I kept agreeing to one more just to spend more time with Levi. When the last log on the fire fizzled out and Levi yawned, I figured it was time to call it a night.

"I'm going to go brush my teeth," I said.

"You mind if I crash out here, too, tonight? Since the boys all slept in one tent, there's an extra."

"Not at all."

"Alright. You go do what you have to do inside, and I'll get my tent ready. I'm guessing you don't want the boys alone for even five minutes anyway, so I'll take my turn when you're done."

I smiled. "That would be great."

When I finished in the house, I came back out and whispered at the door of Levi's tent. "I'm done. You can go in."

Levi unzipped and popped his head out. "Come inside for a minute. This tent has a zip-off sunroof. You have to see the stars."

"Okay." Inside the tent, Levi laid on his back. He patted the ground next to him. "Lie down."

When I did, my mouth dropped open. "Wow. I can't believe how many stars are out. It's absolutely incredible."

"Isn't it?" We lay side by side staring at the sky in awe. Our bodies were so close that our pinkies were touching. That ever-so-slight contact set my entire body on fire. I might've been staring up at the sky, but suddenly I couldn't focus on it. One of the most beautiful things in nature was right in front of my eyes, but all I could see, *all I could feel*, was Levi. My breathing grew faster and shallower, so I closed my eyes in an effort to drown everything out and get control of myself.

But then...his finger moved.

That innocent pinky that lay next to mine suddenly wrapped itself around my pinky and held it. It was so slow and gentle—part of me thought I might be imagining it. Though when I opened my eyes and turned my head to see what Levi was doing, he'd already turned to face me. He hadn't been watching the stars anymore either.

Our eyes locked, and Levi swallowed. The hand not holding my pinky reached up and cupped my cheek. "The sky doesn't hold a candle to looking at you, Presley."

My heart hammered in my chest.

Levi's eyes dropped to my lips. His thumb stroked my skin. "I want to kiss you," he whispered. "I *need* to kiss you."

My lips had gone dry, so I ran my tongue along them before tilting my head up and nodding.

Levi smiled. His hand at my cheek slid to my neck, and he pulled me to him, planting his lips over mine. Even though I knew it was about to happen, the feel of his soft mouth and strong grip made me gasp. Levi's hold on my neck tightened and then...all hell broke loose. Our tongues collided, and the taste of him overwhelmed me, making me absolutely desperate. One minute I was on my back and the next I was rolling us and pushing him down, my body on top of his. We groped and pulled, sucked and bit. Neither one of us seemed to be able to get close enough or kiss hard enough. Levi groaned, and the vibration from it shot straight down between my legs. I felt so needy that I wasn't even sure I remembered to breathe—the moment felt more important than oxygen. Consumed by the kiss, I'd almost forgotten where I was—in a tent, ten feet away from my son and his friends—but then reality broke through.

A damn cell phone started to ring.

Our kiss broke, and we let go, falling onto our backs and panting.

On the third ring, Levi reached between us and grabbed the offending phone. He looked at it and grumbled, "It's yours."

It had to be after midnight. Who the hell would be calling this late?

Squinting, I checked the name on the screen, and my eyes briefly closed. I reopened them with a frown and looked at Levi. "It's Tanner. I guess he finally remembered his son's birthday..."

XOXO

The following morning, I drove a few of the kids home. Alex wanted to stay with one of them for a few hours, so I came back alone, planning to pick him up later in the afternoon.

Last night, I'd never gone back out to the tent after Tanner's phone call. Instead, I'd gone straight to my room where I tossed and turned, thinking about kissing Levi and ruminating over something Tanner had mentioned in passing.

Levi was still in the kitchen, cleaning up the remnants of the boys' pancake breakfast, when I got back from dropping Alex off. This was our first time alone since our kiss. Well, alone aside from Fern probably lurking somewhere in the house.

Levi wiped down the counter without saying anything for a while. The tension in the air was thick.

Then he finally spoke as he continued to move the towel across the counter. "What did Tanner have to say last night?"

It had been odd talking to my ex even briefly after I'd just come off of that amazing kiss in the tent. I'd been guilt-ridden. The phone call had been bad timing, to say the least.

"He didn't have much to say to me, which was good because I couldn't bear to talk to him for any length of time after what had happened between us."

Levi suddenly stopped wiping the counter and nodded. His shoulders rose and fell.

"But before I woke Alex up to give him the phone, Tanner mentioned that he'd seen a photo of you and a *woman* after the fire. He had no clue it was me."

Levi sighed. "I know. When we last spoke on the phone, he mentioned it."

"It spooked me a little, Levi. If he'd recognized me, he might have put two and two together. And after what happened last night..."

He took a few steps toward me. "You feelin' guilty about it?"

"Aren't you?" I asked, his sudden nearness putting me on edge.

"Yeah, I felt guilty. But not enough to take it back." His stare burned into mine. "I'd do it all over again."

My chest heaved. "I don't think we *should* do it again."

He searched my eyes, inching a little closer. "Is that what you really want?"

"This has nothing to do with what I want and everything to do with what I *don't* want. I don't want to mess up your relationship with your brother."

"What relationship?" he muttered angrily before throwing the towel aside. He let out a long breath. "I know what you're saying, alright? And I respect it. In fact, you're right. I have no business wanting you like this. Tanner did you wrong, but he's still my brother. So maybe it makes me a terrible fucking person for what I did last night. I might even hate myself a little. But I *still* don't fucking regret it. I just don't." He placed his big, strong hand around my cheek. "You told me what you *don't* want, but you didn't answer my question." He rubbed his thumb against my skin. "What do you *want*, Presley? And don't say it doesn't matter. Because it *does* matter. What you want matters. Your happiness fucking matters."

I closed my eyes and let those words sink in. "I want you," I whispered. My eyes fluttered open. I meant that with every inch of my soul.

His pupils dilated as he stared into my eyes, but he said nothing.

"I don't know what's happening, Levi. All I can say is, I feel alive again. I'm invigorated whenever I'm with you. This all feels dangerous—but at the same time, you make me feel safe. I could've never predicted that *you* would be the first man to make me feel this way in a very long time." I exhaled. "I had many preconceived notions about you. But you're not the heartless player I imagined. You're caring and protective. I just...love being around you. I love the time we spend together with Alex, too. And I'm as scared about you leaving as I am of something more happening between us."

Levi pulled me into a tight embrace. I could feel his heart thundering against my own. What he said next floored me.

"My life over the past few years—it's been lonely. Even when I came home to visit, it didn't feel the same here. Until this time. When I'm around you, I feel a sense of home again. And it's not because of this house or Beaufort. It's you—your passion, your spirit—which I know is damn ironic, considering how much we butted heads in the beginning." He pulled back to look at me. "I respect you. I respect you as a mother, and most of all, I respect you as a woman. But I'm also deeply attracted to you in a way I haven't felt with anyone else. I don't think I can just pretend like these feelings aren't there. But I will do what you ask of me. If you want me to try to forget about it...I will. I won't pressure you. I know what's at stake."

Maybe it was the mother in me, but my inclination was always to do whatever it took to prevent the people I cared about from getting hurt.

"I think we have to at least *try* to control this," I told him. "Before we know it, you'll be gone again. That's the reality, no matter how strong these feelings are right now."

He said nothing as we stood there, staring into each other's eyes. Despite what I'd just said, the energy in the room felt like it was about to combust. It felt like *we* were about to combust.

I moved to walk past him, and the moment I met his gaze again, he stopped me, gripping my arm and pulling me close. He kissed me so hard that it felt like my lips were slowly burning. I savored his tongue, immediately recognizing the taste from our kiss last night. My heart felt like it was beating out of my chest. And somehow, I knew there was no going back now.

Levi lifted me up as I wrapped my legs around his massive frame. Immediately I felt the heat of his erection pressing against me as he carried me out of the room as if I weighed nothing. I certainly *felt* weightless in his strong arms.

"Tell me to stop and I will," he groaned over my lips.

Him saying that caused me to kiss him even harder, a silent message that the last thing I wanted to do was stop. I hadn't even known how desperate I was for him until this moment, because it felt like I *couldn't* stop, even if I'd wanted to.

When we got to my room, he laid me down on the bed, took my bottom lip between his, and slowly released it. "I have never wanted anyone like I want you. I'm gonna say it one last time. You need to tell me to stop, or I won't." He lowered himself over me and placed a kiss on my lips, gentler than the last. "Last chance," he whispered. "You want this?"

I lifted my hips, pressing my crotch into his erection. "Yes." I nodded, pulling his face toward mine and kissing him hard as I raked my fingers through his thick mane of hair.

"Fuck, Presley. I don't even care if we go to hell for this."

The next thing I knew, he ran out of the room. At first I was alarmed, but then, about thirty seconds later, he returned holding a strip of condoms.

As Levi covered my neck in kisses, I felt myself throbbing. Not only had it been so long since I'd had a man over me like this, I'd never been more turned on and ready for anyone in my life. I was already so wet and could feel my arousal pooling between my legs.

Levi lifted my shirt before lowering his mouth over my breasts, taking each of my nipples into his mouth and sucking until it hurt so good.

"You taste fucking delicious, Presley. Even better than you smell, and that's saying a lot. I want to devour you."

"Please," I begged.

Levi twirled his tongue over my nipples before slowly sliding it down the length of my abdomen.

He stopped short of my bikini line before taking off my shorts and panties. Once I was completely naked, Levi took a few moments to take me in.

"Fuck. Me," he muttered. "You're so freaking beautiful. I swear to God." He shook his head slowly. "Spread your legs wide for me."

I did as he said and watched as he unbuckled his belt, throwing it clumsily to the side. He slid his pants down and kicked them off.

Left only in his boxer briefs, he stopped short of taking them off, instead lowering his head and landing right between my legs. He got right into it, wasting no time before lapping at my clit as I bent my head back in ecstasy, screaming in pleasure as he hit all the right spots.

I yanked on his hair. "Levi..."

"I'm not done..." he teased, flicking his tongue over my clit harder, nearly bringing me to orgasm.

"Stop." I moved his head back. "I almost came."

"I need to fuck you now." Levi reached over to the strip of condoms, took one off, and ripped it open. He flashed a mischievous grin. "I hope you're ready."

I raised up a bit to watch him slide it over his dick, which could only be described as beautiful—long and thick, with a perfect crown.

He squeezed the tip before returning to his spot over me. "If at any point I'm too rough with you, let me know, okay?"

Nothing he could do to me right now would be too much. I wanted him to completely wreck me. Unable to wait a second longer, I boldly placed my hand around his girth and led him into my entrance.

Levi bent his head back and groaned out something unintelligible before pushing himself inside of me, stopping only when he was balls deep.

His movements started slow before evolving into hard thrusts. I'd never wanted a man to fuck me so hard in my life. There was no limit to what I wanted Levi Miller to do to me. The bed shook, and I hoped by some miracle Fern couldn't hear us, but honestly I couldn't have stopped this even if I knew for a fact she was listening in right now. I just didn't give a damn.

Grabbing his ass and squeezing hard, I guided his movements. All the while, our lips never separated. I knew nothing would ever be the same between us after today. *I* would never be the same. Maybe I should have been thinking about the repercussions of this, but they were the last thing on my mind right now. *This man. This body.* It was all that existed.

Moving my hips to meet his intense movements, I screamed from the sheer pleasure of feeling him so deeply inside of me. My hands gripped his hard, round ass as I felt the muscles between my legs contract.

His voice was low and deep. "Come, baby."

It amazed me how well he knew my body, because I *was* ready to explode in that moment. Just as I began to let go, Levi's eyes rolled back as he let out a long, sexy groan.

I didn't think I'd ever forget the sounds he made as he came. Knowing that he was experiencing the same ecstasy as I was made my orgasm even more intense.

He collapsed over me and immediately began kissing my neck, breaking away only to dispose of the condom before returning to me. He continued to shower my body with soft kisses. It felt like he was worshipping me. No one had ever made love to me the way he had, an equal combination of gentle and rough. We soon fell into another passionate kiss as we tumbled around in the sheets.

You would have thought after the amazing sex we'd just had that we'd fall asleep in each other's arms or something—even if it was early afternoon. But after five minutes of kissing, Levi again grew hard as a rock, and before I knew it, he had another condom on and was inside of me again.

We had sex multiple times in the span of two hours, never leaving my room.

At one point, Levi went to the bathroom. His phone lit up with a text, and I couldn't help glancing over.

The message was from *Fern,* of all people.

Fern: Can't wait to collect that ten grand. I'll give you my account information tonight. Don't want to send it via text for security reasons.

What the hell is that all about?

(FOURTEEN

Levi

ALL THROUGH DINNER, I couldn't stop staring at Presley. She had her long blond hair covering the spot on her neck I'd bruised. We'd spent the afternoon holed up in her room all over each other, and I couldn't get enough. I was already plotting how I could sneak into her room later without Alex knowing. *If I'm not already going to hell, that should do it.* Every time thoughts of Tanner entered my mind, though, I reminded myself he'd cheated on her and probably deserved this. But I knew that was a sorry excuse for what I'd done.

Alex sat across from me at the table, telling me all about the game he'd played at his friend's today, and while I nodded and pretended to be listening, all I could think about was getting to fuck his mother again.

Yup. Going straight to hell.

Normally when I was with a woman, after sex I'd immediately go for a shower and want my space. With her? I couldn't wait to get my dick hard again so I could go for another round. And then when we were finally physically spent, all I wanted to do was lie with her and talk. About *anything*. It didn't even matter. I just wanted to listen to her voice. I, Levi fucking Miller, wanted to *talk* after sex. Hell must be freezing over.

What the heck is happening with me? This was definitely not part of my plan in coming here, and I was going to be screwed when I had to leave.

This was so much bigger than my leaving, though. How would I explain it to Alex if he ever found out? He'd only just discovered what sex was—and he'd have to somehow process his uncle doing it with his mother? And then there was the obvious complication of Tanner finding out, which would be *awful* but actually scared me less than the Alex situation.

All of that aside, how the hell could I be there for Presley with my crazy schedule and the fact that I lived in Colorado half the year? There were so many reasons this couldn't work. So many things that should have turned me off. And yet she was all I wanted right now.

Alex's voice snapped me out of my thoughts. "Did you hear what I said, Uncle Levi?"

"Hmm?" I shook my head. "I'm sorry. Repeat it."

"I told Caden that Alex was really short for *Alejandro,* like the Lady Gaga song, and he believed me! So now all the kids are calling me Alejandro."

I chuckled. "I think that suits you."

He turned to his mother. "Can I have dessert?"

"Sure, honey." Presley stood and walked over to the freezer where she took out a carton of ice cream. She scooped some into a bowl and handed it to him. Then she turned to me. "You want some?"

She blushed soon after. The way she said it sounded like she was asking me if I wanted something *else*.

"I do." I ran my tongue across my bottom lip. "And probably seconds."

"Two bowls?" Alex said with his mouth full. "That's a lot of ice cream. You'll get an upset stomach."

I kept my eyes on her. "There are some things you can never have too much of."

She turned redder, and I freaking loved it. I was so damn *hungry* right now.

After dessert, Alex put his bowl in the sink and skipped off to his room. Presley was at the sink when I snuck up behind her. Sensing the heat of my body, she shut the water off and turned around.

"Can I help you?" she teased.

"Yes, actually, you can." I leaned in to kiss her neck.

She arched her head toward the stairs. "We need to be careful."

"I can do that. I can be really quiet, too, if I have to. I'd love to show you that talent tonight."

"Not quiet enough..." Fern said as she waltzed into the room.

Shit.

Goddammit.

Presley yanked her body away from me. Earlier, I'd had to explain to her what Fern's text meant. I'd wired the old lady the ten grand before dinner—not because I felt she deserved it, but because I've never been one to default on a bet. Plus, I needed to do everything in my power to make sure Fern kept her big trap shut. Needless to say, Presley was *not* happy when I told her.

Presley turned to her. "Fern, just to be clear, we need your utmost discretion about what you overheard. You can't mention it to anyone, even people you think you can trust. You know how fast things travel around this town. We can't risk Alex or anyone else finding out."

Fern smirked. "You have my word. The last thing I want is to cause trouble. Thatcher would never forgive me if I did. And for the record, I'm rootin' for y'all. It's scandalous as hell, but it was inevitable." She winked. "And what your brother doesn't know won't hurt him. He certainly ain't gonna hear nuthin' from me."

Just the mention of Tanner made my stomach turn.

"Well, thank you. I really appreciate it," Presley said.

"There's nothing better than living vicariously through young love." She winked again.

Love? I hadn't thought about whether I actually loved Presley, but given that I'd never felt these feelings before, there was a damn good chance this could be developing into that.

Before I could even begin to respond to her statement, I heard footsteps and Alex entered the kitchen. He lifted something up to show us. I soon recognized it as my belt. *My damn belt.* The same one I'd whipped off and thrown on the floor in Presley's room today, right before I buried myself inside her. I couldn't even deny it was mine because it had my friggin' initials monogrammed on the buckle.

Fuck.

Fuck.

Fuck.

"I found your belt on the floor in Mom's room, Uncle Levi. I thought maybe Mom borrowed my iPad again, so I was looking for it in there. This was on the floor."

Presley's face was red as a beet. She was probably ready to shit a brick.

Snapping my fingers, I said, "That's where it is! Thank you. I was looking for it." I took the belt from him. "I ate too much for lunch, and I took it off when I was fixing that light in your mom's bedroom. Totally forgot I did that."

"Too much ice cream, maybe?" He laughed.

He seemed to buy it.

"Yup. I think you were right. I need to stop eating so much before I make myself sick."

Alex shrugged and disappeared again.

Presley and I let out a collective sigh of relief.

"I'd love to know what you were *really* doing with that belt," Fern quipped.

FIFTEEN

Presley

WARM LIPS TOUCHED my bare shoulder as I stood at the kitchen sink. When I turned, Levi was licking his lips. "Why do you taste salty?"

"Umm...that's dried sweat you just had your mouth on. While you were busy sleeping in until almost ten, I finished painting the last of the living room moldings, scrubbed the floors, and polished a set of black candlesticks until they turned silver again."

He grinned and tugged a wayward piece of my hair hanging in my face. "I did sleep pretty late. Must've been all the exercise I got yesterday. You know, if you're already sweaty..."

I felt warmth bloom in my belly, yet I nudged Levi back with a laugh. We'd almost gotten caught a few times over the last week, and we needed to be more careful. "Alex is outside riding his bike. He could burst in at any second."

Levi pouted. It was adorable. "Fine. I guess I'll go to Home Depot to get mollies for the pictures you want me to hang in the living room, then."

"That sounds like a good idea. Thank you."

"You need anything while I'm out?"

I shook my head. "I don't think so."

He winked. "Be back in a little while." But he stopped as he reached the kitchen door, looking into the living room. He held out a hand to me. "Come here."

I walked over and stood next to him. "What?"

"Do you remember what this place looked like when you got here?"

"Yeah."

"Look at it now. Take a good look."

I studied the living room. It looked incredible, if I might say so myself. The walls that had been peeling were freshly painted, old, scuffed-up floors had been sanded and refinished, soot-stained stones on the fireplace had been scrubbed and polished until they sparkled, and colorful new window treatments and matching throw pillows on the couch lit up the room.

I sighed. "It does look pretty great, doesn't it?"

Levi nodded. "It does, and that's all you. I think I was about ten the last time this place looked like this. It even smells awesome. You've done an amazing job, Presley."

I smiled. "Thanks. That means a lot to me."

Levi looked into my eyes. I thought he was going to say something else, but he didn't. Instead, he shoved his hands into his pockets and nodded. "I'll be back."

A few minutes after he left, my cell phone rang. Seeing Harper's face on the screen, I plopped down on the couch and kicked my feet up on the coffee table with a smile.

"Hey, I was going to call you later today," I said.

"I wish you would've called me a half hour ago. I might not have thrown my trash at the new intern."

"You threw garbage at an intern?"

"It was an accident. I was walking by what's usually an empty cubicle while arguing with someone on a call, and from the corner of my eye I mistook her for a wastepaper basket."

"You thought *a human* was a wastepaper basket?"

"She's skinny and was just sitting there, not moving."

I laughed. "I miss hearing your daily mishaps."

"Well, you could remedy that pretty easily. *Call more.*"

"Yeah, I know. I'm sorry. I've just been...busy."

"Does that mean The Palm Inn is almost ready for the grand opening?"

I looked around again. "It's getting there. Two days ago, I quietly started an ad that directed people to our new website, and a few more nights have already been booked for late next month."

"Good. I'm glad you're ready, because I think we're going to be able to sell you out."

My brows furrowed. "How?"

"I got you a two-page spread in *Southern Living* magazine."

"Are you joking?"

"Nope. One of the guys who used to work for me works there as an editor now. We keep in touch, so when I came back from my visit to you, I emailed him a couple of photos I'd taken of The Palm Inn and asked him to keep us in mind if he ever had an opportunity for a feature. He said he would, but I wasn't sure anything more would come of it. Then this morning, he called and said they're running a feature on landmark B&Bs, and one of the buildings they'd planned to showcase fell through at the last minute. He can give it to us with a two-page pictorial!"

I sat up. "Wow!"

"There are two catches, though. First, they're on a tight deadline, so they need a full photo shoot within twenty-four hours."

"Well, I can do that myself, if they're okay with it."

"I figured you'd say that, so I just sent a link to your portfolio over to them. I should hear back pretty fast."

"Okay. What's the other catch?"

"They want Levi Miller in at least one of the photos."

"I don't think he'll have a problem with that."

"But won't that be helping you, and lessening his chances of winning the bet you have going?"

I'd actually forgotten about our bet. "Things have... sort of changed between me and Levi. That's what I was planning to call you about this afternoon. He's not pushing me on selling it anymore."

"Well, that's a good thing." I heard a knock at the door through the phone, and Harper said, "Hang on a sec, will you, hun?"

"Sure."

I listened to the muffled sound of a woman speaking in the background. "Sorry to interrupt, Harper. But your ten-thirty appointment is here. You also have Lyle Druker from the *Chicago Tribune* on line two."

"Thanks, Liz. Just give me a minute." Harper came back on the line. "Sorry about that. I also have a few other things I was able to get lined up for The Palm Inn, but I have to run right now. Maybe we can catch up tonight?"

"Yeah, sure."

"How much time do you need to check with Levi before I can tell *Southern Living* we're a go?"

"He should be back in a half hour. But I really think he'll be fine with it."

"Sounds like things have improved between the two of you."

"Yeah...I, uh, we slept together."

"*What?!*" My best friend screamed so loud, I had to pull the phone away from my ear. "Hang on." I heard the muffling of the phone once again and then, "*Liz!*"

"Yes?" came a voice in the background.

"Tell Lyle Druker I'll call him back in an hour. And my ten thirty is a prospective new client. Can you tell him I have an emergency and to get started on the new client intake form so he isn't just sitting there, please?"

"Sure thing."

"Give me fifteen minutes. Don't interrupt unless the building is on fire. And it better be a big fire, not a little toaster oven."

"Uhhh...okay."

"Thank you. Shut the door behind you." Harper came back on the line. "Start talking."

For the next fifteen minutes, I filled her in on everything that had transpired since the night of Alex's camping party.

"So what are you going to do about Tanner?"

"I'm not going to do anything, because he's never going to know. In less than a month, Levi will be back in Colorado, and that will be it. This was just... We have a strong physical connection, and we let ourselves get carried away."

"So it's just physical? You don't have feelings for him?"

I shook my head. "It doesn't matter if I do. It could never be more for so many reasons."

"You mean Tanner?"

"Well, yeah. But that's not the only reason. Levi leads a very different lifestyle than I do. He's a pro athlete who travels half the year, and I have a son who is in school here, and planting roots for him is my priority. I also don't want to confuse Alex."

"I don't know, Presley. That all sounds logical and smart, but the heart doesn't always do logical and smart. I don't want you to get hurt."

"I won't." I couldn't say the words with enough conviction to believe them myself, so I knew Harper wouldn't buy it.

"I have to go, but I'm calling you later so we can talk about this more."

I smiled half-heartedly. "Okay."

"Let me know what lover boy says about the shoot."

I laughed. "I will. And thanks for everything, Harp."

xoxo

"Why don't I go pick up Alex from camp so you can keep doing what you're doing? I'd say I'd take over, but my idea of decorating is a few footballs and some signed jerseys pinned to the wall."

I smiled. Not only had Levi agreed to be in the photo shoot, he'd also spent the entire afternoon helping me stage bookcases and mantels so they'd look good for the photos. We painted Mason jars and filled them with fresh flowers, went to the used bookstore and bought color-coordinated books to display on shelves, and now I was busy trying to fill in the nooks and crannies with the best pieces from all over the inn.

I set a pale blue vase on top of the mantel, then shook my head and took it down. "Thanks. That would be great. This is going to take me a while."

"No problem."

"Do you mind if I move things around in your room after I finish up here?"

He shook his head. "Have at it. Leave anything heavy that needs to be moved for when I get back."

"Okay."

The plan was to do the photo shoot first thing tomorrow morning. Harper and I had gone back and forth over text and decided the best areas to focus on were the living room, the outside front of the inn, and my bedroom and Levi's. So after I figured out what would go where in the living room, I took some leftover shelf décor to Levi's bedroom to see what I could do about dressing it up. A Broncos duffle bag sat on the dresser, so I grabbed it and went to zip it closed, figuring I'd hide it in the closet for now. But as I rounded the zipper at the corner, a box stuck out. I attempted to tuck it neatly inside, only to realize it was a *giant box of condoms*. Not only that, underneath the mega box was a second box the same size. Both unopened.

My heart sank. *One* of these boxes would have lasted me the past five years. Actually, that was being generous. I could've probably stretched the box to last the final year Tanner and I were together *and* the years that followed. It was a stark reminder of just how different my lifestyle and Levi's really were. He probably blew through these in a month while on the road. That made me feel a little queasy, yet I just stood there, staring down at the box.

I was so lost in my head that I didn't hear Levi until he was in the doorway.

"Hey. Alex wanted to eat over at his friend Kyle's. I texted you, but you didn't answer, so I made an executive decision and dropped him off."

I turned with the box of condoms still in my hands. "Exactly how long does this supply last you? Just preseason, or a few weeks in?"

Levi's eyes dropped to my hands, and his brows dipped. "You think I'm stocking up for when I get back on the road?"

I shook my head. "It's none of my business. I really don't want to know what you do on the road." Suddenly feeling awkward, I shoved the box back in the duffle bag. It still didn't fit. "I wasn't snooping. I tried to zip the bag to put it in the closet, and they were sticking out."

Levi walked over. I'd been avoiding looking at him, but I felt his eyes on me.

"What?" I finally said.

He gently took the box from my hands and tossed it on the bed. "I bought them today. I wasn't stocking up for when it's time to go back to work. I figured I should hide them since Alex already found a belt and asked questions."

I shrugged. "Whatever. It's none of my business."

His eyes narrowed. "What do you mean, it's none of your business?"

"When you bought them and what you plan to do with them is your business, not mine."

Levi held my eyes as he reached into his back pocket. Taking out his wallet, he shuffled through until he found whatever he was looking for. He unfolded a small paper and held it up for me to see. "CVS receipt from today. The date is marked at the top. Is that the only thing you saw? Just the condoms?"

"Yes."

He dug into the bag and held up a small bottle. "I think this will tell you *exactly* what my plans were when I made the purchases today."

I glanced at the bottle and back to him. "Lube?"

"Look closer."

I squinted. *Peach flavored.*

"I thought it would be funny," he said. "But then again, I didn't think I'd be showing it to you while you were accusing me of buying them to get ready to *fuck other women.*"

The anger in his voice pulled my eyes to meet his. "I didn't. I mean...I don't... I wasn't sure if..." I shook my head. "We should probably stop anyway."

"Do you want to stop?"

"It's the right thing to do."

"Wasn't asking about right or wrong. Was asking if you wanted to stop. Because I'm pretty sure the size of the two boxes I picked up today tells you that stopping is the furthest thing from my mind."

"But...we're in business together."

He took a step closer. "Don't care."

"You're leaving pretty soon."

He took another step. "I'm right here, right now."

"Alex..."

His eyes dropped to my lips as he took another step. "...isn't home."

My entire body started to tingle. "This town is so small. Someone will figure it out."

Levi licked his lips as he stared at my breasts. "They can watch, for all I care."

He took another step until we were toe to toe. Arching a brow, he asked, "You done telling me all the reasons us having sex is so wrong?"

I wanted to say no and continue to recite all the reasons we should keep our distance. But he smelled so damn good, and my body felt a magnetic pull to his.

My breathing grew labored, and I groaned. "One more time. I mean it. This is it."

The wickedest grin spread across his face. "Right..." He wrapped a hand around my neck and squeezed as he pulled me close. "Now shut up and kiss me, and let me show you all the reasons it's right."

♂ SIXTEEN

Presley

A WEEK LATER, my warnings had become a running joke. Levi came into the kitchen while I was waiting on the coffee pot to finish brewing. I frowned to see him shirtless—not because the view was disappointing. Just the opposite, really. But I already felt my stance on not having sex again weakening.

"Did you wake up late?" he said.

I nodded. "I also forgot to set up the coffee last night before I went to bed, so I had to drop Alex at camp before getting any caffeine in me."

"So Alex is already out of the house?" Levi's voice deepened. He didn't have to say anything else for me to know where his mind was.

I held up a finger in warning. "No. Yesterday was the last time."

He grinned and moved closer. "Was it?"

"I'm not kidding, Levi." I poked my nail into his chest. "Keep six feet away at all times."

He caught my finger and lifted it to his mouth. Sucking on it, he nodded.

My voice shrank and had zero conviction. "I mean it. No more sex, Levi."

He pulled my finger from his mouth, but nipped at it before releasing it. "Fine. No more sex."

The next thing I knew, my feet were off the ground, and Levi had me up and over his shoulder.

"Levi, what did we just agree to?" I protested.

He swatted my ass as he marched toward his bedroom. "No sex. But we didn't say anything about blow jobs."

"Levi…" I laughed and flailed around. But when he set me down in his bedroom and locked the door, the look on his face was anything but playful.

He pointed to the floor. "On your knees."

"But…" I lost my train of thought when he pushed down his sweats and fisted his cock, which was already hard.

He stroked it up and down. "On your knees, sweetheart."

Considering my mouth was salivating already, I knew it was a lost cause. So I lowered myself. "Fine. But last time…"

He dug his hands into my hair and smiled. "Right."

xoxo

An hour later, we'd both gone down on each other *and* had sex. I stood beside the bed getting dressed as Levi watched me.

"I'm crazy about you…" he said quietly.

"You're crazy about sex. Have you ever had your hormones checked? Maybe that's why you're such a good athlete."

"I'm serious, Presley."

My heart squeezed. "We shouldn't be having this conversation."

"Why not?"

"You know why not."

"You want to know what I was thinking about while you were getting dressed?"

I buttoned my shorts closed. "Nope."

"I was imagining you pregnant with a big belly. I bet you'd look fucking amazing."

My mouth hung open. That might've been the sweetest thing a man had ever said to me. But I had no idea how to respond. So I decided not to. "I have to go to the lighting store to pick up the fixtures I ordered. The electrician is coming to install them tomorrow."

"I also want to fuck you in my old bedroom at my mom's house."

My nose wrinkled. "Really?"

"I was thinking last night that there are two types of women—ones you bring home to your mom, and ones you want to fuck. But you, I want to take you to my mom's for dinner and then sneak you into my old bedroom and fuck you while she loads the dishwasher."

I frowned. "I have to run up to camp. I rushed out of the house so fast this morning that I forgot to give Alex lunch."

Levi was quiet as I picked up my phone and looked around for anything else I might've forgotten. But when I got to the door, he stopped me.

"Tomorrow afternoon, I have to go to the high school. It's their first day of tryouts for next season's team. The coach asked me to stop by and say a few words and sign autographs after."

"Oh, that's nice."

"Yeah, well...it was supposed to be nice. But I made the mistake of mentioning it to my agent when we were on the phone last night, and now he wants to turn it into a PR stunt. He asked me if he could arrange a photographer to come by and take some pics. I told him I might have someone who could do it. If you're not busy, they'll pay you to take some photographs."

"I'd be happy to take some photos. They don't even have to pay me. Lord knows I owe you a thousand favors."

Levi smiled and looked down at my knees. One of them was pretty red. "I think you paid them all back an hour ago, and then some. Sorry about the rug burn on that knee, by the way. I guess I got a little carried away."

I chuckled. "What time tomorrow?"

"Three. Maybe we can bring Alex? He'll probably be playing on that field someday."

"I'm sure he'd love that. Thanks." I smiled and put my hand on the doorknob. "I'll see you later."

"Hang on. Can I ask you something?"

"What?"

"The only time you ever kiss me is when we're in bed. Doesn't it feel weird to leave this room right now without kissing me goodbye?"

It absolutely did. And each time I left him it got harder and felt less natural to just walk out the door. But I forced myself to do it because it also felt like something I needed to do to protect my heart. Though explaining that to Levi would be admitting I had feelings for him out loud, which would only make things worse. So instead, I ignored his question and waved. "I'll see you around."

Later that afternoon at football camp, the boys were taking a water break when Coach Jeremy broke away from the pack to come talk to me.

I'd been sort of keeping a low profile, standing under a shady tree when he approached. I'd ended up canceling our last date, so I'd been avoiding initiating conversation with him.

"Hey, Presley. Long time no speak."

Clearing my throat, I said, "Yeah. How have you been, Jeremy?"

He cocked his head to the side. "I'm good. I've been thinking about you lately. Wondering if maybe we could grab a bite to eat again sometime. It's been a while since we caught up."

I'd thought maybe Jeremy would take the hint that I wasn't interested after I bowed out of going to the music festival with him. But was I really not interested indefinitely, or was I so intoxicated by Levi that nothing else mattered at the moment?

"Things are a bit hectic over at The Palm Inn currently. I think for now, it's best if I don't take you up on your offer."

He looked back toward the kids. "I'm getting a little too old for beating around the bush, you know? And I really like you. If you're not interested in going out with me ever again, I'd prefer you just tell me so I don't make a fool of myself and keep asking. I promise there won't be any hard feelings."

I decided to be as honest as I could right now. "I think you're a great guy, and I did have a really nice time with you. But I have something...personal going on that I'd rather not discuss. And it means I'm unavailable to go out with you for the time being."

"I had a really good time with you, too," he said, crestfallen as he nodded. "Fair enough, though. No pressure. Just know that the offer is always open." He looked past the tree I'd been leaning against and spoke to someone. "Oh, didn't see you there."

I turned around.

Levi.

He held two coffees. My stomach sank. Levi was supposed to have been at the house overseeing the work being done while I was at practice. It must have finished up early.

The tension in the air was thick as Jeremy said, "Anyway, I'd better get back to the boys. See ya around, Presley." He nodded toward Levi and took off.

Levi's cold stare made me uneasy as he silently handed me one of the coffees. He opened his and blew on it, then took a sip, continuing to say nothing.

"How long were you standing behind the tree?" I asked.

"Long enough to hear you promise Coach a date in the near future."

Shit. "That wasn't what I said."

"Oh, you're right. I believe it was that you have something personal going on, and you couldn't go out with him *for the time being*." He fiddled with the lid to his coffee. "This *something personal* guy—does he have a name? Let me guess, is it the chump who actually cares about you, but you only seem to view as a fuckboy?"

"Levi..."

"You're keeping your options open. I get it." He looked out toward the field. "Anyway, I figured I'd surprise you. Looks like I was the one in for a surprise."

"I'm not interested in Jeremy," I insisted.

"Not interested *right now*. Yeah, I got that much. But you might be after I'm long gone. Implying that things might change in the future said it all. Let me translate what you meant. 'When Levi leaves and I no longer have him around to fuck me, I might be interested in fucking *you*, Jeremy.'"

I deserved every bit of his wrath. If the roles were reversed, and I'd overheard him talking to a woman, I would've been just as pissed. But this was my opportunity to set things straight.

"I'm just trying to be realistic, Levi. Pretty soon, you'll leave town and go back to the life you came from. Playing house with me...it's just a phase for you."

Anger filled his eyes. "What have I *ever* done to give you that impression? Don't use my past or even Tanner against me in your answer either. This is about you and me, Presley. *Us*. When have I *ever* given you the impression that I wasn't serious about you?"

I couldn't answer his question. And that terrified me. It made me wonder if my own fear had distorted everything. He'd been nothing but caring, attentive, and dare I say, *loving* with me. But fear was a bitch, and I couldn't seem to come to terms with all of the obstacles we'd have to get through to actually be together. It wasn't a realistic possibility, as far as I was concerned.

"You scare me, Levi, for so many reasons."

"So you're stopping yourself from getting close to me. Same reason you'll let me fuck you in the ass but won't even kiss me outside of the bedroom..."

I winced.

"Shit." He closed his eyes. "I'm sorry. That was uncalled for. I'm just frustrated. This is not the time nor place for this conversation." He turned away.

When I followed and put my hand on his arm, he whipped around. "What is this really about, Presley? Is it just about Tanner, or do you really not trust me?"

I stayed silent, not wanting to admit that I *did* worry about his ability to be a one-woman man, even if he'd done nothing specific to warrant my insecurity. I knew old habits died hard, and I couldn't accept that he'd changed.

He took my silence as an affirmative. "Well, then, I'm fighting a losing battle. If you can't trust me, that's worse than worrying about how Tanner would react. Without trust, we have nothing left to say to each other." He dumped the rest of his coffee on the grass and crushed the cup in his hand. "And by the way, I'm just as fucking scared as you about all this. But I'm not gonna pretend what we have is nothing to try to neutralize it."

He stopped talking suddenly when we saw Alex running toward us.

"Uncle Levi! I didn't know you were coming today," Alex said when he got close.

"Hey, buddy. Figured I'd try to make the end."

"Why were you yelling at Mom?"

Levi blinked. "Did it look like I was yelling?"

"Yeah. It seemed like you guys were arguing about something."

"No. I was just complaining about my day." He lifted the crushed cup. "And this coffee stunk. Put me in a bad mood. Tasted like mud."

"Oh. I thought you guys were fighting again, like you used to when you first moved in."

"No, Alex," I said.

"It's all good, buddy. No one is fighting." Levi ruffled my son's hair.

"You missed a lot," Alex said.

"I'm sorry. I'll be sure to be here for the entire thing next time, okay?"

Alex looked toward his teammates. "I gotta go back!" he said, already running away.

I watched Alex disappear into the distance. "You see how affected he is by everything—just the mere thought of us arguing. If we take things too far and it goes wrong between us, it will devastate him."

"I'm not discounting that." Levi bit his lip and looked down. His ears turned red.

I could *feel* the emotions emanating from his body.

He suddenly looked up at me. "You're right."

"About what specifically?"

"About us. I think we should stop. For real this time. I'm not gonna push for something that's not attainable if you don't believe in me."

He was giving me what I thought was right, but hearing him say that devastated me. We stood staring at each other. I didn't know what to say. I'd essentially asked for this, right? Why did I feel so gutted that he'd agreed?

As he started to walk away, I called after him. "Levi?"

He didn't turn around this time. Instead, he walked to the bleachers on the opposite side of the field. He watched Alex there for the remainder of practice while I stayed in my corner under the tree.

SEVENTEEN

Levi

IN AN EFFORT to follow through on staying away from Presley tonight, I went over to my mother's house for dinner instead of heading back to The Palm Inn.

In fact, I considered spending the night at Mom's if it would put space between Presley and me. I knew nothing good could come of going back there tonight. We needed time to cool off after what happened at practice today.

My mother made corn on the cob and fried catfish. We ate our dinner outside, overlooking the small marsh by her house.

As the last of the evening sun set, she looked over at me.

"Talk to me. What's going on with you?"

"You could tell, huh?"

"When you were younger and you were upset about something, you never used to finish your food. Tonight's the same. That's so unlike you normally. I know something is bothering you."

"I don't think you want to hear it."

"Let's put it this way," she said. "I'm pretty sure I already know what this is about. Or should I say *who*. And my imagination is already running wild, so you've got nothing to lose in telling me the truth." She took a long gulp of her wine. "Now tell me what's happening between you and Presley."

"After today, maybe nothing. I ended it. Well, it was more that I finally agreed to let *her* end it."

"I suspected you wouldn't heed my warnings about getting involved with her. How far did you take things?"

I lifted my brow. "You *really* want me to spell it out?"

"Jesus. How are you even able to get away with that, considering Alex is in the house?"

"Where there's a will, there's a way."

My mother took another sip of her wine. "Okay, so... you ended things. That's good, right? I'll pray your brother never finds out." She sighed. "I assume she wanted more than you could give her?"

"Actually, it was the opposite. She seems to think I'm just playing house and as soon as I go back to Colorado, I'll be back to my old player ways. She doesn't trust how serious my feelings have grown for her."

My mother looked out toward the marsh and shook her head. "I guess I just don't understand how you could let this happen, Levi. Not only how you could do this to your brother, but why you would want to be with someone who left him the way she did. This is not making any sense to me whatsoever."

I'd always felt it wasn't my place to tell my mother what really happened between Tanner and Presley, but I felt compelled to defend Presley, and I couldn't do that without relaying the truth.

"Things didn't go down the way you think," I said. "All those years, we thought she left him because he was injured and down on life when that was far from the case." I gritted my teeth. "Tanner cheated on her. More than once. She never did him wrong. Presley didn't say anything for so long because she wanted to keep the peace for Alex."

My mother narrowed her eyes. "That wasn't the story he gave us."

"Of course, it wasn't. But unfortunately, that's the truth. And it's why I've had a real hard time feeling sorry for him. Not to mention the way he's treated both her and Alex, being virtually absent besides a few phone calls here and there. Yes, I do still feel guilty. But he makes it hard sometimes."

My mother grimaced. "Well, this is the first I've heard of all this."

"I know. I only found out in the course of getting to know her. We certainly weren't gonna learn the truth from Tanner."

"Well, now I feel badly about giving her attitude all this time. I could never help myself, thinking she'd left my son when he needed her most, secretly blaming her in part for his gambling addiction."

"She's a good woman, Ma. A *really* good woman. And a damn good mother to your grandson." I exhaled. "I ended things with her today—or at least tried—not because I wanted to, but because this thing between us is stressing her out. It's complicating her life in a way I never intended. I don't believe for a second that she wouldn't want to be with me if things were different. But I can't push if she keeps letting fear get in the way."

"I've never seen you like this over a woman. I was starting to think you didn't have it in you. I just wish it was *any* woman but Presley Sullivan."

"Yeah, well, we don't always get a choice when it comes to who we—" I hesitated, realizing the word that had almost come out of my mouth.

Was I about to admit I'm falling in love with her?

"You've put me in a difficult spot," my mother said, interrupting my thoughts. "Because the next time your brother calls me, how am I supposed to just pretend I don't know about this? I almost wish you'd lied."

"I'm sorry for putting you in this position."

"I'm not going to be the one to tell him, as much as it will kill me to hide this."

"Thank you."

"But I think eventually *you're* gonna want to tell him. Otherwise, the guilt will eat away at you."

I knew she was right. It would be impossible to keep this from Tanner if Presley and I didn't stop seeing each other. "In a perfect world, he'd never have to find out. I certainly wouldn't unleash the news on him without running it by Presley first. That would be her call. If it were up to me, I'd just live with the guilt. Honestly, my number-one concern is Alex, more than anything."

Mom nodded. "As it should be."

I stared off. "He needs me in his life, especially when Tanner doesn't come around much. I couldn't live with myself if he grew to hate me for any reason."

"Well, I think you should take that thought and let it marinate. There's really no way that Alex finding out about you and his mom could possibly help your relationship with him. That may be reason enough to stick to your guns here. End things once and for all before that boy finds out."

"I get what you're saying. But you're asking me to do something that feels very unnatural. I understand what the *right* decision is. But it's much easier said than done."

Closing my eyes for a moment, I thought back to some of the simple moments Presley and I had shared. "She makes me want things I never knew I wanted. We talk, we laugh about stupid stuff, about Beaufort—all the things I never appreciated before. A year ago, I would've told you I was perfectly fine having one-night stands and meaningless trysts forever. I never wanted the added responsibility of a relationship. But with her, it doesn't feel like that. It feels like it enhances my life, rather than weighing it down. She understands where I come from and vice versa. She just... makes me happy. I don't know how else to describe it."

"Oh goodness, son." My mother let out a long breath. "The sad thing is, all I've ever dreamed for you is that you'd settle down someday, be happy with one woman, and start a family. I'm sorry it's not easier for you to just enjoy this experience, that it has to be marred by scandal. And make no mistake about it, that's exactly what this would turn into if it ever got out." Her eyes widened as something seemed to dawn on her. "Please tell me that old woman you currently live with hasn't gotten wind of this."

Oh boy. She's not going to be happy when I tell her.

"Fern knows. I basically gave her hush money. That's a story for another day. But I do trust that she won't say anything."

"Just great." My mother rolled her eyes. "That sounds really reliable."

xoxo

I ultimately decided not to be a pussy. So I headed back to The Palm that night.

To my surprise, Presley was waiting by the door when I arrived just past 10PM.

She looked worried. "Where have you been?"

"Does it matter?"

"Yes, it does matter when you left things the way you did earlier. I at least thought you'd be home for dinner. You normally tell me when you won't."

The fact that she'd been waiting up made me feel like shit.

"I went to my mother's house to vent."

A look of panic crossed her face. "Did you tell her about us?"

"That we're over? Yes." I sighed and lowered my voice since I knew Alex was sleeping. "She guessed that I was upset over you. She's known for some time about us. She guessed that too. I never really told her anything. She promises she won't mention this to Tanner, even though it's not easy for her."

Presley put her hand on her belly. "My stomach has been in knots all day, Levi. I never meant to upset you. And I don't blame you one bit for being pissed at my response to Jeremy. It was a sad attempt to string him along as some kind of self-protective mechanism on my part. The truth is, you're all I think about. It's almost laughable that you would think I'm interested in Jeremy when I'm pretty sure I'm addicted to you."

"Sexually, you mean," I was quick to add.

"No. Not just sexually. That's the problem."

We were both silent for a bit, until I muttered, "Why couldn't I have found you first?"

She reached her hand out and took my pinky in hers. It seemed my vow to stay away from her was a bunch of bullshit, because I could already feel my walls breaking down again.

"I told myself I was going to come home and not say a damn word to you, Presley. And I'm realizing once again how fucking weak I am. Because all I want to do right now is fuck you till you hurt for making me so damn jealous today."

Her eyes glazed over. "Do it."

"Don't dare me, woman." My dick stiffened.

Whenever I was stressed, I lost my appetite for food, but my appetite for sex was just the opposite. After this day, there was nothing I needed more than to bury myself inside of her. We'd resolved nothing from our argument earlier. Things between us were more messed-up than ever. But somehow my dick had me convinced that fucking her brains out tonight was the answer, like her pussy was magic, and it would solve all of this.

She licked her lips. "Where's the farthest spot in this house from Alex's room?"

"The pantry closet in the corner of the kitchen," I said.

She began to walk toward the pantry before turning around. I stood there frozen, watching her ass sashay back and forth and wondering how I'd gotten to this point again.

Presley turned around to look at me. "Are you coming?"

No, but I will be.

"You're doing a great job with your vow never to fuck me again, by the way," I whispered as I followed her.

We slipped inside the pantry and closed the door. Surrounded by canned food and snacks, Presley dropped to her knees in the darkness.

I couldn't unzip my pants fast enough as I took out my rock-hard cock. Presley wasted no time taking me all the way down her throat, then bobbed up and down as if sucking my dick was her damn job—one she was extremely good at.

Threading my fingers through her hair, I pushed myself deeper into her mouth, and then pulled out suddenly to stop myself from coming down her throat. That had felt better than ever.

I tugged on her hair, prompting her to stand up before flipping her around. She undid her pants, letting them fall to the ground. Thank fuck I happened to have a single condom in my pocket. You never knew what might happen, so I always carried at least one.

Ripping it open as fast as humanly possible, I sheathed myself before frantically locating her hot opening. I pushed deep inside, trying my hardest not to groan out loud.

Her hands were on the pantry wall as I fucked her from behind. My only regret was that there wasn't enough light to allow me a clear view of her beautiful ass as I pounded into her.

When she let out a noise that was a little too loud for comfort, I took my hand and covered her mouth as I continued to pump harder.

Speaking into her neck as I thrust, I said, "You like driving me fucking crazy like this, don't you, Presley?"

She made a muffled sound against my hand.

"I don't give a fuck what you're telling yourself, this beautiful cunt is mine. It belongs to me. Do you understand?"

She nodded, letting out another unintelligible sound.

Within seconds, my orgasm rocketed through me and I emptied loads of cum into the condom. I always tried to wait for her to orgasm first, but this one was intense and came on suddenly.

Luckily, as my movements began to slow, I could sense she was rubbing herself off while I was still moving inside of her. Her breathing became rapid as her muscles contracted around my cock.

I stayed inside of her as we both caught our breath.

Eventually, I pulled out, even though I'd been enjoying her warmth and could have easily gone for round two if I'd had another condom handy.

When she turned around to face me, I whispered, "I want a kiss."

Just as she'd leaned in to comply, I heard rustling in the kitchen.

We froze in unison.

I mouthed silently, "*Fuck.*"

Looking through the small slats in the pantry door, I realized we were about to be way more fucked than we'd ever imagined.

Alex was in the kitchen. He must have come down for a drink, or worse—a snack.

Please don't let it be a goddamn snack. Because most of his options were in here.

We couldn't even react verbally to what was happening, because he might have heard us. All we could do was not move—not even to pull up our damn pants— and pray he came nowhere near this closet. I'd hold the door closed if I had to, with every bit of strength in me. No way in hell was I going to let this kid see me in the closet with his half-naked mother while a fully loaded condom hung off my dick. I'd rather die.

The refrigerator opened. I couldn't see that clearly, but it sounded like maybe he'd taken a drink out of a carton since I didn't hear him going to the cabinet for a cup. Then came the sound of the refrigerator closing, followed by footsteps fading away in the distance.

That was the biggest bullet I'd ever dodged in my life.

Presley and I continued to breathe against each other. I pulled her closer and could feel her heartbeat racing. Mine was going even faster.

I placed my forehead against hers. "It's okay."

"We have to stop," she whispered.

Yeah. We will—for tonight.

EIGHTEEN

Presley

JUST WHEN I thought nothing else could screw with my head, being back at Beaufort High School had me wrestling a kaleidoscope of new emotions.

Behind me were the bleachers. I looked up at the announcer's booth and then counted four rows down to the place my friends and I had sat for every football game for four years of high school. I used to love watching Tanner play. If I closed my eyes, I could probably still see the faces of the cheering Friday-night crowd. Heck, if I inhaled deeply enough, I might even smell hot dogs and pretzels. We'd had some good times here. Thinking about it caused a dull ache in my chest.

But turning around and looking out at the field in front of me caused an even bigger tangle of emotions. Tryouts were over now, though a lot of the kids had hung around after to throw the ball with Levi. He was currently in the middle of a game of two-hand touch, with my son as his running back. Levi dropped back to throw the ball, and Alex ran long. The smile on my son's face lit up the field brighter than the lights at a Friday-night game. I'd already taken all of the photos Levi's agent needed, yet I lifted the camera and shot more. These weren't for PR, but for me.

My camera clicked so fast it sounded like someone was typing.

Alex catching the ball.

Alex in mid-air, high-fiving Levi after they scored.

Levi ruffling my son's hair after he helped him up from the grass.

Levi looking down at my son like a...

Oh my God.

I lost my breath when I realized what I'd been thinking...

Levi was looking down at my son like a *proud father*.

God, I was probably the worst human being on the planet, but in that moment, I *wished* Levi was Alex's father and not Tanner. In the few months I'd been back in Beaufort, the two of them had already spent more time together than Tanner had spent with Alex during his lifetime. That was a pretty sad realization.

I took down my camera and watched how Levi taught him things, how he always seemed to keep his eye on where Alex was, even while throwing the football to another player or running the offensive line. He was protective, truly a natural parent.

Yet here I was, still using my son as an excuse to keep my distance from Levi, while the truth of the matter was, Alex flourished around the man. Of course, if our relationship were to continue and things didn't work out between Levi and me, it would be difficult for Alex. But wouldn't that be a risk I'd have to take with any man? And unlike a random stranger, in my heart I knew Levi was in my son's life for good now, regardless of what happened between the two of us.

A little while later, Alex was playing quarterback instead of Levi. He looked right to find a receiver, and when he dropped back to throw the ball, one of the high school kids on the other team ran at him from the left and tagged him a little too hard. Alex flew in the air and landed on his ass. Levi was by his side in two seconds, making sure he was okay.

Almost a half hour later, Levi wrapped up the friendly game. But he stayed on the field for another twenty minutes signing autographs because a bunch of kids had showed up once word got out that he was at the school this afternoon. Alex stayed dutifully by his side the entire time. When the crowd finally scattered, I'd probably taken over five-hundred pictures.

My son was still smiling when the two of them walked over to where I sat.

"Mom, I'll race you up and down the bleachers!"

I laughed. "Aren't you tired from all that running around you did today? I'm exhausted from watching you."

Alex looked at Levi as he shrugged and thumbed in my direction. "She's afraid I'll beat her."

Levi nodded and folded his arms across his chest. "Yup. Classic chicken response."

They both smirked. So what choice did I have but to set down my camera and accept the challenge? "Fine. But the loser loads the dishwasher after dinner tonight."

"You're on."

Levi chuckled. "Give me your camera. I want to capture my little buddy beating you."

I squinted and stuck out my tongue. But I also passed him the camera and showed him how to use it.

Once we were ready, Levi put his hands out, keeping us behind an imaginary line. "On a count of three. One. Two. Three!"

I took off down the bleachers and turned up the first set of stairs. My son might be fast, but my legs were still longer than Alex's, so my strides had me in the lead until I got halfway up the bleachers. I started to get a little winded as I reached the top, but Alex seemed to grow momentum. The little brat overtook my lead and made it back down and to the finish line a full fifteen feet ahead of me. And I hadn't even let him win.

Levi fist-bumped Alex, and the two of them gloated.

"Mom's doing the dishes," my son sang. "Mom's doing the dishes."

I bent over to catch my breath. Apparently I needed to get my butt to the gym more often. "Fine. But I said the loser loads the dishwasher. I didn't say I was cooking or that there would be any dishes. I think tonight we're having takeout—and Uncle Levi is paying."

Levi laughed. "I'll do you one better. How about I take you both out somewhere?"

"Fine," I grumbled. "But I'm picking the most expensive thing on the menu since the two of you seem to be ganging up on me."

Dinner turned out to be appetizers, a main course, dessert, and another impromptu autograph signing outside the restaurant when some people recognized Levi. By the time we got home, it was pretty late. Alex asked Levi to write down some of the plays he'd run this afternoon, and Levi said he would walk him through them while he put him to bed.

So I sat in the kitchen by myself, having a glass of wine while I waited for the photos I'd taken today to download to my laptop. I'd gotten a ton of great shots of Levi with the high school kids. But when the ones he'd taken of Alex and me running up the bleachers started to populate on my screen, they really caught my attention. Levi had zoomed in and taken some close-ups of me laughing. I studied my face. Typically I always had the same smile in photos. It was practiced and posed—didn't show too many teeth or wrinkle my face too much. But in these photos, nothing was faked. My entire face was smiling; I looked so freaking happy. Staring down, I realized it wasn't that I *looked* happy. I *was* happy—for the first time in a very long time. And much of that had to do with the man behind the camera lens.

I was still looking at the photos Levi had taken when he strolled into the kitchen. He walked up behind me and began to rub my shoulders. "I think he'll be out cold in five minutes. He was yawning while I was showing him the plays."

I closed my laptop. "He had an amazing time today. Thank you for inviting him."

"Of course. He's a great kid."

"Thank you." I let my head drop as Levi dug his thumb into the muscle where my shoulder and neck met. "I got some great shots today. I think your agent and publicist will be happy. Tomorrow morning after I drop Alex off at camp, I'll stop at CVS and print them out so you can see which ones you want me to send them."

"Thanks."

I groaned as he dug his fingers in deeper. "God, that feels so good."

Levi leaned down with his mouth next to my ear and lowered his voice. "Anything *else* I can make feel good for you?"

God, that was a seriously tempting offer, but Alex had just gone to bed, and I still needed to go up and say goodnight. It was safest to do that now before what little willpower I had near this man completely disappeared.

I stood sort of abruptly. "I'm going to go say goodnight to Alex."

Levi nodded.

I took a few steps but stopped at the doorway and turned back. "Levi?"

"Yeah?"

"Alex wasn't the only one who had a great time today."

He smiled. "Oh yeah?"

I nodded. "I'm glad I came. Goodnight, Levi."

"Goodnight, sweetheart."

xoxo

The next morning, my new boss called to ask if I could possibly stop up at the school today to get my picture taken for my identification card. I'd been scheduled to go in next week, but apparently there had been some mix up. So after I picked up the photos from CVS, I needed to jump in the shower and make myself look halfway presentable.

Levi was in the kitchen when I arrived home.

"Good morning, sleepyhead." I smiled. "Here are the photos from yesterday. I was going to sort through them and just give you the best ones to choose from, but I have to take a quick shower and run up to my new job to get an ID card. Do you mind if I leave you all of them to pick your favorites? I know your agent needed them by this afternoon. Maybe you can just make me a pile of the ones you like best, and I'll send those over to your agent electronically when I get home?"

"Yeah, of course. No problem."

"Thanks. Sorry I don't have time to chat. I'm in a rush."

"Do what you gotta do."

I jumped in the shower, dried my hair, and put on makeup. On my way out, Levi was still going through the photos.

"These really came out incredible," he said. "It's hard to narrow it down."

"Thank you."

"Do you mind if I keep a few of them?"

"No, not at all." I grabbed my car keys from the hook. "Take as many as you want."

"Will you be around later?"

"I have some errands to run. But I'll be done in time to pick up Alex and his friend from camp. Alex is staying over at Kyle's tonight, but his mom works late. So I'm going to pick the boys up and feed them, and then drop them over there afterward for their sleepover."

"So you're free after that? I told a few friends I'd go to that new bar that just opened over on Main Street. They have line dancing tonight. Why don't you come? You know most of the people going."

A night out line dancing actually sounded like fun. Lord knows, I didn't do it often. So I shrugged. "Sure. Why not?"

Levi smiled. "Excellent. I have a couple of meetings this afternoon, but I'll probably head out around eight."

"Perfect. I'll see you back here sometime before that."

xoxo

Later that evening, after I dropped Alex and Kyle at Kyle's house, I came back and straightened up the common areas of The Palm while I waited for Levi. He'd left a windbreaker on the kitchen chair, so I thought I'd hang it in the closet. As I picked it up, something fell from the pocket. Or rather a bunch of things—photos. I bent to collect them. They must've been the ones he'd decided to keep. There were probably about a dozen in total, but the one on top of the pile was a close-up of me that he'd taken on the bleachers. When he'd asked if he could keep a few, I'd assumed he meant some action shots of himself. But as I shuffled through the pile, I realized he'd chosen five different pictures of just me. Me laughing. Me running. Me looking directly at the camera and smiling.

And five pictures of Alex playing. Alex celebrating in the end zone. Alex getting ready to throw the football. Alex smiling from the sidelines.

And two pictures of him and Alex together—one where they were high-fiving, and the other where Levi had lifted Alex up in the air to swing him around. There wasn't a single photo of Levi alone.

Over the last few weeks, Levi had tried to convince me that what he felt for me was not something fleeting. He'd tried to assure me it was more than just sexual attraction. But I didn't believe him—*until now*. For my part, I'd done everything I could to keep my feelings shoved down deep inside of me. I was afraid I was alone in what I felt. That seemed ridiculous now.

I was still crouched down, staring at the photos in my hand when the door opened and Levi walked in. He saw the pictures, and his eyes cautiously lifted to meet mine.

I stood and shook my head. "You really do have feelings for me, don't you?"

Levi held my eyes and took a step closer. "I do. Big ones."

I stared at the photos and let out a shaky breath. "I do, too."

He smiled. "I know you do, babe. You just needed to find a way to accept them."

"What are we going to do, Levi?"

He moved closer and took one of my hands, bringing it up to his lips. "See where it takes us."

"But...you're leaving in a few weeks, and your mother hates me, and then there's Alex and Tanner, and—"

Levi pressed a finger against my lips. "Slow down. Let's take 'em one at a time. Okay?"

I nodded, so he took his finger away.

"First, my mother doesn't hate you. Second, just because I'm leaving doesn't mean things have to end. When I pack my bags, my loyalties come with me on the road. Plenty of guys have girls back home. A lot even have wives and families. They find a way to make it work."

I couldn't believe we were even talking about this. Levi read the anxiety on my face and smiled. "I have more to say, but I'm starting to worry you might hyperventilate if I continue."

I let out a big sigh and shook my head. "I'm nervous, Levi."

"Years ago, when I was trying to decide what college to go to, I got offers from a lot of schools. There was one I'd been interested in initially. It had good academics and a solid football program. I went to visit to check it out, and when I got home they tried to push me to give them a decision faster than I was ready to make it. I hadn't gone to see the rest of the schools yet. My grandfather said to me, 'If you're not scared about losing something, it's not worth your time.' For some reason, those words stuck with me over the years and have helped me make more than one important decision. If you weren't nervous, I'd question if I meant enough to you." He paused and squeezed my hand. "When the time comes—when you're ready—I'll deal with my brother and my family. And Alex...we can handle that however you think is best."

I chewed on my lip. "God, Levi."

"For most of my life, I didn't think relationships were worth the trouble. They're harder when you lead the life I do. I'm not gonna sugarcoat that. We'd have to fight for it. But you make me want to do more than fight for us. You make me want to go to war, Presley."

I felt his words in my soul. There was so much I thought I should say right now, but words couldn't express what was in my heart. So I did what felt right and pressed my lips to his. Emotions fed our kiss. Levi wrapped his arm around my back, holding me tight, and I arched to get closer. His other hand lifted to my neck, and his fingers curled into my hair. Our tongues tangled, and I wasn't sure either of us remembered to breathe. When we finally separated, we were both panting.

Levi brushed his nose with mine. "You kissed me. Outside of the bedroom."

I smiled. "I did."

He pulled back to look into my eyes. "Don't run away anymore. Let me show you how things between us could be. Just take it one day at a time."

I nodded. I couldn't believe what a difference a few pictures had made. For the last few months, it was like I'd had a gate locked inside of me, and seeing what was important to him in photos was the key to unlocking it. Not only did I not want to run away anymore, I also couldn't wait to show him how I felt right back.

"Do you think your friends would mind if we bailed last minute?" I asked. "The house is empty. Even Fern is out."

A wicked smile spread across Levi's handsome face. Without warning, he scooped me up into his arms and cradled me against his chest. "Don't give a shit if they do.

Because tonight, we're not fucking, sweetheart. We're making love, and that's going to take all night."

My brows shot up. "All night?"

"All. Night."

♂NINETEEN

Presley

THE NEXT COUPLE of days almost felt like a dream.

Levi and I were inseparable. We worked on the inn together, ate meals together, and took turns sneaking into each other's rooms after Alex was asleep. Last night we'd stayed awake until two or three in the morning, just lying in bed talking. Levi told me about what he wanted to do after he wasn't able to play football anymore, and I told him about my dream of someday having my own gallery, like the one I'd worked at in New York.

Since we hadn't slept much, I was surprised when Levi walked into the kitchen as I was getting ready to take Alex to camp. He smiled, and a swarm of butterflies took flight in my belly.

"Morning," he rasped. I absolutely loved his early-morning voice. It was deep, but sleepy, with a gruff rumble to it.

I smiled. "You're up early."

"A dream woke me."

"Oh? What was the dream about?"

Levi's eyes flashed to Alex, who was reading the back of the Cheerios box while eating his cereal. He lowered his voice. "I was taking a bath."

The thought of Levi dreaming about taking a bath was amusing for some reason. "Was it a bubble bath?"

He shook his head slowly. "Not quite. Do we have any of that rope left from yesterday when I hung the tire swing in the tree out back?"

"I think so. Why?"

Levi checked over his shoulder once again. Alex was oblivious as he slurped the milk from his bowl.

He moved his mouth to my ear and whispered. "How much weight do you think the showerhead can hold? Meet me back here after you drop Alex off. I'll grab the rope from the garage."

Oh. Oh my. I swallowed and cleared my throat. "Alex, you ready to leave for camp? I have to get back home to do some things."

Levi grinned—a wicked, dirty smile that made my heart flutter—as he raised his coffee to his lips. "Yes, it's a very busy day. Your mom will be *all tied up.*"

I'm pretty sure I broke the speed limit driving back home from camp. I also stepped on the gas at a yellow light a few blocks from the house and didn't quite make it through before it turned red. I couldn't get back to Levi fast enough.

At the house, I swung open the front door and could see the back of Levi's head where he sat in the kitchen. For a half second, I considered stripping at the door and walking in naked, but I wasn't sure if Fern was home or not. So I opted to remain clothed—for a few more minutes anyway.

"I think I just got one of those red-light tickets on the way home," I said as I breezed into the kitchen. "And I think you should have to pay for it since—"

I froze. Levi was not alone.

A man sat across from him at the table.

Blinking a few times, I was sure my imagination had to be playing tricks on me. But unfortunately, the smiling face was very real.

The man stood. "There's my girl."

My heart jumped to my throat. "Tanner, what are you doing here?"

He flashed a crooked smile. "Surprise?"

I wiped my sweaty palms on my shorts. "Yeah. It most certainly is."

My eyes shot over to Levi, who stayed seated with his arms crossed. He looked troubled, but sympathetic—as if he were silently telling me he was *so freaking sorry* right now.

I'm sorry, too.

This was not the way this morning was supposed to turn out.

"I thought it was time to come home," Tanner finally said.

With a bitter tone, I asked, "Why now?"

He nodded. "Well, to be honest, it's been a long time coming. From the moment I found out you and Alex were moving down here, I've felt like I was missing out. I decided some time ago that I was going to come join you. But I didn't announce it because I didn't trust myself to follow through. I've just fucked up so many damn times with my son, and didn't want to make any promises I couldn't keep."

"I'm seriously confused, Tanner. You barely came to visit him when we were in New York."

He took a few steps toward me. "I know. This is less about Beaufort and more about where I am in my life right now, Presley. You guys just happen to be *here* right now. But this would be happening if you were in New York, too. I just needed to get to this place in my life first." He sighed. "Look, I know I have a lot of explaining to do, okay? To both you and Alex. I hope you give me a chance."

My eyes once again met Levi's. The happiness I'd seen in his face the past few days was totally gone. It had been drained, replaced by the same fear, anger, and confusion I felt right now.

I turned to Tanner. "Why didn't you call to let me know you were coming?"

"Would it have mattered? I thought about it, but in the end, I thought it would be better if I surprised Alex."

"Where do you plan on staying?" I asked.

He looked around. "Well, given that this place has several rooms, I was hoping you'd let me crash here."

Levi's chair skidded as he got up from his seat. He opened the fridge and popped open a root beer, angrily tossing the bottle cap aside. Tanner likely thought nothing of it, but *I* could see the steam coming out of Levi's ears.

"How long do you plan to stay in Beaufort?" I asked.

"I honestly don't know."

"How can you not know?"

He laughed. "If I didn't know better, I would think you're not happy to see me, Presley. I can't say I blame you, okay? But know that I didn't come back here to cause any problems. I want to spend some time with my son." He turned to Levi before looking back at me. "Big bro told me about all of the stuff you got going on here, all the wonderful plans you have for Gramps's place. You know, when I found out he'd left half of The Palm Inn to Alex, I worried what that would mean. I thought you were crazy for not selling. But Levi told me how much progress you've made. Where there's a will, there's always a way, I guess. And I'm really proud of you."

"Thanks," I muttered, willing my stomach to stop churning.

"I can't thank you enough for helping out," he told Levi.

Levi nodded.

"That's right," I said. "None of this would have been possible without Levi's help. He paid for an entirely new air conditioning system, among other things."

Tanner tilted his head. "I thought you were pushing to sell. What changed, Levi?"

Levi's eyes met mine. "I guess you could say Presley's *passion* rubbed off on me."

My cheeks felt hot as tension formed in the air.

"Well, it's cool that you're seeing eye to eye on things now. That would've been a problem." He looked between us before his eyes landed on mine. "So...uh, you didn't answer my question. Is it okay if I stay here?"

"You didn't answer *my* question as to how long you're staying," I retorted.

"Well, you know I started that new junior sports agent position a few months ago. I can do that from anywhere. I only have to travel to meet new clients, so I do most of my work from home. I was hoping to at least spend the rest of the summer here. I know Levi's heading back to Colorado in a few weeks. Figured I'd be able to fill the void around here once he's gone."

Levi slammed his bottle down on the table.

As much as I wanted to please Alex, who I knew would want his dad to stay with us, my gut told me I needed to stop Tanner in his tracks. "Okay, well, I don't know if you staying here is such a good idea right now."

Tanner looked down at his shoes. "You know what? I shouldn't have thrown all of this on you at once. I'll stay at my mother's for now. If you change your mind, that'll be great. But I understand that you need to get used to me being here first."

Silence filled the air for several seconds before Tanner spoke again.

"Look...I know I've been a shitty father, a shitty brother, and a shitty ex." He looked between us. "But you two are still the closest people to me on Earth, so I feel like I can be open with you right now, even if we aren't on the best of terms." He took a deep breath in. "It's taken me a while to get to the place I am today. I haven't told you just _how_ much I'd been struggling." He exhaled. "You know about my gambling addiction. Well, I finally started seeing a therapist, which is something I should've done a long time ago. He's treating me for not only the gambling issue, but for the generally self-destructive behavior that's gotten me to where I am today."

Levi swallowed, seeming to soften a bit for the first time since I walked in. "I'm glad to hear you're seeing someone."

Tanner nodded. "I look at my life now, and I honestly can't tell you how I got to this place. I'm not gonna stand here and use my injury as an excuse either. I've made that mistake for far too long. Sure, the injury started my downward spiral, but I have to take responsibility for my actions." He turned to me. "Everything I've done has been a choice—from hurting you, Presley, to the gambling, to not being there for Alex. And I'm so damn sorry."

I'd known Tanner long enough to know when he was lying and when he was being honest. I believed he was sincere right now, although I didn't necessarily trust that this newfound conscientiousness would last forever.

Fern waltzed into the kitchen, interrupting our conversation.

Her eyes went wide. "Well, well, well, looks like a party of three in here."

Tanner smiled. "Hey, Fern. Good to see you again. It's been a long time."

"Sure has. What brings you home, son?"

"Just missin' my family. That's all."

She raised her brow. "You stayin' here with us?"

"I plan to stay at my mother's tonight." Tanner looked over at me. "But I'm hoping Presley will change her mind and let me crash here eventually, if she still has the space by then. I know she has a lot going on, so I'm not pushing anything."

"Yeah..." Fern snickered. "It is a little *crowded* at the moment. You being here might be too much for Presley to *ménage—*" She shook her head. "I mean, *manage.*"

Ugh! Sure you did. I glared at her, and she seemed to get the message.

"Well, enjoy your stay wherever you end up sleeping." She winked. "I just came to say hello and see what all the excitement was about."

Levi gritted his teeth, looking ready to explode.

Relief washed over me when Fern went back to her room.

Levi left the kitchen soon after and made himself scarce the rest of the day. He told Tanner he had to meet someone, but I suspected he just needed to blow off some steam in private. It wasn't like we could vent to each other with Tanner right under our noses.

Tanner said he wanted to go with me to pick up Alex. It happened to be the last day of camp, and I knew he was going to be so surprised to see his dad. As much as Tanner showing up here unannounced was jarring, I was happy and excited for my son—as long as this didn't turn out to be another disappointment.

As Tanner and I packed into my car, I made a mental decision not to give in regarding my decision about him staying at The Palm. He could sleep at his mother's for as long as she would have him. I knew Alex would likely push for him to stay with us, but I needed to stand my ground.

As I drove toward the park, Tanner placed his hand lightly on my leg.

"It's so good to see you," he said.

I abruptly shifted my leg away.

"I'm sorry," he said after a moment. "It feels so unnatural not to touch you. But I crossed a line there."

"Yes, you did," I shot back.

"I don't expect anything except for you not to shut me out, Presley. You don't have to say a damn thing to me or pretend to be happy to see me. Just don't tell me to disappear, even if that's what I deserve."

I kept my eyes on the road. "I wouldn't do that, and you know it."

"I do know. Because you're a fucking sweetheart who's always been too damn good to me." He leaned his head back on the seat. "You know, when I got off the plane this morning and stepped outside into the balmy air, it felt like I'd woken up out of a nightmare in a way. I've been stuck in this rut for so long that I've forgotten who I really am. And in that moment—smelling the air—I felt a hint of who I used to be. So much of who I am comes from this place. It didn't take long for me to understand why you wanted to come back here."

"Well, I'm glad you get it now because you were less than understanding when I told you I was coming back."

"I know I was. And I apologize—for that and so many other things."

I gripped the steering wheel. "How many times are you going to apologize to me, Tanner?"

"As many fucking times as I need to," he shouted before lowering his voice. "Do you know how much it hurts to see the disappointment in your eyes when you look at me? And to know I deserve every bit of it? When I look at *you*, Presley, I see everything I've ever wanted and every mistake I've ever made all rolled into one."

When I finally glanced over at him, his eyes were glistening. There was absolutely no doubt he was being honest. Perhaps I might not have felt so sorry for him if I hadn't been having an affair with his brother. But somehow, I *did* feel sorry for him.

I also felt sorry for Levi. He'd been in denial more than I had about the implications of our getting involved—about how hard it would be when the time came to face Tanner. I think his shutting down today proved how difficult the reality was going to be. Neither of us was prepared for this.

When we arrived at camp, my thoughts took a backseat to the excitement of anticipating my son's reaction. The moment Alex spotted his father walking next to me in the distance, his eyes widened. It was priceless when the realization hit.

"*Dad?*" I could see him mouth before he came running toward us.

Tanner held his arms open. "It's me, bud."

"Dad!" Alex ran faster, into his father's arms.

Tanner closed his eyes as he hugged Alex tightly. When he opened them, a lone tear fell.

Jesus. I couldn't remember the last time I'd seen Tanner cry. He'd looked emotional in the car a minute ago, but I certainly hadn't expected him to cry. And he wasn't the only one in tears. My son was crying, too.

Alex seemed understandably confused. "What are you doing here?"

"What do you think I'm doing here? I came to see you."

He wiped his eyes. "Really?"

"Really." Tanner kissed Alex on the forehead. "And I'm not leaving anytime soon either, okay?"

Alex took a few seconds to let that soak in before his mouth curved into a smile. "This is the best day ever."

"For me, too, believe me."

"You're staying with us at The Palm Inn, right? With me and Mom and Uncle Levi?"

Tanner opened his mouth, looking like he didn't know how to answer.

No. I'm not going to bend on this. "Actually, your dad is staying with Grandma," I told him.

My son frowned. "Why?"

Tanner's eyes met mine. "Your mom has a lot on her plate right now, son, with the house and all. She's trying to fix up all the rooms. She doesn't need me in the way. But don't worry, it won't change us getting to hang out."

Alex looked to me. "Mom, can Dad *please* stay with us? He won't be in the way. He can stay in my room."

"I don't think so, Alex."

Alex pleaded. "Please."

The sad look on his face hit me straight in the heart. My son never asked me for much. He'd put up with a lot, given the mess of a relationship his father and I had. *Am I really being fair to him?*

"I suppose...we can make room for your dad," I said, swallowing the anxiety uttering those words brought on.

"You sure?" Tanner asked. When I nodded, he mouthed, *"Thank you."*

I was pretty sure I'd just made a huge mistake. But I'd do anything for Alex, and that proved it.

✗○✗○

Levi was home when we returned to the inn.

Alex couldn't wait to tell him about Tanner staying with us.

"Uncle Levi, Dad is staying with us. Isn't that the best news ever?"

Levi's eyes darted to me. Frowning, I did my best to offer a silent apology.

And he did his best to pretend he was happy about it as he forced a smile. "That's amazing news, buddy."

Tanner ruffled Alex's hair. "Last I recall, your favorite food is pizza. Is that still correct?"

"Well, now it's pizza *and* Iggy's fried chicken."

"Ah. You discovered Iggy's, did ya?"

"Uncle Levi took me. We had dinner there one night when Mom was out. He told me a bunch of old stories from back when you guys used to go there."

Tanner looked over at his brother and smiled. "Thanks for showing him around."

"It was my pleasure." Levi smiled. "We had a good time that night, didn't we, Alex?"

Alex nodded. "We always have a good time."

A look of sadness crossed Tanner's face, as if realizing for the first time that it wasn't only *the inn* Levi had been looking after.

If he only knew...

Looking down at Alex, Tanner clapped his hands together. "What do you say we give your mother a break tonight, and I'll order pizza for all of us?"

"You don't need to do that," I said.

"I want to."

Alex jumped up and down. "Mom, please! Pizza sounds so good!"

He didn't realize my hesitation had nothing to do with the pizza but everything to do with Tanner pushing his way back into our lives at warp speed. But all I could do was sigh.

Tanner ended up ordering three large pizzas to be delivered. Levi and I were quiet throughout dinner while Tanner and Alex made up for lost time. Alex filled his dad in on how camp had gone all summer and the upcoming peewee football season.

After dinner, Alex went to take a shower. Tanner asked Levi if he wanted to grab a couple of beers from the fridge and head out back. He agreed, and I watched them go, only to realize my nerves were shot. What would they discuss during their man-to-man time? I could only imagine what was going through Levi's mind. He'd been forced to keep his emotions inside since Tanner's arrival, and it killed me that we hadn't had a chance to talk.

Later that evening, after I tucked Alex in, I went to my room earlier than normal. The second I closed the door behind me, Levi texted.

Levi: Are you okay?

Presley: I am. You?

Levi: Okay is a relative term.

Presley: I'm sorry I got pressured into him staying here.

Levi: You did the right thing.

Presley: I didn't want to make you uncomfortable.

Levi: The only thing making me feel uncomfortable now is the thought of him upsetting you.

Presley: I miss you. We were supposed to have our day together. Instead, I feel like the world turned upside down.

Before Levi could respond, a text from Tanner came through.

Tanner: I can't tell you how much I appreciate you letting me stay.

Before I could respond to Tanner, another text from Levi lit up my phone.

Levi: I wish I could come to your room right now. This fucking sucks.

And then a text from Tanner.

Tanner: You looked so beautiful tonight.

Then from Levi.

Levi: I need you tonight, Presley. I don't know what's gotten into me. I know he's my brother and I love him and you belonged to him first and all that...but I am feeling SO goddamn possessive right now.

Shit.

Tanner: Seriously, Presley. I know my staying here isn't easy for you.

My brain was spinning.

Levi: Are you there?

I shook my head and responded to Levi.

Presley: Yes. I'm here.

Tanner sent another message.

Tanner: I was hoping you could carve out some time to talk to me tomorrow. There's a lot I need to say to you.

I responded to Tanner.

Presley: I'm not sure we have anything left to talk about.

But it was Levi who answered me.

Levi: What the hell are you saying?

I looked down and realized I'd sent that last text to the wrong brother.

Presley: I'm sorry. That was meant for Tanner.

Levi immediately messaged back.

Levi: He's texting you right now?

I could feel his anger through my phone.

Tanner: Are you there, or are you just choosing to ignore my texts? I'm getting a complex.

It occurred to me that I'd yet to actually respond to Tanner. Before I could type anything, Levi chimed in.

Levi: That's not surprising. When we were out back tonight, he kept asking me questions about you. He wanted to know whether you've been seeing anyone. I felt like telling him about us right then and there. But I fucking couldn't.

My heart began to race.

Levi: You there?

Presley: Yes. I'm just feeling overwhelmed right now.

After about a minute, he responded.

Levi: Alright, baby. Get some sleep. Hopefully he'll leave at some point tomorrow, so we can have some alone time and process this together.

Presley: I hope so.

Levi: Sweet dreams.

Presley: You too.

I clicked on Tanner's name and finally responded to him.

Presley: I'll talk to you tomorrow.

The dots danced as he typed.

Tanner: Cool. Thank you.

I needed to shut down any further communication with Tanner tonight.

Presley: Going to sleep.

Tanner: Sweet dreams.

It wasn't lost on me that his brother had just told me the same thing—"Sweet dreams"—a minute ago. There wouldn't be any dreams tonight, unless they were nightmares about the predicament I'd gotten myself into. I probably wouldn't be getting *any* sleep at all.

TWENTY

Levi

I POPPED INTO Alex's room the next morning. It was his first day of peewee football practice, and the plan had always been that I would take him.

"You ready to go to practice?"

"Dad's gonna take me," he said.

Not gonna lie, my heart sank a little. "He is, is he?"

"Yeah, I am." Tanner's voice came from behind me. "I figured you've been filling in long enough. I have a lot of making up for lost time to do."

I understood that, but I still felt like crap. Alex and I had bonded in Tanner's absence. Now that his dad was here, it felt like he didn't need me anymore. And you know what? That would have been perfectly fine if I didn't worry that Tanner was gonna somehow break his heart and flake out again.

A few minutes later, they were both gone, and the house was quiet for what felt like the first time in forever, even though it had only been a day. The only good thing about Tanner taking Alex was that it gave me a chance to finally be alone with Presley.

The second Tanner's car pulled out of the driveway, I rushed to Presley's side in the kitchen.

She looked so beautiful, leaning against the counter, holding her coffee while lost in thought.

"Hey," I said.

She looked up and smiled. "Hey."

I pulled her into my arms and spoke against her neck. "I feel like it's been forever since I've gotten to hold you."

Presley exhaled. "What the hell are we going to do, Levi?"

I placed a soft kiss on top of her head. "I thought I'd have this all figured out before we had to face him. Clearly, that's not the case."

"Yeah. *Everything* was easier when he wasn't here."

I pulled back to look at her. "Last night when we were outside having beers, he kept saying how good you looked. This mixture of guilt and jealousy hit me like a ton of bricks. And I didn't know who I hated more in that moment—him or myself."

"You have nothing to be jealous of," she said as she ran her fingers through my hair. I closed my eyes, wanting so badly to carry her to my room and bury myself inside of her. But I got the impression she wasn't in the mood. Presley seemed *way* too preoccupied.

I had to know. "What else did he say when he texted you last night?"

"He told me I looked beautiful yesterday and said he wanted to talk to me today."

"Fuck. He wants you back, Presley."

"You don't know that."

"Yeah, I do know it. He didn't say it in so many words last night, but it's obvious." Panic started to set in, and I felt the need to stake my claim. "You're a nervous wreck,"

I told her. "And I feel like I'm about to lose my mind. Not sure how much more of this either of us can take. Maybe I should tell him about us tonight."

She shook her head. "No. Definitely not."

Her adamant stance confused me a little. "No?"

"I don't want him to find out what happened."

Her choice of words jarred me.

"*Happened?* You realize you just used past tense."

"That's not what I meant," she stammered. "It's just... not the best time."

"When will it ever be, Presley? Seriously. You think it's gonna get any easier as time goes on?"

"No. I just don't think it's the right time to hit him with it."

I moved back. "You seem *very* concerned with Tanner's feelings."

Presley shook her head. "I need some time. I feel like the rug was pulled out from underneath us, and I haven't had a chance to regain my footing. Let's just give it some time."

I felt so many emotions, but the one that freaked me out the most was fear—fear of losing her. Unfortunately, I covered it with anger. "Fine. Take all the time you need. Just let me know if it's gonna be forever."

"Levi..." She reached for me. But I took a step back and put up my hands.

"*Don't.* I need some air." I headed for the door.

xoxo

Levi: I'm sorry I acted like an idiot earlier.

Three hours later, I'd finally gotten my shit together

enough to apologize. I'd gotten in my car earlier and started driving, not stopping until I somehow ended up at Folly Beach, just south of Charleston. I didn't even remember the drive here.

I'd parked near the pier and walked down to the end to stare out at the water. I wished I could say it had given me some clarity. But I still felt angry and confused, scared and jealous. Though I did come to the realization that taking those feelings out on Presley wasn't going to do either of us much good.

My phone pinged, and I took a deep breath, unsure what she'd been thinking after the way I'd acted.

Presley: It's okay. I understand. Tanner showing up has thrown us both for a loop.

I smiled. It was just like Presley to be so understanding. It was one of the things I loved about her.

My smile suddenly fell. *Loved. I do fucking love her, don't I?* I'd felt it for a while now, but I hadn't been able to bring myself to accept it. Nothing like the threat of losing someone to make you realize what you have.

Levi: Thank you for understanding.

Presley: I just want to make sure anything that happens with you, Tanner, and me doesn't cause a backlash on Alex. I don't want him caught in the middle. Tanner says he's changed, but I'm not certain he would put his hurt feelings aside for the sake of our son. We can't make any rash, emotional decisions, because it's not just us who will pay the price for them.

I took a deep breath. What she was saying sucked, but I admired her so damn much for keeping her priorities straight.

Levi: You're a great mom.

She responded with a smiley face. A minute later, my phone buzzed again.

Presley: Will you be home for dinner? I know it's not easy to sit at the table all together, so I figured the least I could do was console you with my cooking. I'm making your favorites.

Levi: Fried chicken?

Presley: And buttermilk biscuits from scratch, your grandmother's recipe.

If she didn't already have my heart, that could do it. My stomach growled, as if it were answering for me. So I translated the sentiment.

Levi: Sounds good. I'll be back by dinner, and I'll be on my best behavior.

xoxo

All of the positivity I'd been feeling after the long drive and time staring out at the ocean flew out the window as I pulled up in front of The Palm Inn. The scene unfolding on the front lawn made my heart sink to my stomach. Presley was on the grass with Alex and Tanner, playing football. I watched from the car as Alex threw the ball to his mom. Presley caught it and tried to fake right to run around Tanner, but he grabbed her from behind, wrapping his arms around her waist and pulling her to the ground on top of him. The two of them laughed as they went down, and Alex ran over with a giant smile on his face.

I rubbed at my breastbone and considered driving away again. The happy family probably wouldn't even notice. But before I could, Alex spotted my truck. He waved and pointed.

Fuck.

Now I had to stay. All three of them were looking my way as Alex said something. If I hightailed it out of here now, Alex would be confused, and I'd also have to explain myself to Tanner at some point. So I took a deep breath and turned off the ignition.

"Uncle Levi!" Alex ran toward my truck as I got out. "You can be on Mom's team. Dad and I are killing her. It's like...five million to zero."

I looked over at Presley. The smile that had been on her face before she saw me had morphed into a frown, and her eyes were filled with regret. I wasn't sure if she regretted me seeing her having a good time, or if she regretted that I'd caught her wrapped in Tanner's arms. But there was no damn way I could play anything with them right now.

"Sorry, buddy. Not today. My knee has been acting up."

Tanner smirked at Alex. "Sounds like he's scared we'll beat him, doesn't it?"

Alex grinned. He tucked his hands under his armpits and started to flap his elbows like a chicken. "Buc-buc! Buc-buc!"

I smiled as best I could and kept walking toward the house.

Inside, the kitchen smelled like fried chicken, which normally would perk me up, even on the worst days. But not today. So I went to my room and decided to take a shower. After I was dressed, I debated telling Presley I couldn't stay for dinner. But I knew walking out and leaving her and Tanner together would make me crazy, wondering what was going on while I was gone. So I stuck around to watch the car accident waiting to happen.

Presley was taking biscuits out of the oven when I walked back into the kitchen.

"Hey," she said softly. She looked around to see if the coast was clear. "How was your afternoon?"

I walked to the refrigerator and grabbed a beer. Twisting the cap off, I shrugged. "Fine."

She frowned. "Alex wanted to play, and I couldn't say no."

I nodded and sucked back half my beer.

"It smells like heaven in here." Tanner strolled into the kitchen. "I can't remember the last time I had a home-cooked meal." He walked over to Presley and swiped a biscuit from the tray she'd just taken out of the oven. Biting into it, he said, "Thanks for making my favorites. I miss your cooking, P." Then he winked at me. "Among other things."

Presley closed her eyes and took a deep breath. "We're ready to eat. Can one of you please tell Alex and make sure he washes his hands?"

Tanner and I both said "Sure" at the exact same time. But I needed a moment.

"Enjoy your biscuit." I lifted my chin to my brother. "I'll get Alex."

Once we were all seated at the table, Alex was even more animated than usual. He bit off a chunk of a drumstick and spoke with his mouth full.

"Uncle Levi, did you know my dad probably would've had the highest number of completions in his first year in the pros? Before he got hurt."

I looked up at my brother. He'd had a pretty solid rookie year, though he wouldn't have had the best passer rating in the league if he hadn't gotten injured. I knew that because *I did* hold that title that year. But when I looked over at Alex, who was practically beaming with pride for his father, I didn't have the heart to set the record straight. Instead, I gritted my teeth and nodded.

"I'm sure he would've."

"He also could've been All Pro that year."

I inwardly rolled my eyes. "No doubt."

While Tanner was busy shoveling food into his face, totally undaunted by stretching the truth with his kid, Presley caught my eye. She smiled appreciatively at me. She knew the truth.

"You know," Tanner said. "I realized today that I was just about your age when I first met your mom."

"Really?"

"Yup. We were in second grade together. She was a cheerleader for my peewee football team, and she was the prettiest girl on the squad. Actually, she was the prettiest girl in the school. I remember telling the guys on my team that I was going to kiss her someday."

Alex scrunched up his nose. "Gross, Dad."

Tanner laughed. "Why is that gross?"

"First of all, you're weird for wanting to kiss a girl at my age. And second of all...she's Mom."

"Well, don't worry. Your mom is a nice girl. She made me wait years to get that first kiss anyway." Tanner turned to Presley. "Remember that day? I carved your initials in the tree at Redmond Park."

"You also cut yourself with the pocketknife while doing it."

Tanner leaned back in his chair. "Totally worth it."

I guzzled what was left of my beer and slammed the bottle on the table a little too hard. "I need another one. Anyone else?"

"I'll take one," my brother said.

Presley frowned. "No thank you."

For the next half hour, Tanner continued to walk down memory lane. I had to listen to stories about them going to prom, their first apartment, and how my brother used to fall asleep with his head on Presley's pregnant belly, listening to Alex's heartbeat. Each one was progressively harder to swallow, so I washed them all down with more beer than I normally drank. But it was what came after dinner that made me move to the hard stuff.

"Dad and I are going to camp in the yard tonight together," Alex said.

I knew it was stupid. We'd only camped once, yet selfishly I'd felt like camping was *our* thing. I couldn't even muster a *that's great* to the kid. Instead, I went to the cabinet where my grandfather had always kept the liquor and twisted the top off an unopened bottle of scotch.

Presley looked at me with concern as I poured myself a shot, but said nothing.

"Mom, can we go out and get marshmallows? Dad and I are going to make a campfire when we camp tonight."

"Umm... Sure, sweetheart. Let me just load the dishwasher, and we can run to the store. Why don't you go wash your hands in the meantime."

"Okay, Mom!"

As Alex ran off, Tanner walked up behind Presley at the sink. He put his hands on her shoulders, and I felt heat rise from my toes to the top of my forehead. "Levi and I will take care of all this, babe. You did all the cooking."

Presley turned around, effectively forcing his hands from her shoulders. "Tanner, please stop calling me that."

"Sorry. I guess it just feels so good to be living with you again, I forget we have a ways to go."

Presley shook her head. "We're *not* living together. You're staying in one of the rooms—same as any stranger might be doing once the inn is open again." She lowered her voice. "You need to stop giving Alex the wrong impression, Tanner."

He wrinkled his forehead. "What, that I love his mother? That's not a wrong impression. It's a fact."

"You're making him think we're a couple."

"No, I'm not."

"Yes, *you are.*"

"He's a smart kid. Maybe he just sees what's meant to be."

Presley shook her head again. "I'm going to take Alex to the store. Do you need anything else for tonight while I'm out?"

"Nope."

She glanced over at me before grabbing her keys and yelling for Alex.

Once it was just Tanner and me, another shot of scotch was necessary. I poured to the brim and sucked it back, enjoying the burn as it washed down my pipes.

Tanner rinsed a plate and loaded it into the dishwasher. "You drink more these days than I remember..."

"Not usually."

"Something bothering you?"

"Nothing I feel like talking about."

Tanner chuckled. "Woman problems, huh?"

I said nothing, which made my brother assume he'd hit the nail on the head.

"It was easier when we were eighteen, wasn't it? Now a Ouija board has more answers about what a woman wants than I do."

I poured another shot. "It's not that complicated."

"For you, maybe. What are you pulling down? Twenty, thirty million a year? You just have to flash that Super Bowl ring, and the panties fall to the ground. Us working stiffs have to actually *work* for it."

The muscle in my jaw ticked. "You might want to pull out your Ouija board and have a heart to heart if you think all women only give a shit about money."

Tanner turned off the water. He leaned a hip against the counter and folded his arms across his chest, facing me. "Alright, big brother. If you know so much about women, tell me what Presley wants."

I looked back and forth between my brother's eyes. "Trust, loyalty, and dependability are important to Presley."

Tanner shrugged. "I can give her all those things."

I wanted to say '*Now* you can give them to her? *Where the hell were you seven years ago?*' But instead I just gritted my teeth and motioned to the sink with my eyes. "You got this? I have something I have to do."

"Yeah, sure. Go do whatever you need to." Tanner smirked. "Or *who*ever you need to."

I probably should've walked to the bar a few blocks away and finished getting shitfaced, but instead I went to my room, unable to bring myself to leave the inn. Since my room was at the far end of the hall, away from the common areas of the house, I couldn't hear when Presley came back. Which was probably just as well.

But an hour or so later, there was a light knock at my door. I opened it to find Presley.

She glanced back over her shoulder. "Can I come in?"

I debated saying no for about two whole seconds, but who the hell was I kidding? I was incapable of turning this woman away.

So I stepped aside and held my hand out.

Inside, she stared down at the floor. "This is such a mess. I don't know what to do."

"I do. We need to tell him."

Presley's eyes flared as she looked up. "No, we can't!"

I raked a hand through my hair. "If I have to watch him put his hands on you or listen to him call you *babe* one more time, I'm going to lose it."

She shook her head. "I'm sorry. But I don't know how to make him stop. You've heard me tell him to knock it off. I'm not doing anything to encourage him."

"No? You don't think playing two-hand touch with a man who has made it known he wants to touch you all over is encouraging him? Or making his favorite meal for dinner in the house you invited him to stay with you in?"

"I made *you* your favorite dinner."

I scoffed. "That's not what he thinks."

"I don't care what he thinks."

"Good." I put my hands on my hips. "Then we're in agreement. If you don't give a shit what he thinks, we'll tell him."

"Levi, don't twist my words. You're not being fair."

I narrowed my eyes. "Fair? You know what's not fair? Having to answer my brother when he asks me for advice on how to get you back."

Presley closed her eyes and blew out a deep breath. "God, I'm sorry."

"Are you? Because I'm starting to think maybe you just want to keep your options open."

She pursed her lips and glared at me. "You know that's not true. Stop being an asshole."

"Tell me, *babe*. If I go down on you, are you going to moan my name like you usually do, or might Tanner's slip out?"

If eyes could shoot daggers, I'd be pretty holey at the moment. From the look on her face, I thought I was about to experience the wrath of Presley, but instead she stormed toward the door in silence. I caught her arm as she attempted to pass, knowing I needed to stop her, but not sure what the hell to say.

She spun around, and our eyes locked. So many emotions blazed through my veins: anger, sadness, confusion, *terror*. Presley's chest was heaving; she looked as pissed off as I felt. I took a deep breath to try to calm myself, so I could figure out how to fix this, but all it did was bring in a whiff of her perfume.

Fuck.

She smelled so good. Suddenly, the anger coursing through my veins mixed with something else, and composing myself went out the window. I yanked her arm, pulled her against my chest, and used my teeth to capture her mouth.

Fuck.

Like a salve to a wound, her taste soothed the pain away. I felt greedy, wanting all of her to erase the doubts in my mind. Backing her up against the wall, I wrapped my hands around her cheeks and planted my lips over hers. The last two days seemed to disappear as she moaned into my mouth and lifted her legs to wrap around my waist. Her tits pushed against my chest, and she grabbed for the button of my jeans. *This*. This is what I needed to forget about everything else in the world. When she slipped her fingers into my pants, wrapped them around my cock, and squeezed, the swoosh of blood coursing through my ears was so loud, I wouldn't have heard the fire alarm.

Though it wasn't the fire alarm I needed to hear.

It was the knock at my bedroom door.

TWENTY-ONE

Levi

"WHAT DO WE do?" Presley's eyes bulged.

I held my finger to my lips and prayed Fern would respond when I spoke.

"Who is it?"

"Tanner. Can I come in?"

Shit. I closed my eyes. I wanted to tell him about Presley and me, but this was not the way it should go down. So I pointed to the bathroom and mouthed, "*Go in there.*"

Presley nodded and scurried in, quietly closing the door behind her. My heart raced like a runaway train as I walked to the door. A deep breath did nothing to compose myself, but if I took any longer, I'd definitely raise suspicions. So I opened the door and held onto it, blocking entry and hoping he'd take the hint.

Tanner looked over my shoulder. "Took you long enough. I was starting to think you had a woman in there and I was interrupting something."

I swallowed. "Nope. I was about to jump in the shower."

"Again? You just showered an hour or two ago."

Crap. I shrugged. "Summer in South Carolina."

"Yeah, I'm not used to the heat either. Anyway, I wanted to ask if you knew where the grilled-cheese makers for the campfire are. Alex told me you had them when you camped out for his birthday."

"They're in the cabinet in the garage."

"Great, thanks."

Tanner turned away, and I almost breathed a sigh of relief. *Almost.* But he turned back around.

"Do you happen to know where Presley is? I went to her room first, but she's not there."

I looked into my brother's eyes. Did he know she was in here? Or was he sincerely asking a question? My nerves were frayed, and I couldn't be sure one way or the other. So I answered as truthfully as I could, uncertain how well my face contained the lies.

"I've been in here since she left for the store."

My brother nodded. "She mentioned she might go see her friend Katrina. But I'm wondering if maybe she's seeing someone."

"Why would you think that?"

He shook his head. "I don't know. It just feels like something is in my way."

I swallowed.

"You'd tell me if you knew she was with someone, right? Even if she asked you not to say anything? I mean bros before hoes and all."

I studied his face. *Did he know?* I put the odds about even, because fuck if I had any idea. But I was in too deep now to go off script. So I nodded.

"Of course."

He put his hand on my shoulder. "I'm glad you're here. I miss having someone I can talk to."

And thanks for slamming that last nail in on the coffin of my principles. I think it's safe to lower them into the ground now.

"Yeah. Same."

He waved. "I gotta get back to Alex. You have a good night."

Once I heard his footsteps fade, I turned the lock on the door. Can't be too careful. I wouldn't be surprised if he came back and opened without knocking next time. Then I went to the bathroom and gently opened the door.

"He's gone."

Presley nodded. Her hands were shaking.

"Did you hear?"

She nodded again. "I'm not sure what I feel worse about, the fact that I can't keep away from you and we almost got caught making out, or that I made you lie to your brother."

I dragged a hand through my hair. "It's a fucked-up situation."

She frowned. "It is. And I'm so sorry you're in the middle of things between me and Tanner."

"You didn't put me here. It takes two, and I wanted it as much as you, if not more."

She shook her head. "I should go before he looks for me again."

Normally when she had doubts, I didn't let her walk away without trying to convince her things would work out. But I didn't have the energy at the moment. Or maybe this was the first time I'd started to think maybe they wouldn't...

XOXO

The next day, my brother appeared at the entrance to my bedroom as I was folding my laundry.

"Hey, dude. Does this tie look stupid with this shirt?" he asked.

Tanner wore a blue dress shirt, with a maroon tie hanging off his shoulder.

"No, it looks fine." I gave him a once-over. "Where you going all dressed up?"

"I have an interview."

"An interview? Where?"

"Pinehurst has an opening for a football coach. So I threw my hat into the ring, and they called me."

Pinehurst was a small college two towns over. It hadn't occurred to me that Tanner might be considering locating here permanently, even though I probably should have known with the way he'd been acting lately.

"Why would you want that job? I thought you were liking the agent gig."

"I only have a few clients right now. I can easily swing both for a while. If it turns out I can't, I'll just focus on the coaching. I'm not crazy about travel. And if I want to get serious about settling down and being here for Alex, I need to find something more stable anyway." He knotted his tie. "You don't think it's a good idea?"

I tried to think about the kind of advice someone would give his brother if that someone *didn't* have an ulterior motive. The coaching position sounded like a dream job for someone in his situation. If I steered him away from it, that would be for my own selfish reasons—not wanting him near Presley. And that wasn't fair to him or Alex.

"No. I think the coaching job would be a good thing for you, if you're looking to settle in Beaufort," I forced out.

"Yeah, me too. I really hope I get it. I'm also eager to get back on the playing field. Football is still in my blood, and this'll be one way to get my feet wet again without having to play, which I obviously can't do. It's the perfect opportunity for me."

I sucked in some air. "Well, I hope you get it, then."

Tanner examined my face. "Are you okay?"

No, in fact. Not at all. Apparently, I must not have been doing that great of a job of pretending like I was happy for him. "Why do you ask?"

He leaned against the wall and crossed his arms. "I've been getting a strange vibe from you since the moment I arrived. And then the way you've been drinking... Well, I know a thing or two about addiction."

I *had* been throwing back a few too many lately, but that was directly related to him being here and nothing more; I couldn't exactly admit that.

"There's nothing to the drinking. I'm...just going through my own shit, you know? You're not the only one reassessing your life these days."

He shook his head. "God, I feel like such a crappy brother. I've done nothing but unload all of my stuff on you since the second I arrived, and I haven't bothered to stop long enough to figure out that you're not okay."

Sure. *He's* the crappy brother.

My damn emotions were all over the place. One second I wanted to tell him about Presley and me in order to stake my claim, and the next, I wanted to protect my baby brother from ever finding out. The latter was where I stood at the present moment.

He made it worse when he said, "Listen, I have to apologize to you, Levi."

I held out my palm. "No, you don't."

"Yes, I do." He sighed. "I've intentionally alienated myself from you over the years because I couldn't handle your success. I'm your freaking brother. You don't do that to your only sibling—erase him from your life because you can't seem to be happy for him. My therapist has helped me learn that your success has nothing to do with my lack of it. You deserve every one of your wins. I'm sorry I was insecure for so many years, and that I wasted precious time I could've spent cheering you on from the sidelines. That's where I should've been all along, not off in my own world with my head stuck up my ass. I—"

"Tanner, stop." The guilt inside of me felt like it was overflowing and about to burst. "I always understood why you stayed away. I don't blame you for any of it and can't say I would've acted any differently if I were you."

"You know," he said. "It hit me on the plane ride down here. Dad and Gramps are both gone. You and I—we're the only Millers left besides Alex. That's a big responsibility. We should be setting an example that family sticks together no matter what. It's not too late to do that."

"Yeah, well, it takes two. I haven't exactly been there for you either."

"No, but you've been there for my son as of late. I want to thank you for that. And you at least made an effort to reach out to me these past few years while I've alienated you. I'm the one responsible for our relationship turning sour. But I'm not hiding anymore, and I want to do better."

At a loss, I nodded and bit my lip.

"So, you don't want to tell me what's going on with you?" he prodded.

Tanner's seemingly genuine interest in wanting to help me with my "problem" was like salt in my guilty wound.

What had been so clear to me yesterday seemed like an impossibility now. Had I been crazy for thinking I could start a life with Presley with no serious repercussions?

"I'm a little lost right now," I finally said. "I thought I loved my life until I came back here and realized everything that was missing from it. You could say I'm working things out in the same way you seem to be trying to."

My brother nodded. "Maybe all of this is just a reflection of us getting older," he said. "You start to see things more clearly, including the mistakes you've made. I'm realizing just how much being stuck in my own head has cost me. But I'm determined to get it all back, Levi. Not only my son's trust, but Presley's too. I love that woman. Never stopped. I just didn't know how to be the man she deserved. I truly feel like I've changed, that I'm ready to be that man."

Pain shot through my neck, and I rubbed the back of it. There it was—confirmation of my worst fear. I couldn't manage to conjure up a response to that. Instead, I changed the subject, my head spinning.

"What time is your appointment?"

He looked down at his phone. "Shit. I actually have to hurry up." He headed toward the door but turned around one last time. "I'm not done with this conversation, okay?" He pointed at me. "You and me, we're gonna talk later tonight and figure out our shit—together." He patted his chest and winked. "Miller strong."

I forced a smile before he disappeared down the hall. Grabbing my pillow, I placed it over my face as I fell back on the bed. My heart pounded as I breathed into the fabric.

Presley was right. Telling him would be a huge mistake. My brother had definitely fucked up in his lifetime. But he didn't deserve to hear that I'd moved in on his family while he wasn't looking. He didn't deserve that at all.

I didn't know what to do. I seemed to be waking up from the stupor I'd been in and doubting for the first time whether I could betray him, no matter how much I loved Presley. At the same time, losing her was unimaginable.

I couldn't remember wanting anything in my life as much as I wanted her—not only her, but a *life* with her. It wasn't only about me or what I wanted, though, was it? We had Alex to think about—and honestly, Tanner. He might not have deserved her, but he was still my brother, and I owed him loyalty. It was easier to discount that fact when I thought he didn't care. But now that I knew he apparently *did*, that he wanted to be a better man—it was a game changer.

My phone chimed, interrupting my thoughts.

I looked down to find a text from Presley. My chest tightened.

Presley: Tanner left the house. Can you come to my room?

I had no idea whether she just wanted to talk or whether she was looking for something *else*. But as much as I wanted to be with her right now, I wasn't ready to face her until I better understood what the realization I'd had today meant for us. I couldn't risk getting any deeper into things if I was only going to walk away—even if leaving was the last thing I wanted.

It caused me literal pain to type the words.

Levi: I have a busy day today. I can't. I'm sorry.

TWENTY-TWO

Presley

I COULDN'T TELL you how many times I'd read over Levi's text, trying to decipher the true meaning.

He was busy? That was the biggest crock of shit. And Levi had never been one to shy away from talking, so I couldn't understand why he'd blown me off. This had me feeling a bit panicked. I didn't care how busy he claimed to be; you can always make time for things that matter.

I'd dropped Alex off at a friend's house, so I was alone, aside from the fact that Fern was somewhere in the house.

Deciding to paint an accent wall in one of the bedrooms, I ruminated as I kept going over the same spots unnecessarily—my mind just wasn't in it today.

At one point, Tanner appeared at the doorway, dressed to the nines. I knew about his job interview but hadn't spoken to him before he left this morning.

I put down my brush. "Hey."

"Hi."

"How did your interview go?"

"It went well." He smiled. "They're going to let me know by the end of the week. I think they have to interview a couple more people."

I hadn't known what to think when Tanner announced he was going for that coaching job. While I certainly wanted him to live closer to his son, it had felt hard to breathe with him around lately.

"That's great," I said, finding it difficult to form a smile.

He cocked his head. "You don't sound that enthused."

"Things are just getting down to the wire with these renovations," I lied. "I'm feeling the pressure."

"So, you're good with the prospect of me staying in Beaufort, then?"

"I'm always good with what's best for Alex. He deserves to have his father in his life."

"Fingers crossed this works out. I have a good feeling." He paused. "I have nothing going on the rest of the afternoon. Let me help you paint."

"No, that's really not necessary."

"I insist. Gonna go get out of these clothes real quick." He took off down the hall.

Shit.

Tanner returned a few minutes later, dressed in jeans and a T-shirt. His muscles were noticeably larger than I remembered.

He spent the rest of the afternoon painting alongside me. After we finished, I ended up showing him some of the old photos I'd found in the house, and that led to reminiscing about the old days.

At one point, Fern peeked her head in on her way down the hallway and flashed a snide grin. She was enjoying this soap opera a little too much.

Tanner followed me to the kitchen and lifted a bottle of wine off the rack.

"How about we take this out back to celebrate a job well done? It's just about five o'clock anyway."

Before answering, I checked my phone for the umpteenth time. Once again, nothing from Levi.

What the hell? I could definitely use a little wine to numb this anxiety.

I shrugged. "Sure. I could go for some wine."

Tanner grabbed the bottle of red along with two glasses from the cabinet. We sat out on the porch, and I watched as he poured one for each of us.

As he handed me a glass, he said, "I'm wondering if now would be a good time to have that talk I've been wanting to have with you."

I should've known there was an ulterior motive. I took a long sip. "I'm not going anywhere, so it's just as good a time as any."

"Good." He set his glass down and wiped his palms on his pants. "I don't know why I'm so nervous."

His eyes reflected a rare vulnerability that I only remembered seeing in the early days of our relationship, before the injury changed him.

I stayed quiet as he started talking.

"I don't expect you to give me your trust any time soon, Presley. I know I have to earn that back and then some. But I want to work toward that."

"You only have to worry about earning Alex's trust back," I said.

"And I plan to. But I'm not only here to reconnect with Alex." His eyes seared into mine. "My hope is that we can repair what we lost."

Sweat beaded on my forehead. "Tanner—"

"Please hear me out." He took a long gulp of wine. "I know I've messed up more than once. And you don't owe me another chance. But I am trying very hard to change and be the kind of man you've always deserved. As I told my brother this morning, I'm getting older now, and my priorities are clearer than ever."

My heart dropped to my stomach. "You spoke to Levi about this?"

"Yeah. We talked for a bit before my interview this morning. He said he's going through some stuff, too."

Feeling woozy, I blinked. "What stuff?"

"He wouldn't elaborate, but it sounded like a life crisis—similar to mine. You know, he and I aren't all that different. We're both getting older and wiser and realizing the lives we're living may not be what we want long term." He exhaled. "I talked to him about my desire to get my family back."

I stayed silent, barely remembering to breathe.

"I don't want to be that single guy anymore, Presley. I want a family. And not just any family—*my* family. You and Alex. You're the only family I have, and the only one I will ever want."

My head felt like it was spinning. While I'd known Tanner was trying to get back in my good graces and had been somewhat flirtatious, I hadn't truly believed he wanted us to get back together.

He had no clue just how complicated things were.

"I don't know what to say," I managed.

"Are you seeing someone?" he asked.

I skirted his question. "Tanner, I don't see the two of us ever getting back together."

"Why are you shutting the door on the possibility?"

"I've grown. I'm a different woman than I used to be. I know more about myself and what I want. Not to mention, we just didn't work."

"We *did* work before I fucked everything up. Please try to remember that. There was a time when you loved me. And I've never stopped loving *you*."

My only response to that was to down the rest of my wine. I could have lied and told him I didn't want a relationship with anyone. But that wasn't the truth. Telling him the actual truth—that I was only interested in a relationship with the other Miller—wasn't an option. And knowing Tanner had spoken to Levi about me this morning explained Levi's disappearing act. That made me even more scared of what might have been running through Levi's head today.

"You know what?" Tanner said after a moment. "I can be patient. This conversation was more about me stating my intent. I don't expect you to take me back right now or even respond to any of this. But I want to let you know how serious I am. I'm here for Alex and *you*, Presley. I don't plan to see anyone else, even if you're telling me you won't give me a chance. I'm choosing to hold out hope, and I want to save myself for you."

That's insane. "You're setting yourself up for disappointment, Tanner."

I did wonder what my reaction to this would have been if Levi and I hadn't happened. Even though Tanner had given me many reasons not to trust him, I did feel like he was being genuine right now. Was it possible he had changed and was as determined to get me back as he claimed? Maybe. Might I have caved and been open to giving him another chance if things were different? I couldn't rule out that possibility. But the reality was, I had changed. I couldn't erase what I'd learned about my wants and needs over the past couple of months with Levi, who'd made me feel things I'd never experienced. It was *that* fire I longed for. Even if things were about to end with Levi and me, because of him, I would always know what that level of passion felt like. And I knew I deserved *that*, which was certainly more than what Tanner had to offer.

"Like I said..." He took my glass and poured me more wine. "I don't expect you to be open to this yet. I'm just letting you know I'm not going anywhere this time."

I shook my head. "Please continue to focus on Alex and not me. I'm not interested in anything more than improving our relationship as co-parents. That's definitely something I'd be open to working on."

"We'll start there." He winked. "But I'm still gonna hold out hope."

The tension remained thick as we stayed on the porch and made small talk after Tanner's revelation.

He then told me to stay and relax while he went to pick up Alex at his friend's house and suggested the three of us eat supper together. But instead, I asked if he'd be willing to handle dinner with his son while I ran some errands. He agreed, and after he left to get Alex, I grabbed my keys.

Once I got into my car, I pulled up Levi's name on my phone.

Presley: Tell me where you are. I'm coming to you.

TWENTY-THREE

Levi

CANDY WRAPPERS COVERED the end table by my bed. I had this nervous habit of pigging out on hotel vending-machine junk when stressed. I had no idea how long I'd be staying here, but I needed to be somewhere other than The Palm Inn. Not wanting to deal with questions about this fucked-up situation, I couldn't go to my mother's either.

After Presley's text, I did tell her where I'd checked in, and now she was headed over here. As much as I dreaded what we'd inevitably talk about, I ached to see her. Excitement ricocheted through my body, as it always did when I knew we'd be alone together, except this time it was bittersweet.

The TV was on, but I couldn't have told you what was showing as I paced back and forth. I didn't know what was worse: the guilt or the jealousy.

This wasn't how everything was supposed to go down. I wasn't supposed to care so damn much about my estranged brother. But something *had* changed with Tanner. And I couldn't ignore it. Knowing that he genuinely seemed to regret his actions over the years made it much harder to disregard his feelings, like I'd planned. Now I was second-guessing everything. Hadn't he lost enough when his career ended? Didn't he deserve a chance to have his family back? The problem was, his family now also felt like *my* family. And I didn't want to give up Presley and Alex. How do you choose between the woman of your dreams and your brother? Is blood automatically thicker than water? I honestly didn't have the answer, but losing either of them didn't seem like an option.

Presley was dead set against Tanner ever finding out about us, and I was starting to agree with her, even if I'd been adamant about telling him the truth just a day ago. If he could never find out, how the hell did Presley and I stand a chance? We couldn't hide forever. My stomach churned. It seemed more and more like this decision was being made for us. I just couldn't accept it.

There was a knock at the door.

I opened to find Presley standing there in a short, flowery dress and denim jacket. Her eyes were filled with worry, and despite all of this guilt, I wanted nothing more than to take her on this damn hotel room bed so we could drown our sorrows in each other.

"Why have you been avoiding me all day?" she asked as she stepped into the room.

"I'm sorry."

Her chest heaved. "I know you and Tanner talked this morning."

"Yeah. That's why I left. It shook me."

She nodded, looking down at her feet. "He told me he let you know he plans to try to get me back."

I exhaled. "I'm glad you convinced me not to tell him about us. I don't know what I was thinking. Now I realize it would devastate him." Fighting the urge to pull her into my arms, I looked her up and down. "What else did he say to you?"

"He told me he wants to earn my trust back. He thinks we can get back together once that happens. He has no clue how complicated this situation is."

Jealousy burned through my body. I looked up at the ceiling and shook my head. "Can I ask you something?"

"Of course."

"Would you consider taking him back if you and I had never gotten together?"

She paused. "I honestly don't think so. But it's hard to say, given that I would probably be a different person altogether right now if *we* hadn't happened. But we did happen. I know now that I deserve better. And the way you treat me is the way I want to be treated. I've never wanted anyone like I want you, Levi. I can't just forget about us. At the same time, I don't want him to find out." Her voice cracked. "It's messed up."

While I could tell Presley believed what she'd just told me, it was possible she was confused.

"How do you know your feelings for me are the real deal?" I asked.

Her eyes narrowed. "What do you mean? When you know, you just...know."

"There's no doubt we're addicted to each other sexually, but what if this is just a strong physical attraction that's clouding your judgment?"

Her voice grew louder. "Because I think about you all of the time, even when you're not physically with me, and because you make me happy. I'm not going to deny that I'm extremely physically attracted to you. That *is* a big part of it. But what we have is so much more than sex."

"It means more to me, too," I whispered.

"You make me feel safe, Levi—in a way no one else ever has, certainly not Tanner."

I finally drew her into my arms and held her tight. But the longer I held her, the deeper the seeds of doubt seemed to grow.

Pulling back to look at her, I said, "Even if by some stretch of the imagination we could keep being together a secret, Tanner isn't the only complication. Our relationship has worked thus far because I'm here for you day in and day out, but soon it won't be anything like that. We'd be living apart for a big chunk of the year, and that's the opposite of what you need to continue to feel safe with me. It's unstable. Things are about to change in a big way. And I'm starting to doubt whether I'm really what's best for you and Alex."

Presley closed her eyes, as if my words pained her. When she opened them, she said, "You just told me every reason we shouldn't be together, Levi, and yet I'm still standing here in front of you, wanting you more than anything else. That's not going to change." She placed her hands around my face. "I'm scared to lose you."

The fear in her eyes was palpable. I had no answers. All I could offer her right now was physical comfort, because the words wouldn't come. And I needed her so damn badly, too.

So even though this was the last thing I should be doing, I pressed my lips to hers. Presley melted into me with a sigh, and I knew what she was feeling. All day, my hands had been balled into fists, my jaw locked tight, and my forehead was going to have a few new wrinkles with a matching set of frown lines. Yet the moment we connected, everything seemed to fade into the background, as if nothing in the world was more important than this kiss. Scooping her up into my arms, I kicked the hotel room door closed and carried her into the bedroom.

It felt like a dream as I set her down on the bed. Never in my life had I had such feelings for a woman. Presley lay in the center of the bed with her golden hair fanned out all across the pillow, and I hovered over her, staring down. I ran my thumb over her soft cheek.

"As much as things between us are complicated, falling for you was the simplest thing I've ever done. No matter what happens, I want you to know I will *never* regret you. You've changed me, Presley." I had to swallow to keep from getting choked up.

She smiled sadly. "Make love to me, Levi."

This time when I kissed her, it felt different than all of the other times—more passionate and more intimate. I didn't know what tomorrow would bring, but right now, I was absolutely head-over-heels in love, and I wanted nothing more than to show her with my body.

After I undressed us, I reached for my wallet on the end table to take out a condom. But Presley covered my hand, stopping me.

"I'm on the pill, and I haven't been with anyone other than you in a long time, if you'd want to...not use one."

I blew out a jagged breath. "I would love that. I just hope I don't embarrass myself when I get to feel you without anything between us."

She smiled and slipped my wallet from my hand, letting it drop to the floor. "You can always make it up to me with a second time. Now, c'mere and kiss me some more."

I smiled. "Yes, ma'am."

We kissed for what seemed like hours, slow and deep, just the way I wanted to be inside her when it was time.

But for now, my focus was on lavishing Presley with all the attention I hadn't been able to give her lately. I lowered my mouth to her creamy neck, sucking along her pulse line and trailing wet kisses across her collarbone from one end to the other. Then I kissed my way up to her ear and whispered, "I've dreamed about coming inside of you. Filling that beautiful, tight pussy until it's so full, I watch my cum drip down your legs."

Presley moaned. It felt like I might explode if I didn't get inside of her soon, so I gripped my cock, dragged the head over her clit, and swirled it around before lining myself up at her opening. Without a barrier, her wet heat was already better than anything I'd ever felt, so I pushed inside slowly, hoping I could make it a few minutes. But she was so tight and warm, with only the crown inside of her I already wanted to let go. The urge to fill her was carnal, almost animalistic, like I was a lion who needed to mark my territory to ward off other predators. I squeezed my eyes shut, trying to think of anything that might slow me down, but the feeling of being inside her raw was too consuming to allow my thoughts to wander.

Presley reached up and touched my cheek, making me open my eyes.

"Don't hold back, please. Just let it happen. There's nothing I want more."

I swallowed and nodded before taking one last deep breath and pushing the rest of the way inside. When my balls hit her ass, my body started to shake.

Presley locked eyes with me. She looked as desperate as I felt. "Fill me, Levi. *Please.*"

After that, I lost it. Presley wrapped her legs around my back, and I let go of any attempt to make slow, passionate love, in favor of fucking her into oblivion. We grinded and groped, scratched and screamed, and I penetrated her so hard that I was certain I'd never been this deep inside a woman before.

"Levi...faster...more." She gasped. "Oh God...I'm gonna..."

My body vibrated from head to toe. The sound of our sweat-slicked bodies slapping against each other was the only thing that mattered. There could have been a fire raging under the bed, and I wouldn't have been able to stop. Presley's jaw went slack, her eyes rolled into the back of her head, and then I felt it—her muscles contracting around me, squeezing my cock like a vise, and I started to come with her.

"Fuck...Presley.... Fuck, *fuck*... *Fuuuck*." My cock pulsed inside her as I let go. I visualized what I'd dreamed about—only now it wasn't a dream. It was actually happening, and I could picture it so much clearer—my cum filling her pussy as my cock slid in and out, so much that it seeps out around where we're joined, and warm, thick cream slides down her legs. Imagining it while it's actually happening took things to a whole other level.

After, we both panted as I continued to glide slowly in and out.

"Wow..." Presley breathed out with a smile. "That was..."

"Yeah, it was." I smiled and brushed my lips with hers. "You're incredible."

"I'm glad we did that for the first time without a condom here and not at home. Alex definitely would have heard that."

I smiled. "Fern might've enjoyed hearing it."

We both laughed, but a few seconds later the euphoric look on her face fell, and we locked eyes. Neither of us needed to say what had crossed our minds, but that didn't make it any less of an eye opener.

Tanner would have blown a gasket.

TWENTY-FOUR

levi

I KEPT THE hotel room.

I wasn't sure exactly what had made me do it, but when I'd gone to check out, I slid the key across the counter and then pulled it back, instead asking the front desk clerk if I could extend my stay.

Over the last few days, I'd debated why I'd done it. Was I making sure I had a place to escape to if I needed to get out of the house, or was I hoping Presley and I might meet up there again at some point? If it were the latter, I probably would've given her one of the keys by now, or at least mentioned it. Yet I hadn't done either. Instead, I'd returned to The Palm.

I stood in the dark kitchen, lost in thought while sipping my morning coffee when Presley walked in. She went straight to the refrigerator and took out the half and half. Then she turned around and walked toward the coffee pot. She'd yet to look up.

"Morning," I said.

Presley jumped, and her hand flew to cover her heart. "Oh my God. Were you standing there when I walked in?"

I nodded. "Been standing here about fifteen minutes now."

"I didn't see you."

I sipped my coffee. "You looked pretty lost in thought."

She sighed, setting down the container. "I feel like that's all I do lately—think."

"I know the feeling."

She poured her coffee and leaned against the counter next to me. "You're leaving in fifteen days."

I nodded. "Fifteen days and four hours. My flight is at ten thirty."

Presley lowered her voice. "Will you come back at any point?"

"Most games are on Sundays. Mondays are team meetings and physical therapy appointments. We practice Tuesday through Friday. Saturday we travel for away games or have planning meetings for home games."

"What about the weeks you don't have games? You get a bye week or two, right?"

"There's only one of those this season, and we usually just replace game day with extra practices."

She frowned. "How do...people do it?"

"The majority of guys move their family to the state their home team is in—so they can at least come home at night. The rest just fly their girlfriends in from time to time."

Presley was quiet for a long time. I had no idea where her head was, what she expected or wanted to do once I had to leave. Eventually she turned to face me.

"Alex will be starting school a few days after you leave." She shook her head. "He's just planting roots—"

For a second or two, I wasn't sure why she'd trailed off. But then the light flipped on, and I realized she'd seen Tanner coming.

"Why were you guys standing here in the dark?" he said.

Presley opened her mouth, but nothing came out. So I intervened. "I woke up with a headache. Light makes it worse."

Tanner looked between us. His eyes squinted slightly, as if he might not believe me. But eventually he nodded and flipped the switch back off. When he walked over to pour his coffee, he wedged his body right between us. I had to take a few steps back so we weren't on top of one another.

He lifted his chin to me. "Got a second interview for that football-coaching job today."

"You did?" Presley asked.

Tanner nodded. "Yup. They narrowed it down to me and one other guy. Said they'll have their decision by the end of the week."

Presley's forehead wrinkled. "Well, good luck."

"Yeah," I tilted my coffee mug toward him. "Knock 'em dead." I pushed off the counter. "I'm gonna hit the shower. I have shit to do today."

My eyes caught Presley's, and I nodded before heading back to my room. It made me crazy to walk away and leave the two of them alone in the kitchen. So how the hell was I going to survive walking away completely in two weeks?

xoxo

I'd had an unsettled feeling in the pit of my stomach all morning, since my conversation with Presley in the kitchen. So after I went to the eye doctor and worked out with my trainer, I decided to stop up at Alex's peewee football practice. Presley was sitting in the bleachers with a bunch of women I'd never met.

"Oh my God," one said. "You're Levi Miller—the quarterback."

I offered my standard-issue smile and nodded. "I am. Good to meet you."

"Will you be here for long? My son is your biggest fan. Practice will be over in about twenty minutes, and he would absolutely die if he knew you were here and he didn't get to meet you."

I exchanged glances with Presley. "Well, we wouldn't want that to happen. Sure, I'm gonna watch practice for a while anyway. Which one is your son?"

"He's a running back. Number forty-four."

"I'll keep my eye on him and see if I can give him any pointers when practice ends." I looked at Presley and nodded toward the team. "I'm going to walk down to the other end of the field where the kids are to get a closer look."

She stood. "I'll come."

I heard all of the women whispering as we walked from the bleachers. One said something about my ass.

I shook my head. "And they say men are bad."

Presley smiled. "Can you really crack a walnut with your ass cheeks? I'd like to see it, if you can."

I chuckled. "Is that what she just said?"

"It is, indeed."

"Well, I've never tried. But I'm game to give it a shot if you're into that sort of thing."

We both laughed, and the tension I'd felt since the kitchen this morning waned for the first time. But that fleeting moment of calm was abruptly interrupted by a harrowing scream. *Alex's scream*. When you play a sport where more than half the guys are usually operating with some sort of an injury, you get to be an expert at reading the level of pain from only a yelp. And this one...was not good. The opening to get onto the field was still another twenty yards away, so I hopped the fence and ran to where Alex was lying on the ground. Two coaches hovered over him.

"My ankle. My ankle." He rolled to his side.

I knelt down. "Don't try to move it, buddy."

"Uncle Levi, *it hurts*."

One of the coaches looked up at me. "Holy shit. You're Levi Miller."

I ignored him. "Tell me what the pain feels like, Alex."

"It's sharp—and shooting up my leg."

His little ankle was also starting to bruise and swell. *Not a good sign.*

Presley made her way over. "Are you okay?"

"I think we should run him to the hospital to be on the safe side."

She nodded. "Okay. Yeah, let's do that."

One of the coaches stood and thumbed toward the parking lot. "You want me to grab the wheelchair? I keep one in the back of the van, just in case."

I scooped Alex from the grass, careful not to touch his ankle. "No need. I got it."

My truck had more legroom than Presley's little car, so we drove to the emergency room in it and left hers at the field. She bit her nail as we got on the highway.

"I forgot how nerve-wracking having someone you love play football could be."

"He's going to be fine."

She blew out a deep breath and nodded.

Once we arrived at the hospital, they took Alex into triage with Presley, and I paced in the waiting room. She came out five minutes later.

"They aren't too busy, so they took him right in the back to have him examined," she said. "Only one person is allowed in at a time, so I wanted to let you know. I'll come out when I know something."

I nodded and kissed her forehead. "Okay. Good luck."

An hour or so later, I was fiddling with my phone, trying to keep myself occupied, when I heard a familiar voice.

"I'm looking for Alex Miller."

"And you are?"

"His father."

"He's in the back with his mother. Give me a minute, and I'll go see if I can get you an update. There's only one person allowed with each patient."

"Okay, thank you."

My brother walked to the waiting area where I was seated. He stopped short when he saw me. His forehead wrinkled. "What are you doing here?"

"I was passing by the school on my way home from the eye doctor and saw the boys practicing, so I stopped to check it out."

"You were there when it happened?"

"Yeah. It sounded like it could be a break."

My brother ran a hand through his hair. "Shit."

"How did you know he was here?"

"Presley called me."

"Oh."

I must've frowned, because my brother's eyes roamed my face, and he squinted. "Is that a problem? Should I not be here when my kid is hurt?"

I shook my head. "No...I just meant, I wasn't even thinking. I should have called you. That's all."

My brother nodded, but I wasn't sure he bought the line of crap I was feeding him.

A few minutes later, a nurse opened the door that led back to the exam area. She yelled, "Miller?"

Without thinking I stood, as did my brother. He looked at me funny.

"Oh, sorry. I'm sure they meant you."

I sat down as the nurse walked over. "You're Alex's father?"

"I am. Tanner Miller."

"Your son is doing fine. He just got back from X-ray, and we're waiting for an orthopedic specialist to come down and read the results. But the ER doc on call doesn't think it's broken, just a really bad sprain."

Tanner took a deep breath. "Okay. Great. Can I see him?"

"We usually only let one person in the back with each patient. But it's a pretty slow day, so I guess I can bend the rules." She nodded toward the door. "Come on. Follow me."

My brother didn't look back as he followed the nurse. Once I was alone again, I started to feel like I was intruding on a family matter. As much as I wanted to be there for Alex, it was his father's job—not mine—to be by his side. And that really sucked. Yet I couldn't bring myself to leave. About fifteen minutes passed, and then Presley emerged from the back.

I stood and wiped the sweat from my palms on my pants. "How's he doing?"

"The orthopedist just came in. Luckily it's just a bad sprain. They're going to give him an air cast and some crutches. The doctor said it should heal on its own within a few weeks."

I nodded and blew out a breath. "Good. How's his pain?"

"They gave him some Motrin, and it seems to have helped. But he hasn't tried to put weight on it or anything yet."

"Okay. Well, he's going to be sore. That's normal."

Presley looked down. "I'm sorry if it was awkward when Tanner came in. I called to let him know what happened, but I didn't get a chance to mention you were here because they came to take Alex to X-ray while I was on the phone."

"It's fine. As long as Alex is okay."

A few awkward seconds passed. I cleared my throat. "I should get going. I have to...do some things anyway."

"Oh, okay."

I hated to leave them, but it wasn't my place to be here any longer. Shoving my hands into my pockets, I forced a smile. "I'll see you later."

She nodded. "Okay."

Every step I took as I left that emergency room felt heavier and heavier. I'd made it almost all the way to my truck when Presley yelled my name from the door. I turned, and she ran over.

"I'm sorry. I know you must be feeling really weird right now. I just wanted to say I would rather have you in there by my side than Tanner."

She had enough shit to worry about. I didn't want to make matters worse by pouring on guilt. Besides, I might want to be by her side, but it wasn't my place. It was Tanner's. To reassure her I was fine, I pulled her in for a hug.

"It's fine. Don't think about it for a second. We're good."

She looked up at me for reassurance, and I smiled and brushed a wayward hair from her cheek. "Really."

Relief washed over her worried face. "Okay. Thank you."

I leaned down and kissed her forehead, then tapped her nose with my pointer finger and smiled. "Take a few deep breaths. I'll see you in a little while at home. Everything is going to be fine."

But no sooner than I'd said the words, I began wondering if they were true. Because when I looked up, I saw a man watching us from the door.

Tanner.

⚓ TWENTY-FIVE

Levi

TANNER HADN'T REACTED after he spotted me comforting Presley, and neither had I. Presley didn't need another thing to worry about, so I kept what I'd seen to myself, and after a moment, Tanner had simply turned back around.

I had no clue what he'd actually seen. Was he clueless or just turning a blind eye?

I took a deep breath as Presley went back inside the hospital, and I'd just gotten into my truck when I realized I'd left my hat on the chair in the waiting room.

I went back in to get it and spotted Presley, Tanner, and Alex as they spoke to a nurse just outside the door that led to the examination area. Thankfully their backs were to me, so they couldn't see me spying from this angle.

Tanner rubbed Alex's back while Presley spoke to the nurse. They looked every bit like the family they essentially still were, despite me trying to deny it—the family whose chance at any kind of a future I was slowly destroying behind my brother's back.

My mother's voice from behind me interrupted my thoughts.

"How's my boy?"

I turned around. "He's fine. It's just a sprain."

"Yeah. I know. Poor Alex. Tanner called when I was already on my way here to let me know it wasn't broken." She placed her hand on my arm. "I was referring to my *big* boy, though. How are *you* holding up?"

I let out a long breath. "I've been better."

She nodded. "I can't imagine this situation is getting any easier for you."

I turned back around and looked at them for a bit. "Look how happy Alex seems, to have his dad by his side. I can't compete with that. I'll never be able to." Looking down at my shoes, I admitted, "Tanner fucking saw me hugging her earlier."

My mother's eyes widened. "You think he suspects it was more than platonic?"

"No." I shook my head. "That's the thing. I don't think he'd ever imagine I'm capable of something like that. He thinks I've been a good, stand-up guy looking after them while he was away, and maybe Presley and I got closer because of that. It probably looked like I was just comforting her—at least, I hope. But it was still unnerving."

"This whole thing is unnerving." She sighed. "You're leaving soon. I'm sure you don't feel ready."

"Not in the least."

My mother gestured toward the exit. "Let's go for a walk. I want to tell you something I've never told you before."

That sparked my curiosity. I fell into step alongside her. "What's up?"

"It's actually about your father. Something you don't know."

"I don't know if I like where this is going."

She exhaled as we exited the automatic doors. "By the time he and I separated, both of you boys were out of the house, so you missed some things that happened—well, one particular thing I never wanted you to know about."

My pulse sped up. "What do you mean?"

"I mean the exact circumstances surrounding the end of your father's and my relationship."

"Okay..."

"He and I apparently had different ideas about what the separation meant for us. When we first agreed to it, I was under the impression that even though we were no longer living together, we would remain faithful to each other." She paused. "But your father met someone during that time."

I nodded silently. My stomach felt sick to think about my father with any other woman. Though I'd assumed he dated after their divorce, I'd always tried to block it out of my mind.

"I'd thought the separation was temporary, that we would somehow find our way back to one another," my mom continued. "I figured we just needed some time away to repair things and hoped the end goal would be a stronger marriage. Your father took the separation as a ticket to entertain his midlife crisis."

"Shit," I muttered as I began to wonder what my mother's point was in telling me all of this now.

"Anyway..." she said. "I couldn't get past it. He dated this woman for a while, and then when things ended between them, he tried to mend things with me. He kept using the excuse that we were separated at the time. But I couldn't get past what I saw as a betrayal. So, I told him not only did I want to remain separated, but I wanted a divorce."

The situation she'd described was far from the way I'd imagined my parents' marriage ending. I'd always thought it was a mutual decision that hadn't involved other people—they'd just grown apart.

"So you never really *wanted* a divorce..." I said. "If he hadn't been with someone else, you would've tried to work things out?"

"I loved your father. But I was just...so deeply hurt."

Damn. This was all news to me. "Wow, Mom."

She stopped walking for a moment and faced me. "After fighting me on it for some time, he finally gave in to my wishes for a divorce. But the truth was, neither of us truly fell out of love with the other."

A memory of my parents kissing in our kitchen when I was a kid flashed through my mind. I always thought it was gross and ran out of the room. But knowing they were still in love after all that time gave me some comfort.

"This sort of gives me some solace," I said. "Even though it's bittersweet."

She flashed a sad smile. "When Dad was dying, he told me his biggest regret was ever straying from me. I did believe he regretted entering into a relationship with that woman. Even though I'd been firm in my decision not to take him back, he felt like he hadn't fought hard enough for us—that he could've done more to stop the divorce. Our dream had always been to retire and ride off into the sunset together. Our actual ending was certainly nothing either of us anticipated."

"It breaks my heart that you guys couldn't do that."

Mom's eyes glistened. "It breaks my heart too—that your father died with so much regret and that I played a role in that. If I'd known he was going to get sick and die of cancer a year later, I might've been more forgiving. You think you have endless time to work certain things out in life, but time is one thing that's never guaranteed."

I still wasn't sure why she'd chosen to tell me all of this. "Something tells me you're making a bigger point here than confessing the truth about you and Dad."

"What happened with Dad and me reminds me a lot of what's going on with Tanner and Presley. Your brother made some poor decisions, and now he's trying to rectify them. He has a chance to do something Dad never could."

Shit. Of course that's what she was getting at—more evidence supporting the fact that I was the bad guy in all of this, preventing my brother from getting his family back. I knew letting him try was the right thing to do. That was never in question. It was the feeling that I physically *couldn't* stay away from Presley that made doing the right thing seem impossible.

"I'm not minimizing the feelings you've developed for Presley," my mother said. "But I think you need to look at the bigger picture here. Your career is not going to allow for a sustainable relationship with her anyway. And Tanner doesn't look like he's going to give up on getting his family back anytime soon—what with going for that coaching job here and all. But you also have to think about Presley, about the regret *she* may feel when this honeymoon phase between you and her is over. You two had a summer together. Tanner and she have years of history—and a child."

Yeah, Mother. Tell me something I don't already know.

She placed her hand on my arm. "I know you probably feel like I'm not on your side in this. Please don't feel that way. I feel like what's best for them is *also* what's best for you. Dad's story of regret should serve as a lesson on how you may feel someday when it comes to your brother.

Moving in now that you know he's trying to make things right would be a tremendous betrayal, Levi. I keep waffling on whether or not you should even tell him. I'm starting to think it's best if he never finds out. But the longer you're around Presley, the more likely it is that he will. I feel like you're on the cusp of doing irreversible damage, and now is your only chance to stop before it's too late."

My chest hurt so badly, filled with emotion, thinking about my dad and brother. But what Mom just told me about my father pushed me over the edge. My stepping away would give Tanner the second chance Dad never had. I also believed my father would have given me the same advice as my mother. Was loving Presley worth hurting my entire family? Regardless of that answer, I knew I would be unable to resist her as long as we were physically together. The only thing that would end this was distance.

Suddenly burning up from the stress, I reached into my pocket for my keys. "I gotta go."

My mother frowned. "Have I totally upset you?"

"No. I appreciate you sharing everything with me. It's given me more to think about."

She reached for me. "I love you so much, Levi. Please know that. And I'm so incredibly proud of you, despite seeming disappointed in your actions lately. I know you didn't mean to hurt him. I can see the sadness in your eyes, and I wish I could take it away."

"Thanks, Mom." I hugged her tightly before finally walking to my car.

xoxo

That night, I didn't plan to return to The Palm Inn until after everyone went to bed. Instead, I hung out at a local bar, sitting alone while I pondered my next steps.

Around ten thirty, my phone rang—my agent, Rich Doherty.

"What's up, Rich?" I answered.

"How much do you love me?"

"Depends on how much I've had to drink. And I think tonight might be your lucky night."

"Get it all out of your system now, I suppose. I need you back in tip-top shape."

"Well, I still have two weeks to drink myself into oblivion."

"Actually, back to the question of how much you love me—what if I asked you to come back now?"

"Why the hell would I do that when I still have time off left in my contract?"

"Because the team asked me to reach out. We hoped out of the goodness of your heart, you'd have some sympathy for the new receivers who desperately need your expertise at training camp."

"That's not part of the deal, Rich."

"I know it isn't. This would simply be a favor."

My first instinct was to immediately refuse. Why the hell should I go back now, especially since things were so unresolved between Presley and me?

But then it occurred to me that maybe this phone call happened for a reason. Maybe taking the opportunity to leave early was my ticket out of this whole situation. Maybe it was the right thing to do, even if it wasn't what I wanted.

I pulled on my hair. "Do me a favor. Let me think about this overnight. I've had way too much to drink to make a decision about anything right now. I'll mull it over and let you know in the morning."

"Well, that's not a no, so I'll freaking take it."

"Bye, Rich."

I hung up and dropped my phone on the counter before scrubbing my hand over my face.

A few minutes later, I called for a ride and left a wad of cash for the bartender. I'd planned accordingly and dropped my car off at The Palm Inn earlier before taking an Uber here. The last thing I needed was to be arrested for driving while intoxicated on top of everything else.

xoxo

The following morning, I awoke to find a mane of beautiful, long hair covering my chest. I blinked my eyes as Presley straddled me. She began to kiss down my torso.

Equal parts turned on and panicked, I whispered, "What are you doing?"

"Tanner took Alex for donuts. We don't have much time, but I couldn't wait to wake you up. I missed you so much last night."

Her kisses landed lower and lower.

Hit with a wave of guilt despite my raging hard-on, I didn't know whether to stop this or give in. Before I could think too much about it, I felt her mouth wrapped around my cock. I groaned, bending my head back and allowing myself to enjoy it for a few seconds before forcing myself back to reality. Knowing the decision I'd made as I tossed and turned in the middle of the night last night, I couldn't let her do this.

I yanked my body back. It pained me to see the look in her eyes as she blinked up at me in confusion.

"What's wrong?"

"We can't. It's too risky. They could come back sooner than you think."

If I wasn't feeling so goddamn guilty about my plan to leave early, I could never have refused sex. But I had no right to her now.

Worry filled Presley's eyes as she moved to sit at the corner of the bed.

I sat up and cradled her face in my hands before planting a deep and passionate kiss on her lips. I closed my eyes tightly, trying to burn the feeling into my memory before finally stopping the contact. I licked my lips, unsure if that would be my last taste of her.

"Why don't you go get dressed, and I'll make a quick breakfast for us so we can talk before they come back," I said.

Still wearing a sullen look, Presley nodded before she hopped off the bed and went back to her room.

This was not how I wanted to leave things. I felt sick to my stomach, but for once I needed to do the right thing instead of what made me feel good.

After I threw my jeans and a T-shirt on, I headed to the kitchen and got to work making coffee, eggs, bacon, and toast for Presley and me. I'd likely not be able to stomach any of it, though.

Dread settled in my gut because I had to somehow figure out a way to explain myself. Fuck if I knew how to break the news. Was it easier to just leave in the dead of night? Maybe then she'd hate me and wouldn't care so damn much. She was going to be hurt no matter what, and in some ways, I'd rather she be angry at me than heartbroken.

I was just about to call her to the kitchen when the front door opened.

A few seconds later, Tanner and Alex walked in, just as I was plating the eggs.

I feigned a smile as Alex walked toward me on his crutches.

I put down the pan. "How's my tough guy?"

"My leg still hurts," my nephew said with pink frosting at the corner of his mouth.

"I'm sure it does, buddy."

"I'm still going to the peewee party on Friday night, though, even if I can't play this week."

"That's the spirit."

Tanner didn't say anything as he walked to the refrigerator and took something out.

"You have to come to the party, Uncle Levi. A bunch of my friends want to see you one more time before you leave."

My chest tightened, and I made the impulsive decision to let this be the moment I broke the news. Because, let's face it, this wasn't going to get any easier if I waited.

"Actually, bud, I can't."

"Why not?"

"It turns out, I have to head back to Colorado early. I'm leaving tomorrow."

"Oh no! You can't leave yet. Why?" he asked with a panicked expression.

The sound of Presley's shocked voice rang out from behind me. "What?"

I hadn't realized she was within earshot. My heart sank. Suddenly I could no longer form the words to properly explain myself.

Fuck. Looking into her eyes, I said, "I was gonna tell you over breakfast."

"Tomorrow?" she breathed. "Tomorrow?"

I nodded. "My agent called and said they need me back at training camp early to work with the new receivers.

I figured since I had to leave in two weeks anyway, I might as well head out there."

Presley looked devastated, as if all of the joy had been sucked out of her. I tightened my muscles, vowing to remain strong and reminding myself that ultimately I was doing what was best for her—for everyone.

I regretted telling Alex first, though, and wished Presley and I were having this conversation alone. But it was too late.

"Please don't go yet, Uncle Levi." Alex's voice cracked, and it broke my damn heart. Here I was thinking he had all he needed with his dad here. But he seemed really broken up over the bombshell I'd just dropped.

I knelt and placed my arms around his shoulders. "I promise to come back and visit the first chance I get, okay?"

Come hell or high water, I needed to stick to that promise, even if things would be awkward between Presley and me. My nephew shouldn't have to pay for my indiscretions. Despite Tanner being back in the picture, I'd developed something special with Alex, and I wasn't willing to throw that away, even if I'd forever be second fiddle to his father.

I knew if I could manage to keep what happened between me and his mother secret, my relationship with Alex would remain strong. My relationship with Presley, though? I had no idea what would become of that now that I'd made this decision. But I loved her, and sometimes loving someone means doing what's best for them in the long run.

"Thanks for making breakfast, but I'm not hungry," Presley said as she left the room.

My heart ached. I wanted to run after her but had virtual shackles on me with my brother standing here.

With Presley gone, I finally looked over at Tanner.

"Shame you can't stick around," he said.

Except his tone didn't sound the least bit sincere. I wondered if he hadn't been so oblivious after all.

TWENTY-SIX

Presley

"DO YOU THINK you can run to Home Depot and pick up the bolts we need to hang the swing on the porch?"

Tanner's forehead wrinkled. "The swing I put in the garage the other day?"

"Yes."

"The bolts to hang it come with the swing. I read it on the box."

I'd been afraid he might say that, so I'd snuck into the garage a half hour ago, opened the box, took out the bolts, and hid them in my dresser drawer.

I shook my head and reached into my pocket for the directions. "It says they're supposed to be in the box, but they weren't. I opened it earlier." Unfolding the paper, I pointed to the picture of the bolts included with the parts descriptions. "This is the size we need."

Tanner took the paper. "I'll pick them up tomorrow. I have to go over to the college and do some paperwork. It's right down the street from the Home Depot."

I shook my head. "No. I need it hung tonight. The guy who revamped the website for the inn wants to add a video

275

of it on the homepage before we officially open. Something about giving it movement to catch the eye."

Tanner sighed. "Alright, fine."

"Could you also stop at the grocery store and pick up some coffee beans?"

"There's coffee in the cabinet."

"Not anymore. I made an extra pot this afternoon and finished the last of it." *Or the can is sitting in my underwear drawer next to the swing bolts.*

Tanner nodded. "Okay, sure."

"And...would you mind taking my car and putting windshield wiper fluid in? Oh, and I told Alex he could stay over at his friend Kyle's tonight, if you could also drop him on the way."

Tanner's brows rose. "Anything else?"

"No, that's it." *But only because asking you to drive to Florida to get some fresh oranges might be a bit over the top.*

Normally I felt bad asking people for favors, though today I'd been incapable of feeling bad for anyone but myself. This entire day had been absolute torture. Tanner hadn't left the house, and I thought I might seriously burst if I didn't get some alone time to talk to Levi. So I had no choice but to create a few chores to make it happen. Levi had been scarce all day, holed up in his room with the door closed, like he was right now. So once I got Alex and Tanner out of the house, I went straight to his bedroom and took a deep breath before knocking.

"Come in."

I opened the door. A half-packed suitcase was laid out on the bed, and Levi held a stack of T-shirts in his hand. The look on his face made my heart twist in my chest. He looked as down and out as I felt. Without a word, I stepped into his room and shut the door behind me.

Levi looked over my shoulder at the door and then back at me.

"Don't worry. I sent Tanner to run some errands. He won't be back for at least an hour. And Alex is staying at his friend's tonight, though I promised I'd pick him up by seven AM tomorrow, because he wants to spend every waking moment he can with you before you leave us."

If it were possible, Levi's long face grew even sadder. He raked a hand through his hair. "I'm sorry he's upset about me leaving."

I'd been on the verge of tears all day, but suddenly I felt a different emotion. *Anger.* I put my hands on my hips. "Really? Is it just him you're sorry about hurting? Did you ever stop and think maybe someone *else* might be hurt by your sudden announcement?"

Levi blew out a jagged breath and rubbed the back of his neck. "I'm sorry I didn't get to tell you one on one like I'd planned."

My voice rose to slightly less than a shriek. "So what you're sorry for is telling me the news in an inopportune way, not for leaving early?"

Levi just kept shaking his head with his eyes cast down. "I'm sorry. Work called, and I need to go back early."

"*Bullshit.* I remember how these things go, Levi. I'm not an idiot. If your contract says you have to report at ten AM on July twenty-third, you guys show up no earlier than nine fifty-nine. And the players union doesn't even want you to give the team that one extra minute. So this was *a choice* you made."

He nodded. "You're right. It was. I made a choice to go back a little earlier to help out the new receivers."

I shook my head. Levi still wasn't looking me in the eyes, so I closed the gap between us. "Look at me, Levi. And tell me why you're really going back."

His eyes raised and jumped back and forth between mine a moment before he closed them and took a deep breath. "I'm leaving because things between me and you need to end."

Sadness wrapped around my heart and squeezed out all the anger. I did my best to blink back the sting of tears, but I knew I couldn't keep them at bay too long. "Why? Why does it need to end?"

Levi leaned his forehead against mine. "I'm not right for you. You moved back to Beaufort to give you and your son the life you deserve. That life is here for the taking, and it doesn't include me."

Tears spilled down my cheeks. "But you said we could find a way to work it out."

"We got caught up in the heat of the moment. I care about you, Presley. I really do. And Alex, too. But what happened between us should've never happened. It was a mistake."

It felt like someone had slapped me across the face. Saying it had to end was one thing, but regretting it and calling it a mistake was another altogether. I took two steps back. "A mistake? How can you say that? You told me once that you'd never regret us."

"You should give your family a chance, Presley. Alex deserves to have his father in his life, and you deserve to have someone who can be by your side day in, day out."

"But I don't want to be with Tanner. I want to be with you. I know it's confusing and people will get hurt, but we can figure it out. I know we can. That's what you said all along. You made me believe it could work."

Levi squeezed his eyes shut. He was quiet for a long time. Eventually he looked up and swallowed. "I don't *want* to work it out, Presley."

It felt like someone knocked the wind out of me.

Levi shook his head. "I'm sorry if I led you on and took things too far. I will be there for Alex—that, I promise. But you and me? It was never going to last. We live two very different lives, and I don't want to be tied down while I'm on the road."

My lips trembled. "I see."

He looked down again. "I'm sorry, Presley. I really am."

Levi stepped forward with his arms out, like he was going to console me. But no way could I let him do that. As it was, I was on the verge of breaking down. I just needed to get the hell out of here. So I put my hand on his chest and shoved to stop him. "*Don't.* I'll be fine." I lifted my chin, even though tears were already dripping from it. "Goodbye, Levi."

xoxo

I had to put ice packs on my eyes the next morning to reduce the swelling enough so I could drive to pick up Alex. Last night had been brutal. I kept replaying the months Levi and I had shared over and over in my head to see what I'd missed. There must have been signs that things between us were only a fling to him, signs that I missed because of my growing feelings. People don't just wake up one day and randomly decide a relationship isn't worth fighting for. But no matter how hard I thought back and dissected our time together, I just couldn't see what was coming.

And that scared the hell out of me. I'd been blindsided once before by love—by Tanner—and I'd thought I'd learned from that experience and grown as a woman. Falling for another man, only to be discarded like yesterday's trash *again,* wasn't just heartbreaking; it made me feel like a complete idiot.

Luckily, one of the benefits of being a mom was that you didn't get much time to wallow in self-pity. The minute I picked up Alex from his friend's house, he started rambling on and on about his Uncle Levi, and I had no choice but to suck it up.

"Grandma told me Uncle Levi's team is retiring Grandpa's football jersey this year. The whole family is going to a big ceremony in September. It's in Denver, so Uncle Levi will be there, too. Do you think we can go with them, Mom? Grandma said we could if you said it was okay."

"I'm not sure, sweetie. Things might be busy here. Why don't we talk about it when it gets closer."

"It's in fifty-one days. I looked it up. I'm going to ask Uncle Levi about it this morning."

I didn't have the heart or the energy to tell Alex his uncle likely wouldn't want us to come visit. So instead, I just nodded and forced a smile.

"Next summer, do you think Uncle Levi will come back to The Palm? Maybe he could help coach my summer camp."

It felt like an elephant was sitting on my chest. "I'm not sure what Uncle Levi will have planned for next summer. That's almost a year away."

"Three-hundred-and-forty-three days."

My real smile couldn't help but peek out. I reached over and mussed my son's hair. "Someone found a calendar."

When we pulled up at the inn, Tanner was sitting outside on the swing with his coffee. I hadn't come out of my room after talking to Levi last night to see if Tanner had installed it once he got back from the wild goose chase I'd sent him on.

He stood as we approached. "What's up, killer?" He held a fist out to Alex and the two bumped. "How was your night? You didn't sneak out of Kyle's house to meet up with girls and smoke cigarettes and drink whiskey, did you?"

Alex laughed. "Girls are gross, Dad."

Tanner winked at me. "Just girls? Not booze and smokes?"

"*Daaad*...you're so not even funny."

Tanner chuckled. He nodded toward the house. "Why don't you go inside and get washed up for breakfast? I picked up chocolate chips when I was at the supermarket last night so I could make us double chocolate chip pancakes for breakfast. I'm gonna start making them in a few because I have to drive Uncle Levi to the airport this morning."

"Okay!"

Tanner looked at me after Alex ran into the house. "How do you like your swing?"

"It looks great. Thanks for doing that."

"I knocked on your door last night to tell you it was done, but you didn't answer."

"I guess I conked out pretty early."

Tanner nodded. He seemed to study my face for a minute. "You okay?"

"Yeah, why wouldn't I be?"

He held my eyes. "You look a little swollen...like you've been crying or something."

I looked away. "My allergies are just bad. Actually, I'm going to take a shower right now. The hot water and steam usually do a lot to help my sinuses."

"Make it quick. I'm making those chocolate chip pancakes for all of us. They're not just our boy's favorite, they're my big bro's favorite, too."

I tried in earnest not to frown, but gravity had my lips reaching for the floor. "I'm not really hungry. So don't wait for me to eat." I walked toward the door and looked back. "Thanks again for hanging the swing."

Tanner winked. "My pleasure, sweetheart."

✗○✗○

Today it was apparently my turn to stay in my room. I guess maybe it was only fair considering Levi had done it all day yesterday. I'd seen his flight paperwork on the kitchen table when I'd grabbed coffee earlier, so I knew it wouldn't be much longer before he would be heading to the airport. It was going to kill me not to say goodbye, but I couldn't imagine how I could do that in front of everyone without bursting into tears. We'd made it this far without Tanner knowing anything had happened between us, so there was no reason to blow it now with an overly emotional goodbye. I just needed to keep to myself for a little while longer, and then it would all be over.

Well, it wouldn't be over. Not in my heart anyway. Because you can't just flip a switch and turn love off. But at least the risk of Tanner finding out would be minimal once Levi was gone.

I sat in my room and counted down the minutes with my heart ricocheting in my chest. Then my bedroom door suddenly burst open.

I jumped up from where I sat on the bed, and my hand covered my heart. "Alex, you scared the wits out of me! Remember our rule? We knock on any closed door, especially here at the inn."

"Sorry, Mom. I just wanted to ask if it was okay if I went with Dad to drop Uncle Levi at the airport. Dad said I had to check with you to make sure you didn't have anything else going on."

I sighed. "That's fine. Go ahead."

Just like Tanner had done earlier, my son searched my face before his little one wrinkled. "Are you okay, Mommy?"

I smiled sadly. I hated lying to my son, even when it was for his own good. "I'm fine, honey. My allergies are just bothering me."

He walked over and took my hand. "I'm sad Uncle Levi is leaving, too."

I blinked a few times. "What?"

"When your allergies are bothering you, you sneeze all the time. I think you're just sad like me that Uncle Levi is leaving. He's fun to have around."

I stroked my son's cheek. He was such a perceptive little boy. "How about you and I take a ride to the beach tomorrow? Maybe we can get a hotel room for the night and spend two days surfing the waves in Myrtle Beach?"

My son fist pumped. "Can I get a new boogie board before we go?"

I smiled. "Of course."

"Okay!" Alex squeezed my hand. He then started for the door, but stopped when he realized I wasn't following. "Come on. Uncle Levi is packing the car. You need to say goodbye."

"Ummm..." I couldn't think of a way to avoid doing it, so I reluctantly nodded. "Okay."

Out in the kitchen, Levi was putting his laptop into a backpack when we walked in. He looked up and, if I didn't know better, I would've thought he was in as much pain as I was.

He smiled sadly. "Hey."

"Hey."

Tanner strolled into the room, swinging around a set of keys dangling from a lanyard. He smiled. "You ready to go, superstar?"

Levi's eyes jumped to meet mine again before he looked down to zip his backpack. "Yep."

"Let's hit the road then."

Again, Levi's eyes met mine. Of course, my plan had been to avoid saying goodbye, but now it would seem weird if we didn't at least hug or something. So I took a deep breath and walked over. "Goodbye, Levi. Good luck this season." The hug was awkward, but when I went to pull away, Levi's grip on me tightened.

He whispered in my ear, "Good luck with this place. My grandfather was a wise man."

When he released me and I took a step back, there were tears in his eyes. Levi coughed and turned away. "Let's go. I don't want to miss my flight."

I followed them to the door, completely numb. Levi never looked back as he got into Tanner's SUV and buckled. Alex climbed into the back and the engine started, but at the last second, Tanner opened the driver's side door and jogged up to the porch where I stood. He kissed my cheek and pulled me in for a hug.

"I forgot to say goodbye."

Tanner and I had put a lot of the hard feelings behind us, and we were friendly these days, but we weren't in a place where we hugged and kissed goodbye, so I thought it was odd. Until I looked up and saw Levi watching from the car. That had been Tanner's point. Apparently my son wasn't the only perceptive one in the house, and Tanner wanted to leave his brother with a lasting memory.

xoxo

I allowed myself a solid hour of crying, and then I took a second shower. I'd considered calling Harper to talk through everything, but that would have inevitably led to more tears, and I didn't want to be red faced and swollen when my son arrived back home. So instead, I put the kettle on and made a cup of chamomile tea. As I steeped the bag and stared into space, someone knocked at the front door. More and more people had been stopping by to inquire about renting a room lately. While that was a good thing, I was glad there was still another week until the grand opening, because I couldn't imagine having to smile and welcome strangers right now.

But when I opened the door, it wasn't a stranger on the other side at all.

Tanner's mother took one look at my face and frowned. "Can I come in?"

The last thing I wanted was to discuss anything about either of her sons, but I also couldn't turn her away. So I nodded and stepped aside for her to enter.

She walked into the kitchen and looked at my teacup sitting on the counter. "Mind if I join you?"

Yes. "No, of course not. I'll make you a cup."

We were both quiet as I prepped a second cup. Setting it down in front of her, I took the seat on the other side of the table.

Shelby wrapped her hands around the mug. "I know you're hurting right now. But sometimes the hardest decisions we have to make end up being the right ones."

I swallowed. "Nothing feels right at the moment."

Shelby reached across the table and took my hand. "In life, there are so many different paths we can take. Often we feel compelled to cross one bridge over another to get to a new place. So we don't really give the bridge to the place we've been any true consideration, unless the other bridge is burned, and we have no choice. Right now, you're probably feeling like you lost your way. But I promise you, everything happens for a reason. Just because you're forced to take a different bridge, doesn't mean you can't find happiness on the other side, Presley."

I'd told myself I wasn't going to cry anymore today, but a tear escaped and slid down my cheek. I wiped it away. "I'm not ready to talk about this, Shelby. But I appreciate you trying to make me feel better."

She patted my hand. "It's going to take time. But if you want to talk at any point, you know where to find me."

"Thank you."

"Would you like me to take Alex for a few days?"

I shook my head. "I think we're actually going to go down to the beach for a day or two."

Shelby smiled and nodded. "That's a good idea. You know the old saying: Saltwater cures everything."

She finished her tea and brought her cup to the sink before gathering her purse. Unzipping it, she took out an envelope and extended it to me. "I almost forgot. Levi asked me to give this to you."

My heart, which had felt deflated, suddenly started to pump again. "What is it?"

She shrugged. "I didn't open it, and he didn't say."

I took the envelope. "Okay, thank you."

Shelby was barely out the door when I tore the envelope open. I don't know what I'd been expecting; I guess I'd assumed it was a letter of some sort—the goodbye we didn't get to have, or some attestation of his true feelings for me. But it wasn't a letter at all. Inside was a stapled packet of legal documents, though I wasn't quite sure what I was looking at.

Quitclaim deed?

Grantor and Grantee?

I flipped through the pages, the last of which had Levi's signature on it, then went back and started to read from the top. The meaning of the document didn't become clear until the second full paragraph.

I, Levi Sanford Miller, hereby remise, release and forever quitclaim all of my interest in 638 Palm Court, The Palm Inn, City of Beaufort, State of South Carolina, to Presley Sullivan.

Oh my God.

Levi didn't write me a love letter. He signed over his half of the inn to me.

And cut the last tie that binds us.

TWENTY-SEVEN

Presley

THE WAVES CRASHED as I sat on the sand, watching Alex dig for seashells. It was our first day in Myrtle Beach, and the weather couldn't have been more perfect.

"Look at this one!" Alex came running toward me and handed me an almost-symmetrical white shell with burnt orange spots.

I rubbed my finger along its lines. "This is definitely one for the jar."

We'd brought a large jar from the kitchen with us and promised to fill the entire thing with only the most worthy of seashells to take back home.

When Alex ran back toward the shore, my phone rang. I smiled as I answered. "Hey, Harp."

"I got your text with that breathtaking photo of the ocean. How's Myrtle Beach?"

Breathing in the salty air, I said, "It was definitely a good decision to get away for a couple of days."

"Is Tanner with you guys?"

"No. He wanted to come, but I told him I preferred to have some alone time here with Alex. I honestly needed a breather from him. Levi just left, so I'm still processing everything."

"How did you leave things with him?"

Where do I even begin? I filled Harper in on the days leading up to Levi's departure and ended with the fact that he'd given me his half of the inn.

"Wow. That was amazingly generous of him," she said.

"I wish I could see it that way. I mean, it's obviously generous. But it also felt like a slap in the face—like he didn't want to have anything else to do with me, and that was a way of ensuring he didn't have to. I feel like a fool for ever believing he could love me enough not to run away."

After a few seconds of silence Harper asked, "Do you really think he stopped caring about you, or is this whole thing about guilt over Tanner?"

That was the magic question.

Digging lines in the sand, I shook my head. "I don't know. And I'm not sure which scenario breaks my heart more. In some ways, it would be easier if he truly had lost interest in a future with me. Then I would know for sure he wasn't hurting inside. It's all so confusing. I was pretty sure he'd given up on us until the moment he left when I saw tears in his eyes."

"Oh my God. *Levi Miller* cried?"

It pained me to think about it. "It was subtle, and he was trying to hide it. I still have no idea if he just felt bad for hurting me or if *he* was the one feeling hurt. I'm supposed to be enjoying this time with my son, but that question is haunting me." I sighed. "Even if I knew the answer, it wouldn't change anything. Whether it's a lack of love or guilt driving his decision, it's over. Him giving me the deed proved that, and I need to accept it." Emotion crashed over me, and I whispered, "I miss him so damn much."

"Are you gonna be okay?"

I took a deep breath. "I have to be—for Alex. This is the last I'm gonna speak of it, Harper. As soon as I get off the phone with you, I'm letting it go for the rest of this trip."

"You need me to come down?" she asked.

"No. Of course, I'd love to see you, but I have to do this on my own. Even if it kills me, I'll force myself to move on."

She sighed. "If you change your mind, I'll be on the next plane, okay?"

A friend who'd hop a plane just to make you feel better is definitely a keeper.

"Thanks, Harp. I love you."

XOXO

A couple of days later, it was back to reality after Alex and I returned to The Palm Inn. The trip had turned out exactly as I'd wanted. I'd done the best I could, giving Alex all of my attention as we toured Myrtle Beach. We spent a lot of time together in the water, ate at the local restaurants, had ice cream, and browsed all the shops.

Being back home, though, reignited the emptiness of realizing Levi was gone.

Tanner walked into the kitchen as I was putting away groceries. I hadn't gone shopping since before Levi left and had badly needed to restock the pantry.

"How about we drop Alex off at my mother's tonight and go out to dinner, just you and me?" he suggested.

I paused before making an excuse, which wasn't entirely a lie. "We just got back. I kind of feel like being a homebody for a little while."

He nodded, looking a bit deflated. "Well, then, we can have a date night *in*. I'll cook something for us? Give you a break if you're tired?"

His use of the word *date* forced me to take a more direct approach.

"Tanner, I've already told you where things stand for me. Nothing has changed. We're co-parents, but that's it. Not to mention, my focus right now needs to be on the grand opening next week, and Alex starting school soon." I shut the pantry door. "But even if those things weren't happening, I'm not interested in a romantic relationship with you anymore. I thought I made that clear."

He grimaced. "Oh, you did. But I can't give up without a fight. You mean too much to me. I'll be trying from time to time, fully expecting to get shot down for a while. And you know what? All things considered—the mistakes I've made in the past—this is to be expected. But I won't give up on you, Presley. I will *not* give up on us. You and Alex are the most important people in the world to me. Every day from now on is a step toward earning your trust back." He took a few steps closer. "In the meantime, I'm here to help you. Tell me what you need from me. I'm on your side, on your team. Put me to work, and we'll make this the most kickass grand opening this town has ever seen."

xoxo

Over the week that followed, Tanner definitely turned out to be a man of his word. He'd done so much to help me, from tending to Alex to deep cleaning the rooms in preparation for our guests.

In just a few days, people would start arriving to stay at The Palm Inn, and tonight was the grand-opening party.

We'd invited the local press and arranged for prepared food to be brought in. Two of the reporters would even be spending the night in the recently renovated bedrooms in exchange for write-ups about the inn.

I was getting the kitchen ready for the caterers when Tanner and Alex walked in from back-to-school shopping. Alex carried a bunch of bags to his room while Tanner joined me in the kitchen. I knew I couldn't have focused and been ready for the party tonight if Tanner wasn't here paying attention to Alex. I was more grateful for his presence by the day.

"How's my girl?" Tanner shook his head and corrected himself. "I'm sorry. Old habit."

I sprayed the counter and wiped it down as he came up behind me.

"You're so tense, Presley. You need to relax."

The next thing I knew, Tanner's hands were firmly around my shoulders. He dug his fingers into my muscles, massaging. As inappropriate as this seemed, I closed my eyes and relished the feel of the tension releasing from the base of my neck.

For a moment, as I closed my eyes, I imagined it was Levi touching me. My body stirred before I snapped out of my trance and pulled away.

Letting out a breath, I said, "Thank you."

I swiftly exited the kitchen—and ran into a smirking Fern in the hallway.

"Feeling refreshed?" she cracked.

Great. I could only imagine what that had looked like in the kitchen. But I couldn't be concerned with her assumptions right now.

I walked right past her, went straight to my room, and shut the door before lying down on the bed. My body buzzed from the massage—not because it had been Tanner's hands on me, but because being touched reminded me of everything I still longed for.

I miss Levi. I missed the way Levi looked at me, the way he made me feel, how happy I was with him. I had no idea how I was supposed to just forget all of that and move on with my life.

Rubbing my temples, I started to sweat. I rubbed my legs against the smooth sheets in frustration. I snatched my phone from the nightstand and scrolled through my contacts.

My finger lingered over Levi's name as I debated texting him.

What would I even say? Admitting how much I missed him or that I was thinking about him wasn't going to make either of our lives easier. It would serve no purpose. I tossed the phone and buried my head in a pillow, hoping the moment would pass. And eventually it did. Rather than give in to my need for contact with Levi, I escaped to the shower and began getting ready for tonight.

xoxo

A couple of hours later, I was downstairs, dressed in a floor-length, purple dress as people arrived for the celebration.

Tanner and Alex wore matching navy suits, and even Fern had changed out of her usual house dress into a fancy outfit. She'd finished off the look with a gargantuan hat adorned with flowers.

I made my way around, schmoozing with the guests and answering questions from local reporters.

It was hard to talk about the renovation process without acknowledging Levi, so I gave him credit where it was due. More than one person asked why he wasn't at the party, and I explained with a bitter taste in my mouth that he was back in Colorado for work. Perhaps the most bittersweet fact about this entire shindig was that Levi had arranged the whole thing. Back when things were better between us, he'd made all of the party arrangements—from the invite list down to picking the menu.

By the time everyone left, I was utterly exhausted from having to be "on" so many hours in a row as The Palm Inn's official spokesperson. And I hadn't eaten a morsel of the food Levi paid for.

The kitchen was finally quiet when I opened the refrigerator to see what was left. Staring me in the face was a tray of peach cobbler. Levi had requested that particular dessert for a reason, and at the time, it was likely *not* meant to hurt me.

I took the tray out and grabbed a fork, knowing damn well tonight would be yet another evening consumed by thoughts of Levi Miller.

⚓ TWENTY-EIGHT

Presley

TWO WEEKS LATER, The Palm Inn was officially open for business, and the first guests had checked in. Not only that, we were sold out for two months—until early October. Everything was great, aside from the fact that I was exhausted.

This endeavor was entirely too much for one person. Tanner had started his new coaching job, and was still doing the agent stuff on the side, so he couldn't help me as much anymore. And I'd started the art teacher position at the local high school, which ate up a good chunk of my time.

Tanner had just dropped Alex off at school when he returned to join me for coffee before work.

"You look totally stressed. Did something happen with one of the guests?" he asked as he poured himself a mug.

"No, it's nothing bad. I'm just realizing I need help. We're booked solid for over eight weeks. Preparing breakfast each day is enough work. And now that I've started teaching, I don't think I can handle all the cleaning and turning around the rooms—not to mention the laundry. I know I should've foreseen this, but it's harder than I imagined."

He put his mug down. "Say no more. After I deal with some client stuff this morning, I'll line someone up to come in and clean."

"You don't need to do that."

"I *want* to. And I'll pay for it. Aside from buying food here and there, I've been living at this place rent-free, and that's not really fair. I know I'm still behind on what I owe you, but count on me to handle the cleaning costs and also to start covering more of the other expenses around here."

It was nice to have his support, but I couldn't help feeling like this was another attempt to become a fixture in our lives again. But I certainly wasn't going to turn him down if he wanted to contribute.

After Tanner went upstairs to work, I did something I almost never do. I took my coffee into the living room and turned on the TV. I wasn't a big television watcher, most of the time preferring to read. But I had a little time before I had to report to school to teach my first art class for the day.

For about ten minutes, I watched the *Today* show, and during a commercial, I flipped through the channels.

Normally, I'd blow right by ESPN, except the familiar face on the screen caused me to freeze. Levi's big blue eyes were fixed on the female reporter.

I swallowed the lump in my throat as he spoke.

The beautiful blond had asked him his opinion on a new player who'd been transferred to the Broncos for the upcoming season.

Levi scratched his chin. "Everyone's welcomed him with open arms. It's been fun getting into a groove and being back at camp. The team is stronger than ever, and I'm excited for the season to start."

She continued to ask him questions with a twinkle in her eye. She seemed to be flirting. My stomach sank, and I changed the channel. I couldn't take it.

If I couldn't handle a reporter flirting with him, how would I have ever dealt with all of the rest of the women throwing themselves at him, day in and day out?

XOXO

Two more weeks passed, and things felt more under control at The Palm Inn now that I had regular help. Tanner had hired a friend of Fern's to come in for housekeeping a few days a week, so I no longer had to bear the brunt of that.

Handling the breakfast end of things was also much easier now that I had less on my plate. I didn't have to start my art teaching job until 11AM, so that allowed me plenty of time to prepare coffee and food for our guests. And sometimes, when I was running late, Tanner would step in and take over for me if he didn't have to report to his coaching job. Alex was also settled into the new school year, and I couldn't have asked for anything more right now on the home front.

The only problem was the lingering longing inside of me for a man I couldn't have. The same man whose brother seemed to be doing everything humanly possible to earn another chance.

Speaking of Tanner, I'd finally decided to give in to one of his many requests to spend time outside of the house together. He'd convinced me I deserved a night out and promised not to assume it was a date if I just agreed.

So, one evening, the two of us dropped Alex off at Tanner's mother's house before meeting Lily and Tom

Hannaford at one of my favorite Italian restaurants, Carducci's. Lily and Tom were one of the few couples we'd gone to high school with who were still together. We'd often gone on double dates with them back in the day, so it was definitely like déjà vu to be sitting across from them tonight.

At one point after the waiter took our order, Lily hit me with the dreaded question. "So, what's going on with you two?" She looked between us. "Please tell me a reconciliation is in the works."

I'd hoped Tanner, who set up this dinner, had explained things to them so I didn't have to.

"We're just friends and co-parents, actually," I told her.

Tanner placed his hand on my arm. "That's the plan *for now*." He smiled over at me, but I didn't return it. "I'm holding out hope that she gives me another chance. I messed up royally in the past, so I'm currently working to earn her trust back. Taking it day by day."

Lily grinned. "Well, that's commendable. But what if that never happens?"

Tanner squinted. "What do you mean?"

"What if she can never learn to trust you again?"

He sighed and looked over at me. "Then we'll always be in each other's lives, and I'll always be there for her and Alex—no matter what."

I took a sip of water and felt the need to clarify my position. "There are some things in life that are best not revisited," I explained. "I think you can have respect and love for someone and also recognize that you're better off apart. That's the case with Tanner and me."

A frown crossed Tanner's face.

While it sucked to once again deflate his hope, I needed to continue keeping things real until it eventually sank in for him. He'd clearly misled our friends into thinking this was some kind of double date.

After a few glasses of wine, I managed to finally enjoy myself as the subject moved away from Tanner and me. The four of us reminisced about old times, things like sneaking into movies when we were in high school.

Everything was kosher until Tom brought up the L-word during dessert.

He turned to Tanner. "How's your brother doing?"

"Good," Tanner said. "He's back at training camp, gearing up for the new season."

"I heard the Broncos snagged Chip Reid. That was a huge acquisition."

Tanner nodded. "Yeah. Should be an interesting season."

Tom chuckled. "God, Levi must be living the life. I can only imagine how much ass that guy gets."

My wine felt like it was coming back up as a surge of jealousy hit. It wasn't like he'd said anything I didn't already know, but it sucked to hear. It also sucked that it had such a profound effect on me. But I was no less in love with Levi now than the day he left. In light of that, the way Tom's comment made me burn up was normal. Beads of sweat formed on my forehead as I downed the last of my wine.

Lily tilted her head as she looked straight at me, seeming to examine my face. "Wasn't he here in town for a while?"

I cleared my throat. "Yeah. He was a big help when we were starting the renovations at The Palm Inn."

"I'm totally indebted to him for being here until I got my shit together," Tanner added.

Lily looked at me again. "Was he living there at The Palm with you before Tanner arrived?"

Feeling my cheeks heat, I nodded. "Yes."

"Interesting. Had you ever spent extensive time together before?"

"No, it was my first time really getting to know him."

"I see." She smirked slightly.

And that's when I knew. She had noticed my reaction and put two and two together. Somehow, from the look on my face alone, Lily had figured out what Tanner had yet to—that something had gone down between me and his brother.

How on Earth was I going to hide my feelings for Levi from Tanner forever if this chick had figured it out in a matter of minutes?

TWENTY-NINE

Levi

COACH WILLIAMS HAD asked me to come to his house immediately after camp.

He was quiet as he let me in the front door. I followed him to the kitchen, suspecting he wanted to ream me out for my less-than-stellar performance on the field today.

His wife was arranging a massive bouquet of flowers when we walked in. Kristen was a sweetheart and always treated me like family. I gave her a kiss on the cheek and saw Coach give her a look before she suddenly made herself scarce. I was about to get my ass handed to me, and he wanted to do it in private.

Sure enough, after he passed me a beer, he took a seat and laid it on me. "What's going on with you?"

I pulled out a chair and sat down. "I'm sorry. I know."

"You missed an open receiver downfield. It's not the first time that's happened lately either. You'd better get your head out of your ass before the season starts."

I'd learned the hard way over the years that anytime I tried to hide something from him, he always figured it out eventually. Seeing as though he'd become like a father to me, I felt comfortable admitting the truth. He deserved that, especially when my actions would be affecting his bottom line.

"Some stuff went down back home, and I haven't been able to shake it."

He lifted his brow. "What stuff? Is this about the property?"

"I wish."

"If it ain't that, there's only one other thing I can think of that could be fucking you up so bad." He took a sip. "What's her name?"

I exhaled. "Presley."

"Isn't that the woman you were fighting about the house with?"

"Yes," I bit out.

His head tilted as he began to figure it out. "Your brother's..."

"Yes," I answered under my breath.

"Aw, shit." He shook his head and took a long gulp of beer.

Over the next several minutes, I told him everything and ended with Tanner showing up. "I know what you're gonna say, Coach—"

He held out his hand. "Not so fast. You think I'm gonna tell you to forget about it and get your shit together, but I know it's not as easy as it sounds when a woman is fucking with your head."

I pulled on my hair. "What's the solution, then?"

"Well, it certainly isn't continuing to mess around with your brother's woman..." He chuckled.

"*Ex* woman," I clarified.

"Either way, it's fucked up, and you need to move on from it. But what this proves is that you're needing companionship. Maybe you've outgrown the bachelor life. There comes a time when every man needs a good lady to come home to. Probably the only thing that will get your mind off a woman you can't have is to find a better one and claim her for yourself."

My first thought was: *there isn't a better one*. I knew it. Presley was the best. This wasn't about needing a replacement for her. While I appreciated his advice, I knew I wouldn't take it. I had no interest in starting a relationship that would feel forced with anyone else. What had happened between Presley and me felt natural. It was organic. She felt like home to me, and that couldn't be replicated. I'd rather be alone than try.

"I appreciate your advice. But that's not something I'm interested in right now."

"Okay, then on to Plan B." He slammed his beer on the table.

"What's that?"

"I take you out back and whip your ass into shape. Because we can't have this shit continuing into the season!"

I bent my head back in frustration and rubbed my eyes. "I promise I'll work it out, okay? I won't let you down."

xoxo

Although it had felt good to unload on Coach, I was still in a pissy mood when I returned to my house that night. My place seemed cold and empty compared to being back home with Presley. I hadn't realized just how bad it was until I got back here. I had expensive things, but it wasn't a house that made a home. It was the people in it, and here in Colorado, my home life was nonexistent.

Talking about Presley today had messed with my head. I'd been trying to forget, but the more effort I put into that, the more it seemed to screw with my game. Actually *speaking* about the situation aloud made me feel even worse about how I'd left things with her.

I'd had multiple opportunities to drown my sorrows in other women, but I had no desire to go there. It would be disloyal to Presley, and more surprisingly, I had no desire for sex with anyone else. I wasn't ready to move on, even if I'd tried to encourage Presley to do just that. Instead, I'd close my eyes at night and imagine her smell, her taste, lying next to her, holding her. Then I'd get sick to my stomach imagining Tanner doing the same.

It didn't matter that I was a grown-ass man. When you're feeling this low, there's only one person who has a chance at making it better.

Taking out my phone, I scrolled down to her name.

After a few rings, she picked up.

"Levi?"

"Hey, Ma. What's been going on?"

"It's so good to hear your voice."

"You too."

"You sound tired."

Another way of saying I sounded like shit. "Yeah, it's been hectic at practice. How are things at home?"

"Well, I've currently got your nephew here."

"Yeah?" I smiled. "Put him on."

"Okay. Hang on."

My mother called Alex to the phone, and I could hear him running toward it.

"Uncle Levi!"

The sound of his voice went straight to my heart.

"Hey, buddy. What's going on?"

"Nothing much. Hanging out with Grandma. I miss you."

"I miss you, too." I shut my eyes. "Believe me."

"Did you know I was here at Grandma's? Is that why you called?"

"No. I didn't know, actually. But it's a nice surprise. How's school?"

"It's okay. My friends still ask about you. They say hello."

"Well, tell them I said hey too."

"I wish you were here. We could play Trouble."

"I would much rather be there playing Trouble with you right now than here."

"Grandma always lets me win. It's no fun. I bet you would try to beat me."

"You're probably right." I braced myself. "Where's your mom tonight?"

"She's out on a date with Dad."

His words were a swift kick to the gut. My heart raced.

I hadn't realized I'd fallen silent until he said, "Are you there?"

"Yup." I swallowed. "Did your mom *say* she was going on a date with your dad?"

"Dad told me."

While it brought me some relief to know Tanner was the one who'd referred to it as a date, this still sucked. Whether it was officially a date or not, they were out together, which meant they were bonding.

Fuck. This was supposedly what I'd expected to happen, what needed to happen, but I'd never get used to the idea.

We talked for a few more minutes until Alex put my mother back on the phone.

She'd apparently read my mind.

Mom lowered her voice. "I don't know if they're officially on a date, Levi. From what Tanner tells me, he's still trying to earn her trust."

My heart pounded. "How is she?"

"Presley seems good—good but busy. The Palm Inn is up and running, fully booked for two months."

I smiled. "Wow. That's great."

She paused. "You did the right thing, son. I'm proud of you."

If only it felt right. Instead, my insides felt like they were twisting in knots.

After we hung up, I was desperate for a distraction. Despite knowing I'd pay for it tomorrow, I needed something to numb this feeling. I reached for a bottle of Jack Daniel's and crashed.

THIRTY

Presley

SIX WEEKS AFTER Levi left, I'd finally fallen into a routine. I'd get Alex ready for school, make breakfast for the guests at the inn, teach four periods of art, pick up Alex, come home and make dinner, check in on the guests, eat, do homework and bath time with my son, tidy up the common areas, take a shower, and fall into bed exhausted. Wash. Rinse. Repeat. It was easy to forget what day of the week it was since they all looked the same.

Today I'd just finished tidying up the inn and was about to turn off the lights and head upstairs to take a shower when someone knocked at the front door. Shelby Miller smiled when I opened it. I had to force a similar greeting. It wasn't that I didn't like Tanner's mom, but most of the conversations we had were draining, and it had already been a long day.

Nevertheless, I stepped aside for her to enter and put on my best fake smile. "Hi, Shelby. I didn't know you were coming by. Tanner isn't here. He and the assistant coach are working on some new plays. He said he'd probably be back pretty late."

"I know. That's why I came by. I was hoping you and I could talk for a few minutes alone."

"Ummm... Yeah, sure. Of course. Would you like a cup of tea?"

"If you're having one, that would be great."

We made small talk while I prepped two teas, mostly chatting about Alex and how he was settling into school. After I was done and put out cream and sugar, I sat across from her and sipped my tea.

"How are things going with Tanner?" she asked.

"We've been getting along pretty well. But we're just friends, if that's what you're asking. I don't see Tanner in a romantic light, and I've told him that a number of times."

Shelby sighed. "That's what I thought."

"Did he...say something to you to make you think otherwise?"

She shook her head. "Not directly. But I received all of the confirmations for Jim's jersey ceremony next weekend, and I noticed there was a one-bedroom suite under Tanner's name with three guests listed. So I asked him about it."

"Oh?"

"He said you, Alex, and he would all stay together in one room. Their suites have a separate bedroom and living room, with a king-size bed and also a small couch in the living area, but it's not a pull-out couch. I let Tanner know that, thinking maybe he thought the couch converted to a bed he could sleep on, but he said it wouldn't be a problem, that *Alex* would fit on the couch." Shelby caught my gaze. "He also asked if I'd mind keeping my grandson one of the nights, so you two could have some alone time."

I blew out a deep breath. "I definitely didn't know about that. I only decided to go a few weeks ago because

Alex's begging made it impossible to say no. I've been so busy that I hadn't even considered where we were staying or the sleeping arrangements. I knew Tanner said there were rooms blocked off for everyone. But I had no idea he thought it would be okay for us to share a bed." I paused. "I swear, Shelby, I haven't been leading him on at all. I've been very straightforward about how I feel, even though he keeps telling me he plans to wait me out."

She shook her head. "I wasn't thinking you were doing anything to make him feel that way. But I know how my son can be. Sometimes he gets ideas in his head, and he becomes so focused that he can lose track of reality."

"I don't want to hurt him. Things between us are good right now, on a friendship level. And he's spending a lot of quality time getting to know Alex. But there really is no chance we'll be getting back together." I looked down into my tea. "My heart belongs to someone else, but even if it didn't, I wouldn't be interested in rekindling a romance with Tanner."

Shelby was quiet for a moment. It looked like she might've been deliberating saying more. Eventually, she set down her teacup.

"Have you...spoken to Levi lately?"

I shook my head and frowned.

"This whole situation between my boys is very confusing. I'm never sure what I should say and what I shouldn't. I'm supposed to be loyal to both my sons, but I'm keeping a secret from one, and I hate to see either of them hurting. And you, Presley. I know it probably seems like I've not been the friendliest person since you came back, but I believed some things that I never should've, and for that I'm sorry. You were always like the daughter I never had, and I care about you deeply. I don't want to see you hurting either."

"Thank you. And I'm sorry you've been put in the middle of this mess."

Shelby was quiet for another moment. Eventually, she sighed. "Levi called me last week. It was the evening Alex was over because you and Tanner had gone out with some old friends. Alex told Levi he was over because his parents had gone out on a date."

My eyes widened. "Oh no."

Shelby nodded. "When I got back on the phone, Levi gave me the third degree. I told him Tanner was the one who'd called it a date, and I wasn't sure if that was what you considered it. But he sounded pretty upset."

I felt sick that Levi might think Tanner and I were together so soon after he left, that our relationship had meant so little to me that I could move on that fast—especially with his brother. But I also found Levi's reaction confusing.

"He was the one who broke things off with me."

Shelby reached across the table and squeezed my hand. "I didn't mean to upset you. I just thought you should know—not only because of Levi's reaction, but also because clearly Tanner is feeding Alex some things that aren't exactly the truth. I wouldn't want him to think his parents were back together, only to be let down."

I nodded. "Thank you for telling me. I appreciate it."

After Shelby left, I went to my room to take a shower. But rather than turn in, I decided to wait downstairs in the living room for Tanner to come home. It was time the two of us had a little heart to heart.

XOXO

"Hey." Lips touched my forehead. "You must've fallen asleep."

I rubbed my eyes open to the sight of Tanner. "What time is it?"

"It's almost midnight." He smiled. "You know, you're cute when you drool."

I wiped my face as I sat up. "I was not drooling."

He chuckled. "You want me to carry you to your room, sleepyhead?"

"No, I was waiting up for you."

"Oh yeah?" He grinned. "I like the sound of that."

I frowned. "Let's go into the kitchen to talk. I need some water."

While I was at the sink letting the water run cold, Tanner came up behind me. He stood close, and a hint of something sweet wafted through the air. I turned and sniffed. "You smell like perfume."

Tanner's eyes didn't quite meet mine when he spoke. "Jack's wife hugged me goodbye when I left."

It made sense, and I had no reason not to believe him—that is, except for his *prior track record*—yet for some reason, I sensed he was lying. But unlike when I'd smelled perfume on him years ago, I didn't really care if he'd been out with another woman. In fact, it would make my life easier if he were with someone else.

"Why don't we sit down?" I said.

We settled in at the kitchen table. I took the same seat I'd sat in earlier with Shelby, but rather than take the seat across from me like his mother had, Tanner took the seat next to me. He also scooched his chair closer, so we were practically on top of one another.

Then he took my hand. "What did you want to talk about?"

I untangled my fingers from his. "*This,* Tanner. You've got to stop doing things like taking my hand and putting your arm around me, especially when Alex is around. I don't want to give him the wrong impression."

Tanner frowned. "Fine."

"Also, I called your mom tonight when I realized I'd never reserved a room for your dad's jersey-retirement ceremony. She told me you'd booked a suite for me, you, and Alex."

"I thought it would be nice if the three of us stayed together as a family. The suites usually have a couch, and I figured I would crash there. You and Alex could take the bed."

I didn't want to drag his mother into this, so I didn't mention the version that she'd told me earlier.

"I'm not comfortable sharing a room with you, Tanner."

His face wrinkled, as if he were genuinely perplexed. "Why not? It's not like I haven't seen you naked before."

"That's not the point. We're not a couple. I feel like we've finally gotten to a good place in our relationship, but if you keep insisting on pushing us to a place I don't want to go, things are going to go off track."

"Fine. I'll call the hotel tomorrow and book you a separate room."

"Thank you."

"But I'm still not giving up on us. Eventually we'll be together again, because we're meant to be."

I sighed. Sometimes it was like talking to a wall. "No, Tanner. We're not."

"We'll see."

It was pointless to have this conversation yet again, and my sleep was more important. "I'm tired. I'm going to go to bed. Goodnight, Tanner."

"Goodnight, sweetheart."

THIRTY-ONE

Presley

THE NEXT WEEK flew by, and before I knew it, I was stepping off of a plane in Denver and checking into the Four Seasons Hotel near the stadium. Just being in the same city as Levi had me on edge, and I found myself looking over my shoulder and all around every two minutes, even at the check-in desk.

Shelby had flown in yesterday, but she was waiting in the lobby when we arrived. She walked over and stood next to me as I waited on the clerk to give me a room key.

"He's not staying at the hotel."

"Who?"

She smiled. "Levi."

I sighed. "Am I that obvious?"

She bumped her shoulder with mine. "Well, you're scanning the room better than a Secret Service agent waiting for the president to walk in."

I smiled sadly. "And here I thought I was being so nonchalant. Thank you for telling me. I do feel like I can relax a little knowing I might not accidentally walk into him. At least now I can concentrate all my worry on leaving The Palm in the care of the woman we hired to clean only a few weeks ago."

"Is she not working out?"

"No, no. I'm just teasing. She's been great. Melinda is super organized and capable, but it still feels strange to be away."

Shelby glanced over her shoulder. Tanner had taken the same flight from Beaufort, along with a few of his cousins, but he'd taken a different Uber from the airport, so he was a few people behind me in line to check in. She waved to her son and turned back.

"You also won't have to worry about walking into my other son. I had the manager put you in a room at the opposite end of the hotel from Tanner. I figured if he wasn't in the room next to you, it wouldn't be so easy for him to make excuses to pop over."

I blew out a jagged breath. "Thanks, Shelby. I really appreciate that."

"And as far as Levi, he's at practice now. But he will be at the dinner tonight."

A bunch of Tanner's and Levi's dad's old teammates were in town for the ceremony, in addition to their entire extended family. So tonight there was a dinner in a private room at a nearby restaurant to give everyone a chance to catch up before the ceremony tomorrow.

I nodded. "Okay. Thank you for the heads up."

With no chance of running into Levi, and Tanner on the other end of the hotel, I had about three hours to try to relax—or to worry about how I was going to handle being in the same room with Levi again later. Unfortunately, I was pretty sure the latter was going to win out.

Once I was checked in, Alex and I went to our room. I spent a restless hour flicking through television channels before deciding the best thing to do to conquer my nerves was to take a hot shower and start to get ready. At least it would give me something to focus on. I'd brought a green silk dress that was casual, yet showed off a little cleavage and leg. And since I had time to spare, I put on more makeup than usual, creating a smoky-eye effect and contouring my cheekbones. When I was done, I looked in the full-length mirror and was really happy with what I saw. It had been a while since I'd gotten myself all done up, and it gave me just the confidence boost I needed to get through tonight.

Alex was still in the bedroom watching TV, and when he came out, his eyes widened. "Wow. You look pretty, Mom."

I smiled. "Thank you. I have a hot date tonight, so I wanted to clean myself up."

"Dad?"

"No, silly. I was referring to *you*."

"Oh." Alex smiled.

But because of the way he'd assumed Tanner was my date, I thought it was a good time to set the record straight.

I sat down on the couch and patted the seat next to me. "Come sit for a minute, honey."

"You're not going to put stuff in my hair like you did for that wedding we went to last year, are you? I hate when my hair is hard."

"No," I chuckled. "I just want to talk for a minute."

"Okay, Mom."

I pushed a lock of hair from my son's face and smiled. "I thought we should talk about Dad for a minute, about my relationship with him."

"Are you guys getting married?"

My smile wilted. "No, honey. Your dad and I are just friends. That's what I wanted to chat with you about."

"But you're dating, right? Don't dating people get married?"

I shook my head. "We're not dating. I know your dad has used that term at least once in the past when we went to dinner with some friends, but we're not boyfriend and girlfriend, and we weren't on an actual date. He just kind of called it that. And I know it can be super confusing because Dad is staying at the inn right now while he gets settled, but that's also not the same as me living with Dad. So he lives in the same house as us, but he doesn't really live *with* us."

Alex shrugged. "You guys are weird."

I smiled. "I guess we are. But I've been worried that you might think Dad and I are a couple again, and then you'd be disappointed when you realized we weren't. Someday Dad is going to live somewhere else, and he might even have a girlfriend or something."

"Would that make you sad?" he asked.

"Not at all. I want your dad to be happy."

Alex seemed to mull that around for a minute, and then he shrugged again. "Okay. Can I go back to watching TV now?"

I laughed. He'd certainly taken that talk better than I'd expected. "Actually, it's almost time to go to dinner. Why don't you get dressed? I laid out your clothes on the chair next to the bed."

"But no crunchy-hair stuff, right?"

I patted my son's hand. "No gel. I promise."

XOXO

"Uncle Levi!" My heart nearly stopped when my son yelled. I'd been watching the door ever since we were seated, but when the waitress started making her rounds to take orders, I became distracted, looking down at the menu.

Alex was seated next to me, and both of us across from Tanner. Alex pushed back from the table, scraping the bottom of the chair along the tile, and bolted for the door. When he got to Levi, he leaped into his uncle's arms with a huge smile. My heart squeezed for so many different reasons. They hugged, and then Levi set him down on his feet, and they did some long handshake with slaps, shakes, and fist bumps. I'd been so caught up in my own feelings about seeing Levi, I hadn't stopped to think about how happy Alex would be. They'd grown close over the summer, and the looks on their faces made it clear they'd missed each other.

Seeing Levi, a few of the others in the room got up from the table and walked over to say hello. Tanner's back was facing the door, but he turned to watch all of the commotion, like everyone else. When a crowd started to form around his brother, Tanner remained in his seat. His jaw was set tight, and he raised his hand and called the waitress over.

"I'll take another vodka seltzer." He sucked back the remnants of the drink in his glass and held it up for her, rattling the ice.

She looked across to me. My wine glass was nearly drained, but I needed to take the edge off, not get sloshed. I shook my head. "No, thank you. I'm good."

After a few minutes, the crowd around Levi started to dwindle, and my heart raced as I stole glances at him. He looked beautiful. His hair had grown longer, reaching down to the collar of his shirt, and the ends curled up in a messy sort of way that I found insanely sexy. He wore a French blue dress shirt tucked into navy dress pants, and the outfit really showcased his masculine silhouette. Broad shoulders created the mouth of the V and led down to a narrow waist. *God, he is even more gorgeous than I remember.*

Fawning over him sort of caught me off guard. I hadn't been thinking about what he looked like lately. I missed the man *inside* that body. But seeing the full package on display tonight made me ache for all of him. When Levi finally shook the last person's hand, he scanned the room, and his eyes landed right on me. I felt his gaze all over. My heart jumped into my throat, my body tingled, and my eyes watered. Luckily, my son tugged at his uncle's hand, which caused him to look away. The two of them walked over to Shelby, and Levi hugged and kissed his mother. There were empty seats at her end of the table, but Tanner, Alex, and I were seated in the middle, and there weren't any open spaces.

Levi made his way around the table, saying hello to everyone he hadn't greeted yet, while my son dutifully stayed by his side. When he got to his brother, Tanner didn't even bother to get up. He knocked back half the glass of vodka the waitress had delivered two minutes ago and held his hand up.

"You still know how to make a grand entrance, I see," Tanner grumbled. "Being late means extra attention, all of it on you."

Levi's lips flattened to a grim line. "I came as soon as practice was over." He looked over at me and nodded. "Presley."

I forced a smile. "Hi, Levi."

Alex grabbed Levi's hand and started to tug. "Uncle Levi, come sit next to me."

Levi's eyes flashed to mine before returning to Alex. "There aren't any seats open, buddy. I'm going to sit down at the end near Grandma."

"I got it!" My son took off, darting down to the end of the table. He grabbed a chair that was almost the same size as he was and carried it back to where we were seated. Setting it down, he looked pretty pleased with himself. "Now there's a chair. Mom can move over a little and so can I. There's plenty of room."

There really wasn't. But Alex was on a mission, and before I could say anything to discourage him, he was already moving his chair down and asking the woman next to him on the other side if she could make room.

"Mom, can you move down a little?"

"Ummm... Yes, sure."

When my eyes caught Levi's, I could see he was as hesitant as I felt. But he glanced around the table and found everyone looking at him. Rather than make a scene, he smiled. "Thanks, buddy."

Levi was a large man, so even though my son had managed to squeeze in a chair, his shoulders and legs barely fit when he sat down—which meant our bodies were practically touching. His muscular leg was less than an inch from mine. I could feel the heat emanating from it, and it seemed to travel up my own leg and warm everything below the waist. I had the strongest urge to shift my thigh to rest against his. Because I knew this was the closest I'd be getting to Levi all weekend, and I longed for his touch— even a leg pressed against leg, as sad and desperate as that was.

Instead, I took a deep breath, looked up, and smiled. Surviving dinner sitting all together was going to be a challenge.

Even though other people, including my son, monopolized most of the conversation, there were points when Alex roped me into joining, telling Levi stories about the different guests who had stayed at the inn. The entire time, I had to act like my heart wasn't racing, and that I wasn't utterly and completely consumed by the man sitting next to me. A few times our eyes met, and so many unspoken words passed between us—all under the watchful eye of Tanner, who was now draining his fourth or fifth cocktail. I'd lost track.

Tanner looked around with his empty glass in hand. "Where the hell is the waitress?"

"She's busy bringing out desserts," Levi said. He picked up the full water glass in front of him and set it down in front of his brother. "If you're thirsty, how about some water?"

Tanner scowled. "I'll leave the agua for the *professional athletes* in training." He slid the glass back across to Levi, sloshing it onto the table along the way. Then he looked around again. With the waitress still nowhere in sight, Tanner pushed his chair back. "Looks like I have to go get my own. Anyone want anything?"

Levi and I shook our heads, not that Tanner waited for our responses. He was already heading for the door, presumably to the bar in the main restaurant. He definitely didn't need another drink, but I was relieved to have a minute without him watching me like a hawk.

Levi leaned in and whispered, "Has he been drinking like this a lot lately?"

I shook my head. "Not at all."

Levi's eyes roamed my face. It looked like he wanted to say something more, but then he nodded and turned away.

A few minutes later, the door to the private dining room opened again, and Tanner strolled back in. Only now, he was no longer alone. A tall, shapely redhead wearing a dress that was definitely a size too small for her walked next to him.

I held my breath as he approached the table with a full drink and a vicious smile.

"This is Arielle." He pointed to her and then took a big slug from his glass. "Like from the Disney movie, *Aladdin*."

I mumbled under my breath. "Or *The Little Mermaid*."

"Hey, big bro, Arielle here is a Broncos aficionado." He pointed to the woman again. "Go ahead. Tell him his passer rate last year."

The woman flashed a glossy smile. "Sixty-seven point seven percent. Highest in the NFL."

"And how many yards did he throw for?"

"Four-thousand, seven-hundred and seventy."

"How about the year before?"

"Four-thousand, three-hundred and twelve."

Tanner tilted his glass to his brother. "You're welcome." Then he announced to the table as a whole. "Can everyone please move down to make room for Arielle?"

I wanted to tell him to cut it out, but if I challenged him, I was afraid he would make an even bigger scene. A few people looked over at Tanner with concern on their faces, yet they shifted their seats. Tanner strolled down to the end of the table and grabbed an empty chair, then returned to make it fit next to his seat.

If this was an attempt to make me jealous, he'd failed to realize it wouldn't work. Jealousy only rears its ugly head when something you *want* is threatened.

He held his hand out for Arielle to sit and flashed a wicked smile at me. "Presley, honey, why don't you come sit next to me so Levi can sit with his new friend?"

Levi looked over at me and then at his brother. His teeth were clenched as he spoke. "That's not necessary, Tanner."

"Sure it is. And Presley doesn't mind at all, right, babe?"

Through my peripheral vision, I saw practically the entire table watching the scene. So I quietly got up and walked around to the other side, hoping to diffuse the situation. Arielle squealed a *thank you* and ran around to take my seat next to Levi.

Tanner proceeded to finish his newest drink and snaked his arm around the back of my chair. Levi said nothing, but kept staring daggers at his brother. I began to worry things might come to a head. I did my best to remain calm, but when I noticed Arielle's hand slip into Levi's lap, I'd had enough. I tossed my napkin on the table without touching my dessert.

"It's getting late. I'm going to take Alex back to the hotel."

"What? The night is barely getting started," Tanner said.

"Actually, I think this night has gone on long enough." I stood.

Tanner tried to stand, but he stumbled back into his seat. "I'll go with you."

I placed my hand firmly on his shoulder. "Please don't. Maybe Arielle can find a friend for you."

I looked at my son. "Come on, Alex."

Then I caught Levi's eye. "Goodnight, Levi. Enjoy your evening."

xoxo

An hour later, I was back in my hotel room and still hadn't calmed down. My heart pounded, and I found it difficult to hear with the sound of the blood whooshing through my ears. That was probably why my son had to tell me someone was at the door of our hotel room.

"I didn't hear anyone knock."

"I heard it."

I dreaded the thought of another scene with Tanner. "Okay. You stay in bed. Let me check."

Looking through the peephole, I was relieved to find it wasn't Tanner; it was his mom. But even though I could breathe a little easier, I still wasn't in the mood to talk. Yet I slipped the chain from the top lock and opened the door.

Shelby smiled warmly. "I hope I didn't wake you."

"You didn't. Alex is in bed, but he's still awake, and I was...unwinding."

She nodded. "Pretty sure I'd need two bottles of wine to unwind after what you were tangled up in tonight."

I sighed. "It was not a relaxing evening."

"I understand." She lowered her voice. "I hate to bother you, especially at this late hour, but my son asked if I would come keep an eye on Alex so he could speak to you."

"It's late, Shelby. And to be honest, I don't think it's a good idea for me to speak to Tanner right now. I need to cool off a little."

"Oh...no." Shelby shook her head. "I'm sorry. I didn't mean Tanner. It's Levi who asked me to come."

♂ THIRTY-TWO

Levi

WEARING A HOODIE and sunglasses, I waited in front of the hotel and prayed no one would recognize me. Coming here wasn't smart, but there was no way I could stay away after Presley had left the dinner so upset tonight.

The moment I'd laid eyes on her earlier, it felt like all the willpower I'd tried to muster up since leaving Beaufort had disappeared into thin air. I'd just wanted to leave that freaking dinner and take her home with me, make love to her all night long. Instead, all I'd been able to do was observe her. Presley hadn't looked happy in the least. And Tanner's bizarre behavior only made everything worse.

My heart raced as I continued to pace outside the hotel, hoping my mother wouldn't return to say Presley refused to see me. A man walking by kept staring, and I prayed he didn't come up to me. I adjusted my hood even lower over my head.

I turned and felt instantly calmer at the sight of Presley approaching through the sliding glass doors. She wore what looked like polka dot pajama pants and had a hoodie thrown over her shoulders. Her hair blew in the wind as she walked in my direction.

I waved so she would notice me, considering I was unrecognizable in this getup. When she stopped a few inches away, it took everything in me not to reach out and touch her. I had to remind myself I had no right to do that. She wasn't mine anymore, even if touching her would have felt so natural.

Fumbling with my hands, I said, "Thank you for coming out to see me. Were you asleep?"

She shook her head. "No."

I gently placed my hand on her back and led her away. "Let's move to the back of the building. I don't want anyone to recognize me."

We walked along the grass at the side of the hotel before stopping in a quiet spot, illuminated by a streetlight.

She crossed her arms. "What's going on, Levi? Why did you want to see me?"

"Do you have to ask? I haven't been able to think straight since I saw you tonight. And after the way you abruptly left the dinner—I knew I wouldn't be able to sleep unless I came to you." I could see her face turning red.

"You should've just forgotten about me and taken that woman home," she spewed.

I raised my voice. "Are you kidding? I don't know what the fuck Tanner was even thinking bringing her over to the table. I had no interest in her whatsoever."

"Too many choices, huh? I suppose that's what happens when you can have any woman you want. It's tough being you."

My brows drew together. "That's what you think?"

She exhaled, her tone softening. "I don't know, Levi. I don't know what to think anymore. I just know being around you after everything we've been through is too painful for me. It's way harder than I ever imagined. And just the thought of you with someone else—"

"You think I've been out here messing around with women?"

"I have no idea what you've been doing because you haven't reached out to me!"

My voice shook. "I haven't reached out because it's too damn painful, Presley. All I'm trying to do is the right thing for all of us. But if you think I can just move on and start dating random women again like nothing ever happened, you're underestimating my feelings for you." I moved closer to her. "I haven't been with a single person since I got here. Meanwhile, I find out Tanner's been taking you on dates. I've been freaking *consumed* with jealousy, even though I'm supposed to be accepting all of this."

She shook her head. "Nothing is happening between Tanner and me. Yes, I went out with him, but it wasn't a date. I've sounded like a broken record trying to drill into his head that I'm not interested in him that way."

My pulse calmed down a bit. "I called my mother's house the night she was watching Alex. I thought—"

"I know what you thought. But it simply wasn't the case, Levi. Tanner and I are getting along, but it's nothing more than that. We went out to meet Tom and Lily. And once Tom mentioned your name at dinner, you were all I could think about for the rest of the night. It's so pathetic."

Immense relief came over me. And that was messed up, because it was the opposite of what I should've been feeling. Wasn't I supposed to want her to work things out with Tanner, for Alex's sake? But did he even deserve her? The way he acted tonight had me second-guessing if my brother had really changed all that much.

"I could read your face tonight, could see how upset you were that Tanner brought that girl to our table," I said. "I didn't want you to get the wrong impression and think I went home with her or something. I somehow knew you would be worried."

That set her off.

"You didn't want me worrying or upset?" She lifted her arms into the air. "How do you think I felt when you shut me out of your life and took off to Denver early? Why should tonight be any different for you? You suddenly care about my feelings?"

I tried to defend my actions. "You know why I did what I did. It was a sacrifice."

"You sacrificed me to your brother, like an object that can be passed around. You can't just *give* me to someone, Levi. What you and I had wasn't interchangeable." Her voice cracked. "If you don't want to be with me, then just leave me alone. You don't need to check on me or coddle me. You can't have it both ways. You're either in my life or out of it."

When she started to cry, I couldn't stand it any longer. I took her into my arms and held her so tightly. Surprisingly, she didn't resist. All of the feelings I'd tried to control since arriving back in Denver pummeled me at once.

I kissed the top of her head and whispered, "I'm so fucking sorry."

When she looked up at me with tears in her eyes, I lost all control, lowering my mouth to hers. A hungry groan escaped me as I savored her taste. My dick hardened as I yearned to be inside of her again. Wrapping my hands around her cheeks, I kissed her even harder. *Fuck, I missed this. I missed us.* In my mind, she was *mine*. Despite this time that had passed, there was no part of me that was okay with losing her to Tanner—or anyone else, for that matter.

We got lost in our kiss until she suddenly pulled back.

Panting, we stared at each other. We'd always had a hard time resisting the physical pull between us, and tonight was no different.

What she said next nearly undid me.

"It doesn't matter how much I love you," she said. "I'd rather never see you again than have to see you with someone else or be reminded constantly of the fact that I can't ever be with you."

My chest constricted. *Love?*

She's in love with me?

I'd known *I* was in love with Presley. But to hear *her* use that powerful word came as a shock.

I examined her eyes. "You *love* me?"

Presley blinked repeatedly, looking as if she hadn't meant to utter it aloud. But it was too late. She'd said it. Instead of addressing my question, though, she shook her head. "Does it matter? If I say yes, will it change things between us?"

When I took too long to answer, she looked away.

"That's what I thought." She frowned. "I have to get back to Alex. Goodnight, Levi."

That was the last thing she said before running away and disappearing into the hotel.

She left me in a daze, trying to process how I could continue to abandon someone I loved—who loved me back. I hated that she'd seemed almost ashamed to admit her feelings for me. I looked up at the dark sky and prayed for an answer. Something had to give. I couldn't go on like this. Not only was I going to ruin my career because my lack of focus had rendered me useless to the team, but more importantly, I didn't know how to live without her.

But could I betray my brother? That was the only question left to answer. Was I willing to do that in order to be with the woman I loved?

It took me a full ten minutes of pacing before I made my way back toward my car in the lot at the front of the hotel. I noticed a man stumbling out of a vehicle at the curb. It wasn't until I heard his laugh that I realized it was Tanner.

What the fuck?

I looked inside the car and noticed the person driving. It was the redhead he'd brought to the dinner table earlier. I couldn't even remember her freaking name.

He muttered something to her before slamming the door. My stomach sank. She took off, leaving him on the curb.

My blood boiled. He didn't notice me standing there, so he hadn't seen it coming when I grabbed onto his collar and dragged him a few feet.

"Hey! What the hell are you—"

"What the fuck are *you* doing?" I spat, keeping my hold on him.

"Levi? What are you doing here?"

"Tell me what the fuck is going on, Tanner."

His eyes were glassy. "What do you mean?"

"What were you doing with that girl tonight?"

"It was no big deal," he slurred.

Pulling on his collar tighter, I shouted, "Answer my question."

The alcohol on his breath was pungent. "I was just out having some fun. I needed it."

"Define fun." I roughly let him go. He nearly toppled to the ground before his back hit the hedges in front of the hotel.

He wouldn't make eye contact. "What do you want me to say?"

"I want you to tell me exactly what you were doing with her," I demanded.

When he continued to remain silent, I rephrased my question. "Did you fuck that girl or not, Tanner?"

His silence told me everything I needed to know. But I still wanted to hear him say it.

"Answer me!" I yelled.

"Yes!" he finally admitted. "Okay? Yes. I...went back to her place, and one thing led to another." He hesitated. "We had sex."

My head fell back as I looked up at the sky, feeling ready to blow. *God, give me the strength not to kill him right now.*

I somehow managed to refrain from punching him, instead balling my hands into fists. "How could you do that?"

"You act like it's not something you do every goddamn day of your life."

"Don't you dare turn this on me. This is about *you*. I thought you were trying to earn Presley's trust back. You told her you wanted to be a family again. And *this* is how you show it? By getting drunk and fucking some random woman while your son and his mother are in town with you?"

"Getting a quick fix doesn't take away from my feelings for her. Presley has wanted nothing to do with me sexually. I was feeling stressed and needed relief, for fuck's sake. A man can only take so much. Between the new job and Presley fucking rejecting me over and over—I couldn't deal with it anymore. I just needed to feel good for one damn night."

Something told me this couldn't have been the first time he'd done something like this.

"One night, huh? Look me in the eyes and tell me this is the only time you've fucked around since showing up in Beaufort."

When he looked down at his shoes, I had my answer. *Jesus Christ.* I wanted to murder him. I'd spent all this time miserable, away from the woman I loved out of respect for a man who had no respect for her.

"None of this has anything to do with my love for Presley," he said.

"You don't really love her," I said.

"What are you talking about? Don't tell me how I feel."

"No," I repeated. "You don't love her. You couldn't possibly love her."

"And how would you know that?"

I took a deep breath in. "Because when you love someone, you can't even stomach the thought of being with anyone else. When you love someone, you *belong* to them in every way—mind, body, and soul. And even when you're not physically with them, you respect them. Love and respect go hand in hand. You can't have one without the other."

Tanner's eyes wavered between mine. "You're talking about Presley, aren't you? I saw the way you looked at her back in Beaufort. I figured you were just checking out a piece of ass, like you always do. Then when I saw you two at the hospital…" He shook his head and laughed angrily. "But I put that thought out of my mind, because my brother would never do that to me. *My brother* is a stand-up guy."

I had no idea what to say or do. But apparently he could read me better than I could read him.

He shook his head. "You're fucking my girl."

Whether I was in the wrong or not, I couldn't let him call her that. I gritted my teeth. "She's not your girl. And she hasn't been for a long time."

"She's mine!"

"Presley isn't a possession for you to claim. You hadn't been interested in her for years. Or your son, for that matter. No one thought you were ever coming back. You'd given us every indication that you wouldn't be. What happened between Presley and me wasn't about you—it was about us. And, yes, I felt guilty, but not enough to stop it. You'd hurt her enough already. You didn't deserve her then, and you don't deserve her now."

He stared at me incredulously. "How could you fucking do that to me?"

"I didn't plan it. It just happened. We got close, and it turned into the best thing that's ever happened to me. I'm sorry...but I love her, Tanner."

He swung at me. Luckily, he was too drunk to aim correctly, and he missed. I couldn't afford an injury right now, so I had to rein this in. It wasn't very hard to do, given how inebriated he was.

Managing to get him into a chokehold pretty quickly, I spoke into his ear, "We need to talk more about this in the morning, when you've sobered up. If you know what's good for you, leave her alone tonight. She didn't do anything wrong, and you've hurt her enough already. Go back to your room."

When I released him, he walked backwards toward the hotel entrance, a look of hatred aimed at me. I felt like shit, but at the same time, a huge weight had lifted off my chest.

Then, a wave of panic hit.

What if he goes to her room?

He'd already disappeared into the lobby, so I jogged after him. The automatic doors at the entrance slid open just as he passed the elevator bank ahead of me in the distance. I knew from my mother that Presley was on the top level at the other end of the floor, and I needed to be certain he wasn't going to bother her.

I dropped back and trailed him as he walked through the lobby and turned down a corridor leading to guest rooms on the ground level. At the end of the hall, I ducked out of sight, sneaking peeks to watch him as he stumbled from side to side. About halfway down, he stopped at a door and spent a solid minute trying to dig the key out of his pocket. When he finally pulled it out, it took him a few tries to get in, but eventually he disappeared inside. I waited a while to see if he'd come back out, and then quietly walked down to his room and listened by the door. After ten minutes, without hearing any sign of movement, I figured he must've passed out. I still needed to warn Presley, though, so I took out my phone and started to text her.

But then I thought better of it. She'd had a tough-enough night, and Alex was probably sleeping. Besides, this was a conversation we needed to have in person. She was an early riser, so I'd just get to her bright and early before practice, and before Tanner had a chance to wake up with a belligerent hangover.

✗◎✗◎

The next morning, I wasn't taking any chances. After a shitty night of sleep, I headed over to the hotel at six AM.

The vein in my neck pulsed as I rode the elevator to the top floor. I couldn't remember the last time I'd been this nervous.

What if I blew her trust for admitting the truth to Tanner last night?

What if she won't take me back?

What if the time we've been apart made her realize life with an athlete who spends half of the year on the road isn't what she wants for her and Alex?

Everything that could go wrong kept spinning through my mind.

What if Tanner causes trouble?

Could he turn Alex against me?

Shit, how is Alex gonna take the news?

When the elevator dinged on her floor, my palms started to sweat, and the thoughts circulating through my head began to leak out my mouth. I mumbled like a crazy person.

"Calm down, man."

"You've played in Super Bowls without sweating."

"What the fuck is wrong with you?"

It was a good thing it was early and people weren't around, or they'd run the other way seeing a man my size talking to himself.

When I got to Presley's room, I took a deep breath before knocking lightly. And then I waited.

And waited.

When she didn't come to the door after a few minutes, I assumed she must have still been sleeping. I hated to wake her, but I needed to talk to her before Tanner, and before I had to be at practice. So I knocked again, this time louder.

And waited.

And waited.

Then I knocked again. When she still didn't answer, I started to get freaked out, and the craziest shit ran through my head.

What if Tanner got to her and did something?
What if she's in there hurt?

So I banged on the door. "Presley? Alex? Are you in there?"

I still got no response, but the door to the adjoining room opened, and a pretty pissed-off looking guy walked out. He eyed me. "What the hell are you..." He blinked a few times. "*Holy shit.* You're Levi Miller."

I dragged a hand through my hair. "Yeah. Sorry to wake you. Have you seen the woman who was staying in this room?"

He nodded. "She was coming out when I walked in early this morning. I was out late."

"Was she okay?"

The guy shrugged. "She looked okay to me."

"Did she happen to say where she was going?"

"No. But she had her suitcases and stuff. And the little boy was carrying a bag, so I assumed she was checking out."

Fuck.

"How long ago was that?"

"Maybe four thirty. An hour and a half ago?"

"Thanks." I took off jogging down the hall.

"Wait! Can I have your autograph?"

"Another time!"

I ran to the elevator, uncertain of my next move. The last person to talk to Presley was my mother last night, and she was definitely *not* an early riser. I called anyway.

She answered on the third ring. Her voice was groggy. "Levi? What's going on? Is everything okay?"

"I just went to Presley's room, and she's not there."

"What time is it?"

"It's about six."

"She's probably at the airport by now. She was pretty upset after she got back to the room from talking to you last night. Alex was sleeping, so we chatted for a while. She thought it was better that she go home. It's very difficult for her to be around you, and with Tanner causing scenes at dinner... She asked me to tell everyone there was an issue at the inn and she had to fly home early."

Fuck. I closed my eyes. "I need to talk to her. Tanner knows, Ma."

"Tanner knows what?"

"That I'm in love with Presley. That we were together over the summer."

My mom sighed. "Oh boy. How did that go?"

"I don't even give a shit. I just need to get to her. Can you do me a favor?"

"What's that?"

"Don't mention to Tanner that Presley left."

"Levi, I don't want to get in the middle of this by lying to your brother."

"Then don't lie. Turn off your phone. You're having breakfast with Dad's friend and his wife, right?"

"Yes. And then I'm going to get my hair done before the ceremony."

"So chances are, you won't even see him until later. Just buy me some lead time by not answering your phone. Please."

"Lead time? What are you going to do? Don't you have practice today? And we have the ceremony tonight."

"I'll take the fine for missing practice. And I'm sorry, Mom. But I'm not going to be able to make the ceremony.

I never missed watching Dad play, so I think he'll forgive me. Plus, I'll be able to look up and honor him every time I walk into the stadium for a game."

"Fine. Go. Do what you have to do. I'll tell anyone who asks that you're under the weather."

"Thanks, Mom."

"I hope this is all worth it, son."

"She is. She's the one."

Two hours later, I was sitting on a flight to South Carolina, waiting to take off. I'd called Presley a dozen times, but each time it went straight to voicemail. I hit redial one more time, but the same thing happened. No ring—right to voicemail. So at least she wasn't ignoring her phone; it was probably off. The flight attendant came on overhead to say the cabin door was now shut, and we'd be taxiing for takeoff momentarily. All personal devices needed to be turned off and put away. I was just about to switch my phone to airplane mode when it vibrated with an incoming message. I'd hoped it was Presley, telling me she'd landed okay and saw all my missed calls, but it wasn't. It was my mother.

Mom: Tanner knows Presley left. The front desk told him she checked out. I think he might be heading back to South Carolina.

⚲ THIRTY-THREE

Presley

LAST NIGHT AFTER Shelby and I talked, I'd booked a flight home and turned off my phone. Then when I got up this morning, I'd realized that while I'd plugged the cord into my phone, I hadn't actually plugged the other end into the wall socket. So my cell was dead, and my flight had been so early that I didn't have time to deal with it. Luckily, my plane had been a newer one, and there were outlets at each seat for me to charge it, even if I couldn't turn it on during the flight.

The minute I got off the plane and turned on my phone, messages started pouring in. *All from Tanner.* I knew before I read the first one that it wasn't going to be good news. I needed to take a minute to see what had caused the influx of messages, but my gut told me to do it in private. So I stopped Alex as we passed a restroom just outside our gate.

"Honey, I need to run to the bathroom. Could you wait right out here for a minute?"

"Okay."

I wagged my finger at him. "Don't wander off."

He rolled his eyes. "Yes, Mom."

Once I was alone in the ladies' room, I took a deep breath and opened the text chain.

Tanner: WHORE

Oh God. My heart started to race as I scrolled down to read the rest of them.

Tanner: How could you?

Tanner: My brother?

Tanner: My fucking brother?

Tanner: Where the hell are you?

Tanner: Were you that desperate to get laid?

Tanner: He's using you, you know.

Tanner: He's always wanted anything I had. It's all a game to him.

Tears welled in my eyes.

Tanner: I hope you aren't fooling yourself thinking you were anything special. He's got a girl in every city.

The texts went on and on. They seemed to jump back and forth between angry and sad. Some were both:

Tanner: I've loved you since the eighth grade. How THE FUCK can you do this to us?

But the last text freaked me out the most.

Tanner: I'm coming to find you.

Tears streamed down my face. God, how did he even find out? And what the heck do I do now? I wanted to curl into a ball, but my son was waiting outside alone. So I splashed some water on my face in an attempt to compose myself so I wouldn't worry Alex. But I was so rattled that even the sound of my own phone ringing scared the crap out of me. I jumped and bobbled it in my hands. I couldn't get a good grip on the damn thing. It wound up smacking against the side of the sink before hitting the floor with a loud clank.

Shit.

When I bent and picked it up, the screen had shattered. Worse, it would no longer turn on. I sighed. While I was upset, maybe a broken phone was the best thing for me right now. My eight-year-old son was standing outside, and I needed to get us home without falling apart. So I took a few deep breaths, smoothed down my blouse, and went back out into the airport.

Luckily, Alex was too busy playing a game on his iPad to even notice my red nose. "Come on, honey. Let's go home."

XOXO

Hours later, I was back at The Palm Inn and unpacked, but still very much on edge. I'd used the house phone to call Levi and Shelby, but both went straight to voicemail. They were probably together at Jim's jersey-retirement ceremony, where I hoped Tanner was, too. But his last text kept playing over and over in my head. *I'm coming to find you.* Every time a guest walked in or out, I practically jumped through my skin. I kept expecting it to be Tanner.

When Alex asked if he could go over to a friend's, I was relieved to get him somewhere else. It was a nice day, and Kyle only lived a few blocks away, so I decided to walk him over. I hoped maybe some fresh air and a little exercise would do me good. On the way back, I took a detour and walked through a local park, dreading the thought of what might be waiting for me at home. Tanner had left his car at the airport, so if he was back, that would be my warning sign. I held my breath as I turned the last corner, not breathing until I checked out every car parked on the block. Thankfully, his wasn't there.

Once I arrived back at the house, I didn't feel like going inside. We had a full inn again this weekend, and people were milling around. So I sat down on the porch swing to figure out how I would handle things once Tanner inevitably showed up.

I didn't find any answers, but eventually my thoughts were interrupted when a couple walked out of the house.

They noticed me and stopped. "Oh, hi. Would you be able to tell us how to get to Coyle's Ice Cream Parlor?"

I smiled half-heartedly and pointed down the block. "Sure. You take a left at the corner, go about two blocks, and then make a right on Main Street. You can't miss it."

"Great, thank you."

They walked down the porch steps arm in arm, and then the guy turned back. "Hey, if you're a football fan, there's a pretty famous quarterback inside." The woman smiled and pulled on her T-shirt. "He was very nice. I got him to sign my shirt."

My first thought was *Oh God, Tanner is here.* But then I realized the couple was in their early twenties. They would have been teenagers when Tanner played his *one* season. I couldn't imagine they would know him, or if they did, consider him famous. So I leaned forward on the swing to see the woman's shirt. The signature was pretty much scribble, but the first letter looked a hell of a lot like an L, not a T.

My heart sped up. "What's his name? The quarter-back."

"Miller."

"Do you know his first name?"

"Levi."

"*Levi?* Are you sure? Are you certain it wasn't his brother?"

The guy smiled. "Positive. I'm a huge Broncos fan."

My eyes widened. I'd been sitting on one of my feet, so I practically fell on my face as I leaped from the swing and ran toward the door. Ripping it open, my heart stopped when I found Levi standing on the other side.

"What—what are you doing here?"

He looked over my shoulder. Apparently we had an audience. The young couple I'd completely forgotten about already was eagerly watching us. Levi gestured down the hall.

"Can we talk in your room?"

His face was stoic, so I tried not to get overly excited that he was here. He probably knew Tanner had found out and felt obligated to come try to fix things.

I nodded. "Sure."

I followed him away from all the prying eyes. He opened my bedroom door for me to walk in first, and then closed it behind us.

"What's going on?" I said. "What are you doing here?"

He swallowed. "Tanner knows about us."

"I know. He sent me a bunch of texts. How did he find out?"

Levi raked a hand through his hair. "I guess he's suspected something was going on for a while. We got into an argument last night after I saw you, and when he called me out on it, he read it on my face. I couldn't deny the truth, but I'm sorry it came out the way it did. I'm sure he's been harassing you."

"He's on his way here."

Levi shook his head. "No, he's not. He went to the airport when he woke up, but apparently, the rest of the flights for today were all booked. I just spoke to my mom on my way here, after I got off the plane. He's with her at the ceremony right now."

"Oh my God!" I covered my mouth. "The ceremony! Why aren't you there?"

Levi looked down. "Because I fucked up—in so many ways. I'm so sorry, Presley."

"It's okay. It was bound to come out. I'll deal with Tanner."

"It's not just about him. I fucked up with us. I never should have let you go. I thought it was the right thing to do. But I miss you so freaking much." His voice broke. "I love you so damn much."

The elephant that had been sitting on my chest for the last twenty-four hours finally shifted. I was able to breathe easier.

"You...love me?"

Levi closed the distance between us and took my hand. "I have for a long time. It just felt selfish to admit it. But I'm done giving a shit about my brother or our families, because I realized that by not sharing how I felt with you, I was being selfish to the one person who mattered most: You."

My breathing quickened.

Levi took my cheeks in his hands. "I love you, Presley. I am crazy in love with you."

Tears streamed from my eyes. It was about the fourth time that had happened today, but these were the first ones borne from happiness. "I love you, too."

He wiped wetness from my cheeks with his thumbs before leaning down and sealing his lips over mine. As we kissed, Levi lifted me off my feet and carried me over to the bed. He set me down and looked into my eyes as he reached forward and unbuttoned my pants. I wanted him so badly that our clothes couldn't come off fast enough. So I reached down for the hem of my shirt, but he stopped me.

"Let me, please."

I nodded. It was torture as he took his time taking off my clothes and then slowly stripped out of his own. When he was done, he positioned us both on the bed and looked into my eyes for the longest time as he hovered over me.

"I love you."

"I love you, too."

Our gazes never wavered as he slowly pushed inside. It felt so incredibly right to have him fill me when my heart was so full, too. Once he was fully seated, his arms began to shake, and he leaned down and took my mouth again.

"Fuck. You feel so good," he muttered. "So damn good."

It didn't take long before we were both on the edge. At one point, Levi pulled back and looked down at me again.

His pupils were dilated, his eyes full of love. I wrapped my legs around his back, and together we made love like never before. It felt like the world beyond us no longer existed. After months and months of push and pull, we were finally in perfect harmony. We even came together, at the exact same time. Our bodies, minds, and souls became one as I moaned through my orgasm. It was like nothing I'd ever experienced. And I knew I would never be the same because I'd just given myself fully to this man.

xoxo

Hours later, Levi had gone to pick up takeout. We'd spent the entire afternoon in bed and were both starving. He'd insisted we eat in my room, saying he wasn't ready to share me with anyone yet. Since the inn was packed with guests, and I'd already scheduled my employee to cover me all weekend, I figured why not? Levi would have to go back to the team soon, and who knew when we'd have another chance to be alone. The stars seemed to fully align when Alex's friend's mom called just as I got out of the shower and Levi returned with the food.

"You're never going to guess who that was," I said to Levi as I put the cordless phone down on the nightstand and tucked the edge of my towel in, fastening it closed.

"Who?"

I rummaged in my dresser for a change of clothes. "The mom of the boy whose house Alex is at right now."

"Everything okay?"

I pulled out a lace thong and twirled it around on my finger. "She asked if he could sleep there tonight."

Levi set down the food and walked over. He grabbed the thong out of my hand and tossed it over his shoulder. "Then we won't be needing these."

I giggled.

"Or this." He reached forward, and with a flick of his wrist, my towel fell to the floor.

"You want me to eat naked?"

"Abso-fucking-lutely." He stripped out of his own clothes. "No clothes for either of us until tomorrow."

I was deliriously happy, and would've agreed to pretty much anything he wanted, so I shrugged and smiled. "Okay!"

We sat on the bed without a shred of clothing and ate fried chicken with biscuits and gravy. When I was done, I fell back, holding my stomach.

"That was so delicious."

"I also got dessert. So you better have saved room."

I shook my head. "I think you're going to have to eat two desserts."

He grabbed my arm and pulled me to sit back up. "Nope. I only bought one. And it's most definitely for you."

Levi reached behind him and dug into the bag. He pulled out a silver container and peeled back the lid. Inside was a single serving of *peach cobbler*. Handing me a fork, he reclined on the bed and folded his arms behind his head. "Hop on, cowgirl," he said with a wink. "I plan to make every one of your fantasies come true."

⚓ THIRTY-FOUR

Levi

LIFE WAS A mess. And beautiful at the same time. I reflected on everything that had happened since the summer as I sat on a plane, heading to South Carolina for a short visit. I'd only have two days with Presley, but I'd make the most of them. This trip would be the first time I'd seen her since our confrontation with Tanner after he returned from Denver.

In order to be happy, you have to make hard decisions and overcome the obstacles in your way. Sometimes that means letting go of toxic people you once loved—at least for a while. I loved my brother, and I always would. But I'd made my choice. I'd chosen Presley. And while I hoped Tanner and I could reclaim our relationship, we weren't anywhere near that point.

A month had passed since everything went down, and he still wasn't speaking to me. That was okay, though, because he had returned to speaking terms with Presley—for Alex's sake. That was more important than making amends with me. Still, I had faith that someday we would figure out a way to act like brothers again.

After coming home from Dad's jersey ceremony, Tanner had moved in with our mother, and apparently he'd just found an apartment outside Beaufort, close to the college where he coached. During my last trip home, I'd stayed with Presley until Tanner and Mom returned from Denver, refusing to let her face him alone. As expected, he'd come straight to The Palm to confront us. Thank God Alex was still at his friend's house at the time, because there was a lot of screaming, cursing—and crying on Presley's part.

I knew she blamed herself for ruining my relationship with Tanner. I hated that she felt that way. Because in my mind, I'd chosen all of this and took full responsibility for my part in it. And more than that, Tanner's choices had started all of us down this path, and there was nothing Presley or I could have done to change that.

Thankfully, Tanner and I never got to the point where we threw punches. But Fern watched the entire thing unfold like a goddamn episode of *Days of our Lives*. She was only missing the popcorn. It sucked. Despite his actions in Denver, it pained me to see Tanner hurt. But the truth remained that he didn't love Presley the way I do.

More than anything, I think he was upset because he looked at this situation as another win for me and yet another loss for him. I guess that might have been the case, but my relationship with Presley had nothing to do with him, and it certainly wasn't a game or a competition. We loved each other and deserved to be able to freely express that. If my brother hadn't messed around when he was supposedly trying to win her back, *maybe* I couldn't have gone through with following my heart. But his indiscretion was the straw that broke the camel's back. He'd shown me he was only going to end up hurting her again if she ever let him back into her life. And that had been a long shot anyway because she loved *me*.

She'd made that clear, and who was I to prevent her from being with the man she loved? I was damn lucky to say that man was me. There was a big price to pay in order to be with the woman I loved, but it was worth it.

The *biggest* obstacle, however, had yet to be tackled. That would change shortly after I landed, because today was the day Presley and I had chosen to tell Alex about us. Even Tanner had agreed that we needed to wait for the right time, and he'd also agreed to let Presley and me handle that conversation.

Tanner had told Presley he wanted nothing to do with breaking the news that would "mess his son up." But despite my brother's attitude about it, there was no choice but to be upfront with Alex now. It was a miracle he hadn't figured anything out yet.

When I walked in the door of the inn, the smell of fried chicken greeted me, and I found Presley in the kitchen. She wiped her hands on a towel and rushed to me, wrapping her arms around my neck. I planted the longest kiss on her lips and took in a deep whiff of her scent. The combination of aromas in this place was essentially the smell of home. The Palm Inn was home. This *woman* was my home and always would be, even if I only got to be here a fraction of the year. We'd just have to make the most of every minute together.

"How was your flight?" she asked.

"Went by in a flash with all the thoughts racing in my head. I kept rehearsing what I'm gonna say to him."

She sighed. "I think we just have to wing this. No way I stand a chance of memorizing anything right now."

"You're probably right. Think there's a book on the Internet about this we could read with him?" I winked.

The sound of footsteps approaching pulled us back from each other fast.

Alex came running into the kitchen. "Uncle Levi!"

I gave him a hug. "Hey, buddy."

He looked up at me. "How long can you stay?"

"Only a couple of days, unfortunately."

Alex pouted. "I wish it were longer."

"Me too."

Presley and I looked at each other. My pulse began to race.

"*Now?*" I mouthed.

She shrugged and whispered, "We have some time before dinner. So no time like the present."

I looked back over at Alex. "Hey, buddy. Can you sit down with us for a minute? There's something we need to discuss." My heart pounded. I couldn't remember being this freaked out about anything in my entire life.

Alex's happy demeanor seemed to change as he sat across from us. His face was red, and he was no longer smiling. *Alex is nervous, too.* Did he already know? Had Tanner gone against his word and told him? That didn't make sense... Alex had been so happy to see me only a minute ago.

Presley rubbed her palms on her jeans as she sat down. I knew one of us had to start, and I felt the onus was on me.

I cleared my throat and bit the bullet. "Alex, we have something really important to talk to you about."

His breath was shaky. "Uh-huh?"

"And I want you to know that it in no way changes our relationship."

He fidgeted, looking anywhere but at me and seeming more anxious by the second. The fact that he was so on edge didn't help one bit.

"Are you okay?" I asked him.

"Yeah. Just say it," he shouted.

Shit.

Taken aback by his attitude, I sat speechless for a moment. Presley licked her lips, seeming frozen and just as tense as I was.

I was just about to come out with it when Alex blurted, "I swear I didn't mean anything by it."

I blinked. "What?"

"It was just a silly bet."

Presley's eyes narrowed. "What are you talking about?"

"The bet I made against Uncle Levi before the Dolphins game."

Wait. What? I couldn't help but chuckle. "You bet against me?"

"Well, you've been playing like crap since the season started. And some kids at school started a bet. I bet three months' allowance that the Broncos would lose to the Dolphins. Then the kid who lost the bet got mad and told me he was going to tell you I bet against you."

Alex was practically in tears, and I felt so damn bad for him.

Presley shook her head. "I wish you wouldn't bet your allowance, Alex. That's not very smart. Even if you did win, that's not a habit I want you getting into."

"I won't do it again."

"Look, Alex, I would never get mad at you for betting against me." I shrugged. "You made the smarter business move. For the record, I *have* been playing like crap. It's mostly because I've had a lot on my mind. So I don't blame you."

"I'm really sorry." He looked down at his sneakers.

"Don't worry about it another second. If anything, it gives me a good kick in the butt to do better, so you have a reason to want to bet *for* me and not against me." I quickly corrected myself. "But like your mom says, it's not a good idea to bet again, in general. So no more of that."

Alex looked between us. "Am I in trouble for something else? Why did you want to talk to me?"

"No, honey," Presley said.

I took a deep breath, gearing myself up all over again. "So..." I said. "You know how close you and I got when I was living here this past summer?"

"Yeah." He nodded. "It was the best."

"Well, those were some of the best weeks of my life. Not only did you and I get to know each other better, but your mom and I... We spent a lot of time together too. And we...really grew to care about each other. A lot." I looked over at her. "It wasn't anything we were expecting. But we became more than friends." I paused. "We fell in love with each other, actually, and we want to be together."

Alex blinked several times but didn't say anything. He looked understandably caught off guard and confused. Then he muttered, "Oh..."

Presley finally spoke. "Dad knows, Alex. He's not happy about it, but we're hoping he will grow to accept it. Your dad and I were never going to get back together, honey. I will always care about your father, but I decided a long time ago that we're better off as friends. I told you that before. So this isn't about choosing Uncle Levi over him. And both of them love you very much. This doesn't change anything there. I want to make sure you understand that."

"And I'm not trying to move in on your relationship with your father either, Alex," I said when Presley paused. "Your dad will always be your dad. I'll always be your uncle. And both of us will *always* be here for you."

Presley's voice trembled. "We didn't want to hide this from you. You're the most important thing to us in the world. And I hope you'll be okay with this because Levi makes me very happy."

When Alex remained silent, I decided he needed a prompt. "What are your thoughts, Alex?"

He exhaled and shrugged. "It's kind of gross, but whatever."

Presley's brow lifted. "That's it?"

"I was scared Uncle Levi was mad. I thought he came all the way here to yell at me. Anything is better than that."

Presley and I looked at each other, eyes wide. I'd never been so grateful for a misunderstanding. It definitely took the weight off this announcement.

"Does this mean you're moving in again?" Alex asked after a moment. "I mean, whenever you're in town?"

"Only if you're okay with it."

"Yeah." He nodded. "That's cool."

"Thank you, buddy."

He turned to Presley. "Can I be excused?"

Presley looked over at me, seeming just as surprised as I was that he was done with this conversation.

"Uh...yeah," she said. "But are you sure you're okay? You don't want to talk about this more?"

"No. I'm okay." He hopped off the chair and took off down the hall.

Presley seemed dumbfounded.

I shook my head. "That was almost too easy. Should we be concerned?"

"I'll go check on him in a little while. Maybe he needs to process it alone for a bit. Even if he's upset and not letting on, only time is going to make it easier to accept. The important thing is that he knows, and we don't have to hide anymore."

"Yeah. I'm relieved for sure, although obviously I want him to be okay with it and not just say he is."

She reached for my hand. "I know."

After dinner that night, I was surprised when Alex came to find me in my room. Presley and I had decided we would not be officially sharing a bedroom anytime soon.

"Hey, buddy. What's up?"

He looked hesitant as he stood at the doorway. "Are you and Dad not speaking?"

This was likely the rest of the conversation I'd expected earlier. Presley was right. He'd needed to process the initial shock before he could even begin to ask questions.

"Right now, we're not," I answered as we both took a seat on the edge of my bed. "Did you talk to him tonight? Is that why you're asking?"

He nodded, looking guilty.

"It's okay that you're talking to him about this. You should never feel like you have to hold anything back from any of us. What did he say, if you don't mind my asking?"

"He just said he knew about you and Mom and that he was trying to protect me, which was why he didn't tell me. And then he said you and him aren't talking right now."

I hoped there was nothing more, but if that were all Tanner said, it would be a miracle. "Life is complicated, Alex. One thing we can't control sometimes is the way we feel. In an ideal world, I would've met your mother under different circumstances. Your dad has every right to be upset. I'm his brother, and I hurt him. I have to own that. But I promise you, I would've never considered getting in the middle of your parents' relationship if there were a chance that they'd get back together. I realize I have work to do, and I promise you I will do everything I can to fix things with your dad so you don't have to worry."

He nodded and started toward the door. But before he left, he turned around.

"If Mom is not with my dad, I would rather she be with you than some weird guy."

Immense relief washed over me. "Well, I definitely have my *weird* tendencies, but I can't tell you how much it means to hear you say that, Alex."

"I want her to be happy. She seems happy around you."

"She makes me happy, too, buddy."

"Be nice to her," he added.

"You can bet on that."

He chuckled. "I can't bet on anything anymore, remember?"

I wanted to hug him, but before I got the chance, he took off down the hall.

A few seconds later, Presley appeared at the door.

"I saw him come in here," she whispered. "Is everything okay?"

"Yup." I smiled. "We just had a little man-to-man talk. I'm confident everything *is* going to be okay." I reached for her hand and squeezed. "But this has been quite the damn day. I feel like I need a drink the size of my head right now."

"I think you've earned it." She pulled me toward the kitchen. "I'll hook my man up."

Damn, I loved hearing her call me that. *Her man.* I'd worn many titles in my life and scored in many ways, but snagging Presley and being loved by her? That was better than any touchdown or Super Bowl win.

It was better than anything.

EPILOGUE

Levi - Two Years Later

I SAT ACROSS from my brother and Alex at Iggy's as we finished up our fried chicken dinner. *Fake it 'til you make it.* They say if you want something bad enough, pretend it's already happening until one day the dream becomes a reality.

The situation with Tanner and me was far from totally repaired, but we were a work in progress and had come a long way. From the moment I'd told him I'd fallen in love with Presley, I was determined to work toward fixing things, even if it took a lifetime. I knew I'd broken his trust, and it was my responsibility to make things right. As much as Tanner had hurt Presley, he would always be my baby brother. I would always love him—flaws and all.

Some time ago, Tanner and I had agreed to a once-a-month meetup at Iggy's. Alex had dubbed it The Miller Men Monthly. Except it wasn't just the three of us Miller Men now. There was a *fourth* Miller—two older Miller brothers and two younger ones. Baby Eli was a year-and-a-half. He sat in his highchair at the end of the table, munching on puff snacks while the rest of us ate.

"How's Presley?" my brother asked.

"She's good. The inn's been keeping her busy. She says hello. She's really happy we started doing this every month."

Tanner turned to Alex. "Yeah. The Miller Men Monthly was a good idea, son."

Alex shrugged as he popped a French fry into his mouth. "I know."

"When do you fly out next?" Tanner asked.

"Not for a couple of weeks. The next two games are at home."

My brother chewed. "Oh, nice."

I'd started playing this season for the Carolina Panthers. Games and practices were a few hours away in North Carolina, but it was a hell of a lot better than before and allowed me more time at home, even if it meant lots of long drives down I-77. While leaving the Broncos was one of the most difficult decisions I'd ever made, I had to do it. There was no way I wanted to be away from my family that much—especially now.

"I'm sure Presley is relieved that you're not in Denver anymore," he said.

"Yeah. That would never have worked long term."

My brother nodded.

I never quite knew what he was thinking when he mentioned her name. The ironic thing about our situation? It was a woman predicament that had torn Tanner and me apart, and it was a woman predicament that had brought us together again. I'd never forget that night. A few months after Tanner and I had our blowout in Denver, Presley and I had been hanging out at The Palm during one of my quick trips home in between games. Tanner had called my cell phone for the first time since we'd stopped speaking. He'd asked if we could meet up to talk.

I'd been certain he was going to use that opportunity to ream me out again for ruining his life, but the conversation turned out to have nothing to do with me. My brother had called because he was desperate for advice and needed a shoulder to lean on after receiving news that knocked the wind out of him.

Arielle, the woman he'd hooked up with back in Colorado, had called him out of the blue to tell him she'd gotten pregnant from their one night together. Tanner had been freaking out, and I'd done my best to calm him down and assure him that even the worst-case scenario—that the baby was indeed his—wouldn't be the end of the world.

I'd promised him he'd grow to love the kid just as much as he loved Alex. He'd asked me not to tell anyone until he could confirm that her claim was legit. As much as it had been a nightmare, the fact that he'd turned to me in his darkest hour proved our bond was still there. That night had been a turning point.

Tanner ended up flying to Denver to arrange for a gestational paternity test, which confirmed that he was indeed the father of Arielle's baby. He'd stayed with me at my house there during that trip, and also a few times after that—whenever he'd come to visit Arielle and accompany her to appointments. The following June, my nephew, Eli James Miller, was born. Even after months of mentally preparing, my brother still didn't seem to know what had hit him. He'd moved to Beaufort to be closer to Alex, and now he had another son across the country to look after. It was the craziest twist of fate and proof of life's unpredictability.

During one of his trips to see the baby, he and Arielle had decided to start dating to see where their relationship might go. It had started for the sake of their son, but over time, they fell for each other. Arielle agreed to move to South Carolina, which meant a lot to my brother. I couldn't tell you whether Tanner would remain faithful to Arielle. He'd yet to pop the question. But I could only hope that at some point, he'd grow up and settle down for good without messing things up.

Tanner lifted Eli out of the highchair. "Well, it's been nice, Millers, but this guy here needs a diaper change. And the bathroom here sucks, so..."

I chuckled. I'd never gotten a chance to witness my brother as father to a baby since I wasn't around when Alex was small. It cracked me up to think of him changing diapers.

"Say hi to Arielle," I told him.

"I will. She wants to have you guys over soon."

"Anytime. I'll send you my schedule."

"Cool." He looked over at Alex. "I'll pick you up Friday, buddy."

Alex spent every other weekend at Tanner's and loved hanging out with his little brother.

"Bye, Dad."

When Alex and I returned to The Palm, I found Presley in the bedroom we planned to turn into a nursery. My woman was four months pregnant with our first child, and I was over-the-moon excited. Presley and I had gotten married here at The Palm this past summer during the off-season. It was an intimate ceremony with just our closest friends and family—and yes, that had included Tanner. Presley and I danced to one of Gramps's old recordings for our first song and swapped wedding cake for a tower of peach cobbler. It was the perfect day, without a cloud in the sky.

"What are you up to?" I said as I wrapped my arms around her in the nearly empty bedroom.

"I've just been putting some paint swatches up against the wall, trying to decide on a neutral color. It would be easier if we knew the gender, though."

"My point exactly." I glared at her teasingly.

We'd argued a lot about this lately because I wanted so badly to know what we were having, while Presley hadn't been able to decide if she wanted to find out. She kept going back and forth between leaving it as a surprise or throwing a gender-reveal party.

"I think I still want it to be a surprise," she said.

I kissed her forehead. "Then a surprise it will be."

At the last ultrasound, the technician had written the gender down on a folded piece of paper that Presley had tucked away in an empty cookie jar in the kitchen, both of us vowing not to touch it until we'd made a firm decision.

"How did lunch go?" she asked.

"It was good. Eli is getting so big."

"He must be."

"They want to have us over soon," I said.

"Wow. Okay." She nodded. "That'll be good, I guess. For Alex, especially, you know?"

"Yup." I squeezed her tighter. "I missed you today."

She sighed into my shoulder, and when she looked up at me, I sensed worry in her eyes.

"Are you okay?" I asked.

"Honestly, I've been a little anxious lately."

"About what?"

"Everything is going so perfectly. I sometimes worry it's inevitable that something bad is going to happen. I think it might be my hormones. Every time you travel now, I'm anxious every second until you get home."

I pulled back to examine her face. "How come you haven't told me this before?"

"I guess I don't want you to worry about me worrying."

"You're right. I don't like to think that you're nervous when I'm gone. But I guess it goes to show how much you love me." I knelt down and kissed her stomach. "A part of my heart is in this body, you know."

She ran her fingers through my hair. There was no better feeling than knowing I'd get to sleep next to her tonight. I lived for every moment spent with her at The Palm and longed for the day I could feel comfortable kissing my career goodbye in exchange for the freedom of being able to see my family whenever I damn well pleased. But I had a few more years left to bring home the bacon first.

I stood up. "You know what I think?"

"What?"

"I think some ice cream is in order to get you out of this anxious mood."

She rubbed her belly. "I could go for that."

Taking my hand, Presley followed me into the kitchen.

I called Alex down and served them both bowls of mint chip before scooping some out for myself. We ate together at the table while Alex told us about some of the things happening at school.

Then Fern waltzed into the kitchen.

"Want some ice cream, Fern?" I asked.

"No, thanks. Just lookin' to make some tea. Got a bit of a sore throat."

When she went over to the counter, she opened the cookie jar.

"Don't open that!" Presley yelled.

"Why not?" she asked.

"That's where we hid the piece of paper with the gender of our baby. We don't want to look at it yet."

Alex's eyes widened. "What?"

Presley turned to him. "You're not allowed to look in there either, Alex. Promise me."

Rather than listen and immediately put it back, Fern peeked at the paper before folding it and returning it to the jar. *Great.*

"No worries." She smiled. "Secret's safe with me."

There was no chance of this being secret for the next five months if Big Mouth knew. But more than that, would *I* be able to resist trying to get it out of her? Not knowing what we were having was killing me. Becoming a father was the most exciting thing to happen to me, and I was consumed by curiosity. I would love my kid no matter what, but I *really* wanted to know. I supposed if Fern *accidentally* let it slip, so be it. But I would never go against Presley's wishes to find out.

"The baby is going to be my crother or cister," Alex said with a mouth full of ice cream.

Presley squinted. "Huh?"

"My cousin *and* my brother or sister. *Crother or cister.*"

Damn. Thanks to his uncle boinking his mother, that was true. *Poor kid.*

"I get it now," I said. "Crother or cister like cruncle—crappy uncle." I chuckled.

Alex laughed. "Cruncle used to stand for crappy uncle. Now, it's cuncle—cool uncle."

"Nice! I've been upgraded. Thanks, buddy."

"You're welcome." He giggled and got up to put his bowl in the sink before running off.

Presley yawned as she rubbed her stomach. "I think I'm crashing from the sugar. I'm feeling tired."

"It's either that or, you know, the fact that you're carrying around a little human."

"Thank you for the ice cream." She stood from her chair. "I'm gonna head to the room and lie down."

"I'll join you in a bit." I wriggled my brows. "I promise I got the hint that you're really tired. I won't try anything. I'll just rub your feet if you're not in the mood."

"I'm never too tired for that," she whispered. "I just need a little nap and I'll get a second wind."

Fern snickered from the corner of the room as she prepared her tea. That woman had supersonic hearing.

The old lady and I were the only ones in the kitchen once Presley left.

Fern steeped her tea as she headed toward the hallway to return to her room. "You're just dying to know, aren't you?" she said as she passed.

I stared her down silently. *Of course, I want to know.* But there was no way I'd break my vow and ask.

Fern took a sip of her tea. "It'd be mighty funny if this baby ended up looking like Tanner and not you, wouldn't it?"

"I'm sure you'd be tickled if that happened."

She winked. "Tickled pink."

Then she disappeared down the hall.

It took me a second.

Tickled *pink.*

Holy shit.

I let the euphoria sink in for a few seconds.

Wow—*girl dad.*

ACKNOWLEDGEMENTS

Thank you to all of the amazing bloggers, bookstagrammers and BookTokers who helped spread the news about *Well Played* to readers. You make the book world go round, and we are so grateful for all of your support.

To our rocks: Julie, Luna and Cheri – Thank you for your friendship and always looking out for us.

To our super agent, Kimberly Brower – Thank you for always believing in us and working so hard on our behalf!

To Jessica – It's always a pleasure working with you as our editor. Thank you for making sure Levi and Presley were ready for the world.

To Elaine – An amazing editor, proofer, formatter, and friend. We so appreciate you!

To Julia – Thank you for being our eagle eye!

To Kylie and Jo at Give Me Books Promotions – Our releases would simply be impossible without your hard work and dedication to helping us promote them.

To Sommer – Thank you for bringing Levi to life on the cover. Your work is perfection.

To Brooke – Thank you for organizing this release and for taking some of the load off of our endless to-do lists each day.

Last but not least, to our readers – We keep writing because of your hunger for our stories. We love surprising you and hope you enjoyed this book as much as we did writing it. Thank you as always for your enthusiasm, love and loyalty. We cherish you!

Much love,
Vi and Penelope

CONNECT WITH THE AUTHORS

Enjoy *Well Played?* Then connect with the authors!

Join Vi Keeland's reading group
(https://www.facebook.com/groups/
ViKeelandFanGroup/)
Join Penelope Ward's reading group
(https://www.facebook.com/groups/PenelopesPeeps/)

Follow Vi Keeland on Instagram
(https://www.instagram.com/vi_keeland/)
Follow Penelope Ward on Instagram
(https://www.instagram.com/PenelopeWardAuthor/)

Check out Vi Keeland's website
(https://www.vikeeland.com/)
Check out Penelope Ward's website
(https://penelopewardauthor.com/)

Check out Vi Keeland on TikTok
(https://www.tiktok.com/@vikeeland)
Check out Penelope Ward on TikTok
(https://www.tiktok.com/@penelopewardofficial)

ABOUT THE AUTHORS

 **VI KEELAND** is a #1 *New York Times*, #1 *Wall Street Journal*, and *USA Today* Bestselling author. With millions of books sold, her titles are currently translated in twenty-seven languages and have appeared on bestseller lists in the US, Germany, Brazil, Bulgaria, and Hungary. Three of her short stories have been turned into films by Passionflix, and two of her books are currently optioned for movies. She resides in New York with her husband and their three children where she is living out her own happily ever after with the boy she met at age six.

CONNECT WITH VI KEELAND
Facebook Fan Group (https://www.facebook.com/groups/ViKeelandFanGroup/)
Facebook (https://www.facebook.com/pages/Author-Vi-Keeland/435952616513958)
TikTok (https://www.tiktok.com/@vikeeland)
Website (http://www.vikeeland.com)
Twitter (https://twitter.com/ViKeeland)
Instagram (http://instagram.com/Vi_Keeland/)

ABOUT THE AUTHORS

PENELOPE WARD is a *New York Times, USA Today*, and #1 *Wall Street Journal* Bestselling author. With over two-million books sold, she's a 21-time New York Times bestseller. Her novels are published in over a dozen languages and can be found in bookstores around the world. Having grown up in Boston with five older brothers, she spent most of her twenties as a television news anchor, before switching to a more family-friendly career. She is the proud mother of a beautiful 16-year-old girl with autism and a 14-year-old boy. Penelope and her family reside in Rhode Island.

CONNECT WITH PENELOPE WARD

Facebook Private Fan Group (https://www.facebook.com/groups/PenelopesPeeps/)

Facebook (https://www.facebook.com/penelopewardauthor)

TikTok (https://www.tiktok.com/@penelopewardofficial)

Website (http://www.penelopewardauthor.com)

Twitter (https://twitter.com/PenelopeAuthor)

Instagram (http://instagram.com/PenelopeWardAuthor/)

Made in the USA
Columbia, SC
08 October 2022

69133711R00224